ERIC PICARD

Legacy of the Bitterroots

A Crystal Village Tale

Dragon House
Publishing

First published by Dragon House Publishing 2025

First edition

ISBN: 979-8-218-73090-1

Editing by Andrea Lorenzo Molinari

This book was professionally typeset on Reedsy.
Find out more at reedsy.com

Contents

Prologue

In the beginning of time, darkness covered the world. Raven, who had always existed, was flitting along the coastline, searching for a way to bring light into the world. Raven was a shapeshifter, a trickster, and a being of great cunning. His heart was set on illumination, not just for himself, but for all the creatures huddled in the darkness.

Far off in the distance, Raven heard the faintest echo of a song, a lullaby sung by a beautiful maiden. He followed the sound until he reached the home of Sky Chief, where the maiden, Sky Chief's daughter, was singing to herself in a garden. Raven watched her from the darkness and hatched a clever plan.

Raven transformed himself into a tiny seed of a pine tree, falling into the water that the maiden was drinking. As she quenched her thirst, she unknowingly swallowed the seed, and in time, she gave birth to a boy who had an unusual gleam in his eyes. That boy who was Raven in disguise.

Sky Chief loved his grandson deeply and would deny him nothing. As the boy grew, he became fascinated with the beautiful, glowing orbs that his grandfather kept in a series of boxes. These orbs were the celestial bodies—the Sun, the Moon, and the Stars. But Sky Chief kept them locked away, for he was the keeper of all light in the world.

One day, the boy asked to play with the orbs. Sky Chief, unable to resist his grandson's pleas, allowed him to open the first box, releasing the Stars into the night sky. Some time later, the boy opened the second box, and the Moon was set into the sky.

Finally, the boy pleaded with his grandfather to let him play with the last box, the box that contained the Sun. Reluctantly, Sky Chief agreed. Then as the boy opened the box, he transformed back into Raven, seized the Sun in his beak, and flew through the smoke hole in the roof.

Raven flew higher and higher. As he flew, he dropped the Sun into the sky where it has remained ever since, casting its bright, warm light over the world. Raven's deed brought an end to the perpetual darkness, enabling life to flourish. While Sky Chief was initially furious at Raven's trickery, he eventually forgave him, understanding that Raven had brought about a necessary change.

And so, the world was bathed in light for the first time, thanks to the cunning and determination of Raven.

1

Stakes

The horse screamed. Artillery fire had torn open her belly. Her cry was not a whinny or a battle cry—it was like a woman's shriek of agony. Through smoke-choked air, horses thrashed in blood-soaked mud, broken legs jutting at impossible angles, heads twisting as they writhed. One stood trembling, entrails hanging to the ground, steaming in the cold morning air. A dozen horses screamed across the battlefield, their combined agony drowning out the clash of bayonets and the shouting of men.

Hank jolted awake, his shirt soaked with sweat despite the mountain chill. He drew in the clean mountain air. It was crisp and fresh in his lungs, clearing the lingering stench of death. The screaming of horses was the worst sound he'd ever heard. None spoke of it. None could bear to. It was the true sound of war.

He shifted on the damp ground, heart still hammering in his chest, and tried to fall back to sleep.

Hank wiggled his shoulder to find a spot without roots or rocks. He adjusted his blanket against the cold. Their hand-drawn map showed a few more days of walking to reach the claim. His brother Barney slept on the other side of the fire. They'd traveled five days out of Missoula Mills in Montana. The trip had been difficult but they had experienced beauty as well.

They'd come west seeking gold at the invitation of childhood friend Joe Welch, who had served with them in the War. Joe's package contained gold dust and a garnet the size of a man's thumb, valued at ten dollars by their neighborhood jeweler. This wasn't a gold rush or a stampede—Joe had found a secluded claim far from prying eyes. The claim sat a week's hike beyond Missoula Mills, the last trace of civilization for a hundred miles. Joe had invited them and a few others to stake nearby claims. He sought companionship and safety. Though always jovial, he had wandered west after the War to quiet his demons. His letter arrived with an admonition of secrecy, and Hank agreed.

When the package from Joe arrived, Barney's wife Madeleine pulled Hank into the pantry and clutched his arm.

"Hank, you know how he is. I dearly love the man, but he lacks the resolve to see such ventures through. I cannot bear the thought of him setting out without you by his side. He'll charge ahead until he meets the first obstacle, and then return here, penniless and bereft of prospects," Madeleine said, her eyes full of panic.

Hank sighed. "Maddy, I kept watch over him during the War, true enough. But he's my elder brother, and I've not yet set my own affairs in order. I've no wish to embark on an escapade with Barney and Joe, only to find ourselves back here by autumn with nothing to show for it."

Madeleine met his gaze with a fixed stare. "Hank. You are in disarray. You scarcely rest, barely eat, and you've grown gaunt. Chicago won't mend what ails you. You need this more than Barney does. With you to guide him, I'm confident he'll find his way back to me unharmed and with enough savings that we may cease relying on my father's support. You may be a year his junior, but you are the steady hand we rely on. I beg you—go with him."

Hank rolled onto his back and stared up through the pine boughs. The sky blazed with more stars than he'd ever seen in Chicago. The Milky Way flowed overhead like a river of light. He'd seen more shooting stars on this trip than in all his life. He and Barney had prepared well, pooling their resources to buy two mules and supplies in Missoula Mills. One mule pulled their two-wheeled pack cart; the other was heavily laden.

They'd served in the cavalry together—Hank as a Lieutenant, Barney as corporal. Hank had led his men to victory after victory, earning praise from command. But the War still gripped his mind—his days filled with a constant barrage of sounds, smells, and intrusive thoughts. Barney chattered endlessly about the War, as if only good memories had been created during their service. Hank had agreed to this journey hoping that distance might quiet his haunted sleep.

He rolled over, trying to sleep again. The next thing he knew, low morning light was in his eyes. Barney snored on the far side of the fire. A red squirrel sat on a branch, staring at him with bright eyes as it demolished a pinecone. Hank stood and stretched, groaning as pain shot up from a rock that had dug into his spine. The squirrel chittered and flung the rest of the pinecone at his head.

Hank reached for the pot of coffee they'd left to brew overnight on a flat rock in the fire. He poured a cup and took a sip, it was acrid but warm. He crossed to the other side of the fire and held the cup under Barney's mustache. After a moment, Barney snorted, shuffled in his sleep, and his eyes popped open. He sat up as Hank walked back to the other side of the fire, set his tin coffee cup down, and packed his bedroll. Barney crab-walked to the fire and poured himself a cup. He was balding, with a large handlebar mustache, his face darkened by days of beard growth.

After a quick breakfast, they loaded the mules and returned to the trail. Barney led Bertha, while Hank guided Jim with the cart. The cart held enough supplies to last a winter—Hank's insistence over Barney's protests of extravagance. But Hank had always led, and Barney had always followed, and that was true long before the War.

They walked the Mullan Military Road, cut by Mullan and his crew less than a decade earlier. Though thousands crowded this route at times, it was quiet this year. Near noon, both mules snorted and grew restless. A horse approached from ahead to the west. Without speaking, the brothers moved to the trail's edge and steadied the animals. The Mullan Road was safer than most—unlike the Bannock Road, where more than a hundred murders had taken place last year—but desperate men wandered the West since the War's end. Caution ruled every encounter.

Hank and Barney had passed a few travelers in either direction and made sure even the hard men gave them space. They'd seen plenty of action in the War and weren't easily intimidated. Both carried well-used Colt Army revolvers, worn openly and well maintained. Their dress marked them as former soldiers, though they didn't display Union colors as some did. In the wilderness, a former Confederate who hadn't let go of 1865 might be easily provoked. Still, their Army revolvers were a clear signal that they had once served the Union. More often than not, ex-Confederates carried Navy revolvers.

Hank pulled his new Winchester Model 1866 rifle from the scabbard mounted to the front of Jim's cart. Barney drew his scattergun from its place on Bertha. They kept both barrels aimed at the ground. A few minutes later, a man rode up, slowed his horse, and stood off twenty feet up the trail. Seeing that Hank and Barney were well-armed and ready, he slowly took his hand off his sidearm and politely showed his hands.

"Howdy, friends," he said. "Road clear ahead?"

Hank met his eyes and gave a single nod. "Been a good stretch from Missoula Mills. Not much mud. No trouble."

The rider nodded back. "Quiet here, too. Bit of mud in the lowlands. I passed some Nez Perce horse traders near Lake Coeur d'Alene—they were peaceable. Spent the night at the Cataldo Mission. Padre was friendly, he gave me a free warm meal and a clean bed."

"Much obliged," Hank said. "You get down that way, stop in on Frank Worden in Missoula Mills. Fair trader. Keeps good stock."

The man tipped his hat and edged past them. "Good luck to you."

The Mullan Military Road had been a godsend. After crossing Lookout Pass yesterday, they knew this morning they'd leave it behind for two days of hard hiking into the mountains. They'd counted miles from the pass, watching for a campsite marked with a hidden cart-wide trail heading north. Near mid morning they found it, a tree marked above head height with an underlined double X and an arrow pointing the way. Barney checked their father's pocket watch, it was just before ten o'clock. With no one in sight and the morning having been uneventful, they watered the mules and left the road.

The trail barely took the cart. Sometimes they pushed from behind; other times Bertha helped Jim pull over tangled roots, rocks, or through patches of mud. Tall trees closed in as they followed Nine Mile Creek deeper into the mountains. By late afternoon they reached a fork, where past travelers had left a fire pit and a flat spot for camping. They settled in for the night.

Hank woke Barney in his usual way—waving coffee under his nose. The air was cold but clear, and the dew wasn't too bad on their blankets or gear. They'd staked the mules in a grassy patch the night before. The animals had grazed contentedly, and the creek ran close enough for the animals to drink their fill. After gathering up their gear, the brothers ate cold beans from the night before and started uphill.

By noon, they had crossed two mountain passes, still dotted with snow, and continued following creek beds and gulches toward their destination. That evening, they camped on the banks of the Coeur d'Alene River.

The river churned with snowmelt. The cold struck like a knife when they crossed, stealing breath and burning skin. Even the mules shuddered, steam rising from their flanks as they climbed out. They tracked east along the bank, boots squelching, until the trail demanded another crossing.

A few miles later, they found the small tributary marked on their map and left the Coeur d'Alene. After another mile, they took a hard left, climbing again into the mountains along another branching creek. Despite the freezing crossings and the sweat that followed, they made good time. The trail rose steadily, and the ground turned dry and sandy.

After a few miles of hiking they found a small tributary creek Joe had marked on their map and turned left into the mountains. The ground grew drier and sandy. They entered a ghost forest where fire had swept through. The lower trunks of the pines were scorched black, and the underbrush had burned away. Passage was decidedly easier here, though the air still held the memory of flame, and their boot soles soon blackened with ash. New growth pushed through the charred soil—like tiny, green fingers reaching for light.

In the mid-afternoon, the forest changed. Ancient cedars rose around them, their massive trunks like church columns. Shafts of sunlight pierced the canopy far above, casting golden pools on the cathedral floor. The air was still, heavy with the scent of cedar bark. Their voices dropped to respectful whispers, as if they'd entered a sacred space.

They continued to spot the underlined XX marks with arrows and knew they were still on track. One mark read: <u>XX</u> 3 Mi. They forged ahead, and soon the trail leveled out, opening onto an acre of cleared, flat pasture. A rough pen stood to one side, holding several donkeys and a mule. Beyond it stretched a flat meadow, about a mile long and curving out about a mile wide, before the mountain rose again.

The trail ended abruptly at a graveled outcrop. Hank's breath caught as the land fell away before them—revealing a ravine that plunged easily 100 feet to a ribbon of silver water. To their left, the mountain face rose sheer and towering, a fortress wall of stone sparsely dotted with firs clinging to the near vertical cliffside.

Across the chasm lay something extraordinary: a hidden valley cupped in the mountain's palm. Spring-fed streams laced across the meadowland, catching the afternoon light before cascading into the ravine in delicate falls. The cove of land stretched about one mile wide and deep, a perfect amphitheater of green bounded by granite peaks.

The isolation was complete. No trail led here except the one they'd followed. No eyes had seen this place save those Joe had trusted with his secret. Hank felt something shift in his chest—not peace, exactly, but possibility.

Two cabins stood down in the valley beside separate creeks, set back about a half mile from the ravine's edge. Near one, a man bent over a sluice, working his claim. Barney put his fingers to his mouth and whistled, sharp and loud. The man straightened, shading his eyes, then waved. He rang a small bell, its sound carrying faintly across the open air as he signaled the other cabin.

While they waited, they dropped their packs and unloaded the mules, releasing them into the pen with the others. The new animals and old exchanged brays and snorts. Hank now understood why Joe had asked for some of the items on their list—especially the pulley system and baskets, obviously meant for shuttling gear across the ravine.

A few minutes later, Joe appeared on the far side and hailed them with a shout. They called back, grinning, and watched him scramble across the rope bridge—though Hank felt "bridge" was too generous a word for the contraption.

Joe hugged them both in his bear-like grip. He was a big man: barrel-chested, thick-bearded, with shaggy brows and arms like stovepipes and hands like shovels. He'd grown up with them in the same neighborhood, fought beside them in the War, and now stood beaming at them. He was almost as excited to see the new pulley system they'd brought.

"I reckon you fellas'll take to this place right quick," he said. "One of the prettiest spots I ever laid eyes on. Weather's holding nice! But this basket rig—hell, this is going to change everything." He slapped Hank on the shoulder. "You should've seen me the first time I crossed this ravine. Throwing a rope and a hook like a damn fool, praying to snag a tree on the other side!"

After a few minutes of catching up, they agreed to stack supplies from Bertha and leave the cart loaded while they crossed over to scout for a claim and a place to build their cabin.

That evening, they met Tom and Rick, the miners from the other claim, and all five of them shared a dinner of venison steaks and potatoes baked in the fire. Joe had been here a full year now, and had invited Tom, Rick, Hank, Barney, and two others who hadn't yet arrived. So far, they had found plenty of garnet, a few small gold nuggets, several pounds of gold dust, and even some silver.

But as they spoke, Hank noticed the tightness around Tom and Rick's eyes when discussing the yield. Joe and Barney were cut from the same cloth—optimistic, always chasing the next adventure. Tom and Rick were more reserved, their smiles thinner when they spoke of what they'd pulled from the ground.

After dinner, Joe, Tom, and Rick retired to their cabins, and Hank and Barney settled in by the large group campfire. Joe had spent the evening pointing out good spots for them to set up camp, and Hank did his best to temper Barney's enthusiasm without dampening it. They had plans to reinforce the rope bridge and set up the new pulley system for supplies.

As Hank crawled into his blankets, he felt a spark of real, contented excitement—the first he'd known since the journey began.

I I I I

Tom looked at Hank incredulously. "How in tarnation did you manage that?"

They'd just finished building a much sturdier bridge, lashing rope and wood into place, and incorporated the new pulley and basket system Hank and Barney had brought. All morning they had fought to get the tension on the lines correct, struggling to get the rig stable, all the men bickering and arguing, until Hank finally lost his temper. He told them to take a walk and leave him to it. Tom and Rick had started to argue, but Joe and Barney gave them a funny, quelling look and suggested they give him room. When they returned an hour later, Hank had figured out how to tighten the tensioner and gotten the pulley running smoothly. He only smiled at Tom's question.

"Well, gentlemen," Rick said, "I reckon we've earned ourselves a soak in a hot bath."

Barney laughed loud and sarcastically. The three veterans of the plateau traded a glance. Joe grinned. "Oh, you lads are in for a treat."

The five men walked about a mile inland, toward where the mountain rose steeply and the ground turned rocky. Tall grasses blanketed the flats, broken by thickets of wild rose and scattered juniper in a few varieties. They followed a faint path, climbing flat rocks that formed a rough staircase, and turned past a clump of bushes.

A steaming pool emerged from the shadows. It was fed on the far side by a spring that spilled from a cleft in the rock face, vapor rising all around in wisps and plumes. Sunlight pierced the mist, casting rainbows against the stone. The air carried a pleasant metallic or mineral smell.

"You're joshing," Barney said, staring. "That's a hot spring?"

"As sure as the sky's blue," Joe said, grinning.

Without hesitation, Joe, Tom, and Rick peeled off their boots and clothes and plunged into the water, whooping and carrying on. Barney followed with a laugh, jumping right in. Hank, slower and smiling, waded carefully into the steaming pool. Barney let out a deep sigh as he submerged, and Hank groaned in appreciation as the warmth soaked into his bones. The water was hot, but not scalding—just right.

The five men laughed and drifted into an easy silence, letting the spring work its magic.

"It's a wonder this doesn't reek of rotten eggs," Hank said. "Most hot springs I've been to reek of sulfur—this one doesn't smell foul at all. Kind of brisk. Like iodine."

"Splendid, ain't it?" Joe grinned. "Got me through the winter out here. I built a little shed over yonder for a winter bedroom. Took it apart once the snow melted to add onto the main cabin."

"Stayed warm enough to dip in all winter?" Barney asked.

"Yes, sir, it did—just as warm as it is now," said Joe. "You'd be amazed how many critters it draws. This region's thick with birds year-round. Rabbits, foxes, even mink. One morning I woke up to a herd of bighorn sheep drinking on the far side. Come winter, they all gather here for the warmth. It's quite a sight."

The men sat in the warm water for a while, and Hank looked up at the mountain towering above them. About a thousand feet up, he spotted what looked like the entrance to a cave. For a moment, he thought he saw a person standing there—but when he blinked, it was gone.

He asked, "What's that opening up there, Joe? Any idea?"

Joe looked up. "I've noticed it too," he said, "but I'm at a loss."

Hank leaned back in the water, eyes still on the spot, wondering what wonders this place had yet to reveal.

The next morning, he and Barney ferried their supplies across the ravine and laid out the location for their cabin—close to the bridge and not far from fresh water. They marked the site for their outhouse, carefully placed downstream and downwind. Joe had made several trips to Missoula Mills before their arrival, hauling enough lumber for two additional cabins. With that on hand, all they needed was a foundation of loose stones, gathered from nearby.

A week later, their one-room cabin stood finished—two bed frames inside and the small stove they'd hauled in the cart for cooking and heat. The privy took another day. After that, they were ready to begin mining.

I I I I

Hank and Barney stood ankle-deep in the icy creek behind their cabin, panning for gold. The sun warmed their backs as they joked back and forth. Hank's stomach growled, thoughts turning to lunch, when he spotted a rock that looked like it held silver ore.

"Barn, pass me my knife," Hank called out.

Barney plucked the knife from the creek bank and tossed it in a lazy arc. Hank caught it cleanly, but the scabbard slipped free. The blade bit deep into his thumb, straight to bone.

"Damnation!" Hank cursed and squeezed his thumb in his left hand, and pulled it against his chest. Blood seeped between his fingers, dripping into the clear water. His eyes squeezed shut against the pain.

"I'm so sorry, Hank. I shouldn't have thrown it. Let me see." Barney splashed over, and Hank slowly released his grip to show him the cut. As he did, blood welled out of the deep slash.

They retreated to the cabin where Barney stitched the wound. The needle pierced tender flesh with each careful pass.

"Maybe ease off the panning till this heals up," Barney said, tying off the final stitch.

"Fiddlesticks. We've got a lot of mining to do here, I'll be fine," Hank said.

For the rest of the day, Hank favored his right hand but kept panning. The specimen rock he'd wanted to test had tumbled away in the creek's current, lost among countless others. Over the next few days, he pushed himself harder, especially when Barney inquired about the wound. On the fourth morning, his hand trembled as he tried to sip coffee, splashing it down his shirt front. He jerked his hand away, spilling more. He swore under his breath and his lips pulled back from his teeth in a rigid grimace. When Barney examined the cut, angry blisters dotted Hank's arm and hand. The wound itself glowed an ugly red.

Within hours, Hank's neck stiffened and ached. Barney recognized the signs from his darkest war memories. Hank's muscles betrayed him, twitching and knotting beneath his skin like ropes drawn too tight. The spasms began as small tremors, then escalated into waves that wracked his entire body. His jaw locked shut, teeth grinding like millstones in the cabin's oppressive quiet. Each ragged breath scraped through clenched teeth as Barney watched, helpless.

The next two days brought fresh torment. Between spasms, Hank caught his breath and met Barney's eyes. Fear mingled with grim acceptance.

"Nothing to be done now, Barn." The words came clipped, forced through a rigid jaw. "Seen it before. Just have to see it through."

"Don't say that," Barney's voice cracked. "We'll find a way. I swear it."

But the lie tasted bitter. His mind flooded with memories of field hospitals—the sound of men dying from tetanus—their bodies twisting like branches in a storm. Now those same spasms tortured his brother.

Barney rummaged through their supplies, frantic. He recalled old remedies whispered in hushed tones by desperate soldiers: a poultice of herbs, a concoction of whiskey and honey—anything that might offer relief. He tried what he could, applying warm, wet cloths to the wound, forcing remedies between Hank's clenched teeth, bought from roadside carts on their way west. But the spasms continued, relentless and unyielding.

The other men came by over the next couple of days, sitting with Hank for a while, until things grew so bad that Barney had to send them away at Hank's request.

Barney was working on another poultice at the stove when Hank called out, teeth chattering.

"Barney, sit with me. I don't want to be alone."

Barney left the stove and dropped to his knees beside the bed, clutching Hank's hand. The skin was clammy, the grip weak.

"I'm here, Hank. I ain't leaving."

As the hours passed, Hank's body betrayed him further. His neck arched back under a cruel, uncontrollable force. Muscles strained against skin. Barney watched in silent anguish as the spasms rolled through him.

Now and then, Hank's eyes would find Barney's, and he'd offer a tight smile—a flicker of his old self breaking through the pain.

"Remember those nights in Chicago?" Hank whispered hoarsely. "We'd sneak up to the rooftop of that old tenement? Thought we were on top of the world, looking out over the city."

Barney chuckled softly, eyes misting. "Yeah. We fancied ourselves kings. Silly fools we were."

"Still fools," Hank said, his breath catching as another spasm hit. "But we had good times, didn't we?"

Night settled in, the cabin lit by the soft glow of lantern light. The room smelled of sawdust and sweat. Barney kept vigil, heart heavy with what he knew was coming.

The spasms worsened. Hank's body arched off the bed, muscles tightening to the point of tearing. Barney held him through each wave, murmuring words of comfort—though they rang hollow, even to his own ears.

Hank opened his eyes after a particularly bad spasm. Terror filled, his gaze darted around the room, and in a small, childlike voice he whispered, "I don't like this. I don't like this."

Then his body seized in the most violent spasm yet. His back arched, stiff as a board, only his heels and head touching the mattress. There was a loud crack—the sound of bone shattering—and suddenly Hank went limp, collapsing back onto the bed. Barney gripped his brother's hand, feeling life slip away beneath his fingers.

His heart pounded. He cradled Hank's hand to his cheek as he lost all composure, sobs racking his chest, his own body echoing Hank's final spasms. Tears came freely now. He held Hank's hand to his forehead, to his lips, to his face, over and over—unable to let go.

Time paused. The world fell away into a tunnel of blackness. All that remained visible was Hank's hand, framed in the small aperture of Barney's grief.

When he finally rose, Barney was spent—exhausted and numb. He covered Hank's body with a blanket. The sobs had dwindled to stuttering, involuntary breaths, like a toddler recovering from a tantrum.

He staggered to the door, stepped outside, and sagged down on the rough bench Hank had made for them, and the world began to come back. The morning sun bathed the valley in golden light. The wind whispered through the trees.

2

Connection

March 2028

Jack Seeley shouldered his way from his Uber toward the entrance to LAX's Terminal 4, dodging rolling bags and distracted travelers staring at phones. The air carried hints of burnt coffee and jet exhaust. A flash of white caught his attention—a man in an immaculate linen suit leaning against a pillar, watching him across the crowd with unsettling focus. He was short and lean, with wild, auburn hair escaping from beneath a white Panama hat trimmed with a black band. His handlebar mustache dominated his face, giving him the air of a riverboat gambler. A long, brown cigarette dangled from his fingers, releasing sweet-smelling smoke that seemed to hover around him rather than dissipate on the breeze. He watched Jack through squinted eyes as he smoked.

As Jack approached the man, a woman in front of him suddenly tripped and fell, sprawling headlong onto the pavement, dropping her rolling bag and the handbag strapped to the handle. Both Jack and the man rushed over to help her, Jack on the right, the man in the white suit on her left. They helped her to her feet and despite a bloody palm, she seemed okay. The two men handed her the bags, and she was on her way. Jack noticed that not only was the man wearing a pristine, white linen suit with shiny, black shoes, he was wearing a white linen vest under his suit jacket. In addition, he had a gold pocket watch chain linked to a watch pocket in his vest. In the maneuver to rescue the young lady, the man hadn't once let go of his brown, sweet-smelling cigarette.

The man tipped his hat with theatrical precision, then walked away without any luggage or apparent purpose. Jack filed the odd encounter away and headed for security.

After Jack made quick transit through the PreCheck line and made it to his gate, he noticed that the man was also waiting to board. As these coincidences sometimes work out, he turned out to be sitting right next to Jack in first class. After they both were seated, the man turned to Jack and said, "Hello there, my fellow traveler and rescuer of damsels in distress. My name is Sinclair Lipson," and he paused before adding, "the third." He had a strange, old-fashioned pacing to his speech and an accent that fell somewhere between Yosemite Sam and a third-tier nightly newscaster. He extended his hand, and Jack shook it dutifully.

"Nice to meet you, Mr. Lipson, I'm Jack Seeley. What brings you to Spokane?"

"Ah, Jack, a pleasure. I'm returning to the area after a long absence. I haven't been back there in what feels like... well, forever."

Lipson smiled at Jack in a sort of friendly way, but his eyes were narrowed. His smile was all in the mouth, his eyes looked cold. It gave Jack a chill. He had been about to tell this man that his father was also a "Trip", or third son with the same name, but he thought it better to disengage.

Jack did the universal trick of the frequent flier; he smiled and he reached into his bag for headphones and a book. He pulled out a copy of Hugh Howey's newest novel, slipping on the Nura noise-canceling headphones that he preferred. Lipson asked the flight attendant for a Jack Daniels on ice, and the flight went smoothly. Lipson consumed several drinks during the flight to Spokane.

I I I I

Jack gratefully grabbed his latte in the Spokane airport before continuing his walk to the car rental to drive through to Kellogg. It was early March, and he had gotten a call from his grandmother's caregiver, Amy, that he should make the time to come out. His grandmother was unable to walk, even with the walker she'd used for the last fifteen years. She was now effectively bedridden.

Jack asked the cheerful woman at the Enterprise office for something with all-wheel drive and clearance. An hour later, he pulled off the highway and found his way by memory to his grandmother's house at 620 Chestnut Street. Jack pulled into the driveway of the tiny bungalow. His great-grandfather had built it in 1910, and a cornerstone on the left side that marked it as one of the oldest houses in town. Jack was relieved to see that the yard was in good shape. He'd been paying for a yard service on his grandmother's behalf since she was unable to take care of the property. The modest homes around it told the story of the neighborhood—some showing pride of ownership with fresh paint and tidy yards, others defined by rusty cars and peeling siding.

Jack's great-grandfather had died in an accident in the mountains, and his grandfather had been gifted the house upon his return from serving in the U.S. Army during World War II. Jack's father had been raised in the house until he left for Seattle in the 70s to work as an engineer at Boeing.

His grandmother, Audrey, had been younger than his grandfather, John Jr.; they'd met at a dance for soldiers returning from the War. John had been sent to Fort Lewis upon his return, outside of Tacoma. His grandmother had grown up in Tacoma, and the USO frequently held dances for soldiers on the base. Jack's grandparents often talked about love at first sight and how they had hit it off immediately. They'd gotten married all in a rush when she was only seventeen. Jack's father was born in 1946. Jack remembered how his grandfather would scoop him up when he was small. His grandfather always smelled of aftershave. He was always clean shaven, but in the evenings, his face would have a rough stubble of beard.

His grandfather had been in the infantry and survived D-Day. He told many stories of his adventures in Europe during the War. It wasn't until Jack was much older that he realized all of his grandfather's stories were gentle stories about people. They were anecdotes about personal relationships, funny stories about mishaps, and fun stories like getting lost and finding a bakery where he traded chocolate from his rations for freshly baked bread. Jack's favorite story was how his grandfather had been holed up with his unit for a week in the countryside of France. A little boy came every day and spoke to them in French—but none of his platoon understood. The little boy kept saying, "Oof" and "Loof" to them every day, while his comrades and he survived on rations. Finally, the boy showed up with a basket of fresh eggs and made it clear that *l'oeuf* was the word for egg in French. All that time, the kid had been looking to trade rations for eggs.

None of John Seeley's stories were about the War, the War was just a circumstance, a background against which his stories were set. When his grandfather got sick in his late 70s, Jack would sit with him. It was then that he heard completely new versions of the stories he had grown up with. The darkness underpinning the once light and whimsical stories was transformative for him. After his grandfather died, Jack would still come back to spend time with his grandmother, whom he loved deeply. Still, for all his affection for his grandmother, Jack had been remarkably close with his grandfather.

Jack knocked gently at the front door before entering—his grandmother was laying in a hospital bed in the living room, bright-eyed and smiling as he came into the foyer. The house smelled the same as always, the unique smell of generations of Seeleys and the faint scent of furniture polish. The house was immaculate. His grandmother's nurse, Amy, poked her head in from the kitchen to say hello. Jack walked over to give his grandmother a kiss.

"Hi, Gran, how are you doing today?" said Jack.

"I'm fine. Now step back, and let me look at you," said Audrey Seeley. "Oh, it's so nice to see you, Jackie."

Her hair was pure white and pulled back from her face. Her blue eyes sparkled, and her cherubic face was deeply lined with a fine spider web of broken blood vessels around each eye. She was covered with a comforter and sheet and was wearing a flannel nightgown under that. She was tiny and frail, but her mind was sharp and her sense of humor intact.

The room was filled with various gadgets and medical equipment, all with casters and wheels to allow them to be easily moved and repositioned. The room had been largely emptied of most of its furniture, but there was a relatively new flatscreen mounted on the wall across from her bed, a couple of comfortable, old leather armchairs and her hospital bed.

The living room gave way to a small dining room with a table and chairs for six and then the kitchen. Behind the kitchen was an addition put on in the 90s by his father. It consisted of a handicap-accessible bathroom and bedroom for his grandmother that was now used by Amy since his grandmother needed full-time care.

Jack reached over and gently but firmly planted a kiss on her cheek, giving her a big enveloping hug. She was all bones and dry skin, but she smelled of lavender soap.

"I'm so glad you made it here, Jackie. And for a whole week!" Audrey said quietly, but with excitement. "Why don't you get yourself settled in the guest bedroom upstairs? We can catch up in a little bit."

Jack smiled and politely ignored her instructions by sitting down in the comfortable leather armchair next to her bed. He made small talk for ten minutes or so, then went out to the car for his bags. He carried them back into the house and up the stairs off the front entrance into the bright but cramped second floor.

There were three bedrooms on the second floor and one bathroom; his grandparents' bedroom, his father's old bedroom, and the "guest bedroom" that was mainly his own room from his childhood. He had spent school vacations with his grandparents for most of his childhood, including most of his summer breaks. The room had an antique furniture set of dark wood. He loved that it was wallpapered with a print from 1976 that celebrated the bicentennial. It featured a white background with a colonial theme with various vignettes of colonial scenes in clusters, patriot soldiers in three corner hats, cannons on either side of the liberty bell, colonial era ships, Paul Revere astride his horse, and various colonial slogans such as,

"Spirit of '76," "Don't tread on me!" and "I have not yet begun to fight!"

Jack vividly remembered his childhood in this room. Summertime in Idaho was gorgeous, dry air, blue skies. The climate was ideal, dry and warm. Additionally, he had a personal freedom here as a child that he never could have possessed in Seattle. His grandfather loved to take him for hikes in the woods, and he taught him to fly fish for Cutthroat and Brook Trout. All the little things he'd have learned in the Boy Scouts, had he stayed in Seattle for the summer.

Jack packed away his things, took a quick shower, and went downstairs to have dinner with his grandmother.

"Jackie, I've been meaning to tell you that your great-grandfather's foot locker is upstairs in my old bedroom. It has lots of old papers and pictures and a journal in it that I think you'd enjoy looking through. There's a lot in there about Crystal Village," said his grandmother.

Crystal Village was the mining town his great-grandfather had been born in, somewhere up in the mountains. Funny, Jack hadn't thought about the village in years. He knew that it was one of the mining towns that had been destroyed in the Great Fire of 1910. Anyone who spent time in this area knew about the Great Fire, which had destroyed half of Kellogg, half of Wallace, and completely wiped out more than a dozen towns. Millions of acres of forest land had burned, and there were lots of stories and legends about the Great Fire. During his early childhood, he'd heard stories of Crystal Village from his grandfather, who had never lived there. They'd been passed down from his father, so they were more like fairy tales to Jack.

They finished dinner and dessert, and afterwards, they watched a little television together. His grandmother fell asleep around 7:30, and shortly after, Jack whispered goodnight to Amy and went upstairs.

Jack entered his grandparents' bedroom and reached into the closet to pull out the trunk that was there. He remembered his grandfather showing him a few things in this locker when he was little, but he had completely forgotten about it until his grandmother brought it up. The footlocker was more of a chest. It was covered in black leather that was dried and cracked, and it had bronze straps holding it together. It was heavy, perhaps as much as 80 pounds.

He pulled it open and carefully laid the top back until it touched the floor behind itself. Inside there were some built-in drawers and boxes that were all upholstered in the same, faded material as the rest of the trunk's interior. Originally, it had been decorated with yellow and white stripes. The yellow portion was about an inch wide. Then there was a thread or two of black, a sixteenth of an inch of white, then another thread or two of black, and finally, there was a wide yellow stripe again. The contents smelled old and dusty.

Inside the trunk there were some of his grandfather's things, mementos from World War II and his time in Europe. There was also a photo album from after the War. He'd seen that before. In it there were pictures of Paris, London, the ship that carried him back to the US, and then pictures of New York and his war buddies. He set that aside and found another box that was upholstered in the same yellow and white stripes as the trunk itself. It was about two feet long, a foot wide, and 18-inches deep.

The box yielded faces from another century—first a man with dark hair falling straight as rain with striking light eyes that seemed to pierce through time. His sharp nose and well-groomed mustache spoke of authority. At the bottom, in precise script: Eoinn Seeley. Jack gasped. His great-great-grandfather stared back at him across generations. There was a picture of a beautiful woman with curly, dark hair and arched eyebrows. The pictures were the same size and had the same background. They were three quarter view portraits, with both subjects looking off to the left, behind the camera. Her name, Rose Grady Seeley, was written at the bottom in the same, crisp handwriting. This was Jack's great-great-grandmother.

Stacked underneath the old photos, there were several hand-written letters, each preserved in their original envelopes. The paper was fragile and yellowing, and the seams of the folds were cracking and almost falling apart. So as Jack went through these things, he was careful to take photographs of all of them with his phone.

Inside the box was a smaller box that was heavy and made of plain, thick, old-fashioned card stock, not corrugated cardboard like you'd find today. This was one of the items he remembered from his childhood, his grandfather had shown him this box once.

He pulled it out. It was tied with a red string, which he untied carefully. The inside was lined with black felt, and there were eight stones set into the felt in custom shapes, cut specifically to hold the rock specimens. There was a gold nugget the size of his thumb and three garnets. One of these three garnets was the size of a golf ball, polished to show the rare but beautiful star pattern that sometimes could be found here in Idaho. The other two garnets were cut, seemingly of high quality, and these were each the size of his thumbnail. There was also a piece of silver that was tarnished but also the size of his thumb. Finally, there were three very pretty, large, uncut crystals. He couldn't identify their type but, one was white, one pink, and one a light blue. Drawing in a deep breath, he photographed the contents of the box and carefully closed it up and put it aside.

Among the remaining items in the trunk, there was a framed photograph, with glass over the front of it. It was about 10 by 14 inches, and it showed eight people, seven of them were men and one was a woman. They stood on a cobblestone street in front of a large, brick, Gothic-style building. The caption at the bottom photo read, "The Original Eight." He could see the tall Eoinn Seeley in the center. Yet, there was an even taller man with lighter hair and wild sideburns next to him. That gentleman was muscular and had a great smirk that he was trying to hide by looking serious. He seemed to be in his late 40s, a bit older than Jack was now. To that man's left was a woman in her 20s. She was thin and tall with a very businesslike appearance. She had a pretty face with straight, dark hair pulled back, and she was wearing men's work clothes. To her left was a man about her height, handsome with medium hair and clean shaven. He looked to be in his early 30s. Next to him was a man with light hair and spectacles, he was about 40, taller than his friend, and wearing a light-colored shirt with wool pants. On the other side of Seeley was an older man with a shock of white hair and a scraggly white beard. He seemed to be in his 50s or 60s, and he had a sour look on his face. To his right were two men that looked almost identical, with curly, dark hair and long, dark beards, both in their 40s. On the back was a neat, hand-written legend that said, "From Left to right, Angus and Egan Sullivan, Finn McEnhill, Eoinn Seeley, Liam O'Connor, Sam King, Sean O'Neil, Colin O'Shea." He put the picture to the side.

There was a leather folio that held thick paper and was stuffed with clippings. When he opened it, he got very excited. The first page was a journal-style entry written by his great-grandfather, John Seeley.

September 15, 1910

The Great Fire has scattered us to the winds. Crystal Village, that beautiful dream Father spent his life building, lies in ashes. The bridge is gone. Everything we couldn't carry is gone.

Sam O'Connor and Angus Sullivan have been remarkably generous, considering their own losses. They've provided enough capital for Henry O'Connor and me to establish a proper bank. The region desperately needs stability now, with so many displaced and destitute. Access to credit is paramount.

I cannot fathom Father's choice to remain behind. The stubborn, old man always said Crystal Village was his life's work but to die for it? The other Original Eight who survived speak of their last moments in whispers, but none will tell me directly what happened that night.

Mary has convinced me to build our home here in Kellogg. While half the town burned, the location is ideal, close enough to Wallace for business but removed from its rougher elements. The land I've chosen sits above the river, with a view of the mountains. Perhaps distance from Crystal Village will help ease these dark thoughts.

I must remember to write Sam and thank her properly for the financial arrangements. She's handled everything with remarkable composure, though I know she grieves deeply. Strange to think that skinny girl Father and his men found in the wilderness would become such a force in all our lives.

The surveyor comes tomorrow to mark the property lines. Mary insists on a good foundation, she says if we're to put down roots, we should do it properly. She's right, of course. Time to look forward, not back.

Jack assumed the Sam O'Connor mentioned in the journal entry was the Sam King from the picture. She seemed to have married Liam O'Connor or maybe another O'Connor. He wondered if she was related to his old friend, Susanne O'Connor who had lived a few blocks away from his grandparents.

The pages following this entry contained dozens of yellowing and deteriorating newspaper clippings carefully glued down on the pages. They were all about the Great Fire of 1910. Some called it the Big Blowup. There were articles about people who died in the fire and articles about survivors. Some were heroic tales, others tragedies. There was one, small article about Crystal Village.

REMOTE IDAHO MINING SETTLEMENT LOST IN BIG BLOW UP

The Seattle Post-Intelligencer, August 25, 1910

KELLOGG, IDAHO—Among the countless communities devastated by the recent forest fires that swept across the Idaho panhandle, reports have emerged of a secluded mining settlement known as Crystal Village that was completely destroyed, leaving nothing but ash and rubble. The settlement, which was founded in 1867, was reportedly one of the most prosperous private operations in the region.

Survivors arriving in Kellogg confirm that Eoinn Seeley, the settlement's founder, perished along with one other resident while attempting to save vital records from the mining office. The village's bridge across a deep mountain ravine collapsed during the evacuation, cutting off any possibility of return.

The settlement's exact location remains closely held. Survivors have dispersed to various communities throughout the region, ending an unusual experiment in controlled mining development.

Local authorities expect the final death toll from the fires to rise as reports continue to arrive from remote areas.

There were no other journal entries, just the many articles. Jack imagined that John Seeley had intended to write more, but his focus slipped away.

Tucked into the last page of this folio was a hand-drawn map that showed Kellogg and Wallace and showed a trail to follow up to Crystal Village's location. It was hard to be sure how to follow it, as the references were fairly generic and quite out of date. However, then he noticed Eagle City and Murray listed, both of which were ghost towns in the mountains. He got a sense of where this might be. Jack wondered if he could find the ruins of the old mining town.

Years ago, Jack had asked his grandparents why nobody went back up to find the village. At the time, his grandfather simply brushed off the question, saying nothing was left but ghosts.

3

Crossroads

The skinny boy stood on a fence rail outside a small cabin. His cheeks and eyes were hollow, and the sharp bones of his face were clearly visible. He was nine years old. The boy wore a worn felt hat that was too big, a rough sweater of wool, pants that were too short, and scuffed boots. His dirt-stained face bore the remnants of old tears, leaving pale trails down his cheeks. He stood on the bottom rail of the fence and leaned against the top, idly swinging his left leg. He stared balefully, watching the dust cloud fall to the ground amidst the sound of horses snorting and shifting about as they began to settle.

The six men on horseback had pulled up thirty feet back from the boy, watching him. The small windowless cabin behind him had a wisp of smoke rising from a hole in the roof. The split-log fence the boy stood on was part of a pen for pigs, but there were no pigs to be seen, just their lingering odor. The garden near the house had nothing growing in it. A blanket covered the doorway into the cabin instead of a door.

"Hey, lad, what do they call this place?" asked one of the men from the back of his horse in an Irish accent. The boy just stared, not answering. After a moment, another of the men growled hoarsely, "Where's yer family

at? Anyone else around we can talk to?" The boy glared, chewing the insides of his cheeks, swinging his leg in the air. He didn't answer.

Another of the men stepped down off his horse, reached into a saddle bag, and pulled out a cloth that covered something. He walked toward the boy, unwrapping the cloth, and showed him a hard roll of bread, and some cheese. "Would ye fancy a bit of food?" he asked quietly. His voice was kind.

The boy's eyes were fixated on the roll and cheese. Ever so slowly, he licked at his dry, cracked lips and stepped down off the fence, sliding his legs down on the front side toward the men. He ducked his hat-covered head under the top rail. He took a few steps toward the man, then began to teeter to the left and by his third step, he started to collapse slowly to the ground. The man with the roll strode forward and scooped him up, carrying him toward the house. Behind him the other men dismounted and tied their horses off at the fence.

The man with the boy in his arms was the shortest and youngest of the men in his party. He walked quickly toward the cabin, pulled aside the stained gray wool blanket hanging across the doorway, and pushed through with the boy cradled in his arms. As he did, he called out, "Hallo, the house, are ye home? Yer boy is sick!" He peered around the inside of the cabin, allowing his eyes to adjust.

There was a small fire in one corner of the room. The smoke rising to the ceiling, exiting through a hole in the roof. There was a kettle on a stand over the barely smoldering coals. In the corner opposite the hearth a bed frame stood covered with a jumble of blankets. A woman lay on the bed, her dark hair ragged, pulled back from her face. She was dead, her skin ashen and tight and her eyes open and fixed in a stare. She must've died recently as the place had as of yet no smell of death.

In another corner was a small, rough table ringed about with a few stools. An empty bucket sat on the table. In the other corner a vacant cradle stood abandoned. The whole cabin was no more than ten feet across in both directions. The floor of the cabin was hard dirt, having been raked and swept as clean as a dirt floor can be.

The man looked down at the boy in his arms and saw that his eyes were open, watching him, but still hadn't said a word. He ducked back outside and found a clean spot of grass to lay the boy down. He loosened the boy's sweater and looked down the neck at the boy's bony chest. The boy smelled stale, of old sweat and dirt. His hat fell back from his head. The boy's unkempt, greasy hair stuck out in all directions.

"The name's Sean," said the man softly. "Can ye speak? Are ye thirsty?"

The boy nodded his head slightly, and Sean called out to the other men to bring him a canteen.

A clean shaven, blond man arrived with the water, and checked the boy over with cool, gentle hands. "Hello, Colin's my name," said the man. "Yer in a bad way from lack of water, but we'll have ye sorted out directly."

The other men took turns peeking into the cabin, a few of them spread out into the surrounding area, looking for any sign of other survivors. Sean poured a trickle of water into the boy's mouth, who weakly swallowed it. The other men gathered around watching. Eoinn, the tallest of them with a stern but kind face, walked back from having inspected the area behind the cabin.

"Two fresh graves lie just beyond the cabin, one for an adult and another for a babe. There's also a pig slaughter shed, untouched of late. And the privy reeks of foul fish," he said.

At that, several of the men exchanged worried glances, one shuddered. All of them were well aware that the rotten fish smell was a marker for typhoid fever. Without anyone giving orders or making requests, two of them grabbed shovels from their saddles and walked off behind the cabin to dig a third grave. For his part, Sean got the boy to take some more water and a few bites of bread.

"We'll need to clean him up and make camp a distance from this sorrowful place," Eoinn said. "Two of ye wrap the lady and bear her 'round back of the cabin. Then, let's all of us get cleaned off. We crossed a stream not a mile back—that's where we'll set camp and wash the grime away."

The men did as he bid them, efficiently and without complaint. They rode about a mile upstream from the cabin, then made camp. Two of the men started a blazing fire, then threw a black kettle over it filled with water.

After the water warmed up, Sean and Colin stripped the boy's clothes off to clean him up. To their surprise, the child wasn't a boy at all—he was a girl. They carefully shielded the girl from the others. They ladled warm water over her head and went at it with a bar of soap. They gently untangled her rats' nest of hair until, after a few minutes, Colin finally just cut the last bit loose with his knife. They rinsed and dried her off, and wrapped her in a blanket. With the bath completed, Sean took her clothes along with a hunk of soap down to the river. He scrubbed them over a washboard to scour them until they were as clean as he could get them.

Hours later, Sean sat next to the girl near the evening fire. He had spent the remainder of the afternoon encouraging her to take water and eat a bit of bread softened in tea. While he tended to the child, the other men washed off the grime of the trail with warm water and soap. By sunset, the camp was set up. Food was passed around on plates. The girl, having had water and bread all afternoon, seemed ready for something more substantial. They all sat quietly around the fire eating.

Sean began, softly, "What might they call ye, then?"

"Sam." she replied, her voice small but clear.

"Sam, what's your surname, if you don't mind sharing?"

"King," Sam answered, a bit more confidence seeping into her voice. "I'm Samantha King, but Sam suits me. My ma is Amanda, Papa is Henry, and my sister is Glory."

Sean noted the present tense of her family names. "How many years have ye seen, Sam?"

"Nine."

Eoinn had been quietly listening from the other side of the campfire and gently said, "Miss Sam, it's an honor to make your acquaintance under such trying circumstances. My deepest condolences for your loss. Be assured, your mother was shown all the respects due. Your strength in the face of adversity speaks volumes. Ye've done your family proud."

Sam didn't respond but snuggled down in the blanket a bit more.

Sam looked around the fire, watching these men. They all looked tough but not scary. They seemed nice. She listened to them talk. They all had a funny way of talking, sort of like Mrs. O'Leary who had lived behind them in Quincy, Massachusetts. She felt safe and warm. She had a full belly for the first time in days. Eoinn pulled a small bottle of black liquid out of his pack. He gave a sip of it to Sam, it tasted of licorice and fire. Soon her eyes drooped shut and the world disappeared.

Sam woke the next day feeling much better. The men looked the other way while she dressed in her now clean, dry clothes. Once she was ready Eoinn placed her behind Sean on his horse, and together, they resumed their journey on the trail.

After adjusting to the horse's gait, Sean asked, "Sam, have ye kin, be it here in the West or back East? Is there someone we ought to be seeking out on yer behalf?"

"No, my Papa and his kin were at odds. They didn't talk anymore. So we never met. My Ma, she's without kin as well. There's none left for me," her voice dwindled to a whisper.

"My heart aches for ye, Sam. Losing loved ones cuts deep, but not all is lost. We're here in the West in search of land for mining. Fortune willing, the men will send back for their families. You're welcome to join our venture. There'll be work, but you'll be part of our band. Take your time to decide, no rush. Or if ye'd rather, we'll find a safe place for ye to stay. Either way, you're not alone, and you're welcome ta throw in with us."

Sam rode in silence for a while. Then after a while she asked, "Do you have a wife and children waiting to be fetched?"

Sean laughed. "Nay, lass, no family save for these men here. Colin's akin to a brother to me. Fond as I am of young ones, it's the children of my comrades that are like mine own. That it shan't always be just us men, is what's important. In time, we aim to build a homestead, bringing over families and creating a community where ye'll find other young ones to befriend."

Sam grew quiet after that. Still, by the end of the long day of riding, she felt at home with them. They had shared their food and water with her, and she had helped them water their horses. She liked the funny way they talked too. They joked and cajoled each other. She could see herself fitting in with them. These were kind men, like her papa. They were full of quiet jokes, winks, nods. They seemed calm and at ease. Sean was the one who'd been kindest to her, and he also was a jokester with the other men, frequently making them laugh.

The next day they made camp just outside of Virginia City, Montana—the largest town she'd seen since her family had left Chicago. The men asked Sam to tend the horses while they went into town. She was touched that they trusted her with their belongings. So while they were away, she kept the fire going, ate some venison jerky, and looked at the stars. It was then and there that she decided to stay with Sean and the other men.

I I I I

Liam sat at the bar, the hard wooden stool beneath him, his hands spread out on the bar, fingers wide. He smelled whiskey. Tobacco and wood smoke left a cloudy haze in the air. Across the bar there was a wall with a few shelves sparsely lined with bottles. His face was reflected back at him in a small mirror. He could see his unruly auburn hair sticking out like straw beneath his worn, weathered, navy blue hat. His sideburns were wild, and the rest of his face was covered with five days of stubble growth. His green eyes were bloodshot, a mostly empty, chipped and scratched whiskey glass sat in front of him. His dirty gray linen shirt was rolled up at the cuffs to his mid-forearm. He could see his wool, navy blue pants as he looked down his front. On his right stood an empty barstool, on his left a man leaned against the bar, barely four feet away, staring at him.

"I said I don't like Irish, goddamn potato eaters," slurred the drunk man, his weight staggering back and forth between each leg, wobbling. He had a dark look to him; dark skin, dark hair and beard, and blackish-brown eyes. He wore a brown hat and duster and denim pants. The man's right arm was stretched outwards toward him, his fingers opening and closing but generally pointing in his direction, palm downwards. His hand wavered, moving in a slow, unsteady circle in the man's drunken stupor.

Behind the man, Liam could see a medium-sized saloon, with six round tables and a dozen men sprinkled across them in small groups. Some were playing cards. Some were smoking, and all of them were drinking. The room was dimly lit, what light there was being provided mainly by the grimy windows and a precious few, ancient oil lamps. Liam ignored the drunk for a bit, swallowed the rest of his drink in one gulp, and then slowly turned his head and stood up. He towered over the drunk by a good six inches. Liam measured six foot three and was well-knit with broad shoulders and back, his muscles bunched and cabled under his shirt.

"I reckon the feeling might well be mutual, wherever it is ye hail from," said Liam, his Irish accent on full display, "but I can't recall giving ye cause for ire this day, friend. What say ye to a dram of whiskey on my tab, and then we can part as better acquaintances?"

The drunk stiffened and looked up at Liam's hat, then down at Liam's feet. He looked back over his shoulder to see if any of his friends had stood up behind him, but none had.

He considered the much larger man in front of him, saying shakily, "Well now, tha's... tha's a firs' for me," he slurred, swaying slightly. "An Irishman offerin' to buy me a drink." He squinted up at Liam, his expression softening. "Maybe I was... was wrong 'bout you people."

"Liam O'Connor's the name," said Liam, offering his hand to the dark man.

"Stan Brewster," said the man, accepting the proffered hand.

Liam circled the man's shoulder in a friendly embrace and steered him to the stool next to him at the bar. Then he signaled to the bartender for two whiskeys, saying conspiratorially, "What has brought ye out here to the edge of the civilized world, Mr. Brewster?"

Brewster sat tottering back and forth on his bar stool. He drew in a deep breath as if trying to collect himself. Then he lowered his voice to a whisper and said, "Gold, Mis'er O'Con... O'Connel," Brewster mumbled, struggling as he leaned in too close, his breath heavy with whiskey. "Gold, silver, jewels—whatever treas'res these hills might... might yield." He punctuated his statement with a hiccup.

"O'Connor, if ye please, Mr. Brewster. O'Connor. And have ye found any of these riches here in Alder Gulch? I had thought Virginia City was played out by now."

"Nah, we ain't... ain't found none," Brewster said, his words running together as he tried to focus his bleary eyes on Liam. "Too late... we was too late. They've brought in them big hy-hydraulic mining rigs now." He made a wobbly gesture with his hand. "Gets at the deeper veins, see? An' that's when us... us indepen'ent placer miners gotta move on." He tapped the bar for emphasis, nearly missing it entirely. "Me an' the boys, we're thinkin' of... of headin' off to Cal'fornia. Better luck there, maybe."

They sat together at the bar for a few minutes, then Liam graduated to a table with Brewster and a few of his friends. Brewster nodded off to sleep almost as soon as they sat down, but his friends were more animated. As the afternoon wore on, the conversation ranged from a grim assessment of the prospects for a successful strike here, to questions back and forth about Idaho City and southern Idaho territory, to hopefulness for a fresh start in the hills of California.

One man related some of the rumors of small claims in the Bitterroots in Idaho territory. He gave particular credence to stories about the success some were having in the mountains past Hell Gate, now called Missoula Mills. Liam bought several rounds of drinks for the men, and over the course of the evening, their ranks swelled. He asked probing questions about remote mining stakes that had yet to prove out. He didn't say it, but he was looking for places that hadn't struck yet, but that were nonetheless promising. Before the crowd knew it, all their secrets fell out of them.

As the evening wound down, a group of six men entered the saloon. They were dusty from the road, and they took over a large table. The barman brought them a bottle and glasses, and Liam got up to go sit with them. They all had Irish accents.

I I I I

Sam sat on her horse, Victory, following behind Sean. The saddle felt like home to her now, and she remembered ruefully the sores on her inner thighs from the first few days of travel. Eoinn had bought this beautiful Palouse mare for her from a Nez Perce horse dealer. The mare was a young, but gentle horse, and Sam and Victory quickly learned to love each other. Victory had a handsome gray coat with dark spots, almost like a leopard. Sam was always finding her treats and sneaking them to her. The men pretended they didn't notice. Victory was stable, steady, and never spooked. She was agile too and could jump over a five foot high bush. Fearless to the point of recklessness, the mare could swim any body of water. Sam had never loved an animal like she loved Victory.

As they traversed the trail, the mounted riders were strung out in a line, with Angus and Egan in the lead, Finn next, Eoinn behind him, then Sean, Sam, and Colin. Liam brought up the rear. At the moment, they were passing through a mountain pass in Montana, traveling West from the Butte City camp. As always, Victory was steady, but she started to look around instead of ahead, sniffing at the air. Sean was also suddenly very alert. Somehow without her knowing it was happening, Egan, Finn, Colin, and Liam had disappeared. She sat up straight in her saddle and looked around, trying to see where they'd all gotten off to.

What remained of the party came down a short decline into a clearing where the trail turned off to the right and back uphill. Without any warning, a group of men stepped out into the clearing from behind trees all dressed in hats, long dusters and bandanas pulled up over their mouths and noses. Sean pulled up on his reins, stopped his horse, and told Sam to stay calm. Sam pulled up on her reins, and Victory stopped next to Sean's horse.

The men had their pistols raised, and one of them called out in a gruff voice, "We'll be needin' your valuables, and no funny business, you hear?! Keep them hands where we can see 'em." There were four men, each holding a gun. The one closest to Sean and Sam was nervous and twitchy.

Sean said, "Easy there, friend. No need for any rash actions."

Eoinn said from the middle of the group, "We're all calm.. It's all going to be fine."

The first man who had spoken shouted, "Shut it! Enough chatter! Hand over your loot." He stepped forward a few steps and put his hand out toward Eoinn.

Sam was watching the barrel of the gun the man was pointing at Eoinn, and kept glancing back at the man who had his gun trained on Sean. She, it seemed, was not enough of a threat to concern the men. She considered that for a moment and wondered if there was anything she could do.

There was a sudden sound, and in a flash, all four robbers had a man standing close behind them with a knife pressed to their throats. Finn, Egan, Colin, and Liam had returned without warning, and now the highwaymen were lowering their pistols and handing them over. Eoinn slid out of his saddle and walked to the man who'd been pointing his gun at him. He took the man's gun from Egan. He leaned in toward the man, who was petrified, shaking and covered in sweat. He whispered something. The man shook his head in response and said, "N-no, sir. Just us."

Eoinn sniffed and examined the man's pistol. Then he pulled down the bandit's bandana disdainfully and looked him over. The bandit was about 30 years old. Eoinn leaned back in and said something else to him. Sam couldn't hear what was said, but the tone of Eoinn's voice was unlike anything she'd heard before from him. The bandit suddenly lost control of his bladder and his pants darkened, dark, yellow urine pooling under his boots.

Eoinn grimaced in disgust and then looked at Finn, who pushed his man to the ground. Beside Sam, Sean slid from his horse to take control of the cowed man. Finn walked back into the woods, and they could hear his voice talking gently, soothingly. They heard the winnie of horses, and a few minutes later, Finn led out a line of four horses, pulled off their bridles, and let them go. He went to the first horse, whispered in its ear, and it ran off down the trail in the direction they'd come. The other horses followed, leaving behind them only the sound of their hooves as they galloped off into the forest. Finn went back into the woods for a few minutes and came back carrying weapons, some knives, an axe, and several bags. The robbers looked scared. Finn put the weapons in his saddle bags, and nodded at

Eoinn.

"Gentlemen, I am Captain Eoinn Seeley, formerly of the Irish Brigade, Union Army. Ye've gravely erred today, and your futures now hang in the balance. We've freed your horses and taken your weapons. Ye'll be left with just enough to survive your journey back. But mark my words: if our paths cross again, ye will not be so fortunate. We've no quarrel with former Confederates, but we will not tolerate thievery or threats. Change your ways, or face the consequences! Understood?"

All four men nodded and said they did. Eoinn left the most frightened and nervous of the four untied, Finn tied the rest to trees. He told the fourth man that he could untie his friends once Eoinn and his men had cleared the next turn of the path. He agreed, then Eoinn's men remounted, and they all headed onward down the trail.

When they'd been traveling for a while, Sam asked Sean, "How did Eoinn know that they were Rebel soldiers?"

Sean said, "Their pistols were knock offs of the Colt Navy revolver, with brass handles. Those were made in the South during the War. Also, they had little bits of Confederate kit, pieces of uniforms, just little things ... but ye can tell."

"What did Eoinn say to that man that made him so scared?" asked Sam in a whisper.

Sean chuckled softly, "Let's just say Eoinn knows how to make a man reconsider his life choices. He's got a way with words that can chill you to the bone."

I I I I

July 1867

It had been almost four months since the men had saved her, and Sam had gotten to know them pretty well.

Sean was still her favorite. He was handsome and in his twenties. Sean was the shortest of the men, with a mop of reddish-brown hair and big, green eyes. He was clean shaven, but frequently had a stubble of bright red beard. Sean always carried himself with a bit of whimsy, always making jokes that made the other men snicker and laugh. He was a good musician and singer, and he knew many plays and poems and songs by heart. At any given moment he might be singing an old folk song, or he might be telling a hilarious joke, or he might be reciting Shakespeare.

Colin was a blond doctor who wore spectacles. He had been a doctor assigned to their company in the army, and he was the only one besides Sean who was clean shaven. Sean and Colin were close. Often when they set up camp, they would sleep next to each other. When they stayed in hotels, they would share a room.

There was Eoinn, who led the group. He was quiet and steady, and when he spoke, the other men simply did as he said without ever questioning him. He had dark, straight hair that hung almost to his shoulders and a dark mustache that he would stroke and tug on as he considered a course of action. Sam had thought of Eoinn as tall ... until Liam showed up.

Liam was very tall, strong and charming. But he was always disappearing for a day or two on various missions that were assigned to him by Eoinn. He had wild, auburn hair and long, scraggly sideburns, but he shaved his upper lip and chin periodically.

Angus and Egan, the Sullivan brothers that looked almost like twins, both had dark brown, curly hair and long reddish-brown beards in their late thirties or early forties. Angus was always busy with his hands, always fixing or making things, and he was deadly accurate with a throwing knife. He had the best head for business in the group, and when they had to buy supplies, he would take charge of negotiations. On the other hand, Egan was quiet and let Angus speak for him for the most part. Still, when Egan spoke, all the men stopped to listen. Sam soon realized that Egan was very smart, perhaps a genius. He also had a very dry sense of humor. At first she didn't understand when he was making jokes, but as time went by, she noticed that the other men would chuckle quietly sometimes when he spoke. As the weeks passed, she started to understand his pointed comments and find the humor in them.

Last of all, Finn was the oldest, with white hair laced with bright, red streaks, bushy eyebrows, and a short, white and red beard. While his hair was turning white, he couldn't have been older than fifty. Finn was cranky, always grumbling and complaining, finding fault with everyone's work. But nobody ever took him seriously, and Sam noticed that despite his constant complaining, he was the hardest worker. She realized that he would always lend a hand when someone was struggling to get something done. He was usually the first one up and would get the fire going and make the meals. Beyond that, he was always aware of where everything was across all the men's packs. Sam came to understand that his complaining was like a reflex for him, and the other men always teased him, what they called, "taking the piss".

The men were all Irish. They had all grown up in the same village in the Irish countryside and came to America on the same boat years ago. When the War broke out, they'd answered the call to serve in the Union Army, and miraculously, they had all avoided significant injury despite seeing plenty of fighting.

One night over the campfire, Sam asked Sean where they were from in Ireland, and he had said, "A village called Sedennan, near the town of Omagh." But he implied that they'd left Ireland a long time before coming to America, that they'd gone over to Europe for some time. She tried to sort out how that could be true, since Sean seemed to be about twenty-five years old.

They'd spent most of the summer riding across the West looking for a place to set up a mining camp. There was no shortage of places to stake claims, but Eoinn had very specific things he was looking for in a place to set up his mining operation. One morning over breakfast Sam asked Eoinn about it. "Sir," she said, "it's been months since I joined you, and we've been to many towns, camps, and claims without once picking up a pan or doing any mining whatsoever. What is it that you're looking for?"

Eoinn was quiet for a moment, then he said, "For many a year, I've been in search of a spot to call home, with most precise notions on its requirements. Security and sanctuary are paramount. I have a dream of a community where everyone works for a common set of goals. The main one of these goals being to live together in peace and by working together to achieve prosperity. This is known as an 'intentional community' to many, and that is my goal. To that point, I want to find a place where we might establish mines akin to those we'd built back home, or rather our forebears had. And then to bring all our families to live with us."

That was the same day they'd ridden into Missoula Mills, the last town east of the Bitterroot mountains on the Mullan Military Road between Fort Benton and Walla Walla. The town was small, including most notably the Worden & Co. Mercantile and roughly another dozen buildings. For the most part, it was a tent-town with another twenty or so white tents hosting people and businesses. Sean told her that things had been mighty busy on the Mullan Road a few years ago with miners going west and east. But things had slowed in the last few years. Still, the townsfolk believed that business could pick up any time, perhaps as soon as another find started a stampede. A "stampede" is what they called it when men would swarm like bees over the wilderness looking for gold, silver, and jewels.

They rode up to the Worden & Company Mercantile, which was a small building made from wide boards with a wood-shingled roof. They tied off their horses, and the whole group went inside—except for Finn, who stayed outside because he didn't want to be "shoved and stepped on by ye great oafs."

The interior of Worden & Company Mercantile was absolutely wondrous to Sam's eyes. Every inch of the place was covered in things to buy. Even the ceiling rafters were hung with all sorts of goods. The building smelled of spices and smoked meats. Sam was free to wander the aisles, fingering fabrics and cooking supplies. She saw on the counters that there were pickles, spices, candies, and crackers, some in jars, some in bottles, and some in paper wrappers. Hams and jerky hung from the ceilings alongside dried herbs. A sign read that potatoes and onions were available. A crate marked cheese had a wheel of dry, hard cheese sitting on top, with slices laid out for tasting. Long candies of many colors stood upright in a clear, glass jar.

Behind the counter a man and woman engaged with the various customers, answering questions and ringing up sales. He was handsome, short in height with a long beard and receding hairline, light brown in color. Likewise, the woman was beautiful, with glossy, black hair, wavy and carefully combed, parted down the middle, and pulled back in a bun at the back of her head. Her dress was lovely and reflected the latest Eastern styles. It was a deep, almost purplish red. The fabric was shiny, and it had a corseted waist, flaring out below the woman's hips.

Angus and Egan promptly approached the woman with a list of the supplies that were needed by the group. She glanced at the list, and she walked around the store helping them locate the items. Eoinn was deeply engaged in conversation with the man, who he addressed as Frank and greeted as if he were an old friend. The woman they called Lu, and she was Frank's wife. She saw Frank pass Eoinn a letter, and Eoinn raised his eyebrows in surprise. He thanked Frank and stepped outside to read it in the sunlight.

Sean surprised Sam by tapping her shoulder. When she turned, he handed her a long, thin stick of candy. "Oooh," she said, "may I taste it?" He said, "Of course, I bought it for ye, lass. Ye can eat it all now, or ye can have some now, and save the rest for later."

The woman Lu watched Sam from behind the counter, smiling at her. Sam carefully tore the top of the paper wrapper off the stick of candy, and she put the one-inch long top in her mouth.

She smiled excitedly at Sean and Lu, and said, "Ooh, it's sweet, and spicy, and smells like flowers!"

Lu chuckled and said, "That's an Elderflower candy. We also have ginger candy, lavender, sarsaparilla, and butterscotch."

Sean bustled Sam out of the store, but behind them the other men were buying sweets for Sam as surprises for later.

IIII

Northern Idaho, August 1867

In the cabin, Barney sat in front of the stove. A pang of grief twisted in his chest—he missed his brother, and he missed his wife and daughter back in Chicago. He regretted coming out here.

He'd saved about a hundred dollars in six months of mining. It was barely enough to get him back home—and it was nowhere near what he and Hank had spent coming out. Between them, they'd sunk a few hundred dollars into travel and supplies. He had a bag of garnet crystals weighing nearly twenty pounds, but he had no idea what they were really worth. The hundred he'd made had come from the sale of a similar bag, but the assayer had said the stones' value all depended on quality. He wasn't broke, but he sure as hell wasn't getting ahead either. None of the riches he'd imagined had shown up.

The tin plate rested between his bony knees. He sopped up the last of the broth from his beans and salt pork with the hard, stale bread he'd baked just after Hank died. Their placer mining was steady, but it had yielded only garnets and flecks of gold too small to matter. He knew he'd have to make the decision to leave soon—summer was fading, and Joe warned they'd have twenty feet of snow by Thanksgiving.

Hank had been paranoid about food stores, so Barney knew he wouldn't starve if he chose to stay. They had enough to feed an army. But his heart wasn't in it. Hank was buried out behind the cabin, near the edge of the ravine. Barney's dream had died with his brother. He was lonely, sad, and tired of pretending otherwise. He missed his brother. He missed his family.

He wanted to go home.

As Barney finished his pork and beans, the sun dipped lower in the sky. He scraped out his bowl, then paused at the sound of mules braying. Stepping outside, he made his way toward the rope bridge to check on them in their pen across the ravine.

Halfway there, he stopped. Several men stood on the far side, watching him. His chest tightened, a small pang of panic pinched his heart, but after a moment's study, he relaxed. They looked all right. A few wore remnants of Union blues, bits of insignia and coat trim, familiar signs. He and Hank had worn the same.

Barney raised a hand in greeting. One of the men stepped onto the bridge. There were eight of them in all—seven men and a boy of about ten, climbing on the mule pen fence, studying the animals with open curiosity. Barney felt a flicker of relief that only one man was crossing. He was proud of that bridge. It had taken a lot of work, and he was pleased to see how easy the crossing looked.

The man stepped off the bridge on this side of the ravine, rubbed his hands, and stretched his back as he politely waited for Barney to approach.

He stood tall, just over six feet, with long, dark hair. He wore a waxed duster, leather gloves, and a wide-brimmed hat pulled low. A long mustache framed his face. There was something familiar about him. Then Barney realized that he had met this man before. He was one of Hank's friends from the War, a name Hank had spoken often, always with respect.

The man stripped off his glove and extended his hand. His grip was firm.

"Eoinn Seeley, at your service," he said. His voice held an Irish lilt, deep and refined, almost noble.

"Barney Randall, sir," Barney said, gripping his hand. "We met after Gettysburg. You came with Hank to see me in the infirmary. It's good to see you again, sir. What can I do for you?"

Seeley nodded, standing calm and still. He had the quiet weight of someone used to command.

"My men and I have been traveling from back East. We're looking to do some mining. I'd heard from your brother Hank, back in Missoula Mills, that ye were up here. We've kept in touch over the last few years. I knew he was heading this way, but I hadn't heard where he'd ended up. He left word for me at the Worden & Company Mercantile. His note said a few other men had set up claims on this plateau, but that there might be room for more. Is your brother nearby?"

Barney looked down at his feet, then over toward Hank's grave. He cleared his throat, his voice cracking under the weight of his grief. "He is nearby. My dear brother Hank—may the Lord hold him in His embrace—

died just last week. A mere cut while panning and it festered. Lockjaw. Five days and he was gone. Before that misfortune, our days were joyful, preparing for winter."

"Damn," said Seeley, his voice low. "That pains me dearly to hear, Mr. Randall. I was sore looking forward to seeing your brother again. We spent many an hour talking about life after the War, and how we'd hoped to live it. He was a good man—steady and strong. A true friend. It's a tragedy."

Barney nodded, eyes welling. "From time to time, Hank spoke of you, Colonel Seeley. I didn't know you were still in contact—or that he'd left word for you. He esteemed you highly ..." He choked on the words and looked away, struggling to regain his composure.

Seeley placed a hand on Barney's shoulder and the two men stood there in silence. There were tears in Seeley's eyes too—a shared sorrow for the loss of a good man.

Seeley took a deep breath and let his gaze sweep across the land, right to left, studying the contours in silence. This flat stretch was something of an alpine valley, cut through by the deep ravine. The cove of land stretched about one mile deep and just over a mile wide, bordered by two sharp peaks with a third rising farther back. Between them ran the ravine—silver water winding through stone far below.

On the far side, where his men waited with the horses near the mule pen, the ground flattened for a mile before climbing steeply into forest. The trail they'd followed to the camp had been narrow, weaving through a grove of ancient cedars that towered over the path like a cathedral. It was a place that quieted men—primeval, still, powerful, and somehow removed from the world beyond.

This side of the ravine offered a broad curve of level ground. Four cabins stood apart, spaced along the flats in the shadow of the ridge. Several cold, clear springs emerged from the base of the mountain, feeding slender creeks that threaded through the basin. One stream ran toward them, then bent right, dropping into the ravine in a thin, steady, sparkling fall.

He could feel the throb of the earth here. It pulsed with life and deep, old energy. He could almost sense where deposits of ore lay hidden beneath the mountain, where gems might wait in silence. This was the place he had hoped for, longed for—and here it stood. Real. He felt a deep desire to own this place.

Seeley took in every detail but said nothing. His eyes lingered on the lines of slope and stone, the lay of the water, the cabins, the way the light fell on the grass at this hour. His face remained unreadable, but something in his stillness carried weight.

He exhaled slowly.

"My men and I are seeking a stake," he said, voice measured. "With time, if fortune favors us, we hope to bring our families west. We aren't chasing gold dust from one canyon to the next. We're looking for a place we might keep for generations. For a home."

He turned slightly toward Barney. "I've long watched experiments around the world of the development of intentional communities, where a sense of community, safety, and cooperation rule the day. A utopian dream. Your brother's note suggested your group had made some headway here. And perhaps, after a season's labor, some among ye might consider selling a claim."

There was no press to the words, no demand. Just a quiet invitation.

The sincerity in Seeley's voice was unmistakable. Barney could sense the man's yearning for a stable life, for a future for his family. His heart hammered in his chest, a mix of fear and hope. Even before Hank's death, some of the men had begun to question the venture. The gold hadn't come easily. Lately, even Joe had spoken of returning East. It was as if the infusion of companions had broken through the hard crust of his need for solitude.

And now these newcomers stood at the edge of their clearing, calm and capable—and here, perhaps, to stay.

Seeley paused to gauge Barney's interest. Barney's mind raced. The idea of leaving felt both a relief and a betrayal of Hank's memory. But the thought of home—of his wife and daughter—tugged at his heart. This offer felt like a lifeline tossed to a drowning man.

"We'd be willing to pay a fair sum," Seeley said, "if what ye've done so far looks promising. Some of us come from a long line of miners in the old country. We'd love a spot like this to try our hand again."

Barney sighed, weariness in his voice. "Well, Mr. Seeley, I find myself at something of a crossroads. We've pulled garnets of good quality from the creeks. Gold's been scarce—flecks here and there, the occasional nugget—but hardly enough to suggest fortune lies beneath. Silver's shown itself too, though in modest quantity. The garnets hold promise. We've hoped that, with deeper digging and the proper tools, there might yet be something more. But the West is littered with dreams like ours—men chasing riches and finding only hardship."

He paused, then added, "Your proposal offers a reprieve. And it's heartening to hear that your mission is greater than the hunt for wealth alone."

Seeley had listened closely, his eyes intent. There was a spark of interest in the details of the mining—not eagerness but something focused and alive behind his calm expression.

"That, Mr. Randall, carries the ring of promise to my ears. Our aspirations do stretch beyond mining alone. We seek a haven, a place where our families can live in peace. The West is beautiful, aye, but also lawless. After years of war, our hearts crave sanctuary. We desire a village, modest and well-tended, where our children might grow safely, where neighbors work together, and no man is left to fend for himself. A community built with intent, led for the common good. And this place—it may well be it."

Barney believed him. There was no guile in Seeley's voice, only a quiet conviction. It resonated with his own weariness, his longing for home. He looked toward the mountain, then down at his feet. After a moment, he said, "Mr. Seeley, upon reflection, it seems you may indeed have stumbled upon your refuge. With Hank gone, my thoughts turn more and more toward Chicago. I believe others may feel the same."

Seeley's expression softened. "Sir, my heart weighs heavy at the loss of your brother. He was a cherished friend. On behalf of my men, many of whom know the sting of loss, let me assure ye—your decision to return home casts no shadow upon your character. We've all said goodbye to people we loved. That sorrow drives us, as well."

Barney nodded, then looked out toward the distant cabins. His mind lingered on the faces of the other men, each of them holding his own quiet dreams and disappointments.

"As for the others," Barney said, "I dare not speak for them. But it's fair to say they're as green to mining as Hank and I were. The summer's been fair, this place has a kind of peace to it, but the winter is another matter. I imagine with winter looming, with its isolation and daunting snows, it might well change some hearts."

He hesitated, then added by way of a warning, "The man who found this place survived a winter here. He said by Thanksgiving the snow stood twenty feet deep in the passes. Mining, especially placer work, becomes near impossible. There's been talk of leaving before the snows come. If you were to offer terms that helped them recover their stake and get out in comfort, I think you might well strike a deal."

Seeley nodded, thoughtful. His gaze drifted across the land again, distant but deliberate. "Thank ye, Mr. Randall. We'll make certain your companions are treated fairly. It's not merely claims we seek, but a foundation. For a future worth building."

The challenges of mining in this rugged terrain were not lost on Eoinn. The Bitterroot Mountains were as treacherous as they were promising. The region's history was littered with tales of hardship. His experience in the War had taught him the value of preparation and resilience. Success here would demand careful planning, technological innovation, and a steadfast commitment to the community's vision. Eoinn and his men were determined to apply their disciplined approach and see it through.

He asked if they could corral their horses with the mules and set up camp. The request was met kindly, and once the plan was settled, Seeley crossed back over the bridge to relay it. The men settled the horses, then used the basket to pass their saddlebags, and crossed one by one behind him.

Barney showed them a good spot to set up for the night—a place where earlier arrivals had made camp. Then he went to speak with the other miners, hoping to gather them for a meeting. They usually came together once a fortnight to share some whiskey and company. Since Hank's passing, they hadn't done so.

Over the next few days, Seeley and his men met with each of the miners one-on-one. The conversations weren't without hesitation. Joe, in particular, was cautious—questioning the newcomers' intentions, weighing the worth of what they'd found. But one night of shared stories and a bottle of whiskey softened his heart. It also helped that Seeley had many stories of Hank to share.

Four days after their arrival, the newcomers had reached agreements with each of the men. Seeley's group made a strong impression—quiet, steady, and full of grit. But more than that, they were good men. They'd taken in a young orphan and spoke little but worked hard. The miners felt comfortable passing along their efforts to hands like these.

None of them got rich, but when they gathered together afterward, they spoke openly of relief. There was satisfaction in the terms and a strange peace in letting go. They would return home with heads high—their unfulfilled dreams lightened by the promise of something new.

As the men packed their belongings onto the mules across the ravine, Barney lingered at Hank's grave. The wind carried the scent of pine, and the low murmur of the creek reached his ears. A bittersweet pang rose in his chest, knowing a part of him would remain here, buried with his brother. But in his heart, he carried the hope of home.

I I I I

12th September, 1867
  To: John A. Roebling
  From: Eoinn Seeley

Dear John,

It's been some time since we met for a fine dinner in Cincinnati and discussed our compatible visions for utopian communities. I have thought of that evening often as my friends and I made our way across this beautiful country. We have made our settlement within the Idaho Territory, a week's travel from Missoula Mills in the Montana Territory. I've included an address where you can send your correspondence. We have found a promising location to set up our village, and the mining endeavors have proven most fruitful. We almost feel bad for having bought out the claims of the men who were here, as we quickly found much more than they'd achieved in a season of mining.

I thought of you immediately when I found the location for the mines that my men and I have hoped to put in place. It is a beautiful situation, a flat spot between three peaks—a cove of land one mile by one mile across, at some three thousand feet of altitude in the Bitterroot Mountains. The primary peak rises some six thousand feet to the east, and the secondary to some five thousand to the north, the third to about four thousand to the south, with a ridgeline to the west at about five thousand feet. There is good hunting for deer, elk, and bighorn sheep, and plenty of small birds, with grouse of three types and doves being quite plentiful in season. No bears or cougars have made their territory here.

There is fresh water aplenty, with sweet springs that gurgle and pool delightfully. To our great excitement, there is a wonderful hot spring that smells not of sulfur but faintly of iodine, with waters at the exit point just over 120 degrees Fahrenheit. It drops significantly by the time it reaches the first of the pools, such that it is just tolerable, and by the third pool is like bath water. The skies here are clearer than anywhere I've been, and the atmosphere is most wonderful. The weather has turned colder these last few days, and from what we've been told by the previous inhabitants, we can expect plenty of snow by Thanksgiving, apparently above the top of the existing cabins!

I write to you in part because there is an interesting engineering problem you may be able to help address. The approach to this cove of land is very passable, easily covered by foot, horse, or mule. With only minor improvements it could handle wagons. With an eye to the future, a light-gauge railroad to haul supplies and ore is not out of the question. However, the final approach to the cove is separated from the passable terrain by a ravine with a one hundred foot drop, and about seventy five feet across.

The sides of the ravine are stable and firm, but the current arrangement means leaving horses and mules on the far side. The current traverse is of a simple rope bridge with planks and a pulley system for carrying goods. This obviously will not do for the long term. I have, as always, an eye toward the future. My hope is for my men to bring their families to settle here, and as you know, my Rose is eager to join me as well. But I cannot imagine women and children using such a contraption on a regular basis. I do also have in mind the hauling of larger volumes of ore and supplies, both in and out of the village.

I've included drawings of the ravine and of the approach and landing on each side. For obvious reasons, I do not include any sort of map, but we are a full week's trip by foot from Missoula Mills, at least given current conditions. Improvements to the trail, leading in time to a proper road, could reduce this journey considerably. If you have any thoughts on a design for a bridge that might more permanently straddle this gap, I would be sincerely grateful. I'd like to erect some kind of wooden structure at the outset, but over time, I imagine a beautiful stone and iron span—like those drawings you once showed me for your ideas in bridge design.

I am well aware of the considerable engineering prowess such a task demands. That is why my thoughts turned immediately to you, whose expertise in such matters is unparalleled. The successful construction of such a bridge would not only mark a significant advancement in our mining operations, but also ensure the safety and well-being of our families, including my dear Rose, who is ever so eager to join me in this splendid isolation.

I await your esteemed guidance with great anticipation and extend my sincerest thanks in advance for your consideration of my request.

Please keep all of this in the strictest confidence. Even a rumor of what I've said could cause a stampede of miners, as has happened too often in the West.

Sincerely,
  Eoinn Seeley
  Return correspondence at
  The Worden & Co. Mercantile
  Missoula Mills, Montana

IIII

15th October, 1867
  From: John Roebling
  To: Eoinn Seeley

My dear friend Eoinn,

It was indeed a source of great joy to receive your letter, the first in many months. I find myself ensconced in Cincinnati, and your news from the distant western wilds, detailing the commencement of your ambitious, utopian village in the mountains, has filled me with profound satisfaction. As you well remember, my own endeavors at an intentional community outside Philadelphia did not culminate as I had anticipated. Perhaps, the secluded location you have selected shall prove to be the requisite solution. My son, Washington, extends his heartfelt regards and well wishes to you.

Upon perusing your drawings, I have devised several sketches for a temporary as well as a permanent bridge. The temporary construction, entirely of wood, is designed for the solitary passage of individuals and livestock. I must emphatically advise against its use for large groups of people or multiple horses simultaneously. The permanent bridge, envisioned in stone and steel, awaits our collaborative efforts to procure the necessary steel for the span. Although I believe local sources can suffice for the stone, I implore you to consider the long-term stability of the ravine's banks with great care. My absence from the site precludes me from offering a design guaranteed to endure through the ages.

I eagerly await updates on your progress and the opportunity to lend my assistance. The prospect of beholding the permanent bridge in person is one I cherish. However, my recent proposal for a suspension bridge in New York, connecting southern Manhattan and Brooklyn, has been accepted. Preparations for my relocation to New York are underway. This endeavor will undoubtedly occupy nearly all of my time, yet I harbor hope that upon its completion, I may visit your mountainous village. Washington and I, having deliberated upon your letter, agree that the proposed design offers the optimal solution for stability. Given the presumed steadiness of the ravine's sides and the logistical advantages provided by your remote location, we believe our design will minimize the requisite quantity of steel to complete the project.

With sincere regards,

John A. Roebling

4

Opportunity

Jack Seeley sat in the waiting room of his idol, a man he saw as the greatest living legend in his industry, a man he aspired to emulate. Yomohiro Corporation had flown him to Japan for this meeting, and he was excited, his stomach full of butterflies. The job would be a dream come true, leading a whole new division of the company in the US.

Kisho Yomohiro was a man in his late sixties who walked with a lithe energy in his step. His goatee and glasses look was legendary in Japan, an integral part of the corporate logo. He favored tweed jackets and bow ties, with faded Levis and tennis shoes. Yomohiro was an animator and filmmaker. To many, he was the Walt Disney of the 21st Century. But where Disney had favored fanciful humor, Yomohiro's vision ran a bit to the darker side. Where Disney would turn to a Mickey, Goofy, Dopey, or Donald—Yomohiro would turn to a shadowy figure off in the corner, a playful monster, or mysterious witch. His vision tended to the fantastic, the magical, the wondrous but never to the goofy or silly.

The idea was to bring the spirit of Yomohiro Corporation out of Japan, to create a theme park-based experience tailored to a US aesthetic but with all the advanced techniques proven in the Japanese parks. The balance would be tricky; for out of more than thirty feature films and two extremely successful theme parks in Japan, only a handful of the films were commercial successes in the US. The Japanese theme parks were definitely not designed to a US audience's expectations. There were no rides, just spaces. There were no characters running around signing autographs—there were subtle spirits that were created through amazing special effects using light, sound, and mechanicals.

Yomohiro's vision for theme parks catered more to a sense of wonder, discovery, and mystery when compared to a high throughput US park. Yomohiro's parks were limited to a very small number of visitors at a time. This led to a lottery, and subsequently, it resulted in a secondary auction marketplace where tickets sometimes sold for tens of thousands of dollars. There was a hugely popular, reality television series where a camera crew would follow people through the parks, a new guest every week. In the past, such an idea translated to the US seemed unlikely. Jack wondered if something had changed.

Jack's background was as a Disney Imagineer for the last eighteen years. He designed and created theme park attractions for the various Disney parks. His many designs resulted in some concepts that ended up being made into video games. Eventually, several were made into motion pictures. He saw unprecedented success at an early stage in his career, which led to some significant promotions. But as he got promoted to bigger roles, he found more of his time was spent managing minutia rather than creating bold, breathtaking experiences. He found that his personal vision was diluted, and much of the wonder he liked to evoke in his audiences was simply not realized in the final experience. He was managing his team of Imagineers, not leading them, not doing it himself—a less than ideal situation. Last week he got a phone call on his mobile from a recruiter at Yomohiro Corporation, and today, he was sitting in Tokyo in the waiting room of Yomohiro-san's private office.

The rooms were lush, but darkly lit. They were dramatic and theatrical and evoked a strong sense of wonder.

As Jack sat in the oversized Victorian high-back chair, a high pitched huffing, wheezing sound emanated from under the drapery. As Jack watched a small lump the size of a ping pong ball raced up to the top of the window where it slid under the wallpaper. From there, it moved around the top of the window, then out from under the wallpaper, and under the drapery again. Finally, it slid back down the other side before disappearing when it reached the floor. A very quiet creaking sound evoked the sense that something was crawling under the floorboards heading right toward him. Then there was a quiet thump and a moan rose up from the floor just underneath his feet. A light breeze blew across his ankles, toward the entrance of the waiting room, and the door opened a crack and then shut. Jack watched all this unfold, utterly enthralled, knowing it was all practical effects. He was in awe that this amount of detail was designed into the waiting room. As Jack thought about it, Yomohiro opened the door to his office and beckoned him inside. Apparently, he didn't have an assistant, at least not today.

They walked down a short hallway side by side and entered a large office with two desks, a drafting table, three large wall-screens, and life-size models of characters from Yomohiro's movies, These life-size models included a white, serpentine dragon that wound around the entire room in curls and swirls, his tail to the left of the door, his head to the right of it. Unlike nearly every meeting Jack had ever had in Japan—there was no bowing except a subtle nod of the head. The atmosphere was very casual.

Yomohiro motioned his hand toward one of the chairs urging Jack to sit before quickly seating himself. He sat on the edge of his chair rather than back in it, leaning toward Jack, but not saying a word. Jack sat down and took a neutral position on the chair, but didn't relax back into it. When they were seated, Jack noted that both of their chairs were identical and of the same height. Both were comfortable, leather club chairs, either in actuality worn and faded or done for effect.

"I love the scene in the movie *Brazil*, where Jonathan Price comes home to his apartment to find that the workers have taken apart his heating and cooling systems," said Kisho Yomohiro, his eyes lighting up with childlike enthusiasm. "Bob Hoskins and Derrick O'Connor are fantastic in those roles. Then Robert De Niro arrives as Harry Tuttle, the freelance plumber and extracts revenge before flying away on a zipline." Yomohiro's eyes had a slight glint, wonder shining across his face as he recalled the scene, his voice almost breathless. Yomohiro's English was flawless, with hardly a trace of an accent.

Jack relaxed a bit and smiled as he said, "That's one of my all time favorite movies. De Niro was so beautifully cast in that role. It was so outside the spectrum he usually covered in those days. The scenes of Jonathan Price flying in his winged armor were inspiring."

"I've seen every movie Terry Gilliam made several times. I watch *Brazil* once a year," said Yomohiro. "I thought of that scene, with De Niro swinging away on the zipline, when I rode on the Superhero ride you created in Disneyland Japan. It was elegantly executed, very subtle effects, and absolutely enjoyable. I rode it ten times and saw something new each time."

Jack watched as Yomohiro settled back a bit in his chair. "Thank you," he said.

"You were thinking of that scene when you created that ride, weren't you?" As Jack nodded in response, Yomohiro's face burst into a wide smile. "That's why I need you to run my team in the United States. I can see that we have a compatible vision." He paused thoughtfully before going on. "You know the story of how Gilliam made that movie, eh? That his vision was taken apart, then brought to market as a bastardized piece of vomit? That it almost drove him out of filmmaking altogether?"

Jack nodded, "Yes, it was one of my favorite movies, but it barely made it into the world. It actually inspired me in many ways. I saw his cut of the film in the theater when I was only fourteen years old. It was playing at a film festival, and my friend dragged me in to see it. Then in the first scene, one of the projectors broke down. They had to pause for about five minutes between each reel for the rest of the film. As we waited, my friend and I discussed the previous scenes between reels. It changed the way I thought about movies."

Yomohiro leaned forward in his chair again. "You understand then!" He snapped his fingers. "I thought so, when I rode on your rides, played your video games, and saw the films made from them. You didn't let them change your vision. There was a clear connecting thread between them all."

"Thank you for your kind words," said Jack. "You clearly didn't see Wondergate if you feel that way." He smiled ruefully.

"I gave you the benefit of the doubt on that one," Yomohiro chuckled. "It was the first film made from one of your projects, and that director ... very controversial. I did very much enjoy your commentary on the extended version of the film."

Jack sat back in his seat, surprised. A slow smile washed across his face. "Tell me about what you're trying to do with the parks business in the US," he asked.

Yomohiro leaned forward in his chair as he began to explain where he wanted to go with the US Parks project. His affect was very animated and energetic. "During Covid," he began, "most of the theme parks in the world were in serious trouble. But our parks in Japan had steady revenue. We build our parks' business around the idea that stories come first, that the experience of visiting the park is intimate, not an experience aimed at large scale crowds. When our customers walk into another world, they feel truly immersed in the experience of that world."

Jack nodded. "I haven't been able to get a ticket because of the lottery."

"Yes," said Yomohiro. "The lottery is the trick with the parks. The parks barely break even, but they birth everything else; the television show, the games, the mystique itself. In Japan, we build from movies to parks to shows. The park is the physical extension of the movie universe into the real world. We create the real world around intensely detailed physical exposition of the movie world. The video games expand access to everyone, so anyone can visit that world any time they like. But the parks are exclusive experiences for very few people. We make all the money from the show and the games."

Jack said, "I don't think that the model will translate into the US the same way. The movies are not as widely consumed in the US. You'd need to start over, create a blockbuster US movie just to base the theme parks on. But audiences are fickle. You never know if it will really take off. It could take years to build the audiences and enthusiasm needed to get the excitement flowing for the parks business."

Yomohiro sat back smiling. "You see the problem. Good. Here in Japan we made several very popular movies, which sparked the parks. Which sparked the show. Which sparked the games. In the US, we must start with the park. We must create something that speaks to the American soul. We need to craft a story that is epic, create a park experience that fundamentally taps into the American psyche. We need to create a park that is so real, so detailed, that a whole world can explode from it. From there we will proceed to movies, the US version of the show, and of course, the games. Games are where we have found we make the most money on a recurring basis because it's a subscription."

The two men talked for hours.

I I I I

Oakland, California, May 2028

Jack began unpacking his office late on a Tuesday evening in early May. It was the second day at his new job. Yomohiro-san himself had come to visit him to ensure he was getting settled in, having timed a trip to the US with Jack's first week.

The brand new building where Jack worked was located on the waterfront, on Powell Street in Oakland, California, and it looked out across the bay to San Francisco. From his office window, Jack could see the gantry cranes at the port of Oakland. Those cranes famously were claimed to have inspired the Imperial walkers in *The Empire Strikes Back*, and it couldn't be denied that they were visible from the old Lucasfilm offices at the Presidio on the opposite side of the bay. This building in Oakland was the new U.S. headquarters of Yomohiro Corporation and Studio Yomohiro. They were a few blocks from the Pixar offices, where Jack had spent some time during his Disney days.

Jack had a month of work ahead of him, but he had arranged for a month-long break in June as part of his package. He wanted to get settled into the new role and start his hiring process for the new team before taking time to visit his grandmother again in Idaho. It had been clear during his last trip in March that she didn't have much time left at one hundred years old. He hadn't even found a permanent place to live in Oakland. He was just staying at the Beacon Grand Hotel in San Francisco for now, which was his go-to hotel in the Bay area for decades, going back to when it was the Sir Francis Drake.

Earlier in the day, Jack had been introduced to Bill McKenna, head of the film and attraction gadget shop. Bill who had been working in the motion picture industry for decades and also had a background in designing visual effects for theme parks. He'd done a bunch of work in Japan at the Yomohiro parks there.

It was a bit of a fan-boy moment, as Jack had followed Bill's career for years and always wanted to work with him. McKenna's ability to develop new approaches to filmmaking, new film equipment, and new ways to capture footage were legendary. Some of the things he'd done in Japan were mind-blowing.

Jack also was busy fielding calls and text messages from former teammates and colleagues from Disney. Some were from people he'd worked with years ago, some from people who were still there. Although California doesn't allow non-competes, it is considered bad form to solicit employees from a former employer in the first 12 months. But if they reach out to you, they're fair game. So Jack was very pleased that some of his favorite team members and peers from Disney were reaching out about potentially following along. In the first two days on the job he had already kicked off interview loops with seven people who would have taken months to find using a recruiting firm.

The most critical new hire he was making was Diana Rollins, his former right-hand person from Disney. She had worked directly for Jack for five years. Jack had met her when she was working on a project with another team that had brought him in for some collaborative advice. He was blown away by her organizational skills and ability to keep multiple disparate projects on track simultaneously. Within three months, she'd moved over to his team, within six months, she reported directly to him and was coordinating all the projects in his group. Jack was exactly the person you wanted to come in and figure out what needed to be done and come up with the plan of attack. However, he was exactly not the person you wanted coordinating all the details. Diana did that for Jack and more. She was the organizing force who executed all the projects Jack led.

Diana called him as he was driving into the office on the first morning. "When do I show up? I've already given my landlord notice and have found an apartment in Oakland."

Jack laughed. "I haven't even found an apartment yet. How do you even know I have a role I can hire you into?"

"Jack. Really? You've got to be joking. We both know you need me," laughed Diana. "I was just politely waiting until you started working there."

This is how Jack became the first executive in the history of Yomohiro Corporation to open a job req before finishing his own onboarding paperwork. The head of U.S. HR was nonplussed that he was breaking protocol, but when he had loaded six other incredibly hard to recruit people into the recruiting pipeline by 4 p.m. on the second day, all was forgiven.

Jack sat back in the chair at his new desk, looking at the lights of San Francisco. His mind wandered to the first time he'd driven into the city, on a trip with his parents when he was twenty years old. His parents were John Seeley III, but who went by Trip, and Karen Sullivan Seeley.

It was the summer after his sophomore year in college, during a break from Brown University, when his parents took him on a road trip from Seattle to San Diego. They drove down the entire Pacific Coast, staying in Yachats, Oregon, and Arcata, California, on their way to San Francisco. Jack had told his parents he didn't want to go to his grandparents' that summer, against his usual custom. He was dating a girl from school who grew up in San Diego, and she'd arranged to get him a job at the San Diego Yacht Club for the summer. Her parents had offered to put him up in their guest house.

His father, apparently realizing that this might be his only chance to spend quality time with Jack before he went off on his own, quickly offered to jump in the car and drive him down. His parents usually would drive him out to Kellogg, Idaho, to stay with his grandparents every time he had a school vacation, but this was the longest road trip they'd done together. The highlight of the trip was their time in San Francisco, where they'd stayed for three nights at the iconic Sir Francis Drake Hotel. While they were there they did all the touristy things like riding the Powell Street car over the hill and to Fisherman's wharf. The best meal Jack had eaten so far was during that trip at an amazing Asian restaurant called The Slanted Door. That meal had helped him develop a love for good food.

That road trip was the last time he'd spent with his parents. After ten days driving down the coast, they dropped him off at the estate that his girlfriend's parents owned. He kissed his mom goodbye, gave his dad a hug, and they drove off in the old VW Eurovan that his father meticulously maintained.

After his parents left, he sat down with his girlfriend, who promptly informed him that she didn't want to be in a romantic relationship with him anymore. She explained that she was seeing someone else. He'd been so hurt. However, he was also frustrated and angry that she had waited for him to arrive, rather than telling him before his parents drove him all the way down the coast, and before they left. "But, Jack, that's not something one does over the phone," she had said.

When he finished that conversation, he called his parents on their cell phone to pass along the news, and his mother comforted him. His dad told him to book a flight back to Seattle and gave him the login to his Alaska Airlines account so he could book it on frequent flier miles.

The call came at dawn. It happened on Highway 1, north of El Capitan. A truck driver had fallen asleep. Jack stood in the airport terminal, rebooked into Santa Barbara instead. The funeral director waited at baggage claim, hat in hand. The Pacific stretched endless and gray beyond the airport windows, indifferent to how everything had changed. At twenty, he was too young to rent a car and didn't even have his own credit card, just a debit card.

Jack contacted their family lawyer, who was one of his father's poker buddies. Together they arranged to have his parents transported back to Seattle, and Jack flew back on the same flight with their remains. His grandparents met him at SeaTac and helped make the funeral arrangements.

That summer, Jack learned how to navigate loss and paperwork in equal measure. His parents had left him financially secure—life insurance, his father's careful investments, and to his surprise, a thousand Microsoft shares his mother had purchased at IPO and placed in trust. There was even an unexpected grant from an obscure foundation, apparently for children of Boeing workers. The money gave him freedom but couldn't fill the absence.

Since Jack's mother was an orphan, and his parents and his grandfather had died, his paternal grandmother was now his only living immediate relative. His mother had extended family back in Maine, and Jack stayed in touch, but nobody was as close to him as his grandmother. Time was not on his side, and she was fading when he'd been back in March. His goal was to spend as much time with her in Kellogg as he could, and this new job gave him the flexibility to spend time with her before he got too busy.

I I I I

Kellogg, Idaho, June 2028

Jack was back at his grandmother's house. He had chosen to come back in late June because that had been his traditional time to begin his visits when he was a kid. Every year school would get out, and he'd be driven the five and a half hours to his grandparents' house from Seattle. Wallingford was a great neighborhood to grow up in, but it wasn't the fairyland that he'd experienced here. His grandfather had a huge garden out back, and bees, and chickens. His grandparents' house was right at the base of the Holmes Trail in Kellogg. You could walk for hours or days into the mountains on that trail, and all the others connected to it, if you liked.

Jack spent the morning with his grandmother, catching up on the local gossip, hearing about the locals who had left town or had come back. Amy occasionally would throw in her two cents, stepping out of the kitchen. Jack heard all about the work that had gone on at "the mountain," which always referred to Silver Mountain, the ski resort in town. In 1989, the resort owners had invested in a gondola that went right from downtown Kellogg to the peak, the longest gondola ride in North America at just over three miles. In the mid 2000s, they'd built a giant timeshare resort at the base, and in 2008, they added an indoor water park. As a major employer in the town, any news about "the mountain" was always good to pick through. Kellogg had become a major mountain-biking destination in the summertime because of that gondola, and Jack certainly planned to take advantage while he was here.

As he joined Amy for lunch at the dining room table, they rotated his grandmother's bed so she could participate in the conversation.

They finished their lunch, and Amy said she needed to get his grandmother up for physical therapy and a bath. He asked if she needed any help, but Amy said no. So he announced he was going to go work on his bike for a bit and then take a ride through town. Jack went out the kitchen door to the garage, which his grandfather had always called, "The Barn." Truly it had included a stall for a horse back in the day, but it had been converted into a more standard garage, albeit with vertical barn doors that opened outwards. Jack had converted one stall of the garage into a workshop for his mountain bike when he was in his twenties. His old Bridgestone MB2 was hanging on the wall where he'd left it. It had a green and red frame. It also had a bent seat post from one ill-considered jump off a fairly high rock that still made him wince when he thought about it, and the tires were flat. He hooked up his bike pump, and the tires took air and held it. He could see that both tires really needed to be replaced, not because they were worn out, but because they were old, and the sidewalls were frayed, yellowed, and stiff. When he filled the tires, he could see fine cracks spider-webbing across the sidewalls, and he decided to replace them now while he was thinking about it.

He rode down Chestnut Street, zig-zagged across Mission, and took a left on Riverside for nostalgia's sake. Back in the day, Susanne O'Connor had lived there, and he'd had a huge crush on her. He coasted by her parent's house, a modest bungalow, which looked well kept. Then he took a right on N. Division, flying down under the highway, over the Coeur d'Alene River, and swung right onto Railroad Street, where the Excelsior Bike Shop sat. Jack was surprised to see it had changed names and was now the Coeur d'Alene Bike Company. It was a yellow building with green trim. He wheeled his bike inside. They'd added a bar when changing owners, and there was a small group sitting at a picnic table drinking beer. Behind the service counter a young woman with a bright smile and her hair pulled back in a bandana waved him over. He explained that he needed some things for his bike, pulling it into view.

"Ooh, I love it!" she said. "These old, steel-framed Bridgestones are amazing! What can we do for you today?"

"I need a new set of tires and a new seat post, please," said Jack.

"Do you want to stick with that same style of Continental tires? We have a couple of pairs squirrelled away. People who have used them seem to love them. Or do you want something more modern?" she asked.

Jack smiled and replied, "I'll definitely take another pair. I love them." She informed him that the service department could swap them out now if he liked, so he sat at the bar and bought a bag of chips. When his name was called, he paid for the tires and seat post.

With his bike now sorted out, Jack rode down Railroad Street and stopped at The Beanery for a latte. After paying the barista, he sat out on the porch drinking it, watching kids play at the playground across the street. He brought his cup back inside and put it in the dish basin. Then he got back on his bike and rode down to Hill Street, took a right back over the river and under the highway. He took a left on Riverside, and there, unloading groceries from a beat up Toyota Highlander, was Susanne O'Connor, wearing faded jeans and a white tank top.

He pulled over and called out, "Hi there, Susanne!"

Susanne turned and stared. After a heartbeat, she recognized him and said, "Oh my god, Jack! So great to see you. I always wonder if you're going to show up this time of year!"

Jack pulled his bike to the side of the road, straddled it, and leaned on his handlebars. "So, you're back in Kellogg. Are you visiting, or are you back full-time?"

"Oh, I'm back," Susanne said, brushing her hair from her face. "My mom died last year and left me the house. I moved back a few years ago to help when she got sick. Lymphoma."

"I'm so sorry, Susanne. How are you holding up?"

"I'm good, actually. She was at peace." Susanne leaned against her car. "We were super close those last few years. Things had been hard after Dad died, and we didn't get along. But at the end, things were really good."

"That's great. I'm really glad. I remember things being hard at home for you. We'd stay up late sometimes looking at the stars and talking, waiting until you were sure she'd be asleep, so you could sneak in without an argument."

"Ha, that's true," said Susanne. "You were a good friend to me. I really liked those nights, talking and dreaming together. And boy, you've had quite the career! Your grandmother is so proud of you. She talks about you all the time!"

"Oh, so you've been asking after me?" Jack said, smiling winningly. "What have you been doing with yourself since college?"

"After college I moved to Spokane and worked as a receptionist while writing novels between phone calls. Finally caught a break after a few years of that, and my first book was published."

Jack smiled. "That's really great. It's so hard to make it as a writer. I have lots of author friends who I've worked with over the years who ended up working in the film industry because they couldn't make enough money publishing their work."

"I've published eight books in total, and I just sent my latest off to my editor last month. It's not a way to get rich, but I'm making a living," she said. Then after a pause, she continued, "Well, truth be told, while my fans love me, if I hadn't inherited the house and my Mom's life insurance, I don't know if I could keep going."

"You know, I was aware you'd succeeded as a writer. My grandmother told me, and I've even read a couple of your books," Jack said.

Susanne laughed. "Well, imagine that. You reading my young adult novels about adventures in northern Idaho."

"I thought they were quite good. I especially liked how familiar the main characters were, Skylar and Jake really resonated with me," Jack said, smiling.

Susanne blushed and looked away before saying, "You caught that, eh? Yes, they should definitely feel familiar to you. Even some of their adventures should feel familiar."

They talked for a few minutes, and Jack asked if she needed a hand bringing in the groceries. They carried them in together, and Susanne left most on the counter, putting the cold goods in the fridge and freezer, before pouring them iced tea and moving out to the front porch. They chatted for about a half hour, catching up on the small bits of life, reminiscing about kids they'd known, and where they were now. Susanne talked about her life goals, and how after sending her most recent novel off to her editor, she was in a lull before starting the next book.

Jack watched her talk, he loved her crooked smile, and the way her right dimple was more pronounced when she laughed. To his mind, she looked exactly the same as she had back then, better even. There is something about women's faces after forty, they look more like themselves.

"Well, I should get back to my grandmother," Jack said, "but Susanne, I am so glad we connected. Can we grab breakfast together tomorrow morning? When I was back in March, I found some things that reference my great-great-grandfather and someone named Samantha O'Connor. Might be interesting to find out if she's related to you."

"I'd love that. I really would." She reached over his bike frame and gave him a tight hug, squeezing her face against his. "8:30 a.m. work?"

"It's a plan! I'll come by then."

Jack rode the rest of the way home, dropped his bike in the barn, and walked inside the kitchen door only to be shushed by Amy. His grandmother was asleep in the living room, and so he nodded to Amy and quietly made his way upstairs.

I I I I

Jack and Susanne sat across from each other at Sam's Restaurant. A box of papers and photographs taken from the trunk in his grandparents' bedroom sat on the booth next to him. They'd gone through the box several times, and each of them were reading different letters and documents. They'd spent some time discussing his great-grandfather's journal entry, the clippings, and the map. And they'd poured over the photograph of the "original eight."

The food arrived, and Jack relished the chicken fried steak with over easy eggs and homefries, while Susanne opted for the yogurt and granola.

"I can't believe you're eating that," said Susanne with a laugh.

Jack smiled, "You better believe I'm eating this. It was my grandfather's favorite, and I always get it at least once when I come to town. It isn't how I eat every day, but it's a must-have when I'm in town."

Susanne reached her fork over, cut off a bit of his chicken fried steak, which was smothered in sausage gravy, and took a tentative bite. "Oh. Wow. That's a lot," she said. "I mean, it's really good. But it's a lot."

Jack laughed and cut a big chunk off, pushing it onto the small plate that the waitress reflexively had left for sharing. "Believe me, you won't be able to help yourself."

Susanne chewed slowly, looking towards the ceiling, deep in thought. Susanne pushed aside her empty plate. "Something's not right about this, Jack. I grew up here, and in elementary school, we learned about all the mining towns in the area. Even about Eagle City, which is also marked on maps, and there's nothing left of Eagle City. But Crystal Village? Not a whisper. Not a trace. This place, it's like someone tried to erase it."

Jack looked at her thoughtfully, "I hear you. I asked my grandfather about it once, and he was very cagey. He just said that it was destroyed in the Great Fire, and there is nothing to see. It was like he was ashamed of something."

"Do you think we can find it?" asked Susanne.

Jack paused his eating and looked her square in the face. "I'm sure as hell going to try."

They both fell deeply into thought while they finished their meal. When she finished her yogurt and granola and Jack's contributed chicken fried steak, she pushed her plates carefully to the side and began reading more letters.

5

Home

S am heard the bell ringing down by the bridge and took off running. It was almost four o'clock in the afternoon. The new buildings had gone up quickly; the streets were staked and marked with string. She jumped across the string onto Broadway and could see the wooden bridge at the end of the street. There was a shuffle of people down there, she could see horses and wagons on the other side.

She slowed down to a walk, not to catch her breath, but because she wasn't sure what this all meant. Eoinn and most of the men had gone off to New York to get their wives and children almost three months ago. Over the last two years, groups of them had periodically gone back to visit, but now it was time for all of the families to come West. As none of them had families to visit, Finn, Sean, and Colin had stayed behind to continue working on houses for the men who'd gone back to get their families. Sam had been the only girl, the only child, for so long now that the prospect of women and other children showing up was as daunting as it was exciting.

She had discussed the route with Sean in detail. The families would take the train as far as Winnemucca in Nevada, then proceed by horse and wagon to Walla Walla where they'd join the Mullan Road, finally turning onto the trail leading to Crystal Village. Before departing, each man packed up a gold bar and a sack of highest quality garnets, intending to sell them in New York after reuniting with their waiting families. The journey would be arduous. It included two weeks by rail followed by another fortnight to traverse the 500 miles to their mountain home. All these considerations weighed on Sam's mind as she approached the bridge.

She could see that Finn, Sean, and Colin had already made it there ahead of her. They were embracing people she didn't know, and Sean had grabbed up a little boy and was swinging him into the air. She felt an uncomfortable flash of jealousy at the sight of Sean with that boy, and paused near the horse corral on the village side of the ravine. The wooden bridge they'd built could only handle one horse or a group of people at a time. Beyond the bridge lay the livestock area; separate enclosures for pigs and chickens, a grazing field for cattle, and an open-sided shed that stored tools, carts, and wagons.

Sean spied Sam lurking by the corral and called out, "Sam King, get yer behind over here!"

She waved to him, took a deep breath, and walked toward the bridge. The first wagon had two horses pulling it and was outfitted with a canvas cover for travel. She saw that Liam was there, with a lovely woman with bright, blonde hair, blue eyes, and deep dimples. She was wearing a blue and white checkered gingham dress and a matching bonnet. Four children were with them. The oldest was a boy her own age of twelve or so, with Liam's auburn hair and wearing a straw hat. The other children were a girl of about ten or eleven, a boy who looked to be about six, and a little girl who was about three. The eldest girl was holding the youngest, shy-looking girl in her arms. Sean was holding the six-year-old boy, tickling him under his chin, making him laugh.

Sam walked across the bridge and as she neared the newcomers, Sean said, "Samantha King, please meet the O'Connor family! We've got little Joshua here in my arms, Eva over there is holding Susanne. That monstrous oaf by the wagon is Seamus."

Liam walked over with his pretty wife and said, "Elizabeth, I'd like to introduce ye to Sam King, the young lady I've told ye about."

Elizabeth smiled at Sam, saying, "Hello, Sam. I'm so happy to meet ye."

"Likewise," said Sam, nodding politely at her and nearly curtseying.

Elizabeth said, "Sam, Sean tells me that ye've built some temporary cabins for all of us. I'm wondering if ye could take our children across the bridge and show them around. The Sullivan children are a bit too young to go off with ye yet, but maybe ye could take Joshua by the hand as ye cross the bridge?"

Sam said, "Yes, ma'am, it would be my pleasure to show them."

Elizabeth turned to her children and said, "Mind me now. Please go with Sam; she'll show ye where we're going to be staying for a time. Please mind her. She knows her way around here."

The O'Connor children broke off from the group, and behind them, Sam saw Eoinn and a tall woman with dark, curly hair speaking with Finn. Eoinn looked up at her, caught her eye, and smiled, tipping his hat. She smiled back and took Joshua by the hand. He looked up at her with wonder and followed along. Seamus whistled and a huge white-and-gray shaggy dog ran out from behind the wagon, loping up to the group of children. Seeing Sam for the first time, the dog changed course and bounded up to her. Just as it was about to pounce goodnaturedly on Sam, Seamus whistled again, and the dog stopped and sat.

"This is Dumpling," said Seamus. "She's very friendly but needs to be reminded not to jump up when she meets new people."

Sam knelt down and began scritching Dumpling behind her floppy, right ear. In response, the dog groaned and turned her head, grinding her ear against Sam's hand. "Oh, you like that, don't you, girl?" Sam asked.

She stood up, and all the O'Connor children followed her across the bridge, Eva holding little Susanne tightly and Joshua obediently walking along with her. Dumpling bounded ahead over the bridge, and Seamus brought up the rear.

As they crossed onto the other side of the bridge, Eva said, "I'm so excited to see our cabin! We've been traveling by wagon for two weeks."

Sam replied, conspiratorially, "We've given you the biggest one since you have the biggest family. It's also the one closest to the hot springs."

Seamus interrupted, excitedly, "My Da' said there were hot springs and a swimming hole and caves, and ... well, I'm really glad we're here!" He smiled and his green eyes sparkled as he looked at her.

Then little Joshua piped up. "What's a hot spring?" he asked.

"Oh, you'll love it," said Sam. "We've warm pools of water for soaking in. When water comes out of the ground already hot, it's called a hot spring. The biggest and best pool is really warm, but not so warm that you can't stay in. It's about as deep as my chin in the middle, but there are lots of rocks near the edge that you can sit on."

They walked down Broadway, the widest street in the village, which had been staked off with string and ran from the bridge all the way to the mine opening. Four intersections were marked where future cross streets would be built. At the fifth intersection, a street ran off to the right, and on that corner a wooden sign on a tall pole marked where "Broadway" met "Spring Street." On Spring Street was a row of twelve cabins—most were smaller with just a few rooms, though several larger structures had been built for families. The largest cabin stood at the end of the row on the left, and Sam explained that this was for the O'Connor family. Across Spring Street from that largest cabin stood a communal cooking area. Sam explained that meals would be prepared there for the entire village, though the O'Connor cabin had been fitted with a cooking stove should Mrs. O'Connor wish to prepare some of her own meals.

Sam opened the door and ushered the O'Connor children inside. The cabin's smooth plank floors smelled pleasantly of freshly sawn wood. Eva set little Susanne down, and the children raced from room to room with excited whoops, the toddler determinedly following behind. The cabin comprised four rooms: two bedrooms—a larger one with a parents' bed and another with four smaller beds for the children—a storeroom for provisions, and a bright main room featuring three windows, each divided into twenty-four small panes of glass.

Eva said, "Oh, Mum is going to be so happy when she sees this. Da has been teasing her that we'd be staying in a one-room hut with mud floors."

At that, Sam's face darkened, remembering her own family's cabin. But she quickly covered that up, only Seamus noticing.

She cleared her throat and said, "Okay, and who wants to see the hot springs?"

"And the swimming hole!" Joshua added excitedly. He seemed to equate the hot springs with having to take a bath, but the swimming hole? That had a magical, adventurous sound to it,

"Fine, we can see both. After that, we'll come back and meet your parents here," said Sam.

She headed off toward the hot springs with the other children following. Dumpling raced from bush to bush, sniffing everywhere.

I I I I

The families were all getting settled in. Mrs. O'Hara had sorted out the outdoor cooking area and was just starting to put together a big feast to celebrate the arrival. She had come with them on this trip with the intention of taking over the responsibilities of feeding the camp, with the goal of eventually opening her own restaurant once the town was established. Her husband had served under Eoinn during the War but had been killed. She had stayed with Eoinn's wife, Rose, both during the war and over the last few years, and was now happily engaged with her culinary duties.

Eoinn watched as all the families—both those of the original eight and the families of the newcomers—got settled in their cabins.

Eoinn and Rose had already dropped off their luggage and a few packages in their cabin. Fully aware that there was much for them both to do as far as setting up their new home, Eoinn reached out his hand to Rose and said, "Come with me, I want to show ye something amazing."

Rose had changed into pants, men's boots, and a work shirt once they'd unloaded their things. She considered the disarray of their cabin and sighed. Still, she took Eoinn's hand and walked hand-in-hand with him toward the mine opening in the side of the mountain.

When they reached the opening Eoinn pulled a lantern from the wall and lit it. He walked one step ahead of Rose with the lantern held low toward the ground and simultaneously kept a firm grasp on her hand so she could find her way forward. As he reached intersections in the mine, he lit other lamps. Little by little, he showed Rose places where the walls followed veins of quartz, with gold threading through the quartz, sometimes widening into pockets of rich ore.

Rose paused to admire the minerals, but Eoinn chuckled in amusement at her awe and said, "This is just a taste of what we've found. Come this way."

After traveling about 500 feet into the mountain, only dipping slightly downward, Eoinn came to fork in the tunnel where the path off to the right went downward at a steeper angle. The path was not so steep as to be uncomfortable or slippery, but it had a definite downward grade. He lit the lamp at this fork, and they walked down the right hand shaft.

As they made their way forward, Rose could see a vein of quartz and gold that traveled along on the left-hand wall. Sometimes narrow. Sometimes wide. She marveled at the straightness of the shaft, how clean the corners were, and how well-crafted the supports were. The feeling of confinement was a bit unnerving, but she felt safe and secure walking with her husband into the dark. The air was earthy and damp, cool but not cold. The engineered shaft transitioned to a natural corridor with irregular, rough floor, walls, and ceiling. They took a few more steps forward and suddenly, the air changed. Warmth and moisture surrounded them. She could see by the light of the lamp that the passage was opening up ahead into a larger space. Water gurgled lightly in the distance, the sound echoing as if in a chamber. A pleasant mineral scent reached her nose, medicinal but not unpleasant. By this point, they had traveled about a thousand feet into the mountain. The shaft had angled downward and curved to the right consistently. Suddenly, Eoinn's pace quickened. "We followed this vein of gold down here, and as ye can see, the earth became harder and full of quartz crystals. Then we found this!"

Eoinn had been blocking her view forward. Now he stepped aside. Walking past him, Rose entered a sanctuary of stone. The chamber opened upward, its walls soared into darkness beyond the reach of their lamps. The floor dropped away from the mine entrance in natural terraces of rock, descending into the earth like broad steps. Eoinn lit several more lamps positioned around the entrance. The space revealed itself gradually in the expanding light. Rose gasped in awe. The chamber held an intimate solemnity. Sounds carried differently here; softer and rounder, creating a hushed atmosphere that invited whispers rather than speech. The rock walls curved organically. Light from the lamps caught countless crystal inclusions in the stone, ranging from tiny flakes to larger formations a few inches long. These caught the light, creating a subtle sparkle throughout the chamber. Rose stood transfixed at the threshold.

From where she stood, Rose could hear the sound of trickling water. There was a spot on the right of the shaft entrance where steaming water gurgled into a little stream, emerging from the rock wall at nearly the same level as the doorway. Where the water ran across stone, it left a smooth mineral trail that was lighter and more colorful than the native rock. The hot spring wound its way downward where it collected in a beautiful, glittering pool about fifteen feet across. Wisps of vapor drifted over the surface of the water, dissipating into the cooler air of the cavern. The chamber as a whole felt notably warmer and more humid than the shafts had been on the way here.

Rose saw that the water poured over the downhill edge of the initial pool, streaming down to the next tier of the cavern, where it created a second, even larger pool that was about thirty feet across. From this second steaming pool the water poured off into a third stream that disappeared from the cavern into a dark hole that ran out into the mountain as an underground stream. The water caught the lamplight and reflected it onto the walls, creating shifting patterns that animated the stone. The air tasted clean and slightly medicinal with a hint of iodine rather than the sulfur she might have expected from a hot spring. This wasn't the cold, dank cave she had imagined when Eoinn described a mine. This was something altogether different—a warm, living place hidden within the mountain.

It seemed as if everywhere Rose looked water dripped from hundreds of small stalactites, mirrored below by hundreds of stalagmites pointing upwards. Eoinn busied himself by lighting more and more lamps. The newly kindled light glinted and reflected off millions of crystals across the cave. In some places she could see what appeared to be white plants sprouting from the walls, and she realized they were much larger quartz crystal formations. Some of them were more than two feet in height. After he'd lit all of the lanterns, Eoinn came back and stood on the edge of the first pool.

Eoinn held out his hand. "Will ye join me for a soak?" he asked.

She smiled at him. "Really? We can bathe in these pools?" she asked in amazement

Eoinn said, "Oh yes, I think ye'll find them quite pleasant. The first one is very hot. We could probably only spend five or ten minutes in there. But the second one is more like a bathtub. We could spend as much time in there as you like."

Rose smiled and took his hand and led him toward the second, larger pool.

"Mr. Seeley, I think I'm going to enjoy this Crystal Village of yours."

I I I I

Crystal Village, Idaho, September 1869

Eoinn walked alone on the trail outside of the village. After getting everyone settled in the village and sending Liam back to New York to pick up more recruits, he needed time to contemplate his next moves.

Eoinn particularly enjoyed walking in the area that everyone referred to as "The Cathedral," where a copse of ancient cedar trees ran along a small stream. The space was quiet and spiritual. Songbirds called across the space, which echoed their lyrical strains. He could feel energy under the ground. Eoinn recognized that this was one of those places where multiple ley lines crossed—and in those places, it always felt like anything was possible.

He paused beneath a towering cedar, its ancient bark furrowed like the face of an old friend. This place spoke to him in ways he couldn't explain to the others. It communicated to him in the way the light filtered through the branches. The way the earth seemed to hum beneath his feet. He'd walked countless miles across two continents searching for this feeling, this sense of rightness. Here, he could sense what lay beneath the surface—not just gold and silver veins threading through stone, that was easy. Here Eoinn could sense ... older things. The kind of things to build a dream upon.

A rustle in the underbrush caught his attention. About a hundred feet away stood a coyote, watching him. It was not the scraggly creature he'd expect in these woods but something larger, robust with rusty fur that stood up around its face like a mane. Its eyes caught the dappled sunlight, irises amber-gold and knowing. The coyote held Eoinn's gaze longer than any wild animal should, its head tilted slightly as if considering a puzzle.

When it finally turned and slipped between the trees, Eoinn experienced the strange sensation of having been judged. By what standard, he couldn't say.

Eoinn followed the stream for a few hundred feet and found the spot where a small spring bubbled out from among the rocks. He crouched down and captured clean spring water in his hands, sipping quickly from the bowl made by his palms.

The forest grew quiet. From behind him, he heard footsteps and a throat being cleared. He whirled to find a man standing about twenty feet away, dressed in a white linen suit that seemed impossibly clean for these woods. A white panama hat with a black band sat atop his head. A long knife in a scabbard hung on the right side of his black, leather belt and a small, leather sack dangled at the left. His hair and sideburns were the same rusty color as the coyote's fur, and beneath a bushy, handlebar mustache, his smile never quite reached his eyes.

"Hello. Ye startled me. I wasn't aware anyone was nearby," Eoinn said.

The other man simply stared at him. He was about a foot shorter than Eoinn, and he had a wiry, sinewy build. It was nearly impossible to guess his age; he had one of those faces that could be thirty or sixty.

"My name is Eoinn Seeley. How might I address ye, my friend?"

"You're not from here," said the man, his voice strange with an accent that was hard to place. "I haven't been here in an age, but you people belong to another place, not this one."

Eoinn responded carefully. "We acquired our claims from a group of miners who'd staked up here a few years ago. We're building a village nearby. We're just looking for a safe place to raise our families."

The man sneered at him and spit off to the side. Then he reached down into the leather pouch on his belt and pulled a long, brown cheroot from it. He struck a match on his belt and lit it, taking a series of small puffs, then a long drag. He blew out a stream of smoke that swirled around his head.

He made a sort of growling sound in his throat, then said, "You lot are miners, are you? I see you've built a bridge over that place where the land fell away since I was here last. Not sure why you'd think this place was safe."

Eoinn's eyes narrowed, and he stepped forward a half step. "We've faced danger before. We're not ones to turn tail at the first sign of trouble."

The stranger's smile was thin and unsettling. "Trouble has a way of finding those who dig where they shouldn't. This is a powerful place. It remembers the old agreements. Your people take from the earth but give nothing back to those who dwell beneath. You build without asking permission from those who were here first."

Eoinn stepped forward, his voice firm. "We're not here to make enemies. We respect the land and mean to live with it, not against it."

The stranger flicked ash onto the ground, his gaze never wavering. "Respect is easy to claim, but the land remembers those who forget their place."

Eoinn held his ground, feeling the air grow cold and heavy between them. "We'll make our way. With or without your approval."

The man chuckled, smoke curling from his lips. "You'll need more than approval, Eoinn Seeley." He said Eoinn's name as if savoring an unexpected flavor.

Something shifted in the stranger's face then—it was not quite a change, more like a momentary glimpse behind a mask. His head tilted at that same thoughtful angle Eoinn had seen before.

"You're more than you appear, miner," the stranger sniffed. "Well, so am I." The stranger's voice dropped lower, rough-edged. "You're from far away. This isn't your land. You have power, sure enough. But even the old blood can be spilled."

Eoinn's jaw set. "We've faced worse, and we'll stand our ground."

The stranger's smile widened. "There are none who can be worse than me. It'll be an interesting game." He took a few steps into the forest before pausing and turning back. "The name is Sinclair Lipson." With that, the man turned and disappeared into the forest's shadows, leaving behind only the scent of smoke.

Eoinn stood rooted long after the stranger had vanished among the trees. The forest seemed different now, as if awakening from a spell. Birds called tentatively. Branches moved in a breeze he couldn't feel on his skin.

He'd encountered many strange things in his life, things that didn't fit neatly into the world that men perceived. But here, in this new land where he'd hoped to begin afresh, he hadn't expected ... what? He wasn't certain. All he was sure of was that Sinclair Lipson was very dangerous and unexpected. And something in the back of Eoinn's mind whispered of old stories, tales told around fires in the old country.

He shook his head, trying to clear it. Whatever Lipson was, he'd marked Eoinn as something more than human too. And that meant trouble would follow, sure as winter follows fall.

IIII

In the Fall of 1869, the whole village pitched in to build the central kitchen and dining hall ahead of the coming winter. Feeding and provisioning a growing settlement was not a task for the meek. It required coordination, a crack team of people, and a strong leader. Luckily for everyone in the community, Mrs. O'Hara was the person in charge of feeding the village. Her domain, the central kitchen, was a hive of activity. Pots clattered, knives chopped with rhythmic percussion, and the air was thick with the rich aromas of stews and freshly baked bread. Every meal was a reflection of her skill and dedication, crafted with care, intended to nourish both body and spirit.

Mary Margaret Maguire O'Hara was the heartbeat of the village, a matronly figure whose authority was both respected and unquestioned. Her presence commanded attention, and her sharp eye missed nothing. She moved through her domain with purpose, directing her team with precision. Each member of her crew knew their role, and under her guidance, they worked seamlessly, transforming raw ingredients into nourishing meals that sustained the village.

To the village, she was either Mrs. O'Hara, or Mrs. O, depending on the circumstances and the interactions. Mrs. O'Hara was the general in charge of everything. Mrs. O was the woman who took care of everyone. Her hard edges and her soft edges were distinct, but it was not always obvious to those interacting with her which persona they were talking to, until it was too late. Mrs. O was beloved by everyone, but even Eoinn and Finn tread carefully with Mrs. O'Hara.

Pierre Lemieux, a French-Canadian merchant with a network stretching across three countries, orchestrated the arrival of every nail, sack of flour, and bolt of cloth the village required. His mule trains had navigated the mountain passes of the west for decades before Crystal Village existed. Liam first encountered him during a blizzard in the Rocky Mountains, and claimed that Pierre had saved his life. His efforts were equally vital to that of Mrs. O'Hara. He was the one who ensured that the supplies that were needed to keep the village running smoothly were always in stock. Pierre was a man of many talents, and his contacts included not only a vast number of business relationships, but a sprawling family network of a huge number of cousins spread across Europe, North America, the Caribbean, and Central America. With his keen business acumen, he secured the best deals, often trading for goods rather than relying solely on currency. His charm and silver tongue were legendary, and he had the gift of being able to broker a deal that left both parties feeling they had come out ahead.

While Mrs. O'Hara focused on the dietary needs of the village, Pierre was the logistician behind the scenes, ensuring that every aspect of village life was supported by a steady flow of supplies. His trains of pack mules and wagons, accompanied by well-armed escorts, were a common sight on the trails leading to and from the village, and they were laden with everything from flour and sugar to nails and timber. Pierre's logistical prowess was such that no one ever questioned whether something would run out. It simply didn't happen under his watchful eye.

It was obvious to everyone in the village that Mr. Pierre Sylvestre Lutinel de Lemieux was in love with Mrs. Mary Margaret Maguire O'Hara. It was equally obvious to everyone that Mrs. O'Hara was utterly unaware of his feelings. She seemed to go out of her way to chastise him at every turn. He loved it. No matter how biting her criticism, he would only say, "*Pardon, mon cher.*" When Mrs. O'Hara asked someone what "*Pardon, mon cher*" meant, they fibbed a little and said, "Oh, it means pardon me, my friend." Pierre always referred to Mrs. O'Hara as "*Mon cher,*" meaning my dear.

He took great pleasure in ensuring that her kitchen was always stocked with the finest ingredients, and he often went out of his way to procure rare spices or exotic treats that he knew would delight her. His devotion was evident in the way he anticipated her needs, often delivering supplies before she even realized she needed them. Despite her sharp tongue and frequent chastisements, he cherished every interaction, savoring each "*Pardon, mon cher*" as a term of endearment.

Their dynamic was a source of amusement for the villagers, who watched the pair with fondness. Mrs. O'Hara's priority was the well-being of the village, and she had little time for romantic pursuits. Mrs. O'Hara's husband, her great love, had died in the War. No one, not even Pierre Lemieux, was going to make romantic headway with her until she'd grieved him properly and healed from her loss, which might be never. That she threw herself into caring for the entire village was obvious to Pierre, and he would never think to pressure her. He'd been a bachelor his entire life, and he was content to wait forever if need be.

Pierre's team was an extension of his own capabilities, each member handpicked for their skills and reliability. They were a tight-knit group, committed to the village's success. Like a well-oiled machine, they moved through their tasks with precision. His rapport with his team was such that they operated almost as an extension of himself.

As the seasons changed, so did the demands on Mrs. O'Hara and Pierre. The rhythm of village life ebbed and flowed with the cycles of nature, and they adapted to each new challenge with grace and resilience. In the winter, when the snows blanketed the village and travel became treacherous or quite simply impossible, Pierre's foresight ensured that supplies were stocked well in advance. This allowed the village to ride out the harshest months in comfort. Mrs. O, in turn, crafted hearty meals that warmed both body and soul. Her kitchen was a refuge against the cold.

In the spring, when the earth awoke from its slumber, and the mountains burst into life, Mrs. O'Hara and Pierre worked in tandem to support the agricultural and construction efforts that marked the season. Their partnership was a cornerstone of the village's prosperity, and their contributions were celebrated by all who called Crystal Village home.

Mrs. O'Hara reigned supreme over her domain of cast-iron stoves and copper cauldrons, orchestrating the feeding of the village with military precision. Under her vigilant eye, joints of meat turned on spits, removed at precisely the right moment, loaves emerged golden from the ovens, and not a morsel went to waste—even bones found purpose in her simmering stock pots. The rhythmic chopping of the kitchen girls and scent of woodsmoke mingling with savory aromas announced her authority more effectively than any proclamation. Even Eoinn Seeley himself, who would face down armed bandits without blinking, had been known to take a step back when Mrs. O'Hara fixed him with her stern gaze. Once, after he'd suggested a change to the meal schedule, he learned his place.

"With all due respect, Mr. Seeley," she'd said, hands on her hips, "you may run the mining business, but I run the rest." The matter was never broached again. She had a team of kitchen help that started out with two people and grew over time. She was adept at seeing a person who had a hidden skill that she could deploy in service to her mission, and she would recruit those people, sometimes at a very young age.

Mrs. O'Hara also was in charge of the livestock. Now, many people could claim ownership of the livestock, but ultimately, they didn't make any big decisions without running them by Mrs. O'Hara. She made sure there were enough chickens laying, enough chicks hatching, enough cows available for milking, and enough pigs available to eat the garbage. Mrs. O'Hara also made sure that enough hunting and fishing or foraging in the local forests was going on to supplement what grew or was ordered. When a hunting or gathering party was needed, Mrs. O'Hara would make the call, and hand the planning and organizing of that off to Mr. Lemieux. He would assign a leader and participants. Often Liam would go out to lead those one or two-day trips if he was in the village for enough time.

Every evening after she cooked dinner for the village, Mrs. O would set aside a plate of the finest bits and place it near the stove. Every morning she would take the empty plate and wash it carefully before she started on breakfast. When asked about it, she would always answer without answering. She talked about the wee people, the little cousins or little neighbors. She obviously was referring to fairies, but she didn't ever say the word out loud.

The children of the village loved to swarm around Mrs. O when she was baking, as she would always have cookies, biscuits, hand pies, or other sweet treats to hand out. She would also tell the children stories about fairies and adventures. She'd spin yarns about elves, dwarves, dragons, mischief-making leprechauns, boggarts, and brownies.

One evening, after the day's meal had been meticulously served and the remnants tidied away, Sam, Seamus, and Eva approached Mrs. O with a familiar curiosity. As was her custom, she placed her plate of fancy leftovers near the stove. Eva O'Connor, who often assisted Mrs. O and held her in great esteem, hung on her every word. Finn sat at a nearby table, his hands busy drawing plans for new buildings and the village overall, yet his ears were attuned to the conversation.

Mrs. O caught the children's eager expressions and settled into her chair with a knowing smile. "Ah, here ye are again, wondering about this plate, aren't ye?"

Sam nodded with enthusiasm. "Yes, Mrs. O. It's really for fair ... uhm, for them?"

"For the little cousins, indeed," Mrs. O replied, her eyes twinkling. "But remember, we don't say the 'f' word. They prefer to be known as our little neighbors or cousins. It's a sign of respect."

Seamus, his curiosity ever piqued, leaned in closer. "Have you really seen them, Mrs. O?"

With a soft chuckle, she began repeating her tale. The children never tired of it. "I have, indeed. It was when I was just a lass of seventeen, setting sail for America with my brother on the *Emma Pearl*. That's when I first met a little cousin—a sprite of a girl with the brightest eyes, like starlight."

Eva, always captivated, asked, "Did she follow you all the way here?"

Mrs. O nodded, her expression warm with nostalgia. "She did, through all these years. Even in the bustling city of New York during the War, she'd visit me."

Finn, pausing in his work, offered his thoughts. "And these tales, Mary, they're more than just stories for the young, aren't they?"

With a serious nod, Mrs. O continued, "Much more, Finn. The little cousins inhabit a realm beneath our own. They watch as miners delve into their subterranean kingdom, dreaming of a land where they might dwell unfettered."

Eva, filled with wonder, asked, "What do they long for?"

"They dream of a new kingdom, a place where they can paint their history on the walls and live without the encroachment of men," Mrs. O explained quietly. "A world of peace, away from the iron and machines of our world."

The children sat enraptured, their imaginations fired by the possibilities of what might lie hidden beneath their feet. Finn winked at Mrs. O.

Mrs. O noticed their rapt attention and decided to share more from her past. "When I first left Ireland, life was a mixture of excitement and sorrow. My brother Thomas and I boarded the *Emma Pearl* with hopes of a new beginning. Our parents had died, and this was our chance to see the world and start anew. It was aboard this ship that I first encountered a little cousin. One of the older ladies on board showed us how she would leave an offering for them by the cooking stove the passengers used. I began to help her and noticed that our cabin started to smell fresher and was always clean and neat even before I'd had a chance to tidy up. I saw the little cousin one evening, up on deck, snacking on the treats. She was startled and flew up into the rigging before she disappeared. Over time she'd show herself here and there, just glimpses. She was a guardian, in her own mischievous way."

Seamus's eyes widened. "And did she ever ... talk to you?"

"Not at first, at least not in words," Mrs. O replied, a hint of mystery in her voice. "But in gestures, in the way she'd leave small tokens. Lost or misplaced items would show up on top of the bed covers. Little knots of vines and threads made to look like flowers, small bits of fancy left out that I thought at first were from the sailors, who did very fine work indeed, but now I believe it was her doing. I still have some of those in my cabin."

The fire in the lanterns cast dancing shadows. Sam, Seamus, and Eva listened with rapt attention, their young minds alight with visions of the hidden world beneath them.

Eva, her voice filled with wonder, asked, "And they're here, in Crystal Village?"

Mrs. O nodded, her eyes reflecting the firelight. "Indeed, they are. They watch over us, ensuring that we respect the land, and bringing us good luck. That's why we leave a bit of food out. It's a small token of our appreciation, a gesture of goodwill."

The children remained quiet, absorbing the tales that hinted at the wonders and mysteries of a world just out of reach. Sam was skeptical but kept her thoughts to herself.

The evening drew to a close, and the fire's glow began to fade, Mrs. O'Hara concluded with a gentle reminder. "We share this space with them, our laughter and our stories. It's a bond as old as the hills, a promise to remember the magic that lies just beyond the veil of the everyday."

I I I I

September 1869

Liam O'Connor navigated the bustling streets of New York with the ease of a man who had seen the world and was unperturbed by its chaos. It was his last morning before heading back west. His mission was clear: find and recruit the best talent to join the village. Liam's instincts guided him through the maze of faces and voices. It was in a small cafe that he found his latest quarry.

The stonemason was a bear of a man, his hands calloused from years of labor. His name was Thomas McLeod, and his reputation as a master craftsman in Boston had reached the ears of one of Liam's many cousins. After some negotiation through the mail, they'd agreed to this meeting in New York. Liam's approach was straightforward, his offer enticing.

"Mr. McLeod," Liam began, extending a hand. "It's so nice to meet ye, after all the back and forth through the mail. I'd like to see if we can entice ye to come west to Crystal Village in the mountains of Idaho. We're a community that values skill and dedication."

McLeod looked up, his eyes assessing him. "Aye, it's a fine thing to hear, and I'm excited to discuss it. It's good to speak face to face after all this time." His brogue was a fusion of Scottish and the twang of Boston.

Liam smiled, his voice steady and persuasive. "Crystal Village is a place where your talents will not only be appreciated but celebrated. I've got some photographs and some architectural plans for the work we're doing going forward."

Liam pulled pictures and plans from his satchel, spreading them across the table. The conversation flowed easily, and by the time they parted company, McLeod had decided to join Crystal Village. They agreed that he'd meet Liam that afternoon to start the trip west with Liam's other recruits.

"I just want to warn ye, Tom. This group we're meeting later are fresh off the boat from Ireland. So things might get a bit theatrical with that lot. I don't want it to put ye off," said Liam.

McLeod smiled, "I don't blame you at all. We all got off a boat at some point."

That afternoon, Liam met a group of men at the dock as they exited a ship that had come directly from Belfast. There were fifty of them, all men of Ireland who had come to America at his request. He had sent word over the summer when he'd gone to New York to bring his family west. Now in September, he had fifty good men, all selected by Liam's cousin in Ireland. These Irish recruits were all hard workers, all serious, and all hoping to form families and make their fortunes. None had good prospects in Ireland, so they looked only forward and not back to the old country. They were all from County Tyrone, where he and his mates had come from. He gathered these hand-selected men in a crowd near an Irish bar close to the docks. Tom McLeod was there as well, standing back a bit as he got to know them.

He called out, "Brothers, hear me now, hear me! In a few moments, I'm going to take the lot of ye into that pub yonder, and most of ye'll have yourselves your first pints of beer in America!"

The group cheered. But Liam drew himself up to his full height and crossed his arms in a most serious posture. "Nevertheless, I want to be clear on the plan here. For those of ye looking to come to America to drink yourselves silly, wander from place to place, and end up asleep wherever ye land with nary a care in the world—be off with ye now! If you've come here to America to work and to make a home for yerself, and if maybe ye've a lady back in Ireland who ye'll send for, or maybe you're looking to meet a lass here in the new world, or maybe ye don't care for the ladies at all and just want to get to work ..."

Liam paused for dramatic effect, "... Then ye've found the right place!"

The men cheered, and Liam raised his voice to ensure that everyone heard him, "We're going to go into that pub and drink one, tall pint of beer! Then we're going to walk to the ferry over to Jersey City, and we'll catch the train this very evening that will take us to Chicago! Once in Chicago, we'll get off the train. Then, we'll go to another pub and have another beer! Then we'll get on another train that will take us all the way to Nevada. Once we arrive in Nevada, we'll get off the train in a small place called Winnemucca. There we'll stop at a saloon and have a glass of whiskey! In Winnemucca, horses will be waiting for us, which we'll saddle up and ride north to another strangely named town called Walla Walla. When we get to Walla Walla, we shall spend the evening in a lovely hotel, and in the lobby of that hotel, we shall have ourselves another glass of whiskey. Then from Walla Walla, we're gonna ride the Mullan Military Road for two days. At long last, we'll arrive at our final destination, where we'll have beer, whiskey, and wine."

The men had cheered at the right moments throughout, and then they filed into the bar. The barman, having been warned and paid ahead of time, had fifty-two pints of beer lined up on the bar. The men all sidled up to the bar and drained them down. A few were fast enough and grabbed seconds. Then they all followed Liam out the door and off to start their new lives.

IIII

October 1869

Eoinn gathered with Finn and Egan in the main room of the meal hall. The room was simple, with rough-hewn wooden walls and rows of tables and chairs. One large table closest to the kitchen was covered with scattered papers and sketches.

Finn spread out a large sheet of parchment, his hands smoothing its edges. "These are the plans for the village as we envision it," he began, his voice filled with quiet excitement. "We've drawn inspiration from the towns and cities we've seen in Europe."

Egan leaned in, also excited to unveil the project to Eoinn. "The streets are laid out in a grid," he noted, tracing his finger along the lines. "This will make it easier to navigate, and it allows us to build the infrastructure we'll need efficiently as we grow."

Finn nodded, tapping a finger on one of the sketches. "We've designated spaces for essential buildings—stables, a hotel, a school, a bank, a general store, and an office for managing the business side of the mines. We'll need a place to make bricks with a kiln, and we will also need a place to blow glass. In addition, we've reserved a site for a large, formal bath house, modeled on the ancient Roman baths we've visited throughout Europe. These will be the heart of the village, where people gather and connect with each other."

Eoinn listened intently, his gaze traveling over the plans. "And what about the bridge?" he asked. "That will be our lifeline, ensuring we can bring in supplies and send out our mined goods."

Finn smiled, a hint of pride in his expression. "Roebling's ideas have been invaluable, and with the resources we've secured, we can make it a reality. When we're done, it will support a train that can run right out of the mines, through the village, across the bridge, and down the mountain."

"The bounty of this place is not just the monetary riches of the earth; one of the best resources here are the hot springs," said Egan. "We've found another one inside the mountain that is much hotter than the ones that feed the pools we've been enjoying. We can use this to our advantage. The hot water can heat our homes, providing comfort and warmth during the harshest months. If we run the heating pipes beneath the main street, we can keep it clear of snow in the winter, making it easier for everyone to move about."

Finn's eyes lit up with the possibilities. "It's a natural resource we'd be foolish not to utilize."

Eoinn nodded with satisfaction. "It's a vision worth striving for, Finnegan. Great work, both of you. Egan, the heated streets are genius."

Finn's face lit with an uncharacteristic smile. Egan was beaming. Finn rolled up the plans with care. "We'll make it happen."

IIII

May 1870

Sam sat on the front porch of her little cabin, located next door to the O'Connors' cabin. She'd woken up and couldn't get back to sleep, so she went out to sit on the porch. Sean and Colin had built a small addition to their cabin with a little shed roof and porch. Her cabin had a door to the outside and also one adjoining the main room of Sean and Colin's cabin, where sometimes the three of them would eat a meal or sit and play music together. Colin had taught her to play the fiddle and the mandolin. Sean had the sweetest voice. The three of them would sometimes perform for the whole village. Sean and Colin also could act, and they would put on plays and even musicals with members of the whole village participating.

On this particular evening, Sam was sitting up well after midnight and a full moon lit the sky. Sam looked over at the dining hall, which was across the street. She was wrapped up in a blanket, sitting in a rocking chair with her feet up on the railing. She saw a girl quietly walk into the kitchen. Through the big windows—which could be opened all the way in the summer but were closed tonight—she could see this girl walk over and grab up the sweets that Mrs. O'Hara had left out for the fairies. Still wrapped in her grey, wool blanket, Sam quickly got off her chair, slipped on her boots, and quietly ran across the street to peer in the windows. From a distance, the girl seemed to be eight or nine years old. However, when Sam saw her face, she could tell that she was much older than that, more like a young lady. She was wearing a light dress of silvery wool, and she had light slippers on her feet made of gray leather. She was daintily plucking little tarts and treats from the plate, taking fast, small nibbles and exclaiming with joy each time she ate one.

Sam had initially planned to surprise what she had first imagined to be a girl from the village, for pillaging Mrs. O's fairy snacks. Yet after she got there, she realized this wasn't someone from the village. She'd never seen this person before. She had long, blonde hair that was wavy, pulled up away from her face, and tied in the back with a silver string. The girl quickly cleaned off the plate, then picked up a tiny, silver cup of milk and drank that down, smiling and licking her lips happily.

Once she had finished, she lightly ran out the back door on the opposite side of the building. Mirroring the girl's actions, Sam ran to the corner and peeked around it. She saw the girl running off along the trail heading toward the hot springs. Sam followed her as quickly and quietly as she could. When she got to the hot springs, she saw that the girl had taken off her clothes and was stepping into the hot pool. This was the upper pool that most people only used at the height of winter, because it was a bit too hot during the rest of the year. The girl was laughing and splashing around. Sam stealthily crept to a spot where she was concealed but was afforded a better view. She realized right away that though the girl might be smaller than her with a child's height, she certainly had a woman's figure.

The girl-woman was happily splashing around in the pool and talking to herself in a light, high-pitched voice. Sam couldn't make out what she was saying, but it was clear that the girl-woman had a funny accent. After a few minutes Sam couldn't stand it anymore, she stepped out from the bush she was hiding behind. "Hello!" she called out. The girl-woman shrieked and stared at Sam with wide eyes. She covered herself with her arms and disappeared. Sam stood staring at the empty pool, lit by moonlight. She looked around for a few moments and noticed that even the discarded clothing was missing. "I'm sorry to have startled you," Sam whispered softly into the darkness. "I meant no harm. I only wanted to say hello." Then she walked back to her cabin and went to bed.

In the morning, she woke and couldn't be sure that her memory of the girl was real, or if she'd dreamt the whole thing.

I I I I

June 1870

The late-morning air was crisp in the mountains. The scent of pine and earth were strong in the air. Stelkupmi moved quietly through the underbrush, her eyes scanning for the familiar shape of yarrow, a strong-scented, flowering herb. Her grandmother, Sanhamin, had entrusted her with this task, an important step towards becoming a healer within the Schitsu'umsh people, that the white folk called the Coeur d'Alene tribe.

Nearby, Sanhamin and Stelkupmi's uncle, Hustalk, were foraging for other herbs and other plants that could be used as medicines. The soft murmur of their voices blended with the rustling leaves. Hustalk was a seasoned tracker, his eyes sharp and his movements deliberate. Though Hustalk's demeanor was often serious, Stelkupmi had always felt a deep warmth in his presence. Today, their mission was the gathering of plants and helping Stelkupmi learn their traditions.

As Stelkupmi filled her basket with yarrow, she felt a presence nearby. She turned to see a young white woman stepping cautiously through the trees. Her gaze seemed respectful, and her expression was kind.

"Hello," the young woman said, her voice gentle. "I'm Sam."

Stelkupmi nodded, acknowledging the greeting. "I am Stelkupmi. You may call me Swift Like Deer if that is easier," she replied. They stood for a moment, the forest around them alive with birdsong and the rustle of small creatures.

"Stelkupmi isn't very hard to say, if that is okay with you. I see you're gathering yarrow," Sam observed, gesturing at the basket. "I've heard about its healing properties."

Stelkupmi smiled, pleased by Sam's knowledge. She said, "Yes, it's a powerful plant. We use it for many things—but primarily for stopping bleeding and easing pain."

Sam nodded, her interest genuine. She said, "I'm here with my friends Colin and Sean. Colin is a doctor, and he often looks for plants like these."

Stelkupmi's curiosity was piqued. "A doctor? It's good to know there are others who respect the healing power of the earth."

Sam smiled at Stelkupmi and said, "Your English is very good."

"Thank you. My grandmother has been teaching me," said Stelkupmi.

Their conversation flowed easily. Stelkupmi spoke of her grandmother's teachings, and the spiritual connection her people had with the land. In return, Sam shared tales of her own life, ranging from the struggles and triumphs she had faced since her parents died to various anecdotes of her experiences since she joined the community at Crystal Village.

The sound of crunching footsteps drew their attention. Two men emerged from the trees. One had fair hair, a thoughtful expression, and silver-rimmed glasses. The other was shorter, with darker hair and a quiet strength in his gaze. Sam introduced them as Colin and Sean respectively.

"Stelkupmi is studying to become a healer. She is here in the forest picking yarrow to use as medicine," said Sam. Then she looked at her new friend with an uncertain and nervous gaze. "Did I pronounce your name correctly?" she asked timidly.

Stelkupmi smiled and said, "Very close, it is more ... *Stel-kwp-mi*."

Colin greeted Stelkupmi with a respectful nod. "It's a pleasure to meet ye, Stel-kwp-mi. We're also out looking for healing herbs." Then, as if to prove the truth of his words, he opened the satchel on his waist revealing his treasures.

Stelkupmi felt a warmth in Colin's words, a sincerity that matched Sam's. "It is good to meet others who seek to heal."

Sean, standing beside Colin, offered a small smile.

Stelkupmi felt a sense of peace in their company, a recognition of shared values and respect. Yet, she was also aware of the time and her responsibilities. "I must return to my family," she said, gesturing to the path leading back to camp.

Sam nodded and said cheerfully, "It was nice to meet you. Maybe our paths will cross again."

"I hope so," Stelkupmi replied. There was a genuine warmth in her voice. With a final smile at Colin and Sean, she turned and made her way back through the forest.

As Stelkupmi disappeared from view, Sam watched her go, feeling a connection she hadn't expected.

"Hmmm. Bilingual. Interested in medicine. She seems remarkable," Colin said.

"She is," Sam agreed.

Sean said, "It's important to have these connections. Different people live different ways, we've got a lot to learn from each other."

The trio continued on their journey, moving deeper into the mountains. The forest around them was alive with the sounds of nature.

Time passed, and the sun climbed higher in the sky. Feeling a bit fatigued, they paused to rest beside a small spring that burbled out of the rocks; the water was clear and cool. They all slaked their thirst and filled their canteens. As they sat, the tranquility was broken by a distant cry.

"Did you hear that?" Sam asked.

Colin and Sean exchanged a glance, concern mirrored in their eyes. "It came from downstream!" Colin said, already on his feet. "We should see if someone needs help."

Together, they moved swiftly through the forest, impelled by the urgency of the call. As they neared the source of the sound, they found a scene of distress. Stelkupmi was with two other members of her tribe. A man in his late twenties sat on the ground. He was cradling his left arm, which was bent at a gruesome and unnatural angle. An older woman knelt beside him, her expression calm but worried.

Stelkupmi saw her new friends and said, "He slipped on the rocks." Her voice was steady despite the fear in her eyes. "This is my uncle, Hustalk. And my grandmother, Sanhamin." To her family she said, "These are the people I was telling you about. That one is a doctor." She spoke in Salish to her uncle for a moment.

Colin approached, his medical instincts taking over. "May I?" he asked, gesturing to Hustalk's arm. Sanhamin nodded.

Carefully, Colin examined the injury, his touch gentle but firm. "It's obviously a serious fracture," he said, assessing the situation. "We need to stabilize it before we move him."

Stelkupmi and Sam watched as Colin worked. Sean gathered branches to create a makeshift splint, his actions efficient and precise. "This is going to hurt," he said to Hustalk, "I'm sorry." Sanhamin translated, and Hustalk steeled himself bravely with a grim expression. Colin carefully and quickly straightened the arm, setting the bones of Hustalk's forearm. Hustalk hissed, then groaned quietly. Colin took the wood and cloth for the splint that Sean had set to the side and skillfully splinted the arm.

As they worked, Sanhamin observed Colin's methods, a blend of Western medicine and instinct. "You have a good touch," she said.

Colin met her gaze, appreciating the compliment. "Thanks," he said. "I've learned that there's much to gain from different perspectives."

Sanhamin reached over and gently adjusted the placement of one of the branches, using the shape of the wood to further stabilize the break. Colin smiled at her.

Sanhamin said something to Stelkupmi in her native tongue, who then carefully applied yarrow to help with the swelling.

With Hustalk's arm stabilized, they needed to decide where to go next. Colin offered, "Our village is not far from here. It's only a few hours' away. We would be very happy to invite you to visit and stay while his arm heals. We have plenty of room, and you'd all be welcome."

Hustalk didn't understand English well, but when the offer was relayed to him from Sanhamin, he seemed to consider it carefully. He clearly valued her assessment. Stelkupmi quietly watched and listened as they spoke back and forth. Sanhamin turned to Colin. "We would be grateful to have your help and to visit your village—if you think we would be welcome there."

Colin smiled and said, "Ye'd be very welcome. Ye'd be honored guests."

The journey was slow but the party made steady progress. After a few hours, they arrived at the cathedral of cedars, and all three of their guests were highly appreciative of its beauty. Sanhamin asked if she could pause to grab some red cedar branches if it wouldn't slow them too much. Sean explained that the village was nearby, so they paused and watched as she gathered them.

Finally, they arrived at the village and brought their new friends across the bridge and into the town. Stelkupmi walked alongside Sam, who was explaining everything to her as they walked. Sean dashed on ahead in order to make Eoinn aware of their guests and to find them a guest house to use for a few days. Luckily, there was a tent house that was vacant and just across from the cabin the three of them shared, close to the meal hall.

Quite understandably, Hustalk was exhausted from the journey but also famished. The other felt much the same. So, as Sean and Colin helped their newfound friends settle in at the tent house, Sam raced to the dining hall and brought back food. They helped Hustalk across the street to the porch of their little cabin, and got him settled in comfortably in a chair. Sam and Sean carried more chairs from inside out onto the porch. There the two groups shared their first meal together. .

As they ate, stories flowed freely. Even Hustalk, buoyed by the food, joined in, with Stelkupmi translating. As time passed, many of the villagers stopped by to introduce themselves as they went to and from the dining hall. In between visits, Sanhamin spoke of the history of their people and the traditions that guided them. Colin shared his knowledge of the plants they had encountered, offering insights into their uses and benefits. Sanhamin described additional ways in which the plants could be used, outlining uses Colin hadn't previously known.

Stelkupmi and Sam sat side by side, their friendship solidified by the day's events. "Thank you for your help," Stelkupmi said.

Sam smiled, the warmth of the moment wrapping around her like a blanket. "We're all connected. Of course we would help."

When they finished their meal, Hustalk said that he'd like to sleep. Sanhamin made him a tea that would help with the pain and allow him to sleep through the night. Once Hustalk was settled in, the group continued their conversation on Colin and Sean's porch. Minutes later, Eoinn wandered by. Introductions were made, and Eoinn welcomed Stelkupmi and Sanhamin to Crystal Village and said, "I hope this is the beginning of a long-term friendship between our people, and I also hope that after spending time with us, you will feel welcome to come back as often as you like."

Sanhamin smiled and thanked him, and Eoinn bade them goodnight. "He is the one who leads your people?" Sanhamin asked. Seeing the multiple head nods in response, she said, "He is a powerful leader." All of them agreed with her assessment.

"Stelkupmi," Sam said, "if you would like, we can go to the hot springs. It's my favorite place here. You're of course welcome as well, Sanhamin. The springs are very warm and can help with soreness after a long journey."

All three women walked to the hot springs to soak in their warm, comforting waters.

Over the next few days, their guests grew more and more comfortable in Crystal Village. Sanhamin showed Mrs. O'Hara some native dishes that were easy to make with locally sourced ingredients. The one everyone liked best was camas root and cedar-braised venison stew. It combined venison with slow-roasted camas bulbs, wild onions, and bitterroot. It was flavored with the cedar bark, local yarrow, pine nuts, and huckleberries. Mrs. O added some salt and black pepper, an enhancement their guests heartily approved.

A few days later, when Hustalk was ready to travel, the three new friends were ready to make their way to reconnect with their tribe. Mrs. O packaged up some salt and black pepper to send off with them.

Stelkupmi and Sam exchanged tokens of friendship—a woven bracelet for Sam, a small carved deer for Stelkupmi. They promised to meet again.

Colin expressed his thanks to Sanhamin and Stelkupmi, acknowledging the shared learning and respect that had grown between them. "I hope we can continue to learn from each other," he said earnestly.

Sanhamin nodded. "I hope this is the beginning of a long friendship between us."

Hustalk walked close to Colin. He reached out his good right arm and grasped Colin by the forearm. He bowed his head slightly, and he said, in a way that was obviously something he'd been practicing, "Thank you for helping us. My arm is already feeling much better."

"You're welcome, truly welcome, my friend," said Colin.

With their farewells exchanged, Stelkupmi and her family continued their journey.

I I I I

July 1870

The air this late morning was unusually heavy, and Jonas wiped the sweat from his brow with a relatively clean handkerchief. He got up from his seat and wandered toward the front of the bank. He saw that Mrs. Kane was engaged in a conversation with two young men. They were miners by the look of them, but they weren't hard scrabble. They had a sense about them, like they might know a thing or two. They had curly, dark hair and long reddish-brown beards. They also had enough of a family resemblance so that he assumed they were brothers.

"Mr. Brown, sir, these gentlemen have some business to discuss with you," said Mrs. Kane, from her desk by the door.

Jonas walked to the front and extended his hand to the man who had, by simple shifting of his weight and angling of his torso, made it clear he was in the lead.

"Hello, gentlemen, I'm Jonas Brown, president of the Idaho County Bank."

"It's a pleasure, sir. I'm Angus Sullivan, this is my brother Egan," said Angus, with an Irish lilt. "We've some business to discuss, but I'd prefer it if we could go somewhere private."

"Of course," said Jonas, turning on his heel after shaking Egan's hand and directing them toward his private office. "Right this way, please."

After getting the two men seated and taking his own seat behind his mahogany desk, Jonas said, "Gentlemen, how may I be of service on this fine day?"

"We've a sum of gold we're wishin' to deposit with your fine establishment, Mr. Brown," said Angus. "Yet before we proceed, we sought to assure ourselves that your bank can accommodate us with due regard for security and discretion."

"Indeed, indeed," said Jonas. "A prudent concern, I must say. Might I inquire as to the quantity of gold you would like to deposit with us?"

"We're talking about several hundred pounds, sir," said Egan, from the other chair.

Jonas stared at them.

"Several hundred pounds, you say?" Jonas sputtered, letting the conversation pause for a moment.

Idaho City had been the biggest town in the Northwest a few years ago, having been the epicenter of one of the biggest gold rushes in history. The Idaho County Bank had processed and handled millions of dollars worth of gold a week at the peak of the rush, but since the gold had mostly dried up, the city's population had shrunk from fifteen thousand down to about four thousand, half of them Chinese immigrants. Now a typical month might see twenty or thirty pounds of pure, processed gold, but that gold would need to be extracted from hundreds of pounds of ore. Jonas assumed that these two had found some gold mixed with other minerals and stone, and that's what they were talking about.

"Well, that is most intriguing," said Jonas. "Might I suggest you provide a sample for assay? Meanwhile, I'd be pleased to showcase our vault and discuss the mechanisms we have in place for the safekeeping and transportation of such valuable assets."

As he spoke, he could see Angus fidgeting in his seat. Angus reached into his belt satchel and pulled out three small bags.

"Here are three samples taken from the ore of our first shipment. Each sample was taken from a different part of the shipment. We're willing to await the assay results," said Angus.

Jonas' eyebrows lifted when he heard the phrase "first shipment."

"Of course, of course," said Jonas. "I shall personally see these samples to our assayer. A fire assay, though rigorous, will provide us with the clarity we need. This should take about five hours. In the interim, we can tour our facilities, and then perhaps, we might adjourn for luncheon?"

Jonas left the two men sitting in his office and carried the three bags to the assayer's office. When Jonas entered the shop, Arnold was sitting at his work bench testing little bits of ore.

"Arnold, I have some miners in my office who are looking to get a quick assay on the purity of their ore. Could you please pause your other projects, and test these for me?" Jonas asked. Arnold groaned and complained that he already had a full slate of projects. He asked how much time he had to complete Jonas' assay. Jonas replied coolly, "None." Arnold grunted, grumbled, and then assured Jonas that he would prioritize his request.

Jonas then returned to his office and whisked the two men away for a tour of the vault room. While inspecting the vault, Jonas showed off the several state of the art safes inside the vault room. Then, with the tour completed, he escorted the men to their meal. Afterward, he bought them a drink while they waited. Then he returned to the office while the two men stayed and played cards. Around four o'clock, he looked up from his desk to see a very white-faced Arnold walk into his office.

"Jonas, that gold is the purest ore I've ever seen," exclaimed Arnold. Jonas swallowed hard, his Adam's apple bobbing up and down.

"Which sample?" asked Jonas.

"All three of them!" said Arnold.

A few minutes later, the two brothers walked into the front door of the bank, and Jonas scurried to the front and whisked them into his office.

"Well, gentlemen," he began, "there's good news! It seems that your samples were very pure! I've calculated the value of your find at $18.00 per troy ounce. If the remaining ore is as pure as what you gave us, that could be quite a find indeed! Now, you did say that you've collected several hundred pounds?"

Egan looked calmly at Jonas and said, "Three hundred and fifty-five pounds. All of the same quality."

Jonas's face blanched, "Uhm, that would be ..."

He paused to calculate the amount on paper. Egan interrupted him, saying, "It would be roughly $76,680. Give or take."

Jonas stared at him.

Angus leaned forward in his chair, "Mr. Brown, sir, we're willing to give ye a discounted rate on our ore—if ye can take possession today and guarantee the full amount via a guaranteed bank check, depositable in any major bank. You're authorized to do such things as bank president, are ye not?"

Jonas stammered, "W-what kind of discount were you considering?"

Angus looked over at Egan who said, "Fifteen percent, which means your commission would be $11,502."

It was clear to all three men that the normal percentage given to the bank and assayer was much lower, usually more like one or two percent at most.

"That is very generous!" Jonas said. "If the ore is visually of the same quality throughout, I can agree to that. However, if there is any variation as we examine the ore, I will need to have my man do a fire assay to accommodate this."

Angus looked him directly in the eyes, "We can accept that arrangement, Mr. Brown."

A subdued Jonas Brown nodded his head, reached his hand across the table, and gave Angus a weak handshake. Angus nodded to Egan, who quickly stood, strode from the office, and out the front door of the bank. Jonas saw him walk a few steps past the door, put his fingers to his lips, and let out a loud whistle. Several men who had been standing on the street seemingly busy with the day-to-day of life, suddenly became very business-like. With the practiced ease of men who were comfortable in such situations, they pulled Henry repeating rifles from beneath their coats, taking up positions near the bank.

Angus looked over at Jonas, who smiled brightly at him and said, "We had to be sure ye were our man, sir. I'm happy to hear that ye are."

The sun was setting. The thundering of hooves and wagon wheels approached out of the distance. A crew of at least five, well-armed men with messenger shotguns and Henry rifles accompanied a very well-fortified, steel-reinforced wagon drawn by a team of horses. The whole group barely slowed until they reached the bank building. Then they turned off into the alleyway, where three men stood waiting by the side door. Two armed men stood on adjacent roofs, overseeing the proceedings.

A tall man with dark hair and a long, well-groomed mustache stepped down from his horse. He handed his Henry rifle to Angus Sullivan and unlocked the padlock on the side of the wagon, attaching the steel lockbox to the base. Then he walked over to the other side of the wagon and unlocked the padlock on that side. The two men riding on the back of the wagon holstered their revolvers and were joined by the two men riding in the front of the wagon. All four men lifted the heavy lockbox and passed it down to four more men who had dismounted from their horses. The tall man nodded to Jonas, who led Angus, Egan, the four men carrying the lockbox, and the tall, mustached man in the door and over to the vault. This entire maneuver was executed quickly and efficiently.

The men carefully lowered the lockbox to the floor of the vault, stood up with military precision and then marched out, leaving Angus, Egan and

Jonas in the presence of this new man.

"I'm Jonas W. Brown, president of the Idaho County Bank," said Jonas, reaching his hand out to the man.

The man reached out and firmly took Jonas's hand in a warm, dry grip, "I'm Eoinn Seeley, president of the Seeley Mining Company. We've been researching banks all over the West to find the right one with whom to do business. Mr. Brown, your reputation as a steadfast and honorable man precedes you. You're a lawyer and a damn, good one by all accounts. Rumor has it that you're the most honest lawyer in the West. You're president of a bank in a town that has diminished somewhat from its glory days but still does a fine business. We'd like to build a long-term relationship with ye, Mr. Brown. But today, at this time, we need to finish the work with ye and go. I wish to be far away from here by morning."

Jonas looked at him, confused, "Are you saying that your mining operation is not near here?"

Eoinn smiled, "I think we've picked correctly. No, sir, we're not nearby at all. But I will be giving ye very explicit instructions by post, explaining the need for absolute secrecy regarding our location. Also, I would like to set up some trusts to ensure long-term ownership of the mining property to be kept in my family's name."

Jonas nodded thoughtfully, then asked, "Can you at least tell me, sir, if your operation is within the Idaho Territory?"

Eoinn smiled again, "Yes. Yes, we're within Idaho, which is part of the reason we chose to work with ye."

Jonas inspected the gold ore. Then he had Arnold wheel in the scales and begin to weigh it. He locked Arnold into the vault and passed him the key. He returned to the bank lobby and saw through the window that the wagon and most of Seeley's men had left. Just four horses, tended by a boy of twelve or thirteen, stood outside the bank. He brought Seeley to his office. Meanwhile, the Sullivan brothers took up station outside either side of the door holding messenger shotguns. He sat down at his desk and pulled out the large book of bank checks.

He asked, "To whom shall I address this cheque?"

Seely said, "Eoinn Seeley, that's e-o-i-n-n s-e-e-l-e-y."

Jonas filled out the next available check with all the information necessary but left the amount blank and did not sign the check. He made small talk with Seeley, and then he responded to a knock on the door, which was Arnold coming to give him the final weight.

Arnold said, "Three hundred and fifty five pounds, exactly."

Jonas looked him in the eye and saw Arnold give a small nod and a very slight smile, a huge display of emotion for the man. Jonas thanked him for his efforts and dismissed him. He wrote out the amount on the check, $65,178.00, wrote the date, June 14th, 1870, and signed with a flourish. He marked the amounts in his ledger, then slid the check into a thick envelope, and passed it across to Seeley, who slid it into the inside pocket of his black, leather vest. Seeley stood up, reached across the desk and shook Jonas' hand firmly, looking him directly in the eye. Then he took his duster from the coat rack on the wall and put it on. Finally, he took his hat down from the hook next to the coat rack and put it on his head.

He looked over his shoulder saying, "I'll be in touch soon, sir."

Without looking at his men, he walked straight from Jonas's office to the front door of the bank. The two brothers fell in behind him. The three of them exited the bank, mounted their horses along with the boy who'd been minding them, and rode off. Jonas returned to his office, sat down at his desk, and let out a deep sigh.

IIII

September 3rd, 1870

   From: Jonas W. Brown

   To: Eoinn Seeley

   Dear Mr. Seeley,

It is with the highest esteem that I pen this letter to you, having held our previous exchanges in the greatest regard. I've devoted myself with diligence to the preservation of your legacy, the safeguarding of your assets, and the permanent documentation of your trusts. The bank has warmly received your continued contributions, and I eagerly anticipate your forthcoming visit, for which all requested preparations have been made.

Your lands and holdings have been duly registered with the office of our territorial governor, and I've taken every precaution to ensure the confidentiality of your whereabouts from the public eye. It appears Governor Marston retains a vivid recollection of your valor at the First Battle of Bull Run, mentioning that, but for your intervention, he would have faced the surgeon's saw and lost his arm. Despite governing from afar in Washington, D.C., his influence has been in-strumental in Boise, securing your assets in your name and shielding them for your progeny.

In alignment with your directives, I have established accounts in your name at national banks throughout our great nation. Following your counsel, I have ventured into the realm of long-term invest-ments, identifying a particularly innovative fund in London, the Foreign & Colonial Investment Trust. I have allocated a quarter of your assets to this venture and shall continue to invest therein as prudence dictates.

I remain, with the utmost respect and dedication,

Jonas W. Brown, Esq.

I I I I

September 30th, 1870
  To: Capt. Eoinn Seeley, Retired
  From: Washington Roebling

My dear Eoinn,

Forgive my tardiness in penning this letter. The demands of both convalescence and commitment have left little room for correspondence. It was a mishap, borne of the very labor that consumes my days, that granted me this moment of reprieve to write.

In the summer of last annum, a dire misfortune befell our family with the death of my esteemed father, John. He held you in high regard, Eoinn, and it is with a laden heart I relay the news of his demise. An unfortunate encounter with a ferry at the site of his cherished Brooklyn Bridge project led to the loss of most of his foot—an injury he sought to remedy with a spring water treatment. Alas, his efforts were in vain and tetanus claimed him after several weeks of suffering. I know you well understand the horrors of a death by tetanus.

The mantle of chief engineer for the bridge project has since fallen to me, a role I accepted with mixed emotions, for it was my father's wish to see this endeavor to its completion. Despite the challenges, including a recent fire within one of the caissons from which I am presently recovering, the work has been both exhilarating and fulfilling. My wife, Emily, has been a pillar of strength, assuming the helm of the project with remarkable aptitude during my recovery.

This period of enforced rest has afforded me the opportunity to peruse my father's correspondence, through which I rediscovered your letter. Emily and I are keen to visit your village upon the completion of this engineering leviathan, which has been hailed as the pinnacle of human ingenuity. I remember well our conversations about Europe by the fireside during the War, and my recent travels there in pursuit of bridge-design innovations have only amplified my desire to reunite.

I'm certain that you will remember that I am an avid collector of rare gemstones, and the star garnet you gifted my father now adorns my desk, a constant reminder of the beauty that lies in the natural world—a beauty he, regrettably, never witnessed. To explore your mines and behold the burgeoning town you oversee would fulfill a long-held aspiration of mine.

I would be most grateful for any sketches or photographs of your village, as well as any additional gemstones of interest you might encounter. I have not forgotten your forthcoming need for steel and wire ropes for the construction of your bridge and have taken the liberty of attaching the business card of my own steel procurement manager for your convenience. He has been briefed on your need and the desire for absolute secrecy regarding the project.

Please convey my warmest regards to the delightful Rose.

Yours sincerely,

Wash
   Washington A. Roebling
   Hicks St. Brooklyn Heights, New York

I I I I

October 31st, 1870

From: Eoinn Seeley
   To: Washington Roebling

My Dearest Wash,

It is with a heart heavy laden that I received word of your esteemed father's passing. He was, to me, not merely a friend but a beacon of wisdom and guidance. The cherished moments spent in your company, especially those days in Cincinnati amidst your kin, have left an indelible mark upon my soul. I will forever be in your debt for

106

bringing me to meet him after our time together during the War. I know you had told me years before that I should meet your father, and that he would be like a twin brother of mine taken out of time. This seemed to me then an embellishment. Yet, in truth, our shared vision for a community of purpose was as soothing to my spirit as any salve. Calling us kindred spirits would not have gone far enough.

Enclosed, you will find photographs of our thriving village showing the remarkable progress we have achieved. I have also taken the liberty of sketching plans for a fortification to grace the village's approach, as the wooden bridge your father so ingeniously designed now finds itself outmatched by our cascading needs. I am eager to embark upon the construction of a more enduring bridge come the next year and would value your expertise in securing the requisite steel and wire ropes. The financial barriers that once loomed large are now but shadows, thanks to the prosperous yields of our mining endeavors. I must implore you, however, to guard the details of our success and the location of our village with the utmost discretion.

For your eyes, I have included a selection of gems, the likes of which I am confident will astound you. Our recent excavation unveiled a cavern resplendent with crystals, the vibrancy of which defies adequate capture by photography alone. I earnestly believe a visit to see these natural formations would well justify the journey, and we would be most honored to host you and your family for as long or short a stay as you might wish. Rose extends her warmest regards to both you and Emily.

P.S. Upon the spring, my business manager shall make arrangements with your representative. The winter here approaches, promising snows as deep as thirty feet, yet the thermal springs offer solace against the frost's embrace.

Yours in deepest sympathy and enduring friendship,

Eoinn Seeley

6

History

The morning sun cast long shadows across the valley as Jack and Susanne drove along the winding mountain roads toward Mullan. The small mining town clung to the hillside like a gnarled, old tree, its buildings hinting at stories of boom and bust cycles that had defined this corner of Idaho for over a century.

"Turn left on North 2nd Street," Susanne said. "Aunt Molly's house is up the hill through town, it's blue with a white picket fence."

Jack slowed down as they climbed through the quaint downtown. The road continued as a steep residential street. Houses here were modest, some were modern, others were older, built for miners and their families in the early 1900s. Many showed signs of careful maintenance despite their age—fresh paint, tidy gardens, rebuilt porches. Others sagged under the weight of decades, their windows dark and empty.

"There," Susanne pointed to a small bungalow painted robin's-egg blue. A white picket fence enclosed a garden bursting with flowers. Hollyhocks towered against the house's south wall, their blooms ranging from deep purple to pale pink. Tomato plants with green tomatoes occupied raised beds, and wildflowers bordered the walkway.

They parked on the street and walked through the gate. Before they could knock, the front door opened to reveal a tall, sturdy woman with curly, steel-gray hair cut in a long bob. Her eyes were sharp and bright, and her handshake was firm.

"Hello, Susanne, dear. And you must be Jack," she said, sizing him up with an appraising look. "I can see the Seeley in you. Same jaw as your grandfather, though he was a bit more serious. Come in, both of you. I've got coffee on and stories to tell."

Molly O'Connor Flood's living room was a museum of family history. Photographs covered every surface—wedding portraits, military service photos, children in Sunday clothes, and candid shots of family gatherings. A glass-fronted cabinet displayed china, crystal, and what appeared to be mining artifacts. Books filled built-in shelves, their spines showing a preference for history, biography, and classic literature.

"Sit anywhere you like," Molly said, settling into a worn, leather chair that clearly belonged to her. "Susanne tells me you've been digging into the Crystal Village story. About time someone did."

She poured coffee from a silver service that looked like it had seen better days but was polished to a shine. "This belonged to my great-grandmother, Elizabeth O'Connor. She brought it west in 1869, when she came to Crystal Village with her husband Liam and their four children."

Jack accepted his cup, noting the delicate floral pattern. "You've kept remarkable records."

"Family history was my passion before I retired from teaching," Molly replied. "Forty years in the classroom, and I spent every summer vacation tracking down relatives and interviewing old-timers before they passed on. My husband used to joke that I knew more about dead O'Connors than living ones."

Susanne leaned forward. "What can you tell us about Crystal Village? Jack found some references to it in his great-grandfather's papers but nothing detailed."

Molly's eyes lit up. She rose and walked to a large rolltop desk in the corner. "Let me show you what I've got." She returned with a leather portfolio thick with documents. "This is the O'Connor family archive. Birth certificates, marriage records, letters, photographs, and most importantly, the memoir my grandfather Henry wrote starting in 1952."

She opened the portfolio and withdrew a typed manuscript bound in red leather. "Henry O'Connor was Sam and Seamus's eldest son. He was twenty-six when the Great Idaho Fire of 1910 destroyed Crystal Village and forced the evacuation. He lived to be ninety-one, and after he retired, he wrote down everything he remembered about the village and its people. He founded a bank after the fire with John Seeley, your great-grandfather, Jack. And he worked with his grandfather Liam, helping to manage the bar and shipping company they started together. Henry died in 1976."

Jack felt his pulse quicken. "May we read it?"

"Of course. That's why I had Susanne bring you here." Molly handed him the manuscript. "But first, let me give you the family connections so you understand who's who."

She pulled out a hand-drawn family tree. Its branches spread across several sheets of paper taped together. "Here's where we start. Liam O'Connor married Elizabeth Finnegan in County Tyrone, Ireland, in 1858. They had four children: Joshua, Eva, Seamus, and Susanne."

Susanne traced the lines with her finger. "So there was another Susanne in the family."

"Oh yes, and she lived a full life. The original Susanne survived the fire and relocated to Wallace with the other refugees. She married Patrick McBride there in 1912, and they moved to California. She lived to be eighty-three and died in San Francisco." Molly pointed to another branch of the tree. "Now, Sam and Seamus had five children, including your great-grandfather Henry, who was my grandfather. Henry had three sons— James, Thomas, and Michael. Your grandfather James carried on the O'Connor name in your line, Thomas was my father, and Michael moved around throughout his life to different parts of the country."

Jack studied the tree, noting the careful notations beside each name. "What happened to the other families? The original founders?"

"That's where it gets interesting." Molly pulled out a manila folder. "After the fire, the survivors scattered. Sean O'Neil and Colin O'Shea sailed for Ireland, I imagine to be with their families. It isn't explicitly stated anywhere, but I'm fairly certain that they were a gay couple. When I realized this, I was tickled, because it showed how inclusive that community was—far ahead of its time. The Sullivan brothers went to Maine. Liam and Elizabeth settled in Wallace, while the rest of the O'Connors spread throughout the region. Elizabeth died about the time Prohibition started, and Liam disappeared in the 1930s after Prohibition was repealed. Rumor was that he was a bootlegger during Prohibition. Apparently, this kept him active and engaged, but after it ended, he acted lost and rudderless. He was quite old by that point, and one day he left with a brief note to Henry saying he wanted to go see the world again. He was never heard from again. Sam eventually settled with Seamus in Florence, Italy, with Seamus' sister Eva and her husband Danny. But here's the remarkable part—the younger generation stayed in touch. For decades, they maintained correspondence, sharing news and supporting each other through hard times."

She showed them a bundle of letters tied with ribbon. "These are letters between my grandfather Henry and various members of the other families. They wrote about their new lives, their children, and their memories of Crystal Village. It was like they couldn't let go of what they'd lost."

Susanne picked up one of the letters, noting the careful handwriting. "Did they ever talk about going back?"

"Oh yes. For years, they discussed it. Some wanted to rebuild, to reclaim what the fire had taken. But practical concerns always intervened. The mines were played out, the silver mines in the region were far more valuable than any of the gold that had been found in the various stampedes before then. The world was changing. By the 1920s, most of them had established new lives."

Molly walked to the window and gazed out at the mountains. "But they never forgot. Every Christmas, they exchanged cards. Every few years, someone would organize a reunion. The children grew up hearing stories about Crystal Village, about the community their parents had built and lost."

Jack opened Henry's memoir and read the first few pages. The writing was clear and evocative, bringing to life a world that had vanished over a century ago. "This is incredible! He describes everything—the buildings, the people, and daily life in the village."

"Henry had a remarkable memory!" Molly said, excited that someone else shared her passion. "He could recall conversations from when he was a child, describe the layout of every street, and tell you what Mrs. O'Hara cooked for family Sunday dinner in 1908! When he started writing this memoir, it all came pouring out of him."

Susanne was examining a photograph album. "Look at this, Jack." She showed him a formal portrait of a large group posed in front of a substantial, brick building. "This is labeled 'Crystal Village Original Eight and Families, 1905.'"

Jack studied the faces, noting the mix of ages and the obvious prosperity reflected in their clothing. "I have another photograph of the Original Eight without their families. It was earlier than this one." He turned to Molly, "They look successful. Happy."

"They were ... for a time," Molly said. "Crystal Village was everything they'd dreamed of—a safe, prosperous community where families could thrive. But success brought its own problems. The younger generation started questioning the founders' authority. There were disputes about ownership, about representation in decision-making. By 1910, the village was dealing with some serious internal tensions."

She pulled out another document. "This is a letter from my great-grandfather Liam to his cousin in Ireland, written just three months before the fire. Our distant cousins gave it to me when I went to Ireland for research in the early eighties. He talks about the growing divide between the old guard and the younger families. Some wanted to democratize the village government, give everyone a voice. Eoinn Seeley believed that would lead to chaos."

Jack looked up from the memoir. "What was Seeley like? I keep hearing conflicting accounts."

Molly considered the question. "Complex. Brilliant, certainly. Visionary. But also proud, sometimes to a fault. He'd fought in the Civil War, survived the chaos of the post-War years, and built something remarkable in Crystal Village. From what I could learn, he came from Irish nobility, and he was somewhat paternalistic. He wasn't inclined to share power with people he saw as short-sighted."

"Was he fair to the families?" Susanne asked.

"Mostly, yes. The financial records show that everyone benefited from the village's prosperity. After the fire, everyone was given a nest egg to start over. But Seeley made the big decisions unilaterally. He chose who could join the community, how resources were allocated, and what projects to pursue. Some families chafed under that arrangement. He retained ownership of all the land and buildings. So even though people were doing well financially, some never felt they could set down permanent roots. The last generation of children were starting to leave the village rather than settle down there."

Molly returned to her chair and picked up her coffee. "The irony is that the fire might have saved them from a civil war within their own community."

Jack continued reading, skipping through the volume, he was absorbed in Henry's vivid descriptions. He had loved Crystal Village, and his grief over its loss permeated every page. "He writes about the evacuation like it was yesterday."

"Yes. The train ride haunted him for the rest of his life," Molly said. "He used to have nightmares about it—the smoke, the heat, the sound of the bridge collapsing behind them. But he also talked about the heroism he witnessed, the way people helped each other, the determination to survive."

Susanne had moved to the cabinet and was examining the artifacts. "What are these?"

"Pieces of Crystal Village that survived the fire. That's a chunk of garnet from the original mine. The silver spoon belonged to Mrs. O'Hara, who ran the community kitchen and later lived with Sam and Seamus's family as an adopted grandmother. After the fire, she settled with Glory O'Connor in Wallace. The brass compass was Liam's—he used it to navigate the wilderness when he came west."

Each item seemed to hold its own story. Jack found himself imagining the hands that had held them, the lives they'd touched. "It's like holding pieces of a lost world."

"That's exactly what they are," Molly agreed. "The fire was so intense that almost nothing survived, and since the village was abandoned so quickly, there were very few artifacts. These pieces became treasured family heirlooms, passed down through the generations."

The afternoon passed quickly as Molly shared story after story. She read passages from Eva O'Connor's diary about raising her son in the mountain community. She displayed photographs of the famous hot springs and the elaborate bridge that Eoinn Seeley had commissioned from John Roebling, the famous bridge engineer who had designed the Brooklyn Bridge in New York City. There were pictures of the bustling main street on market day, children playing in the heated cobblestone streets during winter, and families gathering for community celebrations.

"Look at this one," Molly said, showing them a photograph of a group of children building a snowman in wintertime. "That's my grandfather Henry, the tall boy in the back. And that little girl with the curls is Glory O'Connor, Sam and Seamus's youngest daughter."

Susanne studied the faces, trying to imagine these children as the adults who would scatter across the country after losing their home. "What happened to Glory?"

"She stayed in Wallace with Mrs. O'Hara, taking care of her through her old age. Glory worked in Liam's Bar throughout her adult life. After Mrs. O'Hara died, she married a local boy."

Jack set down his coffee cup and looked at the photograph again. "It's remarkable how normal their lives seem in these pictures. You'd never know they were living in such an isolated community."

"That was the beauty of Crystal Village," Molly said. "It wasn't isolated in the way you might think. They had regular supply trains and visitors from across the world. Business relationships brought people from everywhere, even tourists who came to see the hot springs. It was busy enough to support multiple hotels. The village was connected to the outside world, but it maintained its own unique character."

She pulled out another album, this one filled with formal portraits. "These are the wedding photographs. Sam and Seamus's wedding in 1884,

Eva and Danny's in 1885, and several others. The village photographer, Sean O'Neil, was quite talented. He documented everything—births, deaths, celebrations, even the construction of new buildings. Fortunately, he managed to save some of his portfolio from the fire by moving them from his darkroom and studio in the mining offices into the mines."

Susanne leaned closer to examine the photos. "The dresses are beautiful. Look at the detail in the lace."

"The village was a very wealthy community. There were skilled seamstresses working there," Molly explained. "What they couldn't make had to be shipped in, and there were several fashionable boutiques. They wanted beauty in their lives—elegance, even in the wilderness."

Jack found himself drawn to a photograph of the village's main street decorated for what appeared to be a holiday celebration. Bunting hung between buildings, and people in their finest clothes filled the cobblestone street. "What occasion was this?"

"Fourth of July 1908," Molly said. "The last, big celebration before the fire. Henry wrote about it in his memoir—how the whole community came together, how proud they were of what they'd built. There were speeches, games for the children, and a feast that lasted until midnight."

She turned several pages to show them more photographs from that day. "Look at this one. That's Eoinn Seeley giving a speech from the steps of the mining company office. And there's Rose Seeley beside him, looking radiant. She died just a few days later."

"What happened to her?" Susanne asked.

"Heart failure. Her death was a terrible blow to Eoinn and your great-grandfather John. Eoinn was never quite the same after she died, and the relationship between John and Eoinn was strained after her loss."

Jack studied Eoinn's face in the photograph. Even in celebration, there was something serious about his expression. "He looks like a man carrying the world."

"In many ways, he was," Molly agreed. "The success of Crystal Village depended on his leadership, his vision, and his ability to make the right decisions. But that kind of responsibility can be crushing. Especially when you're dealing with strong-willed people who have their own ideas about how things should be done."

She showed them a letter written in Eoinn's distinctive handwriting. "This is from 1909, addressed to his old friend Washington Roebling. I was able to get this from the Roebling Estate in Troy, New York. In it, he talks about the challenges of leadership, the loneliness of command. He was struggling with the political tensions in the village, trying to balance the needs of the community with his own vision for its future."

Susanne read portions of the letter aloud. "'The burden of decision-making grows heavier with each passing year. Those who once trusted my judgment now question every choice. I fear I have become more of a benevolent dictator than a leader, and I'm not certain how to change course without losing everything we've built.'"

"That's heartbreaking," Jack said. "He sounds like he knew change was coming but didn't know how to manage it."

"Exactly. And then the fire solved his problem in the most devastating way possible." Molly closed the album gently. "Sometimes I wonder what would have happened if the fire hadn't come. Would they have found a way to resolve their differences? Would Crystal Village have evolved into something different but equally remarkable?"

The sun was beginning to set, casting long shadows across Molly's garden. Jack realized they'd been there for hours, absorbed in the stories and artifacts of a lost world. "This has been incredible, Molly. Thank you for sharing all of this with us."

"There's more," she said, standing and walking to a closet. "I've got two boxes of documents, a few more photographs, even a few of the original architectural drawings that Finn McEnhill made for the village buildings."

She returned with a large flat portfolio. "These are the plans for the bridge, the mining company office, even the hot springs facility. Finn was a master architect, and his designs were both beautiful and practical. These were rescued by Sean O'Neil as well."

Jack opened the portfolio and found himself looking at detailed blueprints drawn in India ink. The precision was remarkable, every measurement carefully noted, every structural element clearly defined. "These are museum quality."

"They should be in a museum," Molly agreed. "But I've been waiting for the right person to entrust them to. Someone who would understand their value, who might even do something meaningful with them."

She looked directly at Jack. "Susanne tells me you're in the entertainment business. You do theme parks, is that right?"

Jack nodded, suddenly understanding where this conversation was heading. "Yes, I spent the last twenty years working for Disney, designing experiences for their parks around the world. Now I work for a company based in Japan."

Molly nodded and sank into thought.

Susanne reached out and put her hand on Molly's knee. "Aunt Molly, do you know where the village was?"

Molly reached into the bottom drawer of her desk, which was filled with hanging file folders. She pulled out a modern topographical map of the region. "The exact location has been lost, but I'm fairly certain it's somewhere in this area," she said, making a circle with her finger encompassing an area north of Eagle City and northeast of Murray.

Susanne leaned forward, studying the map. "How do you know all this?"

"Grandpa Henry showed me on a map once, but it was a long time ago," Molly answered.

Jack looked her in the eye and said, "And you've never gone looking for it. Why are you passing all this along now?"

She stood and walked to the window, looking out at the darkening mountains. "I'm ninety-three years old, Jack. I don't have much time left, and I don't have any children to pass this responsibility to. I've been waiting for someone from one of the founding families to step forward, someone who might have the resources and vision to do something with all this material. It should be preserved."

7

Rise

April 1st, 1871

Sam King crouched behind the outhouse, her arms wrapped tight around her knees. The morning sun painted Crystal Village in shades of gold and green, but she saw none of its beauty. Terror and shame coursed through her thirteen-year-old body as she tried to make sense of what was happening to her.

She'd woken before dawn with a strange ache in her belly, thinking perhaps she'd eaten something that disagreed with her. But when she'd risen from her narrow bed in her room off the cabin she shared with Sean and Colin, she'd discovered the blood. There was so much blood that her first thought was that she was dying from some grave injury.

Now she sat hidden, her nightgown bunched beneath her, afraid to move. Sean had left early, and Colin was making his morning rounds to check on Mrs. Petersen's rheumatism and young Tommy Wu's persistent cough. She was alone with her terror and had no idea what to do.

The sound of footsteps on the path made her shrink deeper into the shadows. Through the gap between the outhouse and the cabin, she could see Rose Seeley walking toward the hot springs, a bundle of clean towels in her arms. Rose moved with the graceful confidence Sam had always admired, her dark hair caught up in a simple chignon, her dress crisp despite the early hour.

Sam bit her lip, fighting back tears. She couldn't stay hidden forever, but the thought of explaining her condition to Sean or Colin made her stomach churn with embarrassment. Colin would launch into one of his medical explanations, all clinical terms and matter-of-fact observations that would make her want to disappear into the earth. Sean would turn red as a beet and stammer something about fetching Mrs. O'Hara.

"Mrs. Seeley!" Sam called out, her voice barely above a whisper.

Rose paused, looking around. "Sam? Where are you, dear?"

"Behind the outhouse." Sam's voice cracked. "Could you ... could you please come here? I need help."

Rose set down her bundle and approached the outhouse. When she saw Sam huddled in the shadows, her expression immediately shifted to one of gentle concern.

"What's wrong, sweetheart?"

Sam's face burned with shame. "I think ... I think I'm dying. There's blood, and I don't know what's happening to me."

Understanding dawned in Rose's eyes, followed by a warmth that made Sam's chest tight with relief. Rose knelt beside her, her voice soft and reassuring.

"Oh, my dear girl. You're not dying. You're becoming a woman."

"What?" Sam stared at her in confusion.

Rose settled more comfortably on the ground, seemingly unconcerned about her clean dress. "What you're experiencing is called menstruation. It's something that happens to all women, usually starting around your age. It means your body is preparing itself for the possibility of bearing children someday."

Sam's eyes widened. "All women?"

"Every single one. It happened to me when I was about your age. To Mrs. O'Hara, to Elizabeth O'Connor, to every woman in this village." Rose's smile was gentle. "It's perfectly natural, though I understand it can be frightening when no one has explained it to you."

"But the blood ..."

"Will come every month for a few days. It's your body's way of renewing itself." Rose reached out and brushed a tear from Sam's cheek. "I should have spoken to you about this sooner. I've been watching you grow up these past few years, and I should have realized you'd need guidance."

Sam felt some of the terror ease from her chest. "So I'm not sick?"

"Not at all," Rose assured her. "Though you might feel some discomfort—aches in your belly or back. That's normal too." Rose stood and extended her hand. "Come. Let's get you cleaned up and find you some proper supplies."

Sam took Rose's hand and allowed herself to be helped to her feet. "I don't know what to do. Sean and Colin, they're good to me, but ..."

"But they're *men*, and this is women's business." Rose's understanding smile made Sam feel less alone than she had in years. "Let's wrap you in this towel, and you can come to my house. I have everything you need."

They walked together through the quiet morning streets, Rose keeping a protective arm around Sam's shoulders, a towel wrapped around Sam's nightgown. The Seeley house stood grand and welcoming, its windows catching the early light.

Inside, Rose led Sam to a small washroom off the kitchen. She provided clean cloths, showed Sam how to secure them, and explained how often they would need changing. Her manner was matter-of-fact but kind, treating Sam's questions with the same respect she might give to any adult woman. Rose gave her one of her own robes to wear.

"There," Rose said when Sam had cleaned herself and changed into a borrowed wrapper. "Much better. Now, let's have some tea and talk."

They sat at Rose's kitchen table, steam rising from delicate china cups. Sam had never felt so grown-up, sitting in this beautiful house, being treated as an equal by the most elegant woman in Crystal Village.

"Mrs. Seeley," Sam began hesitantly, "how did you know what to do? I ... mean... when it first happened to you?"

Rose's expression grew distant. "I was fortunate, in a way. I was living with my great-aunt in New York—a difficult woman who had little patience for children. She raised me after my parents died, but it was always a trial with her. When my monthly courses began, she simply told me it was the curse of being female and handed me some rags." Rose's voice grew bitter. "She said it was God's punishment for Eve's sin, and that I should bear it in silence like all women before me."

Sam's eyes widened at the harsh words. "That's terrible!"

"It was," Rose agreed. "But it taught me something important—that no young woman should face this milestone alone or with shame." Rose reached across the table and covered Sam's hand with her own. "What's happening to you isn't a curse, Sam. It means you're growing into a woman, as every woman must. There's no shame in it."

"I felt so scared and alone," Sam admitted.

"Of course you did! But you're not alone, and you never will be as long as I'm here." Rose's voice was firm with promise. "Anytime you have questions—about this or anything else that comes with growing into womanhood—you come to me. Do you understand?"

Sam nodded, feeling tears prick her eyes again, but these were tears of gratitude rather than fear.

"Now," Rose said, her tone becoming more practical, "Easter is next week. Do you have something special to wear for the service?"

Sam's face fell. "That's another thing I've been worrying about. Last year I just wore my regular clothes, but this year ... I don't know why, but I feel like I should dress up. Like the other women do. But I don't have anything nice enough."

Rose studied Sam's face, seeing the vulnerability beneath the words. "Would you like me to help you with that?"

"Would you?"

"I'd be honored. I have some fabric that I believe would look absolutely beautiful on you, and I enjoy sewing." Rose's eyes sparkled with enthusiasm. "We could make you a proper Easter dress. Something that makes you feel as lovely as you are."

Sam's face lit up with a joy Rose hadn't seen from her in months. "Really? You'd do that for me?"

"Sam, dear, I lost my parents when I was very young. I know what it's like to navigate the world without a mother's guidance." Rose's voice grew soft with memory. "My great-aunt was ... well, she was *not* a nurturing woman. She saw my presence as a burden rather than a blessing. I promised myself that if I ever had the chance, I would be the kind of woman I needed when I was your age."

"But you have your own family to care for."

"And you're part of that family now, whether you realize it or not." Rose stood and moved to a cabinet, pulling out several lengths of fabric. "Look at these. This blue would bring out your eyes beautifully. And this green is almost the exact color of spring leaves."

Sam ran her fingers over the soft cotton, marveling at the quality. "They're so beautiful. But I couldn't ..."

"You *can* and you *will*. It would give me great pleasure to see you wearing something I made for you." Rose held the blue fabric up to Sam's face. "Yes, definitely the blue. It makes your eyes look like sapphires."

They spent the morning planning the dress, Rose taking careful measurements and sketching out ideas. Sam found herself relaxing completely for the first time in days, caught up in Rose's enthusiasm and kindness.

"Mrs. Seeley," Sam said as Rose pinned fabric around her, "why are you being so kind to me?"

Rose paused in her work, looking up at Sam with gentle eyes. "Because you remind me of myself at your age. Lost, trying to figure out how to be a woman without anyone to show you the way." She resumed pinning. "And it's also because I see something special in you, Sam. You have a strength and resilience that will serve you well in life. But remember, just because you have strength doesn't mean you have to face everything alone."

"I've always felt like I had to be strong. Ever since my family died."

"And you have been. Remarkably so. But there's a difference between being strong and being isolated." Rose's voice was gentle but firm. "True strength sometimes means knowing when to accept help, when to lean on others who care about you."

Sam felt something shift inside her chest, a loosening of tension she'd carried for years. "I'd like that. To not always have to figure everything out by myself."

"Then consider it settled. You'll come to me with your questions and concerns, and I'll share what wisdom I have." Rose smiled. "And in return, you can help me understand what the younger generation is thinking. It will be a fair exchange."

As the morning wore on, Sam found herself sharing things she'd never told anyone—her fears about growing up, her confusion about her place in the village, and her dreams for the future. Rose listened with the same attention she might give to Eoinn's business concerns, treating Sam's thoughts and feelings as important and valid.

"You know," Rose said as she began cutting the fabric, "I think this Easter service will be particularly meaningful for you."

"Why?"

"Because you're experiencing your own kind of rebirth. Leaving childhood behind and stepping into womanhood." Rose's hands were deft at the work, her voice gentle as she talked. "The themes of renewal and new life that we celebrate at Easter—they're not just about religious faith. They're about the cycles of growth and change that touch all our lives."

Sam considered this. "I hadn't thought of it that way."

"Mrs. Wu often speaks about the Buddhist concept of constant change and renewal. Mr. Rosenberg talks about Passover as a celebration of freedom and new beginnings. Even the old Celtic traditions that some of our Irish friends remember celebrate the awakening of the earth in spring." Rose looked up from her cutting. "All these different traditions, they share the same understanding—that life is about growth, change, and the courage to embrace new chapters."

"And I'm starting a new chapter?"

"Exactly. And what a beautiful chapter it will be!"

They worked together through the morning and into the afternoon, Rose teaching Sam basic stitches and sharing stories of her own youth in New York. Rose wrote a note to Mr. Lemieux and sent it with one of the neighborhood children, who brought back a package with new clean pants and a shirt for Sam, in the style she normally wore, and a new nightgown to replace the one she'd soiled. By evening, the Easter dress was taking shape—a lovely creation in soft blue cotton with tiny pearl buttons and delicate white trim.

"It's the most beautiful thing I've ever owned," Sam breathed, running her fingers over the careful stitching.

"And you'll be the most beautiful young woman at the Easter service," Rose replied, folding the dress carefully in tissue paper. "But remember, Sam—the dress is lovely, but your beauty comes from who you are *inside*."

Sam felt her throat tighten with emotion. "Thank you, Mrs. Seeley. Not just for the dress but for … for everything today. For making me feel less alone."

Rose pulled Sam into a warm embrace, and for the first time since her family's death, Sam felt truly mothered. "You're never alone, dear one. Remember that. And please, call me Rose when we're together like this. We're more than neighbors now—we're family."

As Sam walked home, the carefully wrapped dress in her arms, she felt transformed. The fear and shame of the morning had given way to something new—a sense of belonging, of being cherished and understood.

I I I I

June 1871

Angus Sullivan sat at his desk, surrounded by ledgers and papers. Angus's responsibilities as the financial steward of the village were manifold. He managed the village's wealth, ensuring that each coin was accounted for and each transaction recorded. He also worked closely with Eoinn on investing the proceeds of the mines. His wife often joked that he could predict the weather by the rise and fall of the economy. Her joke was not without merit. Angus had an innate sense for the ebb and flow of money.

His sons were often seen around the village, learning the ropes of various trades. The eldest, Robert, had a penchant for numbers, much like his father. Angus took great pride in teaching him the intricacies of finance, hoping that one day Robert would take up the mantle.

"Papa," Robert said, entering the room with a bundle of letters in hand, "these arrived today. One of them is from Mr. Lemieux's cousin Gaspar. He asked me to pass it along to you."

Angus nodded, accepting the letters. His relationship with Pierre Lemieux, who kept the village supplied, was one of mutual respect and trust. Pierre was a vital link in the chain that connected Crystal Village to the broader world. His extended family were all diligent contributors to the life of the village and made up a vast network. Angus scanned the letter's contents, his eyes narrowing with concentration. Gaspar had written about a promising, young bookkeeper he had encountered in Chicago. The man's name was Samuel Townsend, a prodigy with numbers and a keen business acumen. Apparently, Townsend had a young family and was looking to move to the West.

"Robert," Angus said, looking up from the letter, "it seems we may have found someone to assist with the accounts. A young man from Chicago. I'll meet with Liam, and he can arrange to bring him here."

I I I I

Across the village, Finn stood in the shade of a large oak, surveying the construction of a new building. He looked at it with deep satisfaction, each detail had been meticulously planned and stored in the vault of his memory. Finn viewed the village whole cloth, meaning he saw it as it was today and as it would be in the future. His ability to visualize a structure from the ground up was nothing short of remarkable, and his attention to detail was unparalleled.

"Finn!" called a voice from behind him. It was Egan Sullivan, his engineering counterpart and frequent collaborator. "Ye've outdone yourself with this one. The lines are perfect."

Finn turned, a modest smile on his lips. He nodded. Egan's engineering prowess complemented Finn's architectural genius, and together they were transforming Crystal Village.

"Liam's due back soon," Egan said. "I hear he's bringing some talent with him."

Finn's eyes lit up with interest. "Excellent. We'll need skilled hands for the new projects. But first, we need the materials handy. Have ye spoken with Angus about the budget?"

Egan nodded. "Of course. We'll have everything we need."

Egan's domain was a small workshop attached to the mining company offices. Egan was revered among the villagers for his engineering acumen, and the systems he had devised to harness the geothermal energy of the hot springs were nothing short of revolutionary.

Later that day, Egan stood at the mouth of the mine, watching as workers moved to and fro, their silhouettes framed by the golden light of the afternoon sun. "Mr. Sullivan!" called Jacob, one of the workers. "Everything's ready for the new water pipes. We're just waiting on the go-ahead."

Egan nodded, his thoughts already racing ahead to the next phase of the project. The pipes would channel hot water beneath the streets, ensuring they remained clear of snow even during the harsh winter months. This was a stroke of genius that had been born from a chance encounter with a hydrologist whom Egan had met when accompanying Liam on one of his recruiting trips.

I I I I

The laundry in Crystal Village was filled with a mixture of steam, the scent of soap, and the sound of rhythmic scrubbing. Mr. Wu, his sleeves rolled up, orchestrated the operation with precision and physicality. Mr. Wu and his brother had run a successful laundry business in one of the mining camps in the southern part of Idaho. Unfortunately, they had been harassed and threatened by a group of local men who didn't like Chinese merchants working with white folk. Liam had heard the story and recruited them. This had occurred fairly early in the life of the village. Encouraged by Liam's welcoming attitude, Mr. Wu and his brother set up a laundry and brought their families to live in the village. The elder brother was Cheng, and the younger was Jian. Their wives were Mei and Zhong-Ling. They started with a highly productive laundry service but moved beyond that and began to facilitate importing spices and goods from China. Their extended family in San Francisco and beyond were proving highly valuable for Mr. Lemieux's work.

The families Wu shared a large home that was one of the new buildings being constructed in the neighborhood on the east side of Broadway. This was one of the homes with its own kitchen, a desirable trait for a family with its own cooking habits that were deeply connected to their family's traditions. Mrs. O'Hara, ever curious about all things culinary, found herself enchanted by the aromas wafting from the Wu's kitchen. One evening, she knocked on their door, intrigued by the unfamiliar scents. The door swung open, and she was greeted by a cacophony of sizzling, chopping, and laughter. With a warm smile, Mrs. Wu welcomed her in.

Once she learned of Mrs. O's interests, Mrs. Wu wasted no time in engaging her. "Come, try this," Mrs. Wu offered, handing Mrs. O a small plate of steamed dumplings, their delicate skins glistening with a light sheen of oil. They had been sprinkled with a light brown sauce. She bit into one, the flavors bursting forth in a dance of garlic, ginger, and tender pork.

"This is incredible!" Mrs. O'Hara exclaimed, her eyes wide with delight. "You must teach me how you do it."

From that day, Mrs. Wu and her sister-in-law, Zhong-Ling, became regulars in the communal kitchen, their recipes a relished and popular addition to the village's culinary repertoire. Egg foo yong, with its fluffy egg and savory sauce, became a staple at village gatherings. Dumplings were a village favorite. *Bao*, both sweet and savory, were eagerly anticipated treats. Seasonally, they made moon cakes, and they regularly made traditional Chinese baked goods such as sesame cookies and sesame red bean balls.

The introduction of these dishes sparked a culinary revolution in Crystal Village, and soon the community's tables were laden with a wide variety of flavors from other cultures. Mrs. Semanski, inspired by the Wu's creativity with dumplings, shared her family's pierogi recipe, teaching others how to fill the delicate dough with potatoes, cheese, and onions.

Likewise, Mrs. Lombardi introduced the village to the art of pasta making. The community kitchen soon became a haven of flour-dusted countertops. Fettuccine, lasagna, and ravioli took their place alongside the dumplings and pierogi, each bite fortifying the village's growing cultural mosaic. Mrs. Russo, not to be outdone, brought her family's Italian sausage recipes, infusing the air with the rich scents of fennel, red pepper, and garlic.

Mrs. Stein shared the secrets of German sausage-making, teaching eager hands to grind, season, and stuff casings until the kitchen was filled with links of every variety. Mrs. Rosenberg's challah bread, braided and golden, was a weekly delight, its soft, sweet crumb a perfect vessel for chicken soup.

One crisp autumn morning, Mrs. O'Hara joined Mei and Zhong-Ling for their daily *tai chi* practice. The three women moved with grace and fluidity. Soon, others joined them. Before long, the field behind the meal hall was alive with villagers of all ages, their forms silhouetted against the rising sun.

The Wu family shared stories of dragons and spirits, tales that captured the imagination of young and old alike. In the evenings, as the embers of the communal fire glowed softly, Mrs. O and Mrs. Wu wove their stories together, creating a rich melding of myth and magic.

I I I I

Under the dim glow of an oil lamp, Pierre Lemieux sat at a desk in his office. The room was a reflection of his meticulous nature. Every ledger and map was placed meticulously. Liam O'Connor leaned back in his chair opposite Pierre, the aroma of freshly ground coffee mingling with the scent of paper and ink.

"Pierre," Liam said, his voice measured, "ye've orchestrated our provisions masterfully, but I sense ye need someone to share the load."

Pierre nodded, his expression contemplative. "*Oui*, Liam. As our village expands, so do the complexities of our needs. It's no longer a matter of simple provisioning. This is especially true when it comes to meeting the needs of Angus, Egan, and Finn, who are constantly inventing and revising their architectural plans and often finish new construction projects faster than anyone reasonably would expect. I require someone who possesses the foresight to anticipate their needs, someone who can coordinate building supplies with the precision of clockwork."

Liam considered this, his gaze thoughtful. "Ye need someone with a head for planning, a knack for seeing beyond the immediate horizon. Someone who understands building and construction. Let me see what I can do."

Weeks later, Liam found himself in the bustling rail hub of Chicago. The station was alive with the clatter of steam engines, train whistles, and the murmur of travelers. Liam settled onto a wooden bench amidst the chaos, observing the flow of humanity around him.

Nearby, a commotion caught his attention. A large, rotund man with sweat gleaming on his brow and a red face loomed over a smaller, resolute figure. The larger man was a blustering slob, someone who inspired neither respect nor admiration.

"Now see here, Svenson!" the portly man barked. "These delays are intolerable! Fail to get those supplies where they ought to be, and I'll find someone who can!"

Svenson replied with a measured calmness. "Mr. Matheson, it is the mismanagement of orders and the quality of our vendors that is at fault. The delays stem from a flawed process. I've told you for months that there would be issues on these new lines, and that we needed to stock in advance. You wouldn't hear of it. And then when I found a vendor who could do what was nigh impossible to supply our needs, you came in and scuttled a deal that I'd negotiated with nearly impossible terms. You did this all because they wouldn't favor you with a kickback. To perform my duties well, I require autonomy, not meddling. Moreover, our suppliers must be chosen for their quality and reliability, not for the coin they slip into your pocket."

Matheson's visage reddened further, his temper rising like steam from a kettle. "Mind your tongue, Svenson! You're treading on thin ice!"

With that, Matheson stormed off, leaving Svenson standing alone, his resolve unshaken. Svenson looked around, found an empty bench, and sat down with a deep sigh, releasing his tension. Liam saw an opportunity and approached.

"Would ye mind if I took a seat?" Liam inquired, his tone friendly and warm.

Svenson looked up, a flicker of surprise crossing his features. "By all means," he replied, gesturing to the empty space beside him.

"He's a pleasant fellow, isn't he?" Liam remarked with a wry grin as he took his place on the bench.

Svenson chuckled softly. "Not quite the words I'd use for the man. This may well be the final straw. I've been striving to make our superiors see that he's lining his pockets, taking kickbacks from the funds we spend with vendors. But alas, he's the company president's nephew, and I fear my days here are numbered ..."

Liam settled in, and the two men soon found themselves in easy conversation. The man introduced himself as Sven Svenson, from Minneapolis, Minnesota. Liam listened intently as Sven spoke of his background, his dedication to his work, and his yearning for a place where his skills would be appreciated. Liam was on his way to New York, and Sven was heading home to Minneapolis. However, both of their trains were delayed. Liam suggested continuing their discussion over a drink at a nearby tavern.

With pints of ale in hand, Liam painted a vivid picture of Crystal Village—the thriving community, the opportunities it offered, and the role Sven could play in its continued success.

"Angus and Egan Sullivan and Finn McEnhill are all geniuses in their own right," Liam explained. "Angus is the financial steward, a man with a mind like a steel trap for numbers. Finn, on the other hand, is a master craftsman and architect. Egan is a mathematical and engineering genius. They're all brilliant. Finn is a bit of a grumpy old coot, and Egan is eccentric, and they both demand excellence. But they only require it to the bar they have set for themselves. And they're kind men, committed to the vision of

Crystal Village."

Sven listened, captivated by the idea of working in a place where his talents would be valued, where he could contribute to something greater than himself. "Mr. O'Connor, this is very interesting to me. But I have a family, and I've had to travel quite a lot for my current job with the railroad. I've seen the disarray and dangers of the frontier in general and the mining camps in particular with my own eyes. Is this really a place where you feel that my family would be safe?"

Liam leaned in, his voice earnest. "Sven, I've got a large family of my own, and believe me, we're committed to creating a safe community. We want a place where families can thrive, not just survive. With a good school where we could build strong character in our children. We need someone like yerself. Come with me, and see Crystal Village with your own eyes. I think you'll find it's exactly what ye've been looking for. I'll even pay ye for your time, regardless of your final decision."

Sven considered the offer, the weight of his decision clear in his eyes. Yet in his heart, he knew the choice was made. With a nod, he extended his hand to Liam. "All right, Liam. You've convinced me. Let's see what this Crystal Village of yours is all about."

Having come to an understanding, they arranged to meet back in Chicago in two weeks to nail down the specifics. Sven would travel with Liam back to Crystal Village, and if what he found was to his satisfaction, he would return for his family. Liam would buy a round trip train ticket, and would pay him a bonus regardless of his final decision to relocate.

And so began a new chapter for Sven Svenson, one that would see him become an integral part of the community, working alongside Angus, Finn, Egan, and Pierre Lemieux to build a future full of promise and potential.

I I I I

September 1875

Sam walked in the woods behind the village—at the place where the mountain started rising again above the hot springs—and found the trail leading upwards. She'd seen it a few times but had wanted to come back alone. It was three o'clock, and she had a few hours to herself before dinner.

She was seventeen and had grown into a tall, limber, and strong young woman. Her thick, brown hair had a bit of a wave to it, and her expression tended toward the serious, with calm, blue eyes that missed nothing. She was pretty but far too sober to be taken for anything other than the formidable young woman she was becoming. Luckily, her native introspection was tempered by being raised by Sean, whose sense of humor and whimsy were legendary.

Sam had spent her time working in the mines, and she'd been part of the construction of nearly every building on this plateau. However, for the last few months, she had been working with Angus on the mining company business accounts, keeping the ledgers and records of the community's investments up to date. As a result, she was always busy and surrounded by people. Today, she just wanted some time to be alone. Over the last few years, she had repeatedly seen what appeared to be a small cave located high above the village. She didn't quite know how to get up there, and the mountain was very steep. But a few weeks ago, she'd passed what might be a bighorn sheep trail that looked like it might go in that direction.

She followed the trail upwards. She hadn't climbed the mountain before, not in all the years she'd been here. There was always something to do down in the village. Now, as the opportunity to explore this trail presented itself, she was excited to learn something new about her home. The ground was dry but stable, covered in grass and bushes, with the occasional white pine. She followed the sheep path through numerous switchbacks and turns. The path was very steep but passable. Several times she slipped and skidded backwards down the trail, but soon enough she righted herself and set about scrabbling forward. After roughly an hour, she approached an outcropping that she'd noticed ever since coming to the area. There was a copse of trees ahead of the outcropping, and the trail led through it. As she walked through the trees, she thought she heard voices. She slowed her pace and crept forward quietly.

She crouched beneath the pines and peeked at the outcropping. Movement caught her eye. A huge raven was perched on the cliff's edge. It was croaking quietly, hopping and spreading its wings menacingly toward a coyote that stood ten feet back from the edge, eyeing the bird. It was a big coyote, the biggest she'd seen. She wondered if it was part wolf. But still, she thought, it had that rangy coyote body, with a tinge of red to its fur. The coyote was whining and yipping, but quietly; the raven was cawing and croaking. To Sam, it almost looked like they were having a conversation. The raven stretched its beak down and grabbed a rock and tossed it at the coyote, hitting it on the snout. She giggled out loud—louder than she'd meant to—and both animals froze and stared right at her. The raven croaked loudly, jumped into the air, and flew away. The coyote growled at her, walked a few steps toward her, then after getting a better look, tilted its head and ran off up the mountain.

Sam walked forward and approached the outcropping. She could see the whole village laid out below her. It looked fake, almost like someone had made a miniature village like she'd once seen in a store window in Boise. She watched the village and the people moving around in it. Then she turned around to look at the rest of the outcropping and confirmed that there was an opening in the mountain, a small cave entrance, about four feet high. She hesitated for only a second and then walked slowly to it. The entrance was irregular, about six feet high, and it was shaped in such a way that only a small bit of it was visible from the village.

She could see a bit of the cave from the entrance. Every inch of the walls was carved with intricate patterns. The carved lines were then painted with pigments, while the surface of the cave was painted in colors that contrasted the carved lines. The patterns were filled with sparkles that caught the light as some of the surfaces were covered in gold and silver leaf. There were markings carved into the walls in the shapes of animals, birds, stars and moons, and swirls and circles that covered every inch of the cave.

The entire surface area of the interior of the cave was covered with them, going back as far as she could see until the cave disappeared into darkness. She wished she'd brought a lantern, but she had no idea she was going to find a cave.

Sam walked back out on the outcropping, and there was the coyote again. This time it ran toward her. She yelled at it, waved her arms, and made herself big. The coyote stopped short and backed up. Sam turned to walk away, and it started running toward her again. A bit frightened, she turned and ran at the coyote. It barked its funny yelping, yipping sound and ran from her. When she stopped, it stopped. Reaching down, she grabbed some rocks and began pelting the coyote. She was a good shot, and more often than not, the stones found their mark. The coyote yelped at her and retreated, but it didn't run away.

"Stupid coyote," she said, "leave me alone! I just want to go home!"

The coyote cocked its head sideways, just like a dog does when it's confused.

"Away, you! Off with you!" she yelled.

It gave a final, quizzical yelp, turned, and loped off in the other direction. Sam walked down the mountain as fast as she could. When she arrived back in the safety of the village, she didn't mention climbing the mountain, the cave, the coyote, or the raven to anyone.

I I I I

Tom Whitaker stood on the edge of the village square, the late afternoon sun casting long shadows across the cobblestones. Around him, villagers gathered in small clusters, their animated conversations a mix of excitement and anticipation. Today was the day of the village meeting, where Eoinn Seeley and the Original Eight would discuss the allocation of new mining opportunities—a prospect that had the whole community buzzing.

Tom had arrived early, his robust frame standing out among the gathering crowd. He had made a point of coming ahead of the crowd because

134

he was eager to secure a spot towards the front where he could be heard. His broad, sturdy build spoke to years of labor-intensive work, and his deep-set, blue eyes reflected a keen intelligence. With dark-brown hair flecked with gray at the temples and a scruffy beard, Tom embodied the hardworking, principled miner that he was. He had ideas—valuable ones, he believed—that could benefit not just his family but the entire village. Hours spent studying the land had led him to identify potential sites for new shafts, and he had meticulously considered ways to share the wealth more equitably among the villagers.

As he stood there, watching the growing crowd, his mind drifted back to the days when he first arrived in Crystal Village. The promise of prosperity and community had drawn him here, away from the harsh realities of his family's Appalachian mining roots. He had believed in the vision of a tightly-knit community, where hard work and dedication were rewarded, and everyone had a stake in the village's success.

The sound of a gavel brought his attention back to the present. Eoinn Seeley, with his commanding presence, stood at the front of the square, flanked by the other Original Eight. The murmur of the crowd quieted as Eoinn began to speak, his deep voice carrying over the assembly.

"Thank ye all for coming," Eoinn began, his gaze sweeping over the villagers. "Today, we gather to discuss the future of our village, and the opportunities that lie ahead. As ye know, our mining operations have been prosperous, and we are now in a position to expand."

Tom listened intently as Eoinn outlined the proposed plans. The leadership had identified new sites for mining, areas they believed held promise. But as Eoinn continued, it became clear that these decisions had already been made in private, without input from the broader community.

A sense of unease settled over Tom. He had hoped for an open discussion, a chance for the villagers to voice their ideas and concerns. Instead, it felt as though the outcome had been predetermined, the villagers expected simply to accept the leadership's decisions.

As Eoinn concluded his speech, Tom found himself stepping forward, driven by a growing sense of frustration. "Excuse me, Eoinn!" he called out, his voice steady but now tinged with a rising fervor. "I appreciate the work that's been done to identify new sites, but there's value in considering other perspectives. I've spent a lot of time studying the land, and it's high time we all have a say in our own destiny."

The crowd turned their attention to Tom, a mix of curiosity and surprise on their faces. Eoinn regarded him with a measured expression, his eyes betraying no hint of emotion. "And what might those perspectives be, Tom?" Eoinn asked, his tone calm yet carrying the authority of his position.

Tom took a deep breath. "I've identified a quartz intrusion at the western face that shows classic ribbon structure. The gold content in my samples suggests a potential bonanza if we drive a crosscut through the schist layer instead of following the current drift. But more importantly, it isn't just about the technical approach; it's about who benefits from these discoveries. We ought to involve the community in these opportunities. If we risk and invest our time in cutting new shafts, we have the right to share the wealth. Giving miners a direct stake in the mines' success will strengthen our bonds and our village."

For a moment, there was silence as Tom's words hung in the air. He could see the wheels turning in the minds of those around him, the possibility of his proposal taking root, hopeful expressions cropping up around the square. But before he could say more, Eoinn spoke again.

"Tom, your dedication to the village is commendable," Eoinn said, his voice even and authoritative. "But the decisions regarding the mines are made with the community's best interests in mind. The wealth generated by our efforts is reinvested into the village, for the benefit of all. Ownership of the mines is held close in my family's name, not to exclude, but to ensure stability and continuity and to ensure the wealth is reinvested. And we're within a year or two of starting to make the quarterly dividend payments we've been discussing with you all since you joined the village."

Tom felt the familiar sting of dismissal. Five years of practical mining experience before coming here, and still Eoinn regarded his suggestions with the same patronizing patience one might show a child. What Tom couldn't see was the momentary flicker in Eoinn's eyes as he glanced toward the western ridge—the place where Tom had taken his samples—and the almost imperceptible nod to Egan Sullivan, who made a note in his small leather book.

"Stability is indeed vital, Eoinn," Tom pressed, "but what good is stability if it shackles us? We must lift our people, let them grasp their own futures. We came here seeking more than mere survival; we sought a life made richer through our own endeavors and voices. Surely, that is worth the risk, giving us a voice in our future? Giving us more direct rewards for the risk?"

Eoinn's expression softened slightly, his eyes carrying a weight Tom couldn't fully comprehend. "I appreciate yer technical insights, Tom. Egan will discuss the western face with ye tomorrow. As for ownership stakes ..." He paused, seeming to choose his words with unusual care. "There are factors at work beyond what's visible to the eye. The current arrangement ensures protection for all." He didn't add: *protection from forces ye cannot see, from those who would take more than just gold if they could.*

As the meeting continued, Tom moved to a place at the edge of the square, the fire of his frustration simmering beneath the surface. He listened as other villagers raised their hands, their questions and concerns given polite but cursory attention. It was as though the leadership had already moved on, the decisions made, the course set.

I I I I

Sam returned to the cave above the hot springs a week after her first visit. The previous visit had left her curious and eager to explore further, despite the coyote's unwelcome presence. Prepared now, she carried a slingshot and a sturdy walking stick. But much to her relief, the coyote stayed away.

She arrived at the cave after breakfast, savoring the Saturday solitude. She had left a note on her bed, just in case of trouble, then ventured out armed with a lantern and walking stick, a spool of string, a sandwich, a jug of water, chalk, and a small bag of stones to mark her path. She also thought to bring paper and pencil, too, for copying the cave's mysterious drawings.

Reaching the ledge outside the cave's entrance, Sam caught her breath while once again taking in the view of the village below. Her friends moved about, unaware they were being observed. It felt like she was in one of those Greek myths she had read, perhaps like Icarus soaring above the earth. She rested briefly, savoring the perspective afforded her by this vantage point.

Then, with her lantern lit, she stepped inside the cave. The walls had decorations carved into their surface. The dark natural stone of the cave's surface was covered in pigments, the lines carved had been painted in with other colors, creating contrasting lines. On the right, a large bird dominated the scene—a foot across, perched above people and animals. It was a raven, she realized.

She wandered the cave's perimeter, where the floor was packed with earth and gravel. Around the edge, she found still more depictions of the raven. One showed it soaring over a mountain with lightning trailing behind its tail feathers. Another illustrated a gathering of people. Raven stood as a prominent figure among the people.

At the cave's rear, a tunnel beckoned. Holding her lantern aloft, she peered into its shadowy depths. This passage led further into the mountain. The drawings here shifted focus. Here coyote figures took center stage. One coyote held a stick with streamers in its mouth—this portrayed fire, she realized. Another coyote was shown digging into a hill, unleashing a river that teemed with fish.

Above the tunnel entrance, the coyote and the raven met, facing each other, apparently in conflict. Coyote with a fiery stick and raven with lightning. The sight sent a shiver through her.

Sam tied a rock to her string and ventured down the tunnel. The carvings and paint slowly petered out as she penetrated farther into the cave. The passage stretched for twenty feet before opening into a large cavern. Thirty feet high, twenty feet around, the cave was adorned with stalactites and stalagmites—a natural cathedral. In the center, a flat area marked a place for fire, its ceiling blackened with soot. A smoke vent led upwards.

Three exits branched off from this cavern. The central one was tall, the others more humble. The cave's simplicity belied its size. Shelves lined the walls, some large enough for sleeping, others for storage. She found an old basket and a small, carved box. The basket was delicate and fraying, but the box, carved from a single piece of wood, was intact.

Sam explored the tunnels, each led to more caverns, each cavern seemed less touched by human hands. Finally, she reached a chamber where her lantern sputtered, the air becoming thin and hard to breathe. Recalling Sean's tales of gas pockets in the mines, she retraced her steps quickly, wary of the potential for danger.

Outside once more, Sam breathed deeply, savoring the clean mountain air. The cave's dampness and the occasional bat had not deterred her, but the fresh air was welcome. She gazed at the village and the vast landscape beyond, leaving her supplies within the cave. She would return when time allowed, drawn by the mystery waiting in the mountain's depths.

I I I I

October 1875

Sam sat on the porch of her little cabin and saw a small, young woman in native dress coming her way down the street. It was Stelkupmi, her old friend, coming to visit! She sprang up and ran out to meet her shouting a joyful, "Hello!" Sam hugged her friend and invited her up to sit on the porch together.

"I came to visit while our tribe gathers pine nuts nearby. It has been too long since we visited," said Stelkupmi.

"I'm so happy that you came to visit!" Sam said excitedly. "I've been concerned for your people since the Indian Appropriations Act was passed. Are you having any difficulties because of it?"

A cloud passed over Stelkupmi's face. She replied quietly, "My tribe is very worried about the future. We are a peaceful people, but we have had some difficulties with white settlers in some areas. Gathering medicine and food has become complicated. That's part of the reason we haven't been here as often. But this area is still the best place to harvest some medicines and berries and pine nuts, if your people haven't taken them all." She smiled as she said this, to make certain Sam understood she was joking.

"Well, I'm so glad you're here, and I'm glad that your people feel that Crystal Village is not part of the problems you're experiencing. We try to keep to ourselves, and we've been keeping our village's presence a bit of a secret to outsiders," said Sam.

The two women sat and talked for a while. Then Sam went into the kitchen she shared with Sean and Colin, who were out for the day, and brought out tea and some biscuits with honey. As the two sat chatting, Sam asked Stelkupmi about coyotes and ravens and their significance to her people.

Stelkupmi was surprised but delighted by the question. "Sam, let me tell you about Coyote and Raven," she began. "These are not just animals; they are powerful beings in our stories. They can change their shapes, walking and looking like people or in their true forms. This is important to know.

"Coyote, he is a trickster, yes, but he is also wise. He can be both foolish and smart. There is a story about Coyote and fire. Once, the people were cold. They had no fire. Coyote decided to help. He went to the mountain where fire was kept. Coyote tricked the fire keepers. He got close, took a piece of fire, and brought it back to the people. Now they could be warm in the cold months and could cook their food and boil water. This is how he helps, by his tricks. But he also has set fires, sometimes by accident, sometimes as a tool to renew the land.

"Another time, Coyote saw that the rivers were hidden inside the mountains. No fish could swim, no salmon could come. Coyote dug into the mountain and made the rivers flow across the land. Then the salmon came, and the people had food. Coyote, he changes things, brings what is needed.

"But he is also stubborn and impulsive. He takes offense easily and holds his grudges for a long time. If he's not given the courtesy he believes he deserves, he can quickly go from being a friend to a dogged enemy who will not stop until he's destroyed you. Or until he has learned an important lesson of his own and made his peace.

"Raven, he is different. Raven is a bringer of light. In one story, the world was dark because a chief kept the sun, moon, and stars hidden. Raven, clever as he is, changed into a tiny seed and was swallowed by the chief's daughter. He grew inside her, became a child, and cried until the chief gave him the light to play with. When Raven got the sun, moon, and stars, he changed back and flew away, bringing light to the world. Raven, he shows us how to solve problems, how to bring change.

"Both Coyote and Raven walk between worlds. They travel in various forms, always changing with time, sometimes as men, sometimes as animals. They teach us to understand nature, to see beyond what is in front of us. They remind us to laugh, to be humble, and to find light even when everything seems dark. They are always in our stories, always teaching us the ways of the world. They are part of us, in our stories, in our hearts."

Sam listened intently, then said, "That's so interesting! Are Coyote and Raven friends?"

Stelkupmi chuckled a little and said, "Ah, that is a good question! Coyote and Raven, they are not like friends in the way we are friends. They are more like forces in the world, each with their own ways, their own purposes. Sometimes, in stories, they work together; other times, they do not. Sometimes they are rivals, sometimes they cooperate. They both have their own paths, their own lessons to teach us.

"Coyote, he is the trickster, always looking for the next thing to do, sometimes causing trouble, sometimes bringing good. Raven is more of a thinker, solving problems, bringing light and order. They are both important, but they do not always see the world the same way.

"In some stories, they might come together for a purpose, like when there is a great need. Raven can be disapproving and judgmental of Coyote. Coyote often works to gain Raven's approval, but he also plays tricks on Raven. So they're not really friends, more like rivals who sometimes are allies."

Sam considered this and asked, "Are there any stories about Raven and lightning?"

Stelkupmi was a bit surprised by this question, but she was delighted to share her people's stories with her friend. "Yes, there are stories that tell of Raven and lightning. In many tales, Raven is connected to the sky and all its wonders, including lightning. Raven is a being of transformation and power, and sometimes, he is seen as the one who can control the storms.

"One story tells of a time when there was a great fire, and the people and animals were suffering. Raven, seeing their struggle, decided to help. He flew to the highest mountain, where the clouds gathered but refused to rain. Raven, with his cleverness, began to dance and sing, calling upon the lightning and thunder to wake the clouds.

"As Raven danced, the sky grew dark, and the lightning flashed across the heavens. Raven's dance was so powerful that it stirred the clouds, and soon the rain began to fall, putting out the fires and bringing life back to the land.

"Raven, with his cleverness and resourcefulness, can influence the forces of nature. Raven and his stories teach us the importance of harmony with nature."

Sam grew quiet, caught up in her thoughts for a moment, thinking of the drawings in the cave. Stelkupmi gave her time to think, and ate a biscuit smothered in honey, and sipped on tea. Sam smiled at her, and thanked her for the stories.

"How long can you stay?"

"I must go soon. We are harvesting until nightfall. Once we've finished our work, we'll stay at a camp near here, then we'll head back home in the morning," Stelkupmi explained with an expression that revealed to Sam that she wished she had more time. Then she smiled with a sly look. "But I have a couple of hours to spare. And I was hoping that you might be free to visit the hot springs."

Sam laughed and said, "That would be great! It's Sunday, and I'm not working today. Let's go!"

8

Connection

Jack and Susanne left Molly's house in Mullan and drove in comfortable silence to Wallace, both processing the afternoon's revelations. The historic mining town of Wallace was nestled in the valley and looked like a postcard from another era, its Victorian storefronts and brick buildings glowing in the early evening light.

"There's a place called The Fainting Goat that's really good," Susanne said. "It's a wine bar on Bank Street."

Jack parked near the restaurant, and they walked past the old storefronts toward the modern establishment. The Fainting Goat occupied a beautifully renovated space with exposed brick walls and industrial touches—Edison bulb fixtures hanging from the ceiling, polished concrete floors, and reclaimed wood tables that spoke to the area's mining heritage while embracing contemporary style.

Inside, the atmosphere buzzed with energy. Local artwork adorned the brick walls, and a chalkboard menu displayed the evening's specials in colorful chalk. Their table sat near a window overlooking Bank Street, where the occasional car passed under vintage street lamps.

"This is perfect," Jack said, studying the wine list. "Industrial chic meets mining town history. I love the contrast."

Susanne smiled, tucking a strand of hair behind her ear. "I love places like this—where you can feel both the past and the present at the same time." She paused, then added quietly, "Especially after today."

They ordered—Jack chose the braised short ribs, Susanne the pan-seared salmon—and settled back with glasses of local wine. The restaurant hummed with conversation, the clink of glasses and silverware creating a comfortable backdrop of modern life in a historic setting.

"I keep thinking about Henry's memoir," Jack said. "The way he described Crystal Village made it sound almost magical. Like something out of a fairy tale."

"But it was real," Susanne replied, her eyes bright with excitement. "All those people, all those stories! They actually lived there and built something remarkable together." She took a sip of her wine, then looked directly at him. "What are you thinking about doing with all this information?"

Jack was quiet for a moment, turning his glass in his hands. The warm light from the Edison bulbs cast shadows across his face. "Honestly? I keep imagining what it would be like to find the actual site. To see where the buildings stood. There's got to be something left." He looked up at her. "Is that crazy?"

"Not at all." Susanne's voice was soft. "I've been thinking the same thing. Molly's map gives us a general area. With the right research …"

"You'd want to come with me? If I actually tried to find it?"

The question hung between them. Susanne felt her cheeks warm, and she looked down at her hands. "I'd love to. I mean … if you wanted company. I know you're probably used to doing things on your own …"

"Susanne." Jack's voice made her look up. "I can't think of anyone I'd rather explore with. You understand this story in ways nobody else could."

Their food arrived, providing a welcome distraction from the intensity of the moment. They ate in comfortable silence for a few minutes, both stealing glances at the other when they thought the other wasn't looking.

"May I ask you something?" Jack said finally. "When we were kids, I was over the moon about you. I always wondered if you felt the same way I did back then."

Susanne's face flushed a deep shade of red. "When we were kids …"

Jack set down his fork. "Seriously. Did you ever think of me that way?"

Susanne nearly choked on her wine. "You had feelings for me? When we were teenagers?"

"Are you kidding? I was completely gone for you. But you seemed so focused on your writing, your college plans. I figured I was just the geeky friend who hung around while on summer vacations here."

"Jack." Susanne shook her head in amazement. "I ... I was forever imagining what it would be like if you actually noticed me. If someone like you could fall for someone like me."

They stared at each other across the reclaimed wood table, the weight of missed opportunities settling between them.

"We were both idiots," Jack said finally.

"Complete idiots," Susanne agreed, laughing despite herself.

Jack reached across the table and took her hand. "Maybe we could be less idiotic now?"

Susanne's fingers intertwined with his. "I'd like that. Though I should warn you—I'm still pretty awkward when it comes to relationships. I tend to overthink everything."

"I'm probably worse. I get so focused on projects that I forget the rest of the world exists. My last girlfriend said dating me was like dating a very polite robot."

"A very polite robot who designs amazing experiences for millions of people," Susanne corrected. "That's actually kind of romantic, in a geeky way."

They finished dinner talking about everything and nothing—childhood memories, career dreams, favorite books, and travel disasters. The conversation flowed as easily as it had when they were teenagers, but with the depth that came from years of living.

Walking back to the car, Jack took Susanne's hand again. The streetlights mixed with the historic architecture around them, creating the same blend of old and new they'd experienced in the restaurant.

"Tomorrow we start planning our treasure hunt?" Jack asked.

"Tomorrow we start planning our treasure hunt," she agreed, squeezing his fingers.

Above them, stars emerged in the clear mountain sky, the same stars that had once shone down on Crystal Village and its dreamers.

9

Veiled

October 1882

Seeley and Liam stood in the trees quietly watching a man who was standing in Eagle Creek, about fifteen miles from Crystal Village. They noted that he had a full head of dark hair and a dark mustache. His beard had gone white below the chin. The man was panning for gold, doing so with the vigor and energy of a much younger man.

Seeley whispered to Liam, telling him to stay where he was. Then he made his way down through the dense trees, intentionally coming from a direction nowhere near the path to Crystal Village. When he was close enough to be seen, but not close enough to spook the man too badly, Seeley called out, "Hello there, good sir!" At that moment, the man was looking down carefully at the contents of his pan, deep in thought.

The man was startled. He flung the gravelly contents of his pan in the air, and staggered, almost falling into the creek. He spun and looked for the offending party, locking his gaze on Seeley. Clearly, he was unhappy to encounter another person in this area and reached for a non-existent pistol on his belt before quickly adjusting that movement into an attempt to retrieve his hat.

"I beg your pardon for startling ye, sir. My intentions are peaceful," said

Seeley in a soothing tone. "I see that you're panning for gold, and I wanted to introduce myself. My name is Eoinn Seeley. Might I inquire as to whom I have the honor of addressing?"

The man stood staring at Seeley, mouth agape. To him, it was as if Seeley had materialized out of thin air in a landscape he thought he had all to himself.

After a moment of catching his breath and calming down, the prospector said, "My apologies, I had no idea anyone was in these parts. My name is Prichard, Andrew J. Prichard. My friends call me A.J. May I ask, sir, what you're doing all the way out here?"

Seeley replied, "A pleasure to make your acquaintance, Mr. Prichard. I chanced to notice ye whilst on my way homeward. I live near here."

At the notion that there was a homestead nearby, Prichard startled again. "Uhm ... I had no idea there was anyone living up this way."

Seeley said, lightly, "Indeed, I have made my residence hereabouts since the summer of '67."

Prichard swallowed a large lump in his throat.

Seeley continued, "It looks like you're doing some prospecting here, Mr. Prichard. We've tested the waters all around here and haven't found significant value in minerals. But of course, you're welcome to look."

Prichard looked a little sheepish and said, "Should you be intimating that you lay prior claim to these parts ..."

"Oh no," said Seeley, "far from it, sir. Rather, I meant that it would grieve me to see ye expend your efforts in vain. Also, it would be a terrible thing if word were to leak out, and a stampede were to start in this area. I'm a great admirer of the natural beauty of this land, and nothing destroys that natural beauty faster than a bunch of green miners digging up the place. Ye clearly are not green. I've been watching ye, and you're quite experienced. But ye know how things get in a stampede."

"I believe I grasp the direction of your implication," Pritchard replied. "Nor do I wish to see my stake overrun by greenhorns. I've been very careful to keep the locations of my claims secret, and I was pretty surprised that you came up on me like that. I'm surprised to hear that you've been watching me, because I thought I was more observant than that. Beyond all that, it seems clear that someplace nearby you've got a home of your own set up, and that you don't want thousands of miners coming in here. I get that. But you should know that I have several claims, and they're all marked, mapped, and registered, and they all have mineral wealth enough to pursue."

Seeley let out a breath of air and said, "I understand yer meaning, Mr. Prichard. I came out to Idaho Territory because I was looking for land such that I could build an intentional community on, and I found a nice spot not too far from here. We've been here for some time and have built a life for ourselves that is quite rare, and it is something we wish to protect."

At the mention of intentional community, Prichard's eyebrows went up so high that they nearly disappeared under his hat.

"That, sir, is a serendipitous concurrence indeed!" Prichard sputtered, excitedly. "I, myself, hold membership in the National Liberal League, and one of the things I've been trying to do for the last few years is find a plot of land for exactly the same purpose! Are you familiar with the Liberal League, sir?"

It was now Seeley's turn to show surprise. "I am not familiar with it, sir. But this coincidence seems of astronomical unlikeliness. Perhaps, it would be good to sit and chat for a bit."

"You see, Mr. Seeley," Prichard began, "the National Liberal League is dedicated to the principle of absolute separation of church and state. Our vision is for a community where reason and science guide governance, free from the shackles of religious dogma."

Seeley took a moment to reflect aloud, his tone introspective. "It's fascinating how the notion of intentional communities has taken root in this era. From the transcendentalists of Brook Farm to the utopian ideals of New Harmony, and even the religious undertakings of the Mormons and Shakers. America seems alive with the spirit of communal experimentation."

Prichard nodded, his eyes lighting up with recognition. "Indeed, Mr. Seeley. The fervor for creating ideal societies is hardly limited to religious sects. Even secular visionaries are seeking to build communities that embody their philosophies."

"The landscape of America is changing," Eoinn mused, "with people searching for a place where they can forge their destinies, free from traditional constraints. It reflects the spirit of the age, wouldn't ye agree?"

"Absolutely!" Prichard replied, his voice carrying a note of admiration. "It's an age of innovation and exploration, not just in the physical sense but in the realms of thought and community. Our forebears sought freedom, and now we seek the freedom to define how we live together. Without some unifying philosophy, the act of community is tenuous at best. There must be some deep, aligning belief, and in our case, the Liberal League firmly believes in science and reason, not religion."

Eoinn pulled himself up to his full height, arms crossed, his gaze steady. "I appreciate your fervor, Mr. Prichard, but my vision for Crystal Village is different. It's about creating a sanctuary where families can thrive, where children are raised with a sense of belonging and community. We aspire to create a place where—through the collaboration of the community—people can thrive. We don't want our people to have to worry about having enough to eat or clothes to wear. But our community isn't based on any particular adherence to an orthodox set of beliefs, be they religious or political. We're not here to impose our views on anyone."

Prichard's eyes flashed with intensity. "But don't you see? The very foundation of a society must be built on reason and logic! Without it, we're no better than the theocratic regimes that stifle progress. Our communities must be a beacon of enlightenment!"

Eoinn shook his head, his expression thoughtful. "Enlightenment doesn't come from rigid adherence to ideology, Mr. Prichard. It comes from understanding, from allowing people to live their lives without fear of persecution. Crystal Village is a place where diversity of thought is celebrated, not suppressed."

Prichard moved his hands as he spoke, gesturing animatedly. "But how can you ensure progress without a guiding principle?! The Liberal League seeks to create a society where education and rational thought are paramount. We aim to foster a new generation of free thinkers who will lead the world into a new era."

Eoinn's response was measured, his voice calm. "And yet, by insisting on one way of thinking, you risk alienating those who may not share your exact beliefs. Our community thrives because we allow for a multitude of perspectives. We don't demand conformity."

The argument continued, each man delving into the minutiae of their respective ideologies. Prichard spoke passionately of the need for a secular society, where education and scientific inquiry were held in the highest regard. He espoused a community where intellectual pursuits were paramount, a bastion of knowledge and progress.

Eoinn, in contrast, emphasized the importance of balance and harmony. He spoke of a community where people were free to practice their faiths or none at all, without fear of judgment. He advocated for creating a place where families grew strong, supported by their neighbors, where the bonds of friendship and kinship were the true foundation.

"You may call that diversity you cultivate freedom, Mr. Seeley," Prichard said, his voice tinged with exasperation, "but without a guiding light, your community risks stagnation. The world is changing, and we must change with it."

Eoinn met Prichard's gaze, unwavering. "Change for the sake of change is folly, Mr. Prichard. What we need is growth, rooted in respect and understanding. Our community is a living organism, adapting and changing naturally, not through force."

Prichard began raising his voice, and Seeley raised his in return, and rational thought and debate began to disappear from the conversation. Finally Liam intervened. He walked into the clearing and introduced himself, working his charm until Prichard calmed down.

"This isn't a theoretical conversation, friend. Ye see, sir," said Liam, "we've men, women, and families with children living not too far from here. Quite a lot of men, if you get my meaning, many of them Union veterans of the War. And while we harbor no ill will to anyone wanting to have a claim and place of their own, you have to understand that we're going to do what we must in order to keep ourselves safe. Given the kinds of hard men who have been prevalent at these mining camps over the years, that means a lot. We have little children living in our village, sir, several of them mine."

At this, Prichard capitulated.

He took a deep breath and said, "Well, Mr. O'Connor, your timely intercession is much appreciated ... perhaps my passions have gotten the better of me." He extended a hand to Eoinn. "We may not see eye to eye, Mr. Seeley, but I respect your convictions. Perhaps, one day our paths will converge again."

Eoinn accepted the handshake, a wry smile on his lips. "Mr. Prichard," Eoinn replied, "ye seem a decent sort of man, and despite our disagreement, on many things we are very aligned. I would be obliged if ye would join us in Crystal Village tomorrow evening for a dinner in your honor. I will have Liam here come meet you back at this very spot, and he will bring ye to the village.

However, I have to know that ye agree in advance, and swear on yer honor, sir, that ye will not give away the location of Crystal Village. Also I need to be assured that ye will do yer best to continue to keep the location of yer own claims a secret and thus avoid the kind of stampede we've seen so many times in the past."

"I agree to your terms, sir, and I have to admit, I would very much like to see your village. It sounds much like what I am trying to accomplish," Pritchard declared. Then he raised his hand before Seeley could begin to disagree, "I say this despite our differences of opinion about how this all should work."

Seeley nodded and turned to leave. "Tomorrow then. Please meet Liam here at two o'clock in the afternoon. Be prepared to spend the night. I'll reserve a room for ye at the hotel."

Prichard's eyebrows once again nearly disappeared under his hat.

"Until then, sir, I shall eagerly await our rendezvous," said Prichard.

I I I I

Jeremiah Redding wiped the sweat from his brow with the back of his hand, leaving a streak of sawdust across his forehead. The sun hung low in the sky, casting long shadows across the nearly completed row of townhouses. He paused to admire the frame of the building he and his crew had just begun constructing that morning. The clean, straight lines of the balloon framing technique stood like an elegant skeleton against the backdrop of Crystal Village's bustling streetscape.

Standing at five feet, nine inches, Jeremiah was a lean, muscular figure. His sandy-blond hair caught the light as he surveyed the construction site. His piercing, hazel eyes missed nothing, always scrutinizing the work around him. He had joined the crew in Crystal Village with the hope of applying his skills to create something enduring, something that would stand the test of time.

Today, however, Jeremiah's optimism had started to fray at the edges. Finn McEnhill, the village's master architect, strode across the site, his white hair and beard catching the breeze as he approached. Finn carried himself with the confidence of a man who had shaped this town—literally from the ground up, and his presence commanded respect.

"Redding!" Finn called out, his voice carrying over the din of hammers and saws. "What do we have here, lad? This isn't how we do things!"

Jeremiah turned to face Finn, his expression neutral but his jaw tightening. "It's balloon framing, Finn. It's faster and uses less timber. The vertical studs run the entire height of the building, from the sill plate to the roof. It distributes weight more efficiently, and we can get these houses up quicker without sacrificing strength."

Finn's eyes narrowed as he inspected the framework, his fingers tracing the smooth, uniform edges of the studs. "Aye, it's efficient," he said, his tone dripping with skepticism. "But these thin studs—what happens when the wind comes whipping through? Or when the snow piles high on the roof? I've seen timber framing weather storms that would flatten this framework like a house of cards. And what about the risks in a fire? If I'm perceiving things correctly, a fire in any lower wall would race right up to the rafters, creating a chimney all on its lonesome!"

Jeremiah took a deep breath, reining in his frustration. "Balloon framing's been used in cities like Chicago for years now, Finn. It's not some untested experiment. The walls are braced with diagonal sheathing, and it holds up just fine. Plus, it saves us time and materials! And those are two things we can't afford to waste! As far as a fire goes, sure, things could go badly in a fire. But I don't know that it's any worse than in a timber-framed building."

Finn set his jaw, his gaze sweeping over the assembled crew, many of whom had paused their work to listen. "Maybe it works in Chicago, but this isn't Chicago. We're building for the mountains here, not the flatlands. We stick to what we know works!"

The dismissal was brusque. Still, what stung more was the way Finn turned away, already issuing instructions to the crew to replace the balloon framing with traditional timber framing. Jeremiah's hands clenched into fists at his sides, his knuckles white. He could feel the weight of the other workers' gazes, some sympathetic, others wary of challenging Finn's authority.

The moment passed, and the crew returned to their tasks, but Jeremiah's frustration simmered beneath the surface. He had hoped to contribute his expertise, to offer new methods that could benefit the village. Yet, time and again, he found his suggestions sidelined, his ideas brushed aside in favor of tradition.

As the sun dipped below the horizon, casting a warm glow over the village, Jeremiah packed up his tools, his movements deliberate. He exchanged nods with his fellow workers.

Walking home, Jeremiah's thoughts drifted to his family. Margaret, his wife, was a pillar of support, her sharp mind and quick wit a match for his own. Their four children were his reason for enduring. He knew he needed to channel his frustration into something positive, to find a way to be heard.

That evening, around the dinner table, Jeremiah shared his day with Margaret. Her eyes flashed with indignation at the injustice, her voice calm but firm. "You have every right to speak up, Jeremiah. Your ideas are worth hearing. Perhaps, it's time to gather others who feel the same, to make your voices louder together."

Jeremiah nodded, a plan forming in his mind. He would not be silenced. There was strength in numbers, and he was not alone in his desire for change. The village was growing, and with change came the need for a more inclusive approach to progress.

I I I I

Missoula, Montana, January 7th, 1883

The short man stood at the bar with his right boot up on the foot rail. He was wiry and active. His hair was voluminous, tucked under a jaunty, white hat with a wide black band. He looked like a fancy man, with his white, linen suit and shiny, black boots. He wore a vest under his suit jacket that was accented by a gold chain connected to a pocket watch. He had a long knife in a scabbard on his left side and a leather bag on his right. Women liked to look at him; men either admired him or found him boorish.

He had a handlebar mustache and long, jagged sideburns that flared out from his jawbones like a lion's mane. He smoked thin cheroots one after the other, lighting each one from the stub of its predecessor. He kept them in the bag on his belt. His hair was reddish-auburn, his eyes were unusual with surprising golden irises. His face was drawn up in a perpetual sneer, and he had a habit of narrowing his eyes as he listened to people. When he heard something surprising or unusual, he would cock his head to the side. When he was excited, he'd whoop with a high-pitched sound. Other times he'd let out a "Yeehaw!" or he would yip and shout like a coyote. "Hee, Hee, Hee, Haaaa!"

When someone would question the truth of what he said or threaten him, he'd growl quietly from deep in the back of his throat. Then suddenly, he'd smile, laugh, and clap the offender on their back and let them buy him a drink. Somehow when he did that—no matter how angry the exchange had been or how tough the offender imagined themselves to be—their blood would run cold. And suddenly, they felt as if someone had just walked across their grave. And they'd buy him that drink—every single time.

His name was Sinclair Lipson. He was a notorious cardplayer, a teller of tall, self-aggrandizing tales, and a perpetuator of gossip and rumor. To anyone's memory, he'd never actually done anything himself of note. He would just appear in the bar some evening, smoke a whole bag of cheroots, win all his hands at poker, and leave with a woman on his arm before midnight.

On this night, he came into the very busy saloon to see Andrew Prichard at the bar. Prichard had bought a round of drinks for his friends a bit earlier with gold dust as his currency.

Sinclair approached him from the right side. "Mr. Prichard, I declare. Word has it you've been generously pouring spirits for your friends, and lo, I've made my appearance!"

Prichard turned to see who was hailing him in such a friendly manner, but when he saw who it was, he frowned. "Yes, Mr. Lipson, I did buy a round earlier, but you missed it. Sadly, now I'm about to leave."

Lipson growled lightly in the back of his throat and put a hand on the back of Prichard's neck. It was the same hand in which he held his ever-present cheroot. His expression was fierce, but then he laughed. With a crafty smile, he put his arm around Prichard's shoulder and said, "Ah, sir, you had me convinced, you scoundrel." He raised his voice, saying, "Victor, we'll have another pair, courtesy of Mr. Prichard's ledger."

Prichard muttered under his breath but didn't disagree.

The drinks arrived, and Lipson offered a toast, raising his voice loudly to the whole room, "Here's to my esteemed companion, A. J. Prichard, who has unearthed a fortune in gold out in the untamed wilds of Idaho, along the North Fork of the Coeur d'Alene. My felicitations, dear friend!" And he downed the glass of whiskey.

The blood drained from Prichard's face. He wobbled on his stool and whispered, his voice almost a hiss, "What are you about, you daft fool?! Hold your tongue! We'll have a stampede for sure!"

Lipson stood next to Prichard, his back against the bar, his arms spread out wide, resting them on the bartop. He turned his head and blew a long string of smoke in Prichard's face. Prichard coughed. Lipson's eyes scanned across the room, watching the effect of his toast unfold. Men were huddled in groups, stealing glances at Prichard.

Prichard downed his whiskey, got up from the bar, and left, glaring at Lipson as he went, continuing to mutter under his breath. A few people got up and followed him, not very stealthily. Lipson stood at the bar considering the room. A great, hulking man with a dark look and a smaller, lean and sly-looking man got up and approached him. The big man was locally called Big Jim Stanton, and the little man was Anton Duchene.

Duchene, who had bags under his bulging eyes and a pencil mustache, said, "So, Lipson, it sounds like you know something about Prichard's find. What can you tell us?"

Lipson said, "Ah, my friends, why don't you buy me a drink, and we can discuss?"

The men obliged his request, and Lipson began, "Have you heard of Crystal Village?"

I I I I

Prichard returned to the room he was renting in Missoula that night and penned the following note, seeing that he was no longer held to the agreement he made with Seeley. Word was out, and there was nothing he could do to stop it.

January 7th, 1883

From: Andrew J. Prichard
  To: Robert J. Ingersoll, vice president of the National Liberal League

I am writing to share a remarkable discovery: a gold-bearing region that promises employment for 15,000 to 20,000 souls. My investigations have revealed two streams, one extending between sixteen to twenty-five miles, the other from twelve to sixteen miles, both boasting an average breadth of sixty to seventy rods. I have also encountered gold in three additional streams, similar in size, though I must confess, they require further examination to ascertain their profitability.

The two streams I have thoroughly prospected promise rich yields along their entire lengths and likely amongst their tributaries as well. This land is blessed with ample timber and water, bedrock lying between five to twelve feet beneath the surface, and the gold found therein is both coarse and of excellent quality. I foresee the establishment of two cities upon natural town sites within this territory, burgeoning to represent thousands within a mere two years, surrounded by hundreds of mineral-bearing quartz lodes.

For reasons I cannot delve into presently, it is my fervent wish to see this opportunity fall predominantly into the hands of our Liberal brethren. It is within our power to establish a city here, governed by our own laws and sustained by this vast mining region, should we approach this venture with unity and deliberate action.

I have dedicated four years to the solitary exploration and development of this land. My initial discovery was a lode located along the Mullan Road. Despite limited resources, I ventured to seek out placer mines, never anticipating the discovery of potential mines of such magnitude, hidden within the Rocky Range. Should you relay this information amongst our League members on this coast, urging them to convene and maintain discretion, we may secure the majority stake in this venture.

Currently, I reside in the mountains, fifty miles from the nearest post office, where winter snows reach depths of three to four feet, greatly hindering my efforts during the colder months. I have named my claim Evolution, situated on the old Mullan Road to Montana, fifty miles east of Fort Coeur d'Alene and twenty-three miles east of the Old Mission, with the Northern Pacific Railroad running within twelve miles of this location. Prospective parties will require pack animals for the journey, as the mines themselves lie forty miles into the mountains from my location, accessible only by rudimentary pack trails at present. It is advisable to procure supplies sufficient for a month or two before venturing from the post at Rathdrum, as provisions will be scarce thereafter.

Those in need of purchasing horses may find it advantageous to stop at Spokane Falls in the Washington Territory, located thirty miles from the post, where better deals on provisions, groceries, and tools may be found. To ensure that our Liberal colleagues may secure their positions before any widespread excitement, it might be prudent for arriving parties to suggest they are bound for Montana.

With sincere regards,

Andrew J. Prichard

I I I I

Prichard reread the letter to himself several times. Then he wrote the following note to Seeley:

January 7th, 1883

From: A.J. Prichard
To: Eoinn Seeley

Esteemed Mr. Seeley,

I find myself obliged to pen this missive under circumstances most regrettable and unforeseen. It has come to pass that a certain individual of questionable repute, one Sinclair Lipson by name, has laid bare my closely guarded secret. This evening, within the crowded confines of a local saloon, he proclaimed to all and sundry that I have discovered gold on the North Fork of the Coeur d'Alene River. The revelation sparked a tumult akin to pandemonium. Despite the uproar, I retreated to my lodgings without incident. Still, I could not help but note the shadow of several men of dubious character tracing my departure.

In adherence to the pact between us, I have heretofore exercised the utmost discretion in matters concerning my claims, withholding their existence and location from public knowledge. Alas, the proverbial cat has been loosed from its sack. In light of our discourse, I am compelled to dispatch a communication to the National Liberal League, signifying that the opportune moment to dispatch men and lay the foundation for our envisioned community is upon us. It is my sincere hope that several years from now we shall be cordial and esteemed neighbors.

Your achievements in the establishment of Crystal Village have served as a beacon of inspiration to me, imbuing me with a profound sense of reverence for your endeavors. It is with the gravest sincerity that I vow to safeguard the secrecy of your undertaking, fully cog-nizant now of the reasons for your insistent caution. The vision of moral gentlemen and flourishing families within the sanctuary you have forged offers a beacon of hope in the often bleak reality of our frontier existence. It shows the possibility of creating a refuge for women and children in this, at times, forsaken wilderness.

I extend to you my sincerest wishes for your continued well-being and success. May you persevere in maintaining the sanctity of your lands, taking all necessary measures to ensure their protection.

With earnest respect,

A.J. Prichard

IIII

Missoula, Montana, September 9th, 1883

The Summer came and went, and as autumn began to creep into the air, Sinclair Lipson was back in Missoula. He stood at the bar smoking his cheroot and sipping on whiskey. He waited as various people cycled through the bar, smoking and drinking while he waited. Eventually, in came his target, and Lipson sidled up to him. The man was handsome, about five feet ten inches. He wore a fine suit, had a long, handlebar mustache, and carefully combed and parted hair. He smoked a cigar and stood at the bar.

"Good evening, my good sir," said Lipson. "I do believe you're Mister H.C. Davis, who is responsible for ensuring the financial success and growth of the Northern Pacific Railroad in these parts." He knew that only the day before Davis had driven the 'golden spike' in Gold Creek that connected the two halves of the Northern Pacific Railroad. Lipson was also well aware that Davis had previously had the honor of driving the first spike of that very railroad back in 1864.

Davis looked at him, smiled winningly, and said, "My friends call me Henry. To whom do I have the pleasure of making his acquaintance, sir?"

Lipson stepped forward and gave Davis a little bow. Then he reached forward and shook Davis' hand firmly, saying, "Sinclair Lipson, at your service, sir. And I dare say that I have some information for you that could assist you in your mission."

Lipson put his arm around Davis' shoulders and began speaking quietly in his ear, the everpresent cheroot burning balefully from his hand on Davis' shoulder.

The following pamphlet was published by the Northern Pacific Railroad and distributed at stations across the entire network, in the East and the West in the winter of 1883-1884.

Gold in the Coeur d'Alene

The claims are very rich and are located in gulches of the north fork of the Coeur d'Alene river; Eagle, Prichard, and Beaver creeks, streams running into the Coeur d'Alene. Rich placer deposits have been discovered for a considerable distance on Prichard Creek and the same distance on Eagle Creek, them being known by the latter name from the point where they come together. Nuggets have been found which weigh $50, $100, $166, and $200. An intense excitement has sprung up in regard to the quartz deposits of the district.

The immediate occasion of this being a find of a valuable quartz lode at the head of Prichard Creek vein has been traced on the surface for a distance of a hundred feet, and the outcroppings are very prominent. Ore taken from the vein shows a great amount of free gold, in fact it fairly glistens. The most extensive galena belt known at the present day is being developed on Beaver Creek. The vein can be readily traced on the surface for five or six miles. The ore carrying from 80 to 90 ounces of silver and 35 to 40% lead.

Such is a brief sketch of the Coeur d'Alene mines. Which surpass in richness and volume the most fabulous quartz and placers ever discovered. Even the famous deposits of Potosi being inferior to those which underlie the mountains of the Coeur d'Alenes. As the mines of old, some of which have been worked since the eleventh century, are still employing thousands of men, the conclusion to be drawn in regard to the Coeur d'Alenes, a region far superior in every way, is that they are inexhaustible, and although thousands may work them, there will still be room for thousands more.

IIII

February 26th, 1884

Sam was hiding. It was cold and snowing, and it was late. She was silently floating in the center of the big pool of the hot springs. It was very dark, and the shadows were darkest in the spot she was floating, out in the center, with the steam billowing off the water. There was a wide, smooth rock here that she loved to let the balls of her feet rest on while she floated in the water. The snow was falling to the surface of the pool and landing on her face and hair, melting as soon as it landed.

In the winter she spent a lot of time in her little cabin attached to Sean and Colin's cabin. It was next door to the O'Connors'. She enjoyed reading and doing small projects, which gave her the excuse to spend plenty of time by herself, even though she was welcome in any of the homes in the whole town. She and Seamus had been best friends since they met. Now she was twenty-six, and over the last few years, things had bloomed into a courtship. He talked of marrying her, but she was resistant. She wanted to wait before giving up her privacy. She loved him, and she trusted him completely. But this evening she'd had a fight with Seamus, who was sweet, and handsome, and strong, and kind, and funny, and the world's biggest idiot sometimes.

Earlier, Sam had been relaxing with the O'Connors after a delicious and cozy dinner. Mrs. O'Connor brought up the subject of Easter and offered to help Sam make an Easter dress. Hearing this, Eva had exclaimed happily that she'd help. Then Seamus made a joke about Sam only wearing men's clothes, and that he'd pay good money to see her in a dress. Sam had been mortified. She went quiet, thanked the O'Connors for dinner, and left all in a rush.

Sam knew that Seamus was going to come look for her in her cabin, so she took off her clothes and quickly donned the heavy robe and sheep's hide blanket she used when she wanted to go to the hot springs in the cold months. She slipped on her boots and ran off to the hot springs. She knew that it wasn't a great place for her to hide, since most folks in town also knew it was her favorite place. But she was mad, embarrassed, and wanted to soak and sweat and feel better.

As she floated in the water, she heard the fluttering of wings, big wings, on the other side of the pool and saw a large, black shape flying and landing on the edge. It was the huge raven she'd seen around the mountains, and it was dipping its beak into the water and drinking. She'd not known ravens to fly around in the dark, but then, she'd not observed the activities of many ravens.

The raven flew off into the dark a few minutes later, and in the distance, she heard two men's voices talking. The first sounded like Eoinn, but the other voice was very deep, slow, and punctuated his comments with sighs and groans. It was not a voice she recognized. She slowly moved across the pool, trying to get closer to the voices.

Between two trees she could make out two figures. They were standing in a small clearing near the upper pool, close to the origin point where the water exited the mountain. Of the two figures, one was clearly Eoinn, but the other was shockingly large. He was much taller than any person she'd ever seen, far taller than even Liam. He must have been wearing some kind of fur coat, because his body was disproportionately larger than his head, which was topped with a wide-brimmed hat.

When she arrived at the bank on the far side of the pool, she stayed hidden in the shadows. As she settled into the darkness, she heard their voices more distinctly but only well enough to know they weren't speaking English. It sounded like the Salish spoken by the Coeur d'Alene and Nez Perce tribes. She hadn't been aware that Eoinn was so fluent.

The big man seemed concerned about something, not angry or frightened, just sort of annoyed. Eoinn was talking in an even-tempered way, and to her surprise, she saw a third figure appear. This person was much shorter than either of them but harder for her to make out because the figure stood deeper in the shadows. Eventually, Sam heard a small string of words emanate from that third person, and the voice was definitely female. At first, she assumed it was Rose, but then she heard the woman's voice again. Clearly, the voice was too high and musical to be Rose, who had a sultry, deep voice for a woman.

Eventually, the conversation ended, and the huge man turned and disappeared from view. Similarly, the woman disappeared, but Eoinn remained for a few more minutes. It seemed to Sam that he was deep in thought, until finally he turned and went away. She crouched in the steaming water, trying to figure out how two strangers she'd never seen before made it into the village in the late winter when the passes and trails were clogged with twenty feet of snow. She floated there on the edge of the pool, her body submerged and just her nose, eyes, and the top of her head sticking out.

Sam pushed off from the edge of the pool, moving backwards with her feet out behind her, when she heard a voice whisper in her right ear, "Who do you think he was talking to?"

Sam flinched, spun around, and almost let out a shriek, but she saw that it was Seamus, similarly submerged below the water.

"How long were you there?" she asked.

"Just a few minutes," Seamus replied. "I figured you were in here when you weren't in your cabin. When I arrived, I found your robe and boots, so I climbed in and started looking for you. I heard Eoinn talking and went toward the voice, thinking he might be talking to you. But then I saw you at the edge of the pool listening. I didn't want to startle you into making a noise, so I held back until they left. So, who was he talking to?"

Sam paused and said quietly, "I'm not sure. I couldn't get a good look at them, but it was a man and a woman. I didn't know either of them. And they were speaking Salish."

She couldn't see Seamus' face, not clearly, but there was light enough that she could see his outline, and she knew his body language. He was as confused by this as she was. They both knew everyone in the village.

They floated together into the middle of the pool, where the water was shoulder deep. The steam twisted and curled off the surface of the water like a hot cup of coffee on a cold day. Sam heard a fluttering of wings, and the raven landed on the branches of a tree overlooking the pool.

She was very aware of Seamus, whom she'd swam with in the hot springs, the swimming hole, and all over the lakes, waterfalls, and swimming holes of the whole region. But things between them had become more personal lately. Now, she found his presence distracting and his smile disarming. In spite of herself, she found his size and build, which he'd inherited from his father, comforting in a way she never expected. On the other hand, she also found his mannerisms, jokes, and comments infuriating. He could set her off in a way that nobody else could. He was the only one who could get under her skin that way. She was known for being calm, but she couldn't be calm with him. And in the moments she was alone, and lonely, it was presence next to her that she longed. And now here they were, alone in the hot springs, bare skinned and alone in the dark.

Seamus slid closer to her and said, "I'm sorry. I can be a real fool sometimes."

She looked at him and tried to call back the anger she'd felt just a little while ago, but she couldn't. She reached up and put her arms around his neck. He reached around her and pulled her tight against him. She said, "Thank you for apologizing." They floated like this, knees bent, legs intertwined, arms around each other, her face pressed up against his chest, his chin resting against the top of her head. He traced shapes on her back with his finger.

She exhaled, a slow, deep sigh, and he whispered, "I love you, Sam King." She tilted her head upward toward his and kissed him on the lips. They folded in together.

The raven, in his perch, cawed and croaked.

I I I I

March 19th, 1884

It was getting towards dinnertime when Sam heard the sound of horses galloping through the village. She was most of the way down Broadway, just leaving the bakery with some fresh loaves of bread for the O'Connors' dinner. The men who had been working the mine all day were just now emerging from the main shaft, and the crew working at the brickyard were also calling it quits for the day. Likewise, the masons and carpenters who were busy building the brick buildings on Broadway were also finishing up.

As she peered down the road to see who was riding through town at such a clip, she felt a sinking feeling in her stomach and started running for the alarm bell that stood outside the mine. Before she got to it, she heard it ringing. Sean had gotten there faster, and she saw him pulling up and down on the rope with all his might.

The group of men riding into town were armed with Henry rifles and messenger shotguns. Several others among the onrushing horsemen were brandishing pistols and yelling, "Yah, yah!" and discharging their revolvers in the air. They rode fast down the muddy center of Broadway, clods of dirt flying into the air. There looked to be about fifteen horsemen charging down the street, wool coats and scarves flying behind them.

Sam turned and ducked into Finn's cabin, the first cabin the original villagers had built on Spring Street. She knew Finn had two Winchester Model 1873 rifles hanging on the wall. To her surprise, both were missing. But Finn did have a pair of pistols handy, so she checked that they were loaded and she stepped out the back. She took up a position to try to do some good if she was needed.

The group of riders swarmed into the town square at the intersection of Broadway and Spring Street at full gallop. They circled the group of men coming out of the mine and trained their guns on them. They clearly thought this was both great fun, and that they had completely surprised them. They reined in their horses, and a small man with bulging eyes and a pencil mustache urged his horse forward. The unpleasant man wore a dark, gray hat. He brandished a revolver in his right hand and held his horse's reins in his left hand.

"I'm Anton Duchene, who's in charge here?" he cried out in a loud voice.

Eoinn Seeley stepped forward from the crowd and answered, "That would be me. I'm in charge."

The man looked at him and said, "Great, then you'll be coming with us."

Seeley looked calmly back at him and said, "No, ye don't understand. Ye asked who is in charge here, and I told ye. I'm in charge."

The small man sneered and replied, "Well if you're in charge, how come we're the ones with all the guns?"

Seeley smiled confidently at him and said, "Are ye? The ones with all the guns, I mean?"

Suddenly, the sound of many guns cocking echoed around the square.

Sam looked from behind Finn's cabin and saw that there were men positioned all around the square, on rooftops, behind crates and strategically positioned wagons. There were even a few up on the hillside behind her. The riders looked around nervously, and almost all of them slowly lowered their weapons.

Duchene looked unnerved. Then, when he glanced around and saw his men's obvious concession of defeat, he grew angry. Furious, Duchene started to lift his weapon to point it at Eoinn, but two loud cracks rang out almost simultaneously, and two holes appeared in the man's chest, scant inches apart from each other. Duchene's body jerked backward like a marionette with cut strings, arms flailing as he toppled from the saddle. He hit the mud with a wet thud.

A voice from the roof of the canteen shouted out, "Lower those guns now, boys."

The guns of the fourteen remaining riders stayed lowered. Eoinn whistled, and the men nearest to the horses reached up to take the riders' weapons, then they dragged the gunmen to the ground. Once the men were unhorsed, other villagers gathered around them to hold the riders down while others stepped forward with lengths of rope to bind them.

The smell of gunpowder hung in the air. Sam was shocked. Eoinn knew they were coming, and he was completely prepared. He had even allowed them to come into town unopposed. The resulting violence was jarring. Sam couldn't shake the image of Anton Duchene falling from his horse. Eoinn hadn't just defended the town—he'd set a trap and executed that man. It was necessary, maybe even just. But still, the cold calculation in Eoinn's eyes when he gave the signal ... He had taken charge of the situation. He knew that the man was going to try to shoot him, and he'd had him killed when he made his move. Certainly, he was justified, but the very fact that Eoinn could coldly set that man up to be killed was appalling to Sam.

The men were being dragged to their feet and herded off toward the newest of the new brick buildings, where the first floor was completed. She had wondered why the carpenters had put wooden shutters over the first floor windows and had boarded off the back door before they built the stairs up to the second floor. Now, she suddenly realized that they'd prepared that building as a jail cell, knowing that something like this was going to happen.

Sam wasn't sure how she felt about Eoinn. Her hands were shaking as she remembered Anton Duchene's body flying backwards off his horse, like a doll knocked off a shelf by a child. She needed time to think about this whole thing. She needed to decide how she felt. As Sam looked over at Duchene's body, lying quietly in a pool of blood that was mixing with the mud of the street, she shuddered.

The whole town turned out that evening, all three hundred or so villagers squeezed into the music hall on Broadway. They called it the music hall, but it was really just a big open room with some chairs and tables, and space for a stage to be built at some point in the future. They met there because it was the only place where all of them could gather in the same room these days, even the dining hall being too small to fit the whole town.

Seeley spoke loudly to the room, "Folks, settle down, and let's get right to business here! I know some of ye are horrified that this could happen. I am also well aware that others among ye are scared it will happen again. Some of ye are angry, and some of ye are unsure of how we're going to resolve this issue with the men we've captured. Well, listen closely, because I have a proposal for ye. And I think it's a viable solution to all these problems."

The room was silent, and Seeley began again. "I've received a letter from Mr. Prichard, who many of ye met during his visit last year. In that letter, he warned me that word of his claims had leaked out and to prepare for an upcoming stampede into the lands of the North Fork of the Coeur d'Alene River. He kept our secret, but someone discovered the truth, and now the word is out. We all know the stories of hard men in the West. It's no secret that when a mining stampede happens, the people move toward it are often lawless and violent, as we saw today. Many of these people are not the sort we want here in our village.

"I have a pamphlet here from one of the men's satchels. It tells an unbelievable tale of immense wealth in this region, actively recruiting men to come here and mine. I'll pass it along for ye all to read. This was printed by the Northern Pacific Railroad and distributed across the country.

"Ye should know that a new city has been built less than fifteen miles from here. It appeared in winter, at the base of Eagle Creek. They're calling it Eagle City. Consider what that means: a city springing up in the middle of winter. Those men had to come in on snowshoes, dragging toboggans. That's the kind of hysteria we're facing. These are men who are willing to brave the wilderness in winter just to get a head start on those waiting for the snow to melt. Anyone following the creek upward who stumbles across the path to our village is unlikely to miss us." Eoinn paused to take a breath and look out across the room.

"The mine here is doing very well, and we're reinvesting our wealth into the town, but we could move faster. I propose we grow this community over the next year: consider applications to join us, actively recruit new members." Seeley couldn't help glancing at Liam and then continued, "I suggest we invest in fortifications. I've discussed this idea with some of ye. I think that we need to build protections, giving us the ability to defend ourselves should another attack happen here. Like the old, walled cities of Europe. I believe we should make this our next project, even halting construction along Broadway until it's done."

A murmur of agreement rose from the crowd, with several young men cheering Eoinn and a few hands clapping.

Eoinn continued, "The fortifications will require diverting significant resources—timber meant for the new schoolhouse, stone quarried for the bank. But our security must come first. We can't build a future if we can't protect what we have today."

Again, the crowd responded positively.

"As for the men who attacked our village," Eoinn said, "I propose they help construct this fortification. Once complete, they're free to leave. I've spoken with each of them, and while most aren't people we'd want here, a few seem decent enough. They weren't quite sure what they were getting into, and when they saw women and children, they balked at their task. I think we should keep a close eye on these men, and if a few decide they'd like to stay when the defenses are completed, we should consider their application."

A few people grumbled at this suggestion. Sam had carefully watched all the faces in the room. Eoinn had won the town over to his idea of building fortifications and even using their attackers to help build it. But the prospect of welcoming some of these men into their community ... that was a bit too much for some. While everyone agreed on the need for defense, the room had subtly divided itself. Those who had been with Eoinn from the beginning clustered near the front, nodding at his every word. The newer arrivals—tradesmen, shopkeepers, families who'd come in the last year—stood toward the back, their expressions more guarded, more concerned. They clearly opposed welcoming any of their would-be attackers into their community.

Sam spoke up. "Eoinn, sir, many folks here are still frightened from the attack, and not all knew about your protection plan. I'm on your side in this. I've spoken with some of these men and agree with you. One in particular, Callahan, a journeyman blacksmith of eight years, wasn't told the truth when pressed into this crew. He said he owed Duchene money, and he thought they'd just be collecting debts. You've already indicated that others hesitated when they realized what was happening. Callahan seemed decent and truly remorseful. Perhaps, we should form a committee to interview new applicants to the village, starting with any men from this crew who are so inclined."

There were murmurs of agreement, and Sam could see that Eoinn was satisfied with the outcome.

Tom Whitaker, sitting beside his wife Mary, leaned over to whisper in Jeremiah Redding's ear. "This is just another example of Eoinn making decisions without consulting the rest of us. Eight people decide everything for three hundred. And we're supposed to be grateful? We live here, too. We should have a say."

Jeremiah nodded, his eyes scanning the room. "You're right. It's like he's forgotten that we all have a stake in this village. We need more than just a committee to interview new members; we need a seat at the council to make decisions."

Mary said, "If we're going to be part of this community, we deserve more representation. We can't just be passive observers in our own lives."

Jeremiah's wife, Margaret, joined in, her voice barely above a whisper. "We've contributed as much as anyone else here. It's time we had a voice that's heard, not just placated."

Sam, sensing the undercurrent of dissent, approached them after the meeting. "Tom, Jeremiah, I understand your frustrations. It's important that everyone feels like they're part of the decision-making process. Let's work together to ensure that happens. I'll speak to Eoinn about it."

Tom's shoulders relaxed a fraction, but the tension in his eyes remained. "Thank you, Sam. We appreciate it. We just want what's best for our families and the future."

10

Sparks

The morning after their visit to Molly's, Jack and Susanne decided to explore the mountains together. They loaded their bikes into Jack's rental car and drove to the trailhead that went up into the mountains towards Murray, an old mining settlement. Murray was effectively a ghost town, despite some periodic activity on weekends during the peak of summer. While they held no delusions about finding Crystal Village on their first attempt, they wanted to get a feel for the terrain and see if they could spot any promising leads.

The morning air bit cold and sharp as Jack and Susanne pedaled their bikes onto the old dirt road leading to Murray. Jack rode his Bridgestone MB2 while Susanne had an old Trek mountain bike that was well maintained. Their legs burned from the steady climb. The June sun had barely crested the ridge, but already, sweat soaked through their T-shirts. Pine and cedar scents mingled with the musty decay of last year's fallen leaves.

"This is harder than I remembered," Susanne called out, her voice slightly breathless as they climbed.

"When was the last time you rode up here?" Jack asked, downshifting as the grade steepened.

"High school, probably. My dad used to bring me up here to explore the old mining sites." She paused to catch her breath. "I forgot how brutal this climb is."

The road switch-backed up the mountainside. Their bike tires crunched over loose gravel and ancient tailings that sparkled with bits of mica. Jack was grateful for the granny gear as the incline became more punishing. His lungs worked overtime in the thin mountain air. He was in decent shape, but it had been a long time since he'd ridden a mountain bike into actual mountains.

"You doing okay?" he called back to Susanne.

"Define okay," she replied with a laugh that sounded more like a wheeze. "My legs are screaming, but the view is incredible."

After several hours of grinding uphill, the first buildings of Murray appeared through the trees. The town was perched on a narrow shelf carved into the mountainside. To their right, weathered structures leaned at odd angles, their gray, timber walls whispering tales of exciting mining booms now long past. The old hotel still stood, its faded sign barely legible against peeling white paint.

They stopped to catch their breath. Jack's heart hammered against his ribs as he unclipped from his pedals and took a long pull from his water bottle. "Remind me why we thought this was a good idea?"

"Because we're both masochists who are afflicted with an unhealthy obsession with family history," Susanne replied, dismounting and stretching her back. "Plus, look at this place. It's like stepping back in time."

The town stretched before them in a rough line following the contours of the mountain. To their left, a creek tumbled down through a steep ravine, the sound of rushing water echoing off the canyon walls.

They walked their bikes past a row of empty storefronts. Windows stared blank and dusty into the street. A general store, its shelves still visible through grimy glass, sat empty except for a few, ancient tin cans. Next door, the saloon's swinging doors hung askew, creaking softly in the morning breeze.

"It's eerie," Susanne said, peering through one of the dusty windows. "You can almost hear the voices of the people who lived here."

"According to what I've read, Murray was one of the camps that sprang up after the Prichard gold discovery," Jack said, consulting the map in his pack. "It would have been bustling when Crystal Village was at its peak."

"Do you think anyone from Crystal Village ever came here?"

"Probably. Here and Eagle City, both were close to the village. The communities would probably have been connected through trade and travel."

Mercifully, their T-shirts began to dry in patches as they explored the town. Jack counted perhaps twenty buildings still standing, with many collapsed structures between them. Rotting timbers and rusted machinery lay scattered across the slope.

Behind the main street, mining tailings rose in gray pyramids against the mountainside. Susanne studied the terrain carefully, shading her eyes with her hand. "According to Molly's map, Crystal Village should be somewhere up there, right?"

"That's what I'm thinking. The question is which trail to take." Jack pulled out his phone but found no signal. The paper map showed several old, forest service roads branching off from Murray, but none were marked with names.

At the far end of town, they found what looked like a promising trail. It switch-backed up the steep slope, disappearing into thick stands of lodgepole pine. The path appeared well-used, probably by elk and deer. Old boot prints in the dusty earth suggested occasional human traffic as well.

"That looks like it goes in the right direction," Susanne said, studying the trail. "But it's getting late. I don't think we should try it today."

Jack checked his watch. The ride up had taken longer than expected. His legs felt heavy, and the altitude made everything just a bit harder. "Yeah, I think we should head back. But now we have a starting point for next time."

"Next time," Susanne said, smiling at him.

"We'll find it. This was just reconnaissance."

They walked to the edge of town where a cliff dropped away to their right. The valley spread out below, a patchwork of dark forest and lighter meadows. Somewhere up these mountains lay the remains of Crystal

Village.

"It's beautiful," Susanne said, standing close enough to Jack that he could smell her shampoo mixed with the scent of pine and the day's exertion. "I can see why they chose this area. It feels ... protected. Hidden."

"Like a secret kingdom," Jack agreed. The mystery of the place pulled at him like a physical force. "Do you really think we can find it?"

"I think if anyone can, it's us. We have the family connections, the maps, and apparently a shared tendency toward obsessive behavior."

The sound of loose rocks clattering down the slope made them both turn. A mountain goat stood watching them from atop a tailings pile, its white coat bright against the gray rock. They regarded each other for a long moment before the animal bounded away up the mountain with impossible ease.

"Show off," Susanne muttered, making Jack laugh.

They mounted their bikes for the return journey. The descent would be faster but demanded concentration because of the loose surface. "You doing okay?" asked Jack.

"Don't worry about me," Susanne replied. "I may be out of shape, but I remember how to ride downhill."

As they descended, Jack found himself glancing back frequently to make sure Susanne was okay. She handled her bike with confidence, her movements fluid and controlled despite the challenging terrain.

"You're a really good rider," he said, gasping, during one of their stops.

"My dad taught me well. He said the mountains don't care about your excuses, so you better know what you're doing."

The air grew thicker as they descended, carrying the sweet scent of sun-warmed pine needles. Their tired muscles appreciated the easier downhill ride, though their hands ached from gripping the handlebars. Each turn revealed new views of the valley below, and occasionally the mountains above.

"Look," Susanne said, pointing upwards to a distant ridgeline. "Do you see that gap between the peaks? That could be where the village was. Hidden in a valley, protected from the worst weather."

Jack studied the terrain where she pointed. "You might be right. The descriptions mention a sheltered cove of land, natural hot springs. That area looks promising."

"We'll need better equipment for the next trip," Susanne said. "Camping gear, GPS, maybe even some metal detectors to look for artifacts."

"You're serious about this," Jack said, feeling a surge of affection for her enthusiasm.

"Are you kidding? This is the adventure of a lifetime! How many people get the chance to search for a lost piece of their family history?"

They stopped frequently to study the terrain, trying to spot any signs of old trails or structures higher up the mountain. Jack thought about all the references to Eagle City he'd come across in his research.

"You know," he said, "I've been thinking about Eagle City. There's not much left of it now, but there's a road that runs through where it once was. That road leads all the way up to an interpretive site higher in the mountains. It might be a more efficient jumping-off point than trying to bike up from Murray."

"Good thinking. We could drive partway up, then hike from there. Save our energy for the actual search."

By the time they reached the valley floor, shadows had lengthened across the landscape. Their legs trembled with exhaustion as they pedaled the final miles to the rental SUV, but their conversation buzzed with excitement.

"I can't believe we're actually doing this!" Susanne said enthusiastically as they loaded their bikes. "Looking for a lost mining town like we're characters in one of my novels."

"Maybe you should write about it," Jack suggested. "Document our search. Whether we find Crystal Village or not, it's a story worth telling."

"Only if you promise to be good company," she said with a grin.

"I'll do my best," Jack replied, feeling that familiar flutter in his chest when she smiled at him like that.

The trip confirmed their suspicions—finding the ruins of Crystal Village would challenge them but remained possible. The mystery had waited more than a century, but they felt closer than ever to uncovering its secrets.

11

Integrity

Liam sat at the bar of the White Elephant Saloon in Eagle City. To call this a city, he thought, was perhaps overly ambitious. But it helped Eoinn's cause with the rest of the village, since it evoked an encroachment by vile men. The hastily built settlement assaulted his senses. Mud-slicked planks creaked and groaned under boots caked with red clay, and the wafting odor of unwashed bodies competed with wood smoke and the reek of cheap whiskey.

Eagle City was a loose collection of cabins and tents, and the White Elephant Saloon stood out among them. A month earlier, the famous lawman, Wyatt Earp, had arrived in Eagle City with his wife Josie and his brother Jim. They'd bought a circus tent that was about fifty feet tall and fifty feet in diameter and named it the White Elephant. It quickly became the premier saloon of the town, and Earp had been named Deputy Sheriff of Kootenai County to boot. Of course, both Shoshone and Kootenai counties claimed that Eagle City was within their jurisdiction, and each county sent lawmen to keep the peace, which seemed okay with both of them. Earp had established himself as a local celebrity with ease and had thrown in his lot with a group of men, and together they had invested in the acquisition of several parcels of land.

Liam watched the room with a veteran's practiced eye. He noted which men carried their weapons with the easy familiarity of experience, and which ones merely postured. The sound of a hammer being cocked made him tense—just some fool showing off, but the sound brought back memories of darker days.

At a nearby table, two miners argued over their drinks.

"Prichard's got no right to lock up every decent claim from here to the Montana line!" the first miner said, slamming his fist on the rough-hewn table.

"He's got the papers though, don't he?" his companion answered. "All nice and legal with his friends and family names on 'em."

"Legal don't make it right!" the first man spat. "Man can't work fifty claims at once."

Liam absorbed their conversation while nursing his whiskey. Prichard's lockout of all the best claims had nearly led to a revolt in Eagle City. Earp's crew were notorious for jumping claims of others who weren't holding them and using the courts to get their way. Courts and newspapers were always among the first things established in a mining camp, soon after the bars.

On this day, there had been quite a bit of drama over a so-called "city lot" that Jack Enright, a member of Earp's syndicate, claimed to own, attesting that he'd purchased it from a local man named Wyman. Another man, William Buzzard, claimed he'd bought the same lot from a different local man named Sam Black. Buzzard built a small cabin on the back of the lot to solidify his claim. Sam Black, who had sold Buzzard the lot, suggested repeatedly and publicly that there were two lots, and that what he'd sold Buzzard was just the back part of the property, where Buzzard had built his cabin. Enright had stated, at the urging of Earp, that as long as Buzzard kept to his own lot and left the streetfront lot owned by Earp's syndicate, he'd let it be.

Buzzard had inflamed the situation by having a large load of logs and lumber delivered onto the vacant streetfront lot, announcing he was going to build a hotel. Enright heard this story repeated elsewhere in town and rushed off to his lot. He walked around the pile of logs to stumble right upon Buzzard, who shoved a Winchester rifle in his face and ordered him off the lot. Enright had backed off but called out as he left that he'd be back, and that Buzzard should leave the premises if he knew what was good for him.

Liam sat at the bar sipping whiskey. His posture remained deliberately casual, but his mind worked like a chess player, analyzing moves and consequences. Eoinn had tasked him with understanding the power structures that were developing in Eagle City, and the Earps were clearly central to this. Whether they might prove allies or threats to Crystal Village remained to be seen. He watched Wyatt, his wife Josie, and brother Jim as they huddled, deep in conversation at the other end of the bar. Liam caught Wyatt's eye and signaled that he'd like a refill. Wyatt walked over with the bottle to pour another drink for Liam.

Liam said, "Ye know, Mr. Earp, I've been watching this whole story unfold all day. Your man Enright is a hothead, and I think he's likely to start something back up."

Wyatt looked carefully at Liam and said, "You know, I think you may be right, Mr ..."

"O'Connor, Liam O'Connor at your service," said Liam, reaching out to shake hands. He kept his grip firm but not challenging, establishing himself as a man worthy of respect but not seeking confrontation.

Wyatt said, "Mr. O'Connor, I've been standing down the other end of the bar here with my wife and brother talking about that exact situation. Enright's a good fellow, but he is, in fact, a hothead. He also has the added strength of a convincing and inspiring personality. We're just now considering what the best approach might be so as to ensure things don't escalate."

Liam gave him a wry smile and said, "Well, sir, this seems like one of those situations that are worth avoiding, which likely means I'll be dragged right into it."

Wyatt placed his finger against the side of his nose, winked and nodded at him and returned to the conversation at the other end of the bar.

A few minutes later, a skinny young man rushed into the bar and whispered in Wyatt's ear, and the Earp brothers donned their dusters and hats, looped on their gun belts, and headed for the door. Liam rushed to follow them, leaving some coins on the bar and signaling to Josie so she'd know he wasn't skipping out on his tab. His tab settled, he followed the Earp brothers down the street, about twenty paces behind, keeping a strategic distance that allowed him to observe without seeming to be too eager to involve himself.

The afternoon sun cast long shadows across the muddy street. Liam's ears caught the unmistakable sound of weapons being readied—the metallic click of rounds being chambered, the soft scrape of holsters. As Liam got closer to the contested lot, he could see four men carrying rifles, shotguns and pistols standing in the street. William Buzzard was standing amidst the construction of his hotel that he'd started building over the course of the day. Behind him, three loyal men stood cradling their weapons.

Enright called out, "Listen here, Billy Buzzard, I warned you I'd be coming back, and that you had better be off my property. But here you are, and you've started building, and you've got friends backing you up. This doesn't need to end badly, Billy Boy, you can leave now, and if you disagree with my claim, we can work it out in the courts."

Buzzard scoffed at Enright, saying, "Oh sure, we can settle it in court!"

The crack of Buzzard's first shots split the air. He'd fired two quick shots from his Colt revolver, before diving behind the low log wall. Then all hell broke loose. Bullets flew in all directions, and gunsmoke obscured the street. Enright and his crew advanced on the hotel foundation through the hail of bullets. Splinters flew as Enright's return fire struck the fresh-cut timber. As Enright's crew drew closer, Buzzard and his men retreated to the cabin on the back of the lot, firing from the door and windows.

The Earp brothers arrived and walked right in the middle between the two parties, shots firing from side to side the whole time. Liam marveled at their composure—he'd seen generals with less command of a battlefield.

Wyatt called out loudly, "Well, isn't this a fine picture, Jim? I don't think I've seen this many bad shots in my whole life. These boys couldn't hit a snowbank in a snowstorm!"

Jim laughed and called back, as bullets whizzed through the air around the two brothers, "Wyatt, I feel like these boys really need some shootin' lessons. But maybe first we can get them to stop shooting at us?"

Liam stood nearby, on the opposite corner from this vacant lot, assessing the situation with a soldier's eye. He noted how the Earps used humor to defuse tension, filing that away in memory for his report to Eoinn. As he watched, a carpenter named John Burdett who was standing near him was shot through the thigh and crumpled to the ground. Liam rushed over to help, applying pressure to the wound. As he tended to Burdett, he positioned himself so as to keep both the gunfight and the Earps in view. Liam hadn't seen this much gunfire since the War.

Wyatt called out loudly, his arms pointing simultaneously at the two parties, gesturing at the men to lower their guns, "Okay, you foozlers, you just hit a bystander across the street! If you don't want to hang for manslaughter, I strongly suggest we end this. Even shots as bad as all of you might hit someone by accident."

Enright and his men ceased their shooting, and the matter appeared to be over. Wyatt lowered his arms just as another shot rang out from the cabin, whistling past his head, breaking a window in the building across the street. Wyatt grimaced angrily and shouted, "Goddammit! That's enough now! Don't make me come over there, Billy!"

Buzzard called out in a muffled and apologetic tone, "Sorry, Wyatt."

Around that time, the Shoshone County Deputy Sheriff W.F. Hunt arrived on the scene carrying a Winchester rifle. Deputy Hunt shouted, "That's enough with the shooting! All you boys, put down your weapons!"

Jim Earp said, sarcastically, "You tell 'em, Deputy Hunt! Just in the nick of time!"

Wyatt called out, "Okay, Enright and Buzzard, get your asses over here! We're gonna settle this thing." Wyatt led the two men over to a spot where Buzzard had set up a couple of chairs near his cabin. He motioned to them to sit down. Reluctantly, both men sat, Enright taking a chair first, then Buzzard. Wyatt pulled out his pipe and tobacco and asked if either of the men would like a smoke. Buzzard said yes, pulling out his pipe, and Wyatt handed him his own tobacco pouch. Enright pulled out his pipe and took the bag from Buzzard, who looked sheepishly at him. The three men lit their pipes and took a few puffs.

Liam watched the transformation with fascination. The shift from deadly conflict to peaceful negotiation happened with a speed that would have seemed impossible anywhere but on the frontier. This was information Eoinn needed to understand—how quickly alliances could form and dissolve in Eagle City.

Buzzard said, "You know, Jack, you sure cut yourself a fine figure walking across that street guns ablazin'. That was some cool-handed shooting, if I do say so."

Enright replied to Buzzard, "Yeah, Billy, I have to say, you have some *cojones* on you. I don't think I've seen someone return fire without panicking before, but I'll hand it to you that you're a cool hand yourself."

Jim Earp sidled up to the impromptu conference with Deputy Sheriff Hunt and said, "Now if any of you lot could shoot, you'd be a real hazard to this here town. But, Billy, you're going to have to work things out with that carpenter that your lot hit with a stray round. It was obviously accidental, but you best hope he's not of a mind to press charges. I think a kind word and dare I say, an offer to cover his doctor's bill and a gift of some gold dust and some whiskey might win him over."

The Earp brothers left things in the hands of Deputy Sheriff Hunt and began walking back toward the White Elephant. Wyatt spied Liam on the side of the road helping Burdett and nodded. Liam nodded back, and after making sure Burdett was in good hands, he headed toward the stable where he'd left his horse. His first contact with the Earps had gone well. He'd positioned himself as a voice of reason, someone they could trust. It was a start, and he had much to report back to Eoinn about the delicate balance of power in Eagle City.

I I I I

The whole village came out to celebrate the marriage of Sam and Seamus. Everyone had been waiting for this for years. There had even been some bets laid at one point, although nobody ultimately won anything as Sam had held out for so long.

Despite her reputation as a serious and reliable woman, those who knew her well were not surprised when she chose April Fool's Day as her wedding day. It was cool and dry that day. Sean led a crew who put together a small stage outside of the main opening to the mine, at the head of the square where Broadway and Spring Street met. It was decorated with an arbor and pine boughs and featured a special array of flowers that had been gathered and arranged by the children of the village. There were shooting stars in vibrant purple and pink, yellow bells, lavender-colored pasqueflowers, and brilliant-yellow sagebrush buttercups.

Eoinn presided over the ceremony, and the whole village filled the square. Sam wore her Easter dress, a light-pink dress she'd made with the assistance of Mrs. O'Connor. Sean and Colin walked her down the aisle between the parted crowd, one on either of her arms.

The couple exchanged vows, Eoinn pronounced them husband and wife, and the whole town cheered. Then they went off to the music hall and enjoyed a delicious meal made by Mrs. O's crew. When the meal was finished, the tables were cleared and moved to the edge of the room, the musicians took their places for the dancing. But before the dancing started, Sean stood up and motioned for quiet. He and Colin picked up their guitar and mandolin, and Sean made an announcement. He met Sam's eyes as he spoke.

"My friends, I've written a song in the style of my people. Some of ye know the story of how we found Samantha King and brought her into our clan. And I've heard some folks telling the tale as if we'd saved Sam, and there may be a bit of truth to that, aye. But ye don't know the whole story, which is that as much as we brought Sam into our hearts, it was Sam who saved us."

He choked up just a bit for a moment and paused. After he regained his composure, he continued, "Sam brought a bit of sunlight into the hearts of a bunch of rough fellers, who'd been to war, who'd seen terrible things that would freeze the heart of a saint. Many of the men were missing their own children and wives at that point, and to have a young lass with us was a balm to the spirits."

"So I've written this song here, and I'd like to play it for ye. It's called ..."

The Maiden of the Wilds

In the untamed, open lands where the wild breezes sigh, a lass walked on with heavy heart 'neath the boundless sky. Her kin were gone, her path unclear, her spirit nearly spent. In the wild embrace of nature, her lonely days were lent.

In a vale of hidden wonders, a circle she did find, with warmth and gentle laughter, they welcomed her inside. Their kindness wrapped around her and nurtured her with care, a haven in the wilderness, where dreams took root to dare.

Oh, hear the whispers rising from the wilds so wide, where the spirit of kindness and gentle hearts abide. Guiding stars are shining with wisdom firm and bright, to lead a lost one homeward through the shadowed night.

Through their strength she flourished, her spirit bold and free. With courage and with wisdom, she sailed life's endless sea. In time she found her heart's own song, and love became her guide, a beacon in the darkness, where hope and dreams abide.

Now tales are told of courage, of the maiden's steadfast ways, who found her place and purpose, in the wilds where she stayed. Her story lights the evening, a legacy of grace, a tribute to strength and love, in every heart's embrace.

Oh, hear the whispers rising from the wilds so wide, where the spirit of kindness and gentle hearts abide. Guiding stars are shining with wisdom firm and bright, to lead a lost one homeward through the shadowed night.

As the final strains of the chorus ended, Sam, tears streaming down her face, ran to Sean and hugged him. The rest of the seven men stepped forward and joined the huddle, wrapping their arms around the group, even Finn, who looked a little uncomfortable at first.

After a few minutes, a teary Sam stood and thanked Sean for the lovely song. She also thanked him and Colin for taking such good care of her in her hour of need and every hour since. And all seven of the men who'd taken her in and made her a part of their families.

"I lost my parents and my sister when I was nine, and nothing will ever replace them. But what I gained, what the universe conspired to give me, was the best a person in need could ever have hoped for. I've been given seven fathers and seven families to join, with a host of mothers, aunties, uncles, and extended family." Sam paused as the room cheered, and many of those present dabbed at their eyes.

Sam looked at Seamus and nodded, and he stepped up and said, "All right, all right, thanks for that wonderful gift, gentlemen. But now it's time for us to get to the dancing!" With that, the musicians settled in and began to play. Seamus grabbed Sam by the wrist and pulled her out on the floor, and they began their first dance as a married couple.

The celebration went on late into the night, and when Sam and Seamus finally made their way back to Seamus' cabin, he scooped her up and carried her across the threshold to begin their new life together.

I I I I

For weeks, Sam and Seamus had been pestering Liam to take them into Eagle City. Liam initially resisted, insisting it was no place for them to spend time. Sam argued vehemently that they'd visited many cities all over the West for missions involving banks, supplies, and other matters. Now, with a city just a few miles away, it seemed absurd to be denied access.

The allure of meeting Wyatt Earp captivated her imagination. What finally tipped the scales was the news of Calamity Jane's return for a repeat performance, following a first visit with her stage show a month earlier. Upon hearing this, Liam came up to the village, collected Sam and Seamus, and they headed down with him. They arrived at the edge of the camp, where Liam paid two bits for a stablehand to watch over their horses for the evening.

Sam was taken aback by the dismal state of Eagle City. The forest was devastated. It had been brutally cleared, and the town was littered with holes and mine tailings. It was appalling what the miners had done. No real buildings existed, only platforms supporting white tents. The largest tent was the White Elephant, an old circus tent erected by the Earps to house their bar. It was here Calamity Jane and her group of eight fancy ladies were set to perform.

As they strolled through the town, Sam noticed the attention she received. Standing between two large, muscular, well-armed men, she felt secure. Liam had explained that the camps had few women, most of whom were either prostitutes or accompanied by their husbands, making any woman in town a subject of considerable interest to the many men.

Liam led them into the White Elephant, and once inside, they approached the bar. A pretty woman bartender greeted Liam as an old friend.

"Welcome back, Liam!"

Liam replied happily, "Hello, Josie, please meet my son Seamus and his wife Sam." Liam turned to Sam and Seamus and continued, "This here is Josie, wife of Wyatt Earp."

Josie smiled warmly at them, saying, "Imagine! Liam with a son—and one who looks so much like him too! It's wonderful to meet you both. Seamus, your pa has been a big help to us here at the White Elephant. And it's very nice to meet you, Sam."

Soon, Wyatt and Jim Earp joined them, and introductions were made all around. Sam was surprised that nobody asked where they lived and said so quietly to Liam when she had a moment. Liam replied under his breath, "Miners are pretty close-mouthed about the location of their claims. Nobody presses too hard to know where anyone else spends their days."

The Earps set up near the bar, and the group enjoyed a pleasant evening as they awaited the show. On the opposite side of the tent, a small stage had been erected. It had red, calico curtains drawn before it. Beside the stage, a man with an accordion prepared to accompany the evening's entertainment. Sam had heard of such instruments but had never heard one played. It resembled a tiny piano attached to a box with a bellows, producing music akin to a harmonica but louder and more beautiful.

A woman peeked out from behind the red curtain and spoke to the accordion player, who began playing introductory music. The room fell silent, all eyes fixed on the stage as the curtain parted to reveal a woman dressed in a man's woolen suit. Her leathery face bore the marks of exposure to sun and wind. She perched on a stool and introduced herself as Jane, launching into her life's tale.

While her stories were clearly embellished for effect, they were entertaining. She recounted her days scouting for the U.S. Army, her friendship with Wild Bill Hickok, and various escapades in which she had played a part. When she finished her stories, the room erupted in cheers, and eight dancing girls took the stage, performing a jig.

Other musicians joined the accordion player, and tables were moved to make space. The ladies danced with the men for $1 each—a steep price for a five-minute dance, but the men were clearly starved for female interaction.

As the evening wore on, tensions rose. Men were reluctant to yield their dance partners when their time had expired. Of course, this led to arguments and fights outside in the snow. Inside the Earp's establishment, however, no one dared throw a punch.

The evening soured for Sam when a large, drunk, and smelly man noticed her at the bar. Though he wasn't as tall as Liam and Seamus, he seemed twice as wide, with a great bush of a beard. He stumbled over and asked how much she wanted for a dance. Seamus placed a hand on the man's shoulder, stating that Sam was his wife.

The man misunderstood and asked Seamus for a price to dance with Sam. Liam intervened, putting an arm around the man's shoulders and saying, "Listen, feller, she's not selling dances tonight, ye should go over, and join the line." Wyatt and Jim Earp were watching and chuckling, but they nodded to Liam. When the man began to argue, Wyatt's gun butt came down on his head. The dazed man was lifted off the ground, and then Liam, Seamus, Wyatt, and Jim carried him to the door. On the count of three, the men heaved him into the muddy street.

Jane approached the bar for a whisky.

Wyatt said, "Jane, these fine folks are Liam O'Connor, his son Seamus, and Seamus' wife, Sam."

Jane smiled at them and said hello. Sam said, "I loved your storytelling. I've heard about you and read about you, but it was wonderful to hear it directly from the source."

Jane smiled and replied, "Thank you kindly, Sam. I hate to dodge out on you here, but there's right to be a revolt if I don't get back to the dancing."

Jane tilted her head back, downed her whiskey, and disappeared.

Deciding it was time to leave, Liam, Seamus, and Sam bid their farewells and exited the tent. The ejected man was long gone, and they still had a journey back to the village. They collected their horses at the stable and walked them to the trail. Though it was dark, Liam knew the way to the hidden Crystal Village trail. So Liam led, with Sam in the middle and Seamus bringing up the rear. As they rode along, they discussed the night's events. Sam admitted to Liam that he'd been right. Although she was glad to have gone, it wasn't what she'd expected—less thrilling and more horrifying.

Victory, Sam's reliable horse, moved steadily despite her age, making the ride back uneventful. It took them about five hours to get home in the dark. When Sam and Seamus finally tumbled into bed, they talked at length before sleep eventually claimed them.

Over the course of the following spring and summer, Liam spent a good bit of time in Eagle City. During that time, the population started shifting over to Murray, a new town downriver where gold had been found. Eagle City was starting to unravel, but Liam kept his eye on things there, since Eagle City was the closest of the mining camps to the village, and where problems might most likely arise.

Liam also continued to develop his friendship with the Earps and their friends, including a young man of twenty-three named Danny Ferguson. Ferguson had been one of the men supporting Enright in the shootout he'd had with Billy Buzzard. He was a good young man who was passionately loyal to his friends, and who tried to do the right thing.

IIII

June 19th, 1884

Danny Ferguson was twenty-three years old, and five feet, ten inches tall. He was handsome with deep, blue eyes, dark-blond hair, long sideburns, and an otherwise clean-shaven face. One evening, Danny was leaving Donnelly's Saloon in Eagle City. As he stepped out the door, he saw a man named Thomas Steele slapping a woman across the face repeatedly in the street. He was holding the front of her bodice with his left hand, striking her with his right. She was bleeding from her nose, sitting up in the muddy street outside the saloon.

Danny couldn't abide men who beat women. He shouted, "Hey there, Steele, don't you hurt that woman!"

Steele looked up from the woman and said, "Maybe you want some of this?! Damn you, I'll fix you!" In one fluid motion, Steele tossed the woman aside and drew on Danny, the click of his cocked Colt chilling the air. Danny backed off as Steele stepped up onto the boardwalk. He raised his hands in peace, but Steele wasn't done. A cruel backhand across the nose with his pistol sent Danny reeling, cutting him deeply, blood welling up in the wound.

Steele said, "Now, what have you got to do with this, boy?"

Danny said, "Nothing, only I wouldn't hurt a wom—"

He was cut off mid-sentence as Steele whipped his pistol hand back, striking Danny's left temple and discharging the gun, which ripped off a chunk of skin and hair, knocking him back hard against the tent wall of the saloon. Steele jumped back a few feet and fired two shots in quick succession, both missing their mark. Danny bounced back off the canvas and pulled his own pistol. Both men fired. Danny's shot went wide and missed altogether, but Steele's shot grazed Danny's right cheek and clipped his ear. Danny fired again at the spot that Steele had been standing. When the flash from his muzzle dimmed from his eyes, he ducked under the cloud of gunsmoke, and Steele was gone. He heard footsteps running down the boardwalk into the dark.

He wondered aloud, "Could I have missed him?"

He saw that a bystander had jumped down into the mud to help the woman out, and a few others lit out after Steele.

Danny left the scene immediately. Blood dripped from three separate wounds on his head. He staggered through the dark to find Wyatt Earp. He started at the White Elephant, where Liam was sitting at the bar. Liam grabbed hold of Danny, whose face was a mess of blood and gunpowder. He was bleeding from the bridge of his nose, down the left side of his head from the pistol whipping, and from the discharge of the gun, which blew off a chunk of his scalp to the bone, leaving the flesh hanging by a flap of skin. He had been grazed by Steele's bullet on the right side of his cheek, and he was missing the edge of his right ear. Liam grabbed up a bandana from his belt and wrapped it around Danny's head, covering his wounds. As he tended to Danny, he shouted to the bartender to give him a cloth for Danny's nose.

Once Liam had tended to Danny's wounds, he dragged him out of the White Elephant and helped him walk a few buildings over to Wyatt's cabin. Wyatt was standing at the open door in his long underclothes, and he ushered the two men inside. Josie was there. She slipped on her robe and came over to listen.

"Those pistol shots sounded like a fight up the street," said Wyatt.

Danny groaned and said, "Yes, I had one."

Wyatt paused, then asked, "Did you win it?"

"Yes," said Danny, "I think so, I don't think I could have missed him. He run off into the dark."

Wyatt grunted. "Okay, Danny, you sit here. I'll get my clothes on and go up and look over the battleground."

Wyatt pulled on his pants and buttoned up his shirt. He asked Danny to tell him exactly what happened. Danny recounted the events as he remembered them, making a point to inform Wyatt there were several other people on the street who saw the whole thing. Wyatt nodded to Josie, who rushed over to tend to Danny's wounds. Satisfied that the young man was in good hands, Wyatt asked Liam to accompany him, and the two men walked out the door.

They walked down to the scene of the shootout in front of Donnelly's Saloon. Upon arriving, they met Deputy Sheriff Hunt, who asked if they knew where Danny Ferguson had gone. They saw that Hunt was standing next to two trees at the end of the boardwalk, and that Steele had collapsed between the trees. He was sure enough dead.

After a cursory examination of the dead man, Wyatt turned back to Hunt and said, "Danny is back at my cabin. He's all beat to hell. Steele pistol whipped him across the nose and the left temple. That blow discharged the gun and nearly blew his head off. He took considerable damage to his scalp and is damn lucky that it wasn't much worse! He also was grazed by another bullet from Steele at close range. That bullet caught him on the right cheek, and he lost a bit of his ear as well. He should be okay, but Danny was the hero here. He got caught up by Steele because he called him off of a young lady, who he was beating."

Deputy Hunt said, "Wyatt, I know he's a friend of yours, but he done killed this man. He shot him right through the chest and left him to die."

Liam walked over to talk to a few men who were part of a small crowd. They were comforting the woman who Steele had been beating. Liam inquired as to her part in this grim affair, and she confirmed Danny's version.

Liam spoke up, "Deputy, I think if ye come and question this woman, ye'll find that she backs up Danny's version of the story."

Hunt said, "You keep your nose out of this, Liam! The Sheriff is on his way and will want to come to his own conclusions."

Things had soured between Wyatt, who was the Kootenai County Deputy Sheriff, and Shoshone County Sheriff Dunwell, who felt Earp was acting without any jurisdiction. Dunwell also didn't like the Earps on principle, since they were involved in several business endeavors in Eagle City and were caught up in several cases where they were accused, probably accurately, of claim jumping.

Liam could see that Danny was not likely to receive a fair hearing due to his friendship with Wyatt. So he nodded to the deputy, caught Wyatt's eye, and turned to walk back to the Earp cabin. When he arrived, he found Danny being tended to by Josie's capable hands. She was stitching up the wound on the side of his head, and she asked Liam to hold him still, which he did.

When they were all done, Josie left to refill the water bucket and Liam took Danny aside.

"Danny, if things go afoul on ye, and ye need a safe place to go, ye should come up to Crystal Village. It's where I live, and there are many families, places to stay, and plenty of jobs. We'll sort ye out and keep ye safe. Nobody here knows about Crystal Village, not even Wyatt and Josie, and we need to keep it that way. There are families with small children that we need to keep safe. Hear me clearly on this—ye can't ever tell anyone about us! Ye can't ever mention Crystal Village in public. If ye talk about us, if ye tell anyone that's where you're going, then I'll disavow ye, and ye'll be on your own."

Danny paused thoughtfully and said, "I understand, and I promise to keep it a secret, whether I come up to the village or not."

Liam carefully explained the path to Crystal Village and how to follow it. Just as they finished that conversation, Wyatt entered the cabin.

"Well," Wyatt began, "I told Sheriff Dunwell that I'd vouch for you for the night, and I'd release you to them once the coroner's inquest is done. That's why they're not hauling you off to jail. But there's a chance they're going to pin this on you, Danny. You could hang for it. Now what are you going to do, ride or stay?"

Danny thought for a moment then he said, "I ain't done nothing wrong, Wyatt. I'll stick."

Wyatt nodded curtly and looked over at Liam. Liam nodded back, said good evening to the group, and left.

I I I I

193

July 1st, 1884

Danny walked on the trail that Liam had directed him to. His nose was scarred and healed but didn't look too bad. The stitches on the side of his head had left a scar that wasn't easy to see through his hair. The wound from the bullet grazing his cheek also had scarred as well. He hoped that the ladies would think that the scar gave him a roguish look and didn't make him look sinister. He enjoyed the trip along Eagle Creek. He crossed back and forth a few times as he went, and after a few hours, he came to the "cathedral of cedars" and walked onward until he came across the road. The road was well built and had railroad tracks on the right side that ran parallel to it. He took a right turn and followed the road until he came to a farmstead on the right with cows, chickens, and pigs. Then passing the farm, he came to a beautiful bridge made of stone and steel. The surface of the bridge was tightly set Belgian blocks, and on the right side of the road the train tracks continued right on over the bridge, through the gate, and onward through the center of the village in a northerly direction.

He saw a sign on the side of the bridge nearest to him that read, "Welcome to Crystal Village. No guns allowed. See the constable and check your weapons. All visitors must register."

He crossed over the bridge, admiring the fine craftsmanship of the structure. On the far side of the span, two, large, stone gatehouse buildings stood, one on either side of the bridge's landing, with a large gate between them that stood open. Danny thought that this was like some European medieval castle he'd read about in children's books, where a walled city had a main gate and a moat with a bridge across it. Above the gate there was a steel catwalk that crossed over the road, spanning the distance between the two buildings on their second floor. Integrated into the catwalk was a great wood and iron gate. Its doors were open, pulled back against the walls of the buildings on either side, and as Danny walked through them he saw that they were held back with large steel hooks. Where the bridge ended the road turned into a cobblestone thoroughfare that continued on into the village. As he passed through the gate, Danny noted that there was an armed man standing on the catwalk above him who gave him a friendly wave.

Beyond the main entrance to the village, the stone building on the left had a wall with a series of arched entry gates that opened onto the road. The second floor of that structure had firing slits or loopholes that allowed a rifleman positioned on the inside of the building to aim down onto the road and fire at any attacker with almost complete immunity. Another man was stationed there. Similar openings on the second floor of the building across the road were staggered, presumably so people on either side wouldn't accidentally fire on each other. A sign read, "Stables" with an arrow pointing off to the right.

There was a small sign over the opening on the left that said, "Constable On Duty, all visitors please register." Danny walked to the entry gate, poked his head through, and saw a small office behind metal bars. A man was sitting at the desk, and Danny approached him. The man was about fifty years old. He was a bit overweight, had a long, waxed mustache, and was clad in a dark-blue coat.

He looked up, smiled, and said, "Hello there! Who have we here?"

Danny paused, then said, "I'm Danny ... Miller. I was invited up here by Liam O'Connor."

The man nodded. Then he stood up behind his desk, extended his hand, and said, "Mr. Miller! It's so nice to meet you. Liam has told us to expect you. I'm Constable Stanley J. Finch, but folks call me Stan. I look forward to getting to know you!"

Stan picked up a pen and wrote in the open book in front of him, noting Danny Miller as the visitor and the date and time. Once finished, he stood up and walked around the desk.

He said, "Mr. Miller, I must ask for your pistol and any other guns you've brought. We keep them in the gun safe here. We'll put your name on it, so you can pick it up whenever you leave. But we don't allow anyone to bring guns into Crystal Village."

Danny nodded and unhooked his gun belt. He handed it to Stan, saying, "That's fine. I like this much better. It's Danny, by the way. You can just call me Danny."

Stan smiled, accepted Danny's gun belt, and hung it in the large, steel gun safe that stood behind his desk. He pulled a small tag with string out of one of his desk drawers, squinted as he wrote "Danny Miller", and the date on it, and tied the tag to the gun. He motioned to Danny in a congenial way and walked him out onto the street.

He looked carefully at Danny's clothes and pack, and he asked, "Is this everything you've brought? No horse or luggage on the other side of the bridge?"

Danny said, "No, sir, I was traveling light."

Stan said, "That's good, very good, Danny."

Stan looked up to the man standing watch on the wall and said, raising his voice, "Jacob, please hold down the fort for me while I bring Danny here to meet with Liam and Eoinn."

As they walked through the town, Danny noticed that the street was beautiful. It ran south to north and was paved with more of the same Belgian blocks made of granite. It had a slight curvature to the center to allow for good drainage. The sidewalks here were made of slate and had slate curbstones standing on their ends with the grain of the slate pointing upwards. The gutters dipped a few inches down and were made of long, flat pieces of slate, each about a foot wide. There were openings covered with cast-iron grates every twenty feet or so for the water to drain down underneath the roadway. The street was only paved for the first few hundred feet, and there was a crew working to lay additional blocks. Nearby, a cart filled with Belgian blocks was being pulled by two mules. Further up the street there was a crew laying long rows of thick pipes made of cast iron into the street. They were working out ahead of a team laying gravel, who were themselves working ahead of the team that was setting the blocks.

Between the pipe layers and the block setters and among the men laying the gravel, a man with a large iron roller was tamping down the gravel. He was working with another man who was checking to make sure the street was graded properly. Here and there other teams were working on brick buildings up and down both sides of the street. Each building had a team of five or ten men working on it, with each building being in various states of construction.

Stan walked with Danny up the street, explaining that this was called Broadway. There were several cross streets with buildings in various states of construction that ran off in both directions, east and west. On some roads were lines of platform tents, the standard setup across the frontier, but a bit nicer. Clearly the intent was to replace these with permanent structures.

The Constable spent the walk naming and describing the intended purpose of the various buildings that were under construction. He explained that they were laying the gravel and block paving on the street over pipes that would be fed directly from the hot springs. The intent was to utilize the hot water to melt the snow and ice in the winter so nobody would need to shovel or plow this main road. He turned back and pointed out the new stables that had been built across from the armory, the building they'd started out in. He turned back around and nodded north into the distance toward the end of the street, where a big square had been staked off.

Stan said, "That's where the mine entrance is, at least the main entrance. The mining company office is to the left of the mine entrance. Mind you, it's just a wood building today, but that will get replaced with a big, brick building at some point. Sprouting off each side of the square going east to west is Spring Street, where many of the first houses have been built. If you go right on Spring Street you will find the meal hall. They serve breakfast, lunch, and dinner."

Each time they passed an intersection, Stan would point out the name of the cross street and explain what was planned to go down each side of them. Soon they came to the end of the road and to the mining company office that seemed to be their destination. He saw that there was a fancy, scrollwork sign above the door that read, "Seeley Mining Company" in gold leaf against a navy-blue background. Off to the right at the base of the stairs, there was an iron boot scraper. It had two, short-bristled brushes mounted next to it facing down and up. That way, you could put your whole boot in-between them to scrub both top and bottom at the same time. Both men cleaned their boots off and wiped their feet on the mat. Stan opened the door and walked inside, motioning to Danny that he should follow. In the entryway there were heavy hooks on the wall about half-full of various mining equipment and hard metal helmets.

Stan said, "Danny, please take a load off, and hang your pack here."

Danny happily slung his pack onto one of the empty hooks, and they continued into the building. The entryway opened up into a large, open space with several desks and offices at the back, each with glass windows looking into the main room. A pretty, thin young woman with thick, brown hair sat at a desk in the middle of the room. She was a few years older than Danny and dressed in men's clothes. When Stan and Danny entered, she was chatting with a man in his forties. The gentleman had curly, brown hair and a reddish-brown beard that was going a bit gray in the red bits, and he sat on the corner of her desk as he conversed with the woman.

Stan spoke up, "Sam and Angus, I'd like you to meet Danny Miller. He's a friend of Liam's, and he's been invited to join the village. Danny, this here lovely lass is Sam King, I mean Sam O'Connor, as she recently married Liam's son Seamus. The gentleman with whom she is chatting is Angus Sullivan. They're two of the original eight founders of the village."

Danny reached out to shake hands with them both, saying, "It's really nice to meet you both."

Sam smiled at him and said, "Mr. Ferguson, you're most welcome here. Liam has told us the story of how you came to be invited to join us, and he also described the dustup with your name changing to Miller. You're safe here, and your secret will not leave this building. I'm sorry that you got railroaded for standing up for a woman in distress."

Danny had quirked his eyebrow at hearing himself called Ferguson, but he smiled at Sam and said, "Thanks, ma'am. I really appreciate it. I thought the truth would prevail in my favor, but I've learned that the world isn't always so interested in truth. So I lit out for the hills and changed my name. I'm pleased to hear that you don't think less of me for it."

Sam looked approvingly at him and said, "Not in the least. You did the right thing, and you fought for your legacy. Sometimes the world is corrupt."

"Agreed!" Angus interjected. "Sir, I think based on what we've heard, you'll be a great addition to our little village."

Sam turned to the Constable and said, "Stan, Eoinn's in his office, and it so happens that Liam is with him. Go right inside."

Stan thanked them and walked Danny toward the big office on the right side of the room. The office had a large, glass window that allowed people to see in and out. It also had a window in the door. Two men were inside, and Danny was relieved to see Liam was one of them. The other man was a tall, gray-haired man with a well-groomed mustache. Liam saw them coming and smiled broadly at Danny. He threw the door to the office open and strode across to meet them. He embraced Danny in a huge bear hug, lifting him off the ground and laughing out loud. He turned around, setting Danny down, and pushing him toward the door to the office, thanking Stan for bringing him.

Stan laughed and said, "Danny, I'll leave you in Liam's tender embrace and head back to the armory. Please do look me up once you're settled in."

Danny waved weakly at Stan and thanked him.

Liam brought Danny into the office and said, "Danny, please meet my eldest friend, Eoinn Seeley. We grew up together in Ireland, we traveled the world together, we emigrated to these United States together, we fought in the War together, and we've made our homes here in Crystal Village together. Eoinn, this is Danny Ferguson, who now goes by Miller. He's coming to stay here in order to avoid being thrown in prison—or worse. And his troubles are all because he did the right thing! He tried to stand up for a woman who was being beaten by a drunkard, ne'er-do-well, son of a doctor who did his best to kill our man here. Still, it was Danny who got the better of him, gunning him down in self-defense. But sadly, politics being what they are, Danny fell on the wrong side of a county dispute on police jurisdiction, and now he's here."

Eoinn walked over and firmly grasped Danny's hand in both of his. "Danny, I have to say I was really taken by your story. You're welcome to stay here in Crystal Village for as long as ye need."

"Thank you, sir," replied Danny.

Eoinn continued, "We've our own need to bring in more good people to ensure that this enclave of culture, family, and strong values is perpetuated for generations to come. Liam, have ye got a place for Danny to stay?"

"I'm going to put him in the tent housing that just went up on Long Street," Liam replied. "That should keep him for a month or so until more permanent housing is available."

"Excellent," Eoinn said. "Tell me about yerself, Danny, where are ye from? What brought ye to Idaho? What do ye do? What's your ambition for a career look like?"

Danny thought for a moment and said, "Well, I grew up outside Omaha, Nebraska, on a farm. Pa was a good man. He raised me and my sister right. Ma died giving birth to my sister, but I was only two years old, so I barely remember her. Sadly, my sister died of the Typhoid when she was thirteen. Pa was heartbroken, and a few years ago, he died from his sadness. After that, I sold the farm and came out here."

Eoinn nodded sympathetically, "I see, my condolences."

After pausing a moment, Danny continued. "As to what I want to do for work, sir, I'm not really sure. I'm not particular. I've done some mining and did okay with that. I've done some farming, and I can say that I'm good with animals. On the other hand, I'm a decent carpenter. I built several buildings both with my Pa and again here in Idaho. I'm not a great shot with a pistol, but I've never backed down from a fight. I'm a good shot with a rifle, and I can hunt. Pa made sure I knew how to read and cypher. I'm good with numbers, and I have been successful in a few businesses. I guess I'm open to whatever comes along."

Eoinn leaned back in his chair, the leather creaking. He studied Danny with eyes that seemed suddenly ancient.

"Ye'll need to understand how we operate here," Eoinn said. "We're not like any place ye've been before."

He reached into a desk drawer and pulled out a small, leather pouch. From it, he extracted several metal tokens, each stamped with the Crystal Village

Mining Company seal. They clinked as he set them on the desk between them.

"No cash inside our walls. These tokens—our scrip—handle what ye might need beyond the basics." He pushed the tokens toward Danny with a calloused finger. "Housing is provided. Food comes from the common kitchen. Mrs. O'Hara runs it like a general, and God help ye if ye make any suggestions for improvement."

Danny picked up one of the tokens, turning it over in his palm. The weight felt substantial, reassuring.

"Those are for you. Friday evenings, Angus handles the payroll. Ye'll get scrip based on your work. Lemieux's store stocks most anything a man needs. Anything exotic, Pierre can order it, though he'll talk your ear off about the trouble it causes him."

"And if I need something from outside?" Danny asked.

Eoinn's expression hardened slightly but then softened again. "If necessary, Angus can exchange limited amounts for currency. We prefer to keep our business internal."

Liam, who had been silent, cleared his throat. "Tell him about the long view, Eoinn."

Eoinn nodded, his eyes taking on a distant quality. "This is temporary. As the village grows, we're planning on establishing a proper bank. Then we'll move beyond scrip into official U.S. currency. The mine's proceeds build our infrastructure now, but eventually, quarterly dividends will flow to every resident. A share in what we build together."

He fixed Danny with an intense gaze. "This isn't just a mining camp. It's a new way of living. Everyone contributes, everyone benefits. No man gets rich off another man's labor here."

Danny nodded. "Seems more than fair, sir."

"Fair has nothing to do with it," Eoinn said, rising from his chair. But then his expression softened, his eyes focusing on Danny. "No. It's about building something that lasts beyond any one of us." He extended his hand and smiled warmly. "Welcome to Crystal Village, Danny. My son John will show ye around. Get your bearings before ye start working tomorrow."

"Thank you, sir." Danny said.

Liam clapped him on the shoulder as they walked out of Eoinn's office. "Don't mind Eoinn's intensity. He carries the weight of this place on his shoulders. Has since the beginning."

Liam called out into the room. "Sam, could ye please have John Seeley swing by the last tent on Long Street to meet Danny and take him on a tour to get him settled in?"

Sam waved at him, nodding. Without any further discussion, Liam led Danny back to the door where they grabbed Danny's pack and then out the door. Admittedly, Danny was in a bit of a daze, but he felt happier than he had in months. He followed Liam quietly down Broadway to Long Street, which was the second on the left heading back toward the bridge.

They walked toward the row of canvas tents that housed the newest arrivals. They passed the place where the crews had gotten to installing Belgian blocks in the street, with the pipes below them.

Danny clutched the tokens in his pocket. They represented something he'd hadn't had in some time—stability, perhaps even belonging.

I I I I

John Seeley led Danny through Crystal Village, his small boots kicking up dust from the half-finished street. Belgian blocks were being laid in precise rows, the new sections gleaming against the packed dirt. John was ten, with unruly, brown hair and clothes that showed signs of frequent mending.

"See those frames going up?" John pointed to a row of wooden skeletons rising from stone foundations. "That's gonna be a bank and a general store. Mr. Lemieux says we'll stock everything from boots to sugar candy."

The street buzzed with purposeful activity. Men and women carried lumber and tools, nodding to each other as they passed. No drunks sprawled in doorways. No painted women called from balconies. The air held the scent of fresh-cut pine and baking bread instead of whiskey and vomit.

"We have a small general store now," John explained. "Back by the stables. And over there—" he swung his arm toward a large, timber building with smoke rising from a stone chimney "—that's the meal hall where everybody eats together. Mrs. O'Hara runs the kitchen. She makes pies that'll make you weep. Dinner's in an hour."

They passed a field where several children played with a leather ball, their laughter carrying on the mountain air. Danny couldn't remember the last time he'd heard children laugh.

"Sometimes we play there," John said. "When we're not in school or helping with chores."

School. The word struck Danny as foreign. In most mining camps, children worked alongside adults or ran wild.

John led Danny along a faint path through tall grasses and thickets of wild rose. They climbed flat rocks that formed rough steps, turning past a clump of juniper. The path opened to a series of steaming pools fed by a spring that spilled from a cleft in the rock face. Vapor rose in wisps and plumes. The air carried a pleasant, mineral smell.

"These are the hot springs," John announced. "Best thing about Crystal Village. The water comes up hot from under the mountain."

A wooden shed stood nearby. "We keep towels and swimming clothes in there," John said, handing Danny a rough, linen towel and dark, woolen drawers. "Nobody swims naked except after dark."

John stripped down, revealing he already wore swimming drawers under his clothes. Danny changed quickly, conscious of the knife scar that ran from his shoulder to elbow, a souvenir from a Virginia City card game.

The water was warm enough to make Danny gasp as he eased himself in. Heat penetrated his travel-worn muscles. He sank to his neck, feeling the tension of the journey begin to dissolve.

John settled across from him, only his head visible above the water. "Pa says the springs are like magic. They make you forget all the bad things."

Danny doubted water could wash away the memories of what had happened in Eagle City, but he had to admit the heat was working on his body in ways that whiskey never had. His thoughts slowed. His breathing deepened.

After several minutes, Danny ducked his head under the water. The world disappeared into heat and pressure. When he surfaced, water streaming from his hair, he felt something he hadn't experienced in years, something that was starting to feel like home.

"Thank you, John," Danny said. "For showing me this place."

John smiled, his face flushed from the heat. "You're gonna like it here, Danny. We all take care of each other."

The meal bell rang in the distance, a clear tone that echoed off the mountainside. Danny listened to its fading resonance and realized he'd been holding his breath, waiting for gunshots or shouting to follow. But there was only the sound of the wind in the pines and water lapping against stone.

For the first time since he could remember, Danny felt safe.

I I I I

With the warmth of the hot springs still clinging to his skin and somewhat damp hair, Danny followed John back to the meal hall. The boy chattered excitedly about the neighbors walking into the hall, each with their own stories. Danny listened intently, absorbing the names and faces, committing them to memory as best he could.

As they entered the meal hall, the rich aroma of baked bread and hearty stew filled the air. The large room buzzed with the murmur of families gathered around communal tables, sharing the day's events and laughter. John led Danny to a serving table where a woman with kind eyes and a welcoming smile beckoned them over.

"This is Mrs. O'Hara," John introduced. "She's the best cook in the whole village!"

Mrs. O'Hara extended her hand to Danny. Her voice had that same Irish accent that Liam and Eoinn and Angus had. "Pleasure to meet ye, young man. Welcome to Crystal Village. Ye must be famished. Here, have some of this stew—it'll put the strength right back into ye."

Danny thanked her. As he ate, John bounced around, introducing Danny to anyone within earshot.

Soon, a blonde woman approached, her hair tied back in a practical bun, and flanking her, there was a young man and woman about his age. "Danny, this is Mrs. Elizabeth O'Connor and two of her children, Eva and Seamus. You met Seamus' wife, Sam earlier. Liam's off doing something important, as always," John said with a hint of mock seriousness.

Mrs. O'Connor extended a hand, her grip firm and confident. "Welcome, Danny. Liam's spoken highly of ye. We're glad you're here safe with us now."

Eva, a pretty young woman who was tall and thin, offered a shy smile, her eyes alight with a curiosity that matched her brother's. Seamus clapped Danny on the back with a grin. "Good to have another strong back around. There's always work to be done and fun to be had."

The meal passed in a blur of introductions and friendly exchanges. Danny felt enveloped by the generosity of the village. The laughter and camaraderie of the hall filled him with a profound sense of belonging.

As the evening drew to a close, John led Danny back to the tent on Long Street that would be his home for the foreseeable future. The tent was spacious and well-furnished and was set up on top of a raised platform, making it comfortable and dry.

"Thanks for everything today, John," Danny said, ruffling the boy's hair.

John beamed, "You're welcome, Danny. Sleep well. Tomorrow's another big day!"

With that, John scampered off into the night, leaving Danny to reflect on the unexpected turn his life had taken. Danny marveled as he climbed beneath the sheets on a real bed, and the sounds of the village carried him into a peaceful sleep.

I I I I

Danny woke early and went to the meal hall for breakfast. He was happy to see Liam, who greeted him warmly. When Danny expressed interest in joining a work crew, he quickly found himself amidst a bustling crew tasked with laying Belgian blocks on Broadway. The street was a hive of activity, the clatter of tools mingling with the voices of men as they worked under the morning sun. The work was laborious and precise, demanding a meticulous attention to detail that Danny was eager to learn, though he felt like a fish out of water in this new environment.

Egan Sullivan was in charge of overseeing the work. His instructions were direct and efficient, leaving little room for interpretation. "Listen up, lads," Egan called out, his voice carrying over the noise. "First, we lay the pipes for the hot spring water. Make sure they're aligned properly and secured. Then comes the gravel and sand substrate. It needs to be evenly spread and compressed. After that, we place the Belgian block, ensuring they're level. Finally, the finishing layer of sand to fill the gaps. Got it?"

Danny nodded along with the others, eager to prove himself. To his left, Tom Whitaker and Jeremiah Redding exchanged a glance, their expressions sour. Both men had been pulled from their usual duties to work on this project, and their dissatisfaction was obvious.

Jeremiah grumbled under his breath, his frustration bubbling to the surface. "This isn't what I signed up for, Egan. I'm a carpenter, not a laborer."

Egan, oblivious to the tension, continued with his instructions, seemingly unaware of Jeremiah's protest. "Make sure the blocks are tight. We can't afford gaps or uneven surfaces."

Jeremiah's patience snapped. "Egan, this is a waste of my skills! There are buildings that need my attention, and I'm stuck here laying blocks like some greenhorn!"

Egan turned to Jeremiah, his eyes wide and surprised. "We're all here to do what's needed, Jeremiah. This is important for the village, and everyone has a part to play."

Their exchange drew the attention of the rest of the crew. Danny watched, unsure of how to react. As a newcomer, he felt torn between respecting the established hierarchy and understanding the grievances of the villagers. Egan was a bit odd, clearly he wasn't someone who normally led crews of men, more of a thinker than a leader.

Tom Whitaker stepped forward. "Egan, maybe you should let those of us who know what we're doing focus on our strengths."

Egan looked at Tom with a mixture of confusion and irritation. "It's about what the village needs, Tom. We need this road, and we need it done right."

Before the argument could escalate further, Eoinn Seeley approached the group. He had been walking along Broadway, and the raised voices had caught his attention.

"Gentlemen, what's the issue here?" Eoinn asked, his tone calm but firm.

Jeremiah, emboldened by Tom's support, spoke up. "Eoinn, this isn't the best use of our skills. We have other projects that need attention, and we're being pulled away for this."

Eoinn considered Jeremiah's words, his expression thoughtful. "I understand your point, Jeremiah, but this road is part of the infrastructure that will support everything else we build. It's all interconnected."

Tom answered, "We're putting in this work, but what do we get in return? It's always about what's best for the village, but when do we get a say in how things run, in real meaningful decisions?"

Eoinn's eyes met Tom's, a flicker of frustration crossing his features. "You have a voice, Tom, and it's heard. But we must balance individual needs with the needs of the whole community."

Danny, observing the exchange, felt a pang of sympathy for both sides. He understood the desire for recognition and agency, yet he also saw the necessity of getting this road laid before winter.

Egan addressed the crew. "Let's get back to work. We have a deadline to meet, and the sooner we finish, the sooner we can move on to other projects."

As the men returned to their tasks, the atmosphere remained tense but focused. Eoinn watched for a few minutes, then continued on his way. Danny resumed his work, laying the blocks with renewed determination. He glanced at Jeremiah, who was muttering under his breath, and Tom, whose demeanor suggested he was far from satisfied.

IIII

The last vestiges of sunset were fading from the sky as Danny made his way to the hot springs. The air was crisp, and the promise of the steaming waters beckoned him forward. He had come to cherish these late evening soaks after a hard day's work.

He stepped into the pool, settled into a comfortable spot, closed his eyes, and let the tension of the day melt away. This had been his third day working with the crew installing granite Belgian Blocks on Broadway. He hadn't done that kind of work before, and he would be happy never to do so again, although he guessed that once they finished Broadway there wouldn't be much call for the skillset.

Of course, his exhaustion wasn't merely a result of the physical demands of the current job. There was also the effect of the thin air at this elevation. He was slowly getting used to living at such a high altitude. The first few days he'd been a bit parched, but now he was getting acclimatized. The trick seemed to be to keep drinking water throughout the day. One of the men on the crew had warned him the first day. "The air up here will suck the spit right out of you!" Teenage boys with water buckets and ladles followed the work crews closely. He was struck by how organized everything was here. Everything was planned, people cared about the quality of their work, and really seemed to watch out for each other.

The sound of approaching laughter stirred him from his reverie. Opening his eyes, he saw two figures making their way to the water's edge. As they drew closer, he realized that it was Sam O'Connor accompanied by Eva O'Connor, Liam's daughter. Eva was a vision of beauty to Danny, her cheeks flushed with the cool evening air and her laughter as they chatted. She shyly held back as Sam stepped forward.

"Evening, Danny," Sam greeted with a smile. "Mind if we join you? The springs are too lovely tonight to pass up."

"Not at all," Danny replied, his heart skipping a beat as he nodded to Eva. "The more, the merrier."

The women, dressed in dark woolen drawers and simple swim blouses—

practical yet demure garments for the occasion—slipped into the water with a shared giggle. The trio exchanged pleasantries and caught up on the day.

Sam playfully nudged the conversation towards the lighter side of village life. "You know, Danny, the young folk have a tradition of late-night swims here—completely skyclad," she said, using the local term for nude bathing. "It's quite the liberating experience, or so I've been told." Eva's eyes widened slightly, and Danny fancied he could see a blush creeping up her neck in the thickening darkness, but her smile remained. Danny found himself longing to know her more.

As they spoke, the sound of someone whistling cut through the night air. Seamus O'Connor strolled up to the springs. Without a hint of reservation, he shed all his clothes, revealing a lean and athletic form, and with a whoop of delight, leaped into the springs, disturbing the serene water with a playful splash. Eva let out a startled laugh, her eyes dancing with amusement at her brother's antics, while Sam shook her head with an affectionate roll of her eyes at her husband. "That's Seamus for you—no sense of modesty whatsoever."

Danny chuckled, the sight of Seamus's unabashed joy was infectious. In that moment, beneath the stars and amidst the laughter of new friends, he felt a sense of belonging.

As the night wore on, the four of them shared stories and dreams, the barriers of acquaintance falling away in the warm embrace of the hot springs. Danny found himself drawn to Eva, her quiet and gentle nature enticing and calming all at once. As they eventually said their goodnights, Danny wondered again at his luck at finding this place.

I I I I

As dawn's first light graced the mountain peaks, a hunting party organized by Mr. Lemieux and led by Liam O'Connor set out from Crystal Village, their spirits high and their steps light. The air was crisp and filled with the promise of the hunt. Among them was Danny, his eyes scanning the treeline for signs of game, his rifle resting comfortably across his folded arms.

For a brief time, the hunting party was accompanied by a group of women who were setting out to gather various items from the forest including pine nuts and mushrooms—both porcinis and the delicious morels that sometimes hid beneath the fallen leaves of the aspen groves. Eva O'Connor was one of these ladies, and she walked alongside the women who chattered about various topics of interest. Her basket swung from her arm, her gaze occasionally crossing the clearing and meeting Danny's with a spark of shared anticipation.

As expected, the groups eventually split, men and women veering off to their respective pursuits, the sound of laughter and camaraderie fading away as the parties separated. Among the hunters, Danny moved stealthily, his senses attuned to the rustle of feathers and the soft call of mountain quail. He took in the beauty of the high mountain forest, with its scraggly pines and the soft carpet of needles.

It wasn't long before Danny saw a mountain quail strutting awkwardly along underneath a thicket of trees. He moved around to the far side of the trees, threading his way through the woods until he got positioned to fire without putting any of the party in harm's way. As he scanned for any stray people, he saw a shadow move further up the ridge. A mountain lion, its tawny coat blending with the dappled sunlight, stalked closer, its golden eyes fixed on something. Danny sidled to the right to get a clearer view, and saw that the cat was positioning itself above the unsuspecting Eva. Danny's heart froze. He felt a shift in the air, his vision tunneled in on the big cat.

With deliberate care, he circled back, his boots making no sound. He caught sight of the cougar crouched low, its muscles coiled, ready to spring. Danny's heart pounded in his chest. He moved over towards the ridge line and prepared himself to interrupt the path of the cougar as it moved towards Eva, who strolled along obliviously about forty feet away from him. He raised his rifle, the weight familiar and reassuring in his hands, and took aim.

Eva walked towards the ridge line, where the view went on for a hundred miles. Her fingers brushed against the rough bark of a pine tree, when the hairs on the back of her neck suddenly stood up. She turned suddenly and saw the danger. A gasp escaped her lips as she locked eyes with the cat. Time seemed to slow as she stood frozen, the cougar's focus tangible in the air between them as it began to spring.

In that heartbeat, Danny's shot rang out, its sharp crack echoing against the mountainside. The bullet found its mark, hitting squarely on the cougar's shoulder. With a snarl of pain and surprise, the great cat lost its footing. It tumbled down the rocky edge of the ridge, its claws scrabbling for purchase.

The cougar tumbled over the side of the ridge, head over tail. Danny raced to Eva and grabbed her in a tight embrace. Their bodies pressed close in the aftermath of such a terrifying experience. In both adrenaline still courses through their veins. Eva's heart raced against Danny's, their breaths mingling in the cold morning air. Danny's hand trembled as he reached up, catching a loose strand of Eva's hair. Eva's response was a tender lean into his hand, her eyes locking with his in gratitude for his intervention.

The hunting party, alerted by the shot, converged upon them. Liam arrived, his face a mixture of relief and stern fatherly worry. He had seen the whole incident unfold and ran to them with urgency. But as he took in the scene, his expression softened, and he placed reassuring hands on both Danny and Eva's shoulders.

"Great job, Danny. I'm glad ye were here today," said Liam with relief. Eva reached out to her father, and they embraced.

As the two parties went back to their hunting and gathering work, Eva ran to Danny and gave him one last hug and a quick kiss on the cheek. "Thank you," she whispered softly.

12

Formation

Jack and Susanne sat in the same booth at Sam's Restaurant where they'd first spread out the contents of his great-grandfather's trunk just days earlier. The worn Formica table held only coffee cups and the remnants of breakfast.

"I can't believe you ordered that again," Susanne said, gesturing at Jack's empty plate with her fork. The chicken fried steak had been demolished with the same enthusiasm as before.

"What can I say? I'm a creature of habit." Jack grinned, stealing a piece of bacon from her plate. "Besides, you helped me finish it. *Again.*"

"Only because you're a terrible influence," she said with feigned annoyance. She swatted his hand away playfully, but not before he managed to snag another piece. "I'm going to have to start running marathons if I keep eating breakfast with you."

Jack leaned back in the booth, studying her face in the morning light streaming through the diner's windows. Three days of poring over family documents and planning their expedition to find Crystal Village had brought them closer. The shy glances and careful conversations of their first reunion had given way to an easy back and forth.

"So," he said, reaching across the table to brush a crumb from the corner of her mouth, "are you ready for our treasure hunt? I picked up those topographical maps yesterday, and I think I've identified at least three promising areas to explore."

Susanne's smile faltered slightly. She set down her coffee cup and looked out the window toward the mountains. "Actually, that's what I wanted to talk to you about."

Something in her tone made Jack straighten. "What's wrong?"

"Nothing's wrong, exactly. It's just ..." She turned back to him, her expression a mix of excitement and frustration. "My agent called last night. There's been a development with my books. Apparently, someone at Netflix has been reading my series. They want to talk about optioning it for a streaming show." The words came out in a rush, as if she couldn't quite believe them herself. "My agent wants me to fly out this afternoon to LA for meetings tomorrow."

"Susanne, that's incredible!" Jack reached across the table and took her hands. "This is huge! You must be thrilled."

"I am. I really am." Her fingers tightened around his. "But the timing couldn't be worse. I've been looking forward to going into the mountains with you, and now ..."

"Now you have to go chase your dreams," Jack finished for her. "Which is exactly what you should do."

Susanne's eyes searched his face. "You're not disappointed?"

"Disappointed that you're getting the recognition you deserve? That someone wants to turn your brilliant stories into a television show?" Jack shook his head. "I'm proud of you. And maybe a *little* jealous that Skylar and Jake are going to be famous."

A blush crept up Susanne's neck. "You know those characters are based on us, right? When we were teenagers?"

"I suspected as much." Jack's thumb traced across her knuckles. "Though I have to say, you made Jake much more heroic than I ever was in real life."

"You were plenty heroic. You just never knew it."

They sat for a moment, the weight of unspoken feelings settling between them.

"How long will you be gone?" Jack asked finally.

"Just a couple of days." She pulled one hand free to run it through her hair. "My agent told me that the first meeting is just to begin a conversation, and if it goes well, we'll need to stay over for another night. I can't believe I've got this kind of opportunity."

"You deserve it, you've been working hard on this for years," Jack said firmly.

Susanne leaned forward, her voice dropping to almost a whisper. "What if this changes everything?"

The question hung in the air between them. Jack felt something shift in his chest, a recognition of how much her presence had come to mean to him in just a few short days.

"Then I'll be happy for you," he said, meaning it. "You know that Netflix's main office is in Los Gatos, only a short drive from Oakland where I work? And their LA offices are where most of the entertainment stuff happens. I lived in LA for fifteen years when I worked for Disney. I'm pretty comfortable there."

She smiled, but her eyes looked suspiciously bright. "I guess I hadn't realized that. You could come with me for the trip if you like."

Jack considered it for a moment, then shook his head. "This is your moment, Susanne. You don't need me tagging along, playing the role of supportive friend while you're trying to impress television executives."

"Is that what you are? A supportive friend?"

He froze. The question caught him off guard. He looked at their joined hands, at the way her thumb was now tracing patterns on his palm, at the way she was looking at him like the answer mattered more than anything else in the world.

"I hope I'm more than that," he said quietly. "But I also don't want to complicate things for you right now."

Susanne was quiet for a long moment, studying his face.

"I'm going to go for these meetings. To see what's possible. But then

I'm coming back to the people who matter."

"And I matter?" Jack asked, his heart hammering against his ribs.

"You matter," she said simply. "More than I probably should admit before getting on a plane to chase my dreams."

Jack lifted their joined hands and kissed her knuckles. "Then go chase your dreams. And when you're ready, come back, and help me find our lost village. It's waited over a century. It can wait a little longer."

Susanne laughed, the sound slightly shaky. "You shouldn't wait. I know you only have a few weeks left on your vacation. And if you find it, we can go back up there together! And if things work out with Netflix, maybe I'll be coming to California on a regular basis."

"Either way, we're going to find a way to spend time together," Jack said. "I promise."

She pulled her hands free and reached for her keys and phone. "I should go. I need to pack, and my flight leaves from Spokane this afternoon."

They stood together, the moment suddenly awkward as the reality of her departure settled between them. Jack wasn't sure if he should hug her, kiss her, or simply wave goodbye.

Susanne solved the problem by stepping forward and wrapping her arms around his waist. She fit perfectly against him, her head tucked under his chin.

"Find the village if you can," she murmured against his chest.

"I'll try," he replied, breathing in the scent of her shampoo.

She pulled back just far enough to look up at him. "And Jack? When I come back, maybe we can figure out what this is."

"I'd like that," he said, and then he leaned down and kissed her.

It was soft and brief and tasted like coffee. When they broke apart, Susanne's cheeks were flushed and her eyes were bright.

"That's definitely going to make it harder to concentrate in meetings," she said.

"Good," Jack replied with a grin.

"Good," she said and turned toward the door.

Jack watched her walk away, noting the confident set of her shoulders and the spring in her step. She turned back once at the door, gave him a wave that was equal parts excitement and regret, and then she was gone.

He sat back down in the booth and signaled the waitress for more coffee. Outside the window, the mountains beckoned. He'd explore them alone if he had to, but he found himself already counting the time until Susanne would return.

13

Reward

Sam and Seamus walked arm in arm down Broadway, admiring the decorations. The road was clear of snow due to the ingenious laying of pipes under the cobblestones that pumped water from the hot springs. The snow would melt as fast as it fell and leave the street clear for passage. The side streets still needed to be shoveled, but this long, beautiful street lined with stately buildings made from brick and stone was a respite in winter where people could take long walks. The air was cold, and a light, powdery snow was falling. The railings of the porches were strung with garlands of pine and other evergreens. Giant wreaths hung from second floor balconies, and a large evergreen fir tree had been cut down and then set up in the square at Broadway and Spring Street. It was absolutely covered in decorations, red bows and tin ornaments, and someone had strategically placed some of the lanterns from the mines into spots within the tree, lighting it beautifully.

The electrification of Crystal Village had started the year before. Several Pelton water wheels and large General Electric dynamos had been installed in various locations where pressurized springs exited the mountain and also down in the river at the bottom of the ravine. The electric street lamps that Egan had teams working on all summer were temporarily colored red and green, hand colored. The hotels had purchased the new GE string lights and hung them around the inside of their windows. The whole town had a magical feel, the roofs of the buildings white with snow, the green garland everywhere, the children running to and fro throwing snowballs at each other. A group of carolers were going from house to house singing songs of the season.

They arrived at their new home, a townhouse with three floors and six bedrooms, located on the west side of Broadway, near Long Street. They walked into the house, entering the front hallway that had a parlor off to the left and her office to the right. As they walked down the hallway into the interior of the house, they encountered a sitting room that was decorated for the holiday. The star of the show was a well-decorated Christmas tree, strung with electric lights. It was positioned to the left of the fireplace, yet it was situated far enough away that the fire wouldn't dry it out. The fire itself was cheerful but small, made up mostly of banked coals and one large log pushed all the way to the back. Seven stockings were hung on the mantle. From the back she could hear Mrs. O'Hara working in the kitchen. She yelled out, "Hello, family! We're home!"

From upstairs she could hear the thundering of little feet as the youngest children ran down to meet them. The tradition they had was for each person to open one gift on Christmas Eve, and this was Sam's favorite night of the year. Sam and Seamus had five children. The oldest, Henry, was fifteen. Susanne was second oldest, she was twelve. Next were the twins, Albert and Andrew, who were nine, and the youngest, Glory was five years old.

Mrs. O'Hara came out of the kitchen. She often cooked for the family and did a little cleaning. She was like a grandmother to the children. She'd moved in with them after retiring from her job running Mrs' O's restaurant and maintaining logistics for the whole village. She had a bedroom on the first floor, next to the kitchen. For years, everyone had hoped she would end up with Mr. Lemieux, but Pierre had died unexpectedly of a heart attack in his late sixties. Sam's family was more than happy to have her come to live with them.

The children all came and sat in the sitting room, and Seamus went into the front office and carried a large bag of presents into the room. He sat down next to Sam, and they handed out the gifts together. They gave each of the children their Christmas Eve present in reverse order of age, since the littlest always had trouble being patient. The children were understandably exuberant, each holding up their special gift for all to see. Finally, after all the children had received the present and had calmed down, the family gave Mrs. O'Hara her gift. It was a brightly wrapped box containing a bracelet of finely woven strands of silver, silver being her favorite metal. Seamus had crafted it for her. He was a gold and silver smith, an expert at working with precious metals, and his handiwork was available in his jewelry shop across town. Next it was Sam's turn. Seamus gave Sam a gift of a fine set of pens. Finally, Sam presented Seamus with his gift—a brand new knife for his belt.

With the gifts distributed and the annual tradition upheld, everyone enjoyed some fresh cookies that Mrs. O'Hara had baked. The children set out a plate of them out for Santa Claus. Mrs. O'Hara put a second plate of baked treats on the mantel, this one for the Fairies. It had a little fruit cake, a cookie, and two, small, silver cups with milk. The children gathered around for Mrs. O to tell them a story, another tradition that had developed over the last few years.

"Gather 'round, children," Mrs. O'Hara said in a hushed, almost reverential voice. "Let me tell ye a Christmas tale my grandmother used to share with me when I helped in her kitchen. Mind ye, she had quite the imagination, that one.

"Many years ago, our family kept the provisions store in Bangor, and my grandmother's restaurant sat right next door. As you can imagine, Christmas Eve was always bustling—the store filled with last-minute shoppers and wonderful smells drifting over from grandmother's kitchen.

"Now on one particular Christmas Eve, Gran told me she'd seen something peculiar in the back room. Gran had seen a tiny man in a red coat with green trim! He was sitting at her sewing table, mending a pile of children's shoes! Now all these shoes actually belonged to the Murphy children, whose father had lost his job at the mill only a couple of months previously.

"'He worked with such speed,' Gran'd say, her eyes twinkling, 'that his hands were nearly invisible. When he noticed me watching, he gave me the quickest wink and kept right on working.'

"The next morning, Gran found those shoes wrapped neat as ye'd like near the front door, each one perfectly mended and polished. Inside each shoe was a bright gold sovereign! My grandmother took those shoes straight to the Murphy house herself.

"Now, my father always said it was grandmother who mended those shoes late into the night. But she'd just smile and say, 'Perhaps. Or perhaps some magic finds its way into kind hearts at Christmas.'

"Years later, when I asked why she told me that story, she laughed and said, 'Mary, dear, sometimes the best magic isn't about what's real or make-believe—it's about the stories that remind us to be generous.'"

Mrs. O'Hara adjusted the plate of treats on the mantel with a knowing smile. "And that's why we leave these offerings on Christmas Eve. Just in case."

Glory asked Mrs. O'Hara to put her to bed and tell her more stories. Of course, Mrs. O'Hara consented, as she was unable to refuse the little child any good thing. At that Glory, ran over to hug and kiss her parents before being whisked away by Mrs. O. The other children lined up to kiss their parents good night, and marched off to bed. After settling the house for the night and doing their parental duties of laying gifts under the tree, Sam and Seamus said goodnight to Mrs. O'Hara, who was just then making her way downstairs. After an exchange of Christmas pleasantries, Mrs O'Hara went off to her bedroom, and Sam and Seamus went up to bed.

The couple's room was on the second floor of the townhouse. It had large windows and a set of doors that opened out onto the balcony, which was what they called the porch that ran the whole length of the block. It was like a second-storey sidewalk, two levels up. At the point where each building ended on the higher floors, the railing that ran along the front of the balcony turned and blocked access between the buildings. This was mostly for privacy. Some of these corner railings had gates in them, but as Sam and Seamus' home abutted the Hawthorne Hotel, theirs didn't have a gate. Instead the barrier was a beautiful floor-to-ceiling, metal screen made of copper and bronze that looked like lattice, with vines growing on it. The screen's patinated copper showed up as the green of the vines, and its dark bronze showed up as squares of lattice.

As was her habit, Sam stepped out on the balcony in her nightgown and robe before going to bed. She walked to the edge of the balcony and leaned out to look up and down the street. Silently, she thanked her seven benefactors, the men who had found her and raised her up. Then she came in to climb into bed with Seamus. He had taken the bed warmer—a huge bottle of water with a handle that they left on top of the hot-spring-fed radiator—and run it over the bedclothes, warming them before they got in. This little ritual had started when they first were married, in the old cabin they shared after they first wed.

They turned off the electric lights and climbed into bed. After sleeping for an hour or so, Sam was awakened by a small voice. She rolled over and opened her eyes to see Glory next to the bed.

"Mum, can you get me a drink of water and tuck me back in, please?" pleaded Glory.

Sam groaned internally but smiled and said, "Of course, sweetest. Let's get you settled in."

She got out of bed and scooped up her littlest one. Glory was tiny, with a body all skin and bones and a largish head, with fair blonde hair. The child snuggled up against Sam, who carried her up the stairs to the nursery she still shared with the twins. Sam laid her down in her bed and filled a cup with water from the bathroom adjoining the room. She sat on the edge of Glory's bed and helped her drink her water without spilling it.

"Thank you, Mum," whispered Glory. "I'm sorry to wake you, but I saw the girl outside my window again. I know you said she's not real, but she was eating a cookie, sitting on the railing."

Sam said, "Ah, Glory, you were dreaming, sweetness. But I'll go look just so we can be sure."

Sam winked at Glory, got up, and walked to the window. She looked out onto the fourth floor balcony, which was just the roof of the third floor balcony, and she saw tiny footprints in the snow. They were made by small feet, larger than Glory's but smaller than an adult. They traced a path around the balcony, entering from the right and leaving to the left. But it was clear that the person who left the footprints had paused to look in the windows. Then they walked over to the railing of the balcony, which now had a spot on the top of the railing where the snow had been wiped clean.

Sam was alarmed but didn't show it. She sat back on the bed, whispered to Glory that she should go back to sleep, and waited for her breathing to change before she got up. Satisfied that Glory was asleep, she walked back over to the windows and checked all three to make sure they were locked. To her relief, all three windows were locked. However, when she looked out again, she saw a huge raven sitting on the railing looking at her. It croaked once, and then jumped up into the air and flew away.

I I I I

September 4th, 1906

To: Capt. Eoinn Seeley, Retired
  From: Washington A. Roebling

Dearest Eoinn,

It was such a pleasure finally to come out to see your astonishing Crystal Village. I have had adequate time to reflect as I traveled back to New York by train. I so thoroughly enjoyed seeing you and your lovely Rose and meeting your son John for the first time. To see the village in reality, to travel the length of the country to get there, to ride the carriage up from Wallace into the mountains, and to cross that lovely bridge that my father and I designed, and to cross over the ravine and into the arms of your town was just breathtaking. The greatest disappointment was that I had waited so long, and that my Emily did not live long enough to accompany me on the trip.

As much as I miss her, and as saddened as I have been by her loss, this trip was a balm to my soul. It has helped me grow and has matured that loss to more of a dull ache and less of a sharp wound. I am back here in Troy, and I am spending time with the fine members of the Rensselaer Polytechnic Institute Alumni Association. But my mind wanders back to the streets of your village, and the spectacle of a modern but antique looking town in the wilds of the West just tickles me in the strangest way.

I do believe that my favorite moment of the entire trip was seeing the hot springs in Crystal Cave for the first time, and the ensuing visits to the cave and those springs were rejuvenating and enthralling. I thank you for enabling my passion for rocks, gems, and minerals, and please pass my sincerest thanks to your son John for taking the time to help me find exactly the specimens I was seeking.

Of course, my favorite part of the trip was spending time with you, the men of your company, and your families as we reminisced about the days of the War, and as we told each other stories of the days since. I know that my father was looking down on this reunion. How much he would have approved of what you have accomplished there in Crystal Village! Your ability to inspire and build such a great community and to lead it to success and long life is clearly unsurpassed in the history of intentional communities.

It is with fond memories and a slight melancholy that I say farewell,

Wash

Washington A. Roebling
Troy, New York

I I I I

June 29th, 1908

Jeremiah Redding and Tom Whitaker walked purposefully along Broadway engaged in a deep discussion. They had spent the morning complaining to each other about the recently disclosed plans for growth in the village. As they approached Monsieur Lemieux's General Store, they saw John Seeley and Joshua O'Connor standing and chatting pleasantly. "Look there," Jeremiah said, nodding toward the two young men. "That's Eoinn's son and Liam's boy. Let's see if they have anything worthwhile to say about the latest decisions."

Tom nodded, his jaw set with determination. "Same old thing. It's time they heard us, Jeremiah. For years, it seems as if we are being heard. Little by little, Eoinn showed signs that he was taking our concerns seriously. Here and there small changes get made, but then all of a sudden, he reverses course and makes these sweeping decisions!"

The men met on the street alongside the boardwalk, right at the spot where the general store had set some tables and racks outside in the sun to showcase some items that were being featured for sale. The air was alive with the chatter of villagers, but as Jeremiah and Tom approached John and Henry, a hush fell over those nearby, sensing the tension that crackled between them.

"John!" Jeremiah called out, his voice carrying a hint of challenge. "Got a moment to talk? I'd like to hear your thoughts on the recent plans your father put forward."

John turned to face them, his expression guarded. "Jeremiah, Tom. What can I do for you?"

Jeremiah wasted no time cutting to the heart of the matter. "It's about your father's plans for the mines and expanding the village. Once again, decisions are being made without any discussion with the rest of us. Look, John, we work just as hard, if not harder, and we deserve a say in how things are run."

John shifted uncomfortably, the weight of his father's legacy pressing down on him. "I understand your concerns, Jeremiah, but these decisions are made with the village's best interests in mind."

Tom stepped forward, his voice laced with frustration. "You're great at repeating your father's party line! Who decides what's in the village's best interest? It's always the same people making all the calls, while the rest of us are left to follow orders!"

Joshua, who was John's closest friend and who had been listening quietly, now spoke up, his tone measured but firm. "I understand where you're coming from, Tom, but the Original Eight have been leading this village since it was founded. They've seen us through tough times and know what's needed. If you have concerns, or ideas, just talk to any one of them. Or all of them."

Jeremiah's eyes narrowed, his patience wearing thin. "We're not questioning their past contributions, Josh, but times are changing. We need new blood involved in the decisions. Representation. A voice in the decisions that affect us all!"

Josh met Jeremiah's gaze, unwavering. "And you think bullying John into submission is the way to get it? This village was built on principles. Our way isn't about tearing things down, it's about building together. We need to find common ground, not resort to intimidation."

Tom bristled at Henry's words, his temper flaring. "We're not bullying anyone! We're standing up for what's right, for the future of our families!"

Josh remained calm, his voice steady. "By trying to strong-arm John, you're only creating division. We need to work together, find a way to give everyone a voice without undermining the progress we've made."

The crowd around them had grown, villagers drawn by the confrontation. Some nodded in agreement with Josh, while others murmured their support for Jeremiah and Tom.

Jeremiah felt his frustration boiling over, his vision narrowing as he locked eyes with John. "You talk about progress, but all I see is a system that benefits a select few! We need change, and we're not going to sit by and wait for it!"

John's hesitation was evident, the weight of his father's expectations heavy on his shoulders. He opened his mouth to speak, but Joshua interjected.

"Change doesn't come from tearing each other down," Josh said, his gaze unwavering. "It comes from communication, from understanding, compromise, and respect. We all want a better future, but we need to find a way to achieve it together."

Tom's anger simmered beneath the surface, his fists clenching at his sides. "You're naive if you think things will change without pressure. We've been arguing this point for decades. We're not asking for much—just a fair share in helping to shape what we've built together!"

Joshua held his ground, his voice calm but resolute. "And you have a right to speak your piece but not at the expense of the community's harmony. Go and talk directly to Eoinn and the others of the Original Eight. They're reasonable and will listen. But backstabbing folks, gossiping, going after John, and trying to divide him from his da' is not the way. You're better than this, Tom."

The crowd watched as the two sides faced off. "Enough," Jeremiah said, his voice low and edged with defiance. "Every time we try to discuss this with Eoinn he just shuts us down. He's not interested in any kind of self-governance! This isn't a democracy, it's Eoinn's own little kingdom! If he isn't going to entertain any change in the way we make decisions, we'll find another way to make our voices heard."

With that, Jeremiah and Tom turned on their heels, striding away from the square, their anger evident in every step. The villagers watched them go, a sense of unease settling over the crowd.

Joshua watched them leave, a mixture of relief and trepidation in his heart. He turned to John, placing a reassuring hand on his shoulder. "We need to talk with your da' about this. He's got to know that there's a storm brewing. We have to make him listen."

John nodded, grateful for Joshua's support but aware of the challenges that lay ahead. Truth be told, he was more inclined to agree with the dissenters than with his own father. He heard echoes of his own arguments with his father in what these men were saying.

"Maybe we can go talk to Finn," said John. "At least, he listens."

Joshua stood thinking, as the crowd that had gathered began to disperse. He rubbed his jaw and muttered, "Maybe Sam can help. She seems to be good at getting Eoinn's ear."

I I I I

The afternoon sun slanted through the tall windows of the Seeley home, casting geometric patterns across the polished hardwood floors. John Seeley stood in the doorway of his mother's sitting room, his shoulders rigid with tension. Rose looked up from her embroidery, the delicate white threads forming intricate patterns on the linen stretched across her wooden hoop. Her curly, dark hair had gone steel gray, with the occasional pure-white hair running through the curls, like lightning.

"Come in," she said, setting her work aside. "You look as though you're carrying the weight of the mountain on your shoulders."

John entered the room but remained standing, his hands clenched at his sides. The familiar scents of his childhood surrounded him—his mother's lavender water, the beeswax polish on the furniture, the faint aroma of bread rising in the kitchen. However, his frustration overwhelmed these positive memories.

"I don't know what to do, Mother." His voice cracked slightly, betraying the boy he'd once been. "I feel caught between two sides, and neither one will listen to reason."

Rose gestured to the chair beside her, a piece upholstered in deep-blue velvet that had been his favorite spot as a child when fever or nightmares had driven him to seek her comfort. "Sit with me. Tell me what's troubling you."

John remained standing, pacing to the window that overlooked Broadway. Below, villagers went about their daily business, children chasing a wooden hoop down the cobblestones.

"It's Father," John said, his back still turned to his mother. "And

Jeremiah. And Tom. And half the village, it seems." He pressed his palm against the cool glass. "They cornered me today. Jeremiah and Tom, I mean. Right there in front of everyone."

Rose's expression grew concerned. "What did they want?"

John turned from the window, his face flushed with frustration. "The same thing they always want. A voice in how the village is run. Ownership of their homes. Some say in the decisions that affect their families and their long-term financial legacy." He ran his hands through his hair. "And the terrible thing is, Mother, I think they're right."

The admission hung in the air between them. Rose studied her son's face, seeing the conflict that tore at him.

"You think your father is wrong?" she asked gently.

"I think—" John's voice broke, and he sank into the blue chair, burying his face in his hands. "I think Father built something beautiful here, but he can't see that it's grown beyond what one man can manage—or even should manage!"

Rose reached over and placed her hand on his arm. "Tell me what happened today."

John lifted his head, his eyes bright with unshed tears. "Jeremiah and Tom approached Joshua and me outside Lemieux's. They were angry, Mother. Angrier than I've ever seen them. They said Father makes all the decisions without consulting anyone. That we're living in his 'little kingdom,' as Jeremiah put it."

"And what did you say?"

"Nothing." The word came out as barely a whisper. "I stood there like a fool while Joshua defended the Original Eight. While he talked about building together and finding common ground." John's hands clenched into fists. "But what common ground can there be when one side holds all the power?"

Rose was quiet for a long moment, her fingers tracing the pattern on her embroidery hoop. "Your father has carried this village on his shoulders for forty years, John. Every decision, every risk, every burden—he's borne it all."

"I know that!" John said, his voice rising. "I know what he's sacrificed. What you've both sacrificed. But that doesn't mean he should carry it forever. Or that he can, he's not immortal. And it doesn't mean other good people shouldn't have a say in their own lives."

"And you've tried to discuss this with him?"

John let out a bitter laugh. "Have you tried to discuss anything with Father when his mind is made up? He sees any questioning of his authority as betrayal. As ingratitude for everything he's built."

Rose sighed, recognizing the truth in her son's words. Eoinn's strength had created their world, but his inflexibility was legendary.

"He loves this place," she said softly. "Sometimes, I think he loves it more than anything else in the world."

"More than us?" The question escaped before John could stop it, raw and painful.

Rose's heart clenched at the hurt in her son's voice. "Oh, John. No. Never more than us. But his love for the village and his love for his family are so entwined in his mind that he can't separate them. To him, protecting the village is protecting us."

"But what if protecting the village means listening to the people who live here? What if it means sharing the responsibility instead of hoarding it?"

Rose stood and moved to the window, gazing down at the street. "You know, when we first came here, your father was our leader, yes, but we all had voices. Somewhere along the way, as the village grew and prospered, that changed."

"You see it too, then. The problem."

"I see a man who's afraid," Rose said, turning back to her son. "Afraid that if he loosens his grip, everything he's built will crumble. Afraid that the people he's protected and provided for will make choices that destroy what he sees as perfect."

John stood and joined his mother at the window. "But it's not perfect, is it? Not if people are unhappy. Not if families are talking about leaving."

"No," Rose agreed. "It's not perfect. But I've lived in other places, John. And it's by far the most perfect place I've lived."

They stood in silence, watching the life of the village unfold below them.

"I don't know how to talk to him about this," John said finally. "Every time I try, he shuts me down. He tells me I don't understand the complexities of leadership, that I don't see the bigger picture."

Rose placed her hand on her son's arm. "You're thirty-four years old, John. You're a grown man with a wife and child of your own. You have every right to voice your concerns about the community where you're raising your family."

"Then why does he make me feel like a child every time I disagree with him?"

"Because he's afraid of losing you too," Rose said quietly. "Afraid that if you start questioning his decisions, you'll eventually question your place here. Your place in the family."

John stared at his mother in surprise. "That's not ... I would never ..."

"I know that," Rose replied. "You know that. But your father sees threats everywhere these days. The mines are playing out. Young people are leaving for opportunities in the cities. He feels the world changing around him, and change has never been easy for Eoinn Seeley."

"So what do I do? How do I reach him?"

Rose was quiet for a long moment, considering their options. When she spoke, her voice was firm but gentle. "You approach him not as his subordinate but as his heir. Not as someone asking permission but as someone offering partnership."

"I don't understand."

"Your father built this village, John, but you're going to inherit it. Whether he likes it or not, whether he's ready or not, the future of Crystal Village rests with your generation. He needs to hear that you're not trying to tear down what he's built—you're trying to ensure it survives and thrives."

John felt a spark of hope. "You think he'll listen?"

"I think he'll have to, eventually. But you have to be strong. You have to stand up to him not in anger or frustration but with the confidence of a man who knows his own mind." Rose cupped her son's face in her hands, the way she had when he was small. "You are not your father, John. You don't have to lead the way he leads. But you do have to lead."

Tears finally spilled down John's cheeks. "I'm scared. Scared I'll disappoint him. Scared I'll make the wrong choices. Scared I'll destroy everything he's worked for."

"Oh, my dear." Rose pulled him into her arms, and for a moment he was seven years old again, seeking comfort after a nightmare. "Fear is not the enemy of good leadership—arrogance is. The fact that you're afraid of making mistakes means you'll be careful with the trust people place in you."

They held each other in the golden afternoon light, mother and son finding strength in their connection. Finally, John pulled back, wiping his eyes.

"Will you talk to him?" he asked. "Before I try again?"

Rose nodded. "After the Independence Day celebration. Let him enjoy the holiday, see the village at its best. Then I'll help him understand that the village's strength comes not from his control but from the love and commitment of its people."

"And if he won't listen?"

Rose's expression grew resolute. "Then you'll do what you must do as a leader. You'll find a way forward that honors the past while embracing the future. You'll remember that this village was built by people working together, and it will only survive if people continue to work together."

John stood straighter, feeling some of the weight lift from his shoulders. "Thank you, Mother."

"Thank you for caring enough to fight for what's right, even when it's difficult." Rose picked up her embroidery again, but her eyes remained on her son. "Now go home to Mary and little John. Hold your family close, and remember what you're fighting for."

As John left the sitting room, Rose remained at her window, watching the village she'd helped nurture from its earliest days. She was concerned about this rift forming in the village. And she was concerned that her son hadn't grown into the confident man she'd seen him growing into when he was a child. Eoinn didn't raise John to stand on his own, he raised him to follow his lead. John wasn't who he could have been, who he still could be with the right support. She felt that she'd failed John to some degree, but recognized he was a grown man who needed to find his own way through the world.

She pressed her hand to her chest, feeling the irregular flutter that had been troubling her more frequently of late. There was so much still to do, so many bridges to build between the past and the future. She could only pray she'd have time to help her husband and son find their way to each other. John was so different from his father, so unsure of himself. So caught up in emotion.

The sound of children's laughter drifted up from the street, and Rose smiled despite her worries. Whatever came next, Crystal Village would endure.

I I I I

July 4th, 1908

Independence Day preparations were well underway. The scent of fresh pine commingled with the mouthwatering aroma of sweet pastries and savory meats being baked and grilled for the day's festivities.

The usually calm streets were abuzz with activity as villagers adorned their homes and the public square with red, white, and blue bunting. Children laughed and scampered about, their hands were already sticky with sweets. A group of boys were rolling hoops down Broadway. Many of the children were dressed in red, white and blue or other celebratory accessories.

Eoinn Seeley stood on the balcony of his stately brick home, surveying the scene below. Beside him, his wife Rose shared her warm smile.

As the day progressed, the square across from the mining office became the heart of the celebration. A platform had been erected for speakers, and Eoinn was scheduled to address the crowd. His speech would be one of cultivating a sense of gratitude, reflection on the community's many accomplishments, and hope for the future. He wanted to offer a reminder of the freedoms they cherished and the bonds that held their community together.

White-haired Liam O'Connor, still spry and healthy, still the heart and muscle of the village, worked alongside his fellow villagers. Together they set up the games and competitions that would entertain young and old alike. His grown children, Susanne, Joshua, Eva and Seamus, were eager organizers of the day. His grandchildren, much like the others in the village, were excited for the upcoming festivities, sack races, pie-eating contests, and the much-anticipated tug-of-war. And of course, everyone was excited about the fireworks display that would be fired off just after dark.

Across the square, fifty-year-old Sam King O'Connor moved through the crowd with ease. She was a respected leader in the community, and her keen eye ensured that everything was in place.

At six o'clock, Eoinn Seeley, with Rose at his side, addressed the village.

"Friends, on this day, we celebrate not just the birth of our nation but the strength and beauty of our community. Crystal Village stands as a beacon of hope, a place where freedom and unity reign. Let us never forget the sacrifices made for our independence and our freedom, and let us always strive to uphold the values that make this village so special."

The crowd erupted in cheers, their voices joining together in a chorus of gratitude and pride.

The setting sun bathed Crystal Village in a warm, golden light. Music pulsed through the square, couples swaying on the makeshift dance floor. Sizzling meats and buttery corn scented the air as volunteers served a continuous feast.

In the midst of it all, Eoinn and Rose Seeley stood together. Eoinn surveyed the scene with a contented smile. They greeted friends and newcomers alike. They revelled in the tight-knit community they had nurtured.

Not far from them, Danny and Eva Miller strolled along with their son, Ned, now ten years old and brimming with youthful energy. He zigzagged between the adults, occasionally joining packs of roving children who darted in and out of the crowd.

After sunset, the square stood illuminated by the soft glow of lanterns. Each structure, from the stately Seeley residence to the cozy homes that lined the side streets, was adorned with patriotic decor.

John Seeley and his wife Mary, the daughter of Angus Sullivan, made their way through the crowd, pausing to exchange pleasantries with neighbors and friends. Their son, John Jr. toddled along behind.

At a corner table of the lively café, Finn and Egan Sullivan raised their glasses in salute to the village and its people. These men had helped shape the very stones of Crystal Village more than any others, and now they sat back to enjoy the fruits of their labor, their faces aglow with pride and satisfaction.

Nearby, Mrs. O'Hara, the matriarch of the meal hall and a beloved figure in the village, leaned on her cane as she was escorted by Glory O'Connor, her ever-vigilant attendant. Despite the weight of years, Mrs. O'Hara's spirit remained undiminished, her eyes sparkling as she took in the sights and sounds of the celebration.

Sean and Colin, inseparable as ever, strolled along the street arm in arm. They wore matching boater hats with flat crowns and a round flat brim, adorned with red, white and blue striped ribbons. They frequently were stopped by their neighbors for hugs and to snuggle babies that Colin had delivered to the world.

There, in the center of it all, stood Eoinn and Rose Seeley, hand in hand. The anticipation for the night's fireworks display was tangible, a collective breath held as villagers and guests alike turned their gazes skyward. Children clutched the hands of their parents, their eyes wide with delight. The music swelled, and villagers gathered in the streets. A hush fell over the crowd as the first rocket soared heavenward, exploding into a cascade of shimmering color that reflected in the eyes of every onlooker.

It was at this moment, as the sky bloomed with the brilliance of a hundred flowers of fire, that Rose Seeley's grip on Eoinn's hand tightened unexpectedly. Her breath caught, and a pallor spread across her features.

Eoinn turned to her with concern, his own heart skipping a beat at the sight of her distress.

"Rose, what is it?" Eoinn's voice was steady, but the worry that creased his brow betrayed his fear.

Rose attempted a smile, "It's nothing, Eoinn ... just a little faint, is all."

But as she swayed, Eoinn knew it was more than a momentary weakness. With a swift motion, he swept her into his arms, his body showing unexpected strength for a man of his years, as he moved her to a nearby bench.

The celebration of those villagers who were nearby paused as they took notice, their joy giving way to concern. John and his wife rushed to their side.

"Fetch Colin," Eoinn commanded, his voice carrying an authority that mobilized the community into action. John ran over to where he'd last seen him. As if blissfully unaware of the drama that was playing out, the fireworks continued.

Sean emerged from the crowd, Colin by his side. Together, they reached Rose, Colin's practiced hands working swiftly to assess her condition. A hush fell over the nearest onlookers as Rose was carefully carried away.

The fireworks continued, their beauty bittersweet as the news of Rose's collapse swept quickly through the village. In that moment, the true strength of Crystal Village was on display—not in the grandeur of its celebration but in the solidarity and love of its people.

I I I I

As the soft rays of the morning sun filtered through the delicate curtains, the room held a somber stillness. Eoinn Seeley, his once robust frame now hunched with the weight of concern, sat beside the bed, his eyes never leaving the frail figure of his wife. Her breaths, once even and strong, now came in shallow, labored gasps, each one a fragile thread tethering her to the world they had built together.

Colin entered the bedroom with a quiet grace. He approached Rose and gently but thoroughly examined her, his heart aching for the woman who had become the village's matron.

Outside the bedroom door, the muted tones of a heated discussion ebbed and flowed. John Seeley spoke with urgency. Beside him, Finn's more seasoned timbre, thickened with the wisdom of eighty-odd years, provided a grounding counterpoint.

Finn looked back at him thoughtfully, a furrow forming on his brow. "I share your sentiment, lad. We are at a crossroads, and the path we choose now may very well define the legacy of Crystal Village."

"Finn, the whispers grow louder each day. People are speaking of depleted veins. Young folks are ready to start their life, and they're not looking to do it here," said John emphatically.

Finn nodded slowly. "Aye, but we mustn't act in haste. Eoinn's vision has steered us true for so long; we owe it to him to proceed with care. He has ideas about other industry we can make beyond mining. Just give him time."

In the adjoining room, Sam stood with the Sullivan brothers. The brothers' hair and beards were salt and peppered and their formerly red hairs were now bright white. What was once dark brown was now a steel gray. The gravity of the moment was not lost on them, as they too sensed the changing tide. Sean entered the room quietly and enveloped Sam in a comforting embrace. His silver hair caught the light coming in the windows. Their shared sorrow needed no words. Sam clung to Sean, her tears highlighting the love and respect she held for the woman dying in the room next door, the woman who had helped raise her.

Colin entered the room, letting the bedroom door close gently in his wake. His expression was grim. John and Finn walked over to hear the news. At Sean's hopeful expression, Colin very quietly addressed the room. "It's her heart."

All their faces fell. John turned and walked to the door, entering to be with his parents. The rest of them took comfort from each other.

Outside, the village stirred with life, unaware of the quiet vigil being held within the Seeley home. Children played in the streets, their laughter flying upon the summer breeze. People carried on with both the important and the mundane tasks of everyday life.

As night fell, Eoinn remained at Rose's side, his hand finding hers, their fingers entwining as they had through countless seasons. In the quiet of their room, with only the soft whisper of Rose's breath and the distant echo of the village's heartbeat, Rose quietly went to her final repose.

14

Embers

September 15th, 1909

In the pre-dawn dark, Sam floated in the hot springs, her head barely protruding from the steam-cloaked water. These early morning soaks had become a ritual, infusing her with vitality for the day ahead. As she floated, she heard someone walking along the far shore of the pool. She scanned the shore and saw two figures engaged in hushed conversation. One was somewhat familiar: Sinclair Lipson, a recent arrival to the village who had caused quite a stir, especially with Liam. His reaction to him had been decidedly negative. Lipson stood just off the trail, murmuring flirtatiously to a young, petite woman, who appeared captivated by his attentions. Sam recalled seeing Eoinn and a towering man with a small woman at this very spot some years ago, but this woman was not her. This woman was younger, obviously in awe of Lipson and receptive to his romantic advances.

Curiosity piqued, Sam attempted to approach them quietly in the water of the pool. Lipson seemed to sense that he was being watched and reacted with the cunning of a predator. He whisked the woman away before Sam could glean anything from their exchange. The woman was unfamiliar to Sam, but her knowledge of Lipson was vague at best. The village was bustling, with visitors and newcomers amidst the ongoing project of cutting a new shaft into the mountain. Finn had expressed doubts, claiming it was a waste of time, but Eoinn insisted on keeping the miners busy.

Sam was privy to the true story. While plenty of the mountain's treasure remained, the real wealth of the village lay in the investments made over the years by Eoinn, Angus, and Egan. The village's prosperity no longer depended on the mines, yet Eoinn, since Rose's death, had become increasingly secretive and suspicious of outsiders, choosing to restrict his trust to the Original Eight and their families. Even his relationship with his own son was strained.

Later that day, as Sam prepared to leave work to meet Seamus for lunch, she saw Sinclair Lipson enter the office, standing out in his white linen suit. He walked in as if he belonged there and strode towards Eoinn's office, a long cheroot leaving a smoking trail from his left hand.

She stood up from her desk and stepped into his path. "Mr. Lipson," she asked, "how may I help you?"

He pulled up abruptly and stared at her with surprise. "Dear lady, have we met?"

Sam looked back at him coolly. "No, Mr. Lipson, we haven't. But your reputation precedes you. I'm Sam O'Connor. I believe you know my father-in-law, Liam. Do you have an appointment here?"

Lipson was obviously unused to being challenged. "An appointment? No, but I do rather feel that Mr. Seeley will be happy to meet with me." He acted as if that would be the end of the conversation and stepped lightly to the side, intending to go around her.

Sam stepped back in front of him, placing her hand on his chest. "Mr. Lipson," she began, "why don't you take a seat on the bench over there, and I'll check to see if Mr. Seeley can take the time to see you now."

Lipson stood very still and looked carefully at Sam, as if seeing her for the first time. His mouth curled into a tight smile, and he slowly and deliberately took a drag from his cheroot. He blew a slow stream of smoke into her face before growling, "Ah, Mrs. O'Connor. I do believe I know who you are, now."

Sam felt the hairs on the back of her neck stand up. The threat implied in Lipson's tone was very clear. The world seemed to slow down. Out of the corner of her eye, she saw Angus Sullivan stand up at his desk and begin to come towards them. Behind her, she heard Eoinn's office door open.

"Mister Lipson," said Eoinn in a booming voice that had been honed on battlefields, "what an unexpected surprise."

Lipson's attention was diverted from Sam to Eoinn, as if one predator was confronted by another predator just as it was stalking its prey. Sam shifted to the side, and Lipson stepped past quickly, heading towards Eoinn's office. Just before he went in, he turned his head towards Sam, staring with calculating eyes, his head cocked at an odd angle. She again felt the hairs on the back of her neck rise.

Sam watched as Eoinn allowed Lipson to enter his office, not taking his eyes off of his unexpected guest for a moment, and closed the door behind them. She turned to Angus, who looked at her with raised eyebrows.

They both returned to their desks, no longer thinking of leaving for lunch. Soon, raised voices emanated from the office, abruptly followed by momentary silence. Sam heard Eoinn speaking. She couldn't make out the words, but Eoinn's quiet, commanding tone, reminiscent of the time he had faced down the robbers on the mountain trail—the time he'd made that man piss his pants—was unmistakable. Then suddenly, the door flung open, and Lipson stormed out, leaving a lingering trail of smoke from his cheroot. He flew through the office like an arrow fired from a bow, not looking left or right, and slammed the door behind him as he left.

Sam excused herself and followed him outside at a distance. She was already late to meet Seamus, but she watched as Lipson stalked angrily down Broadway towards the stables, moving so quickly and deliberately that people were scrambling to get out of his path.

That evening at dinner, the entire family sat at the table. Mrs. O'Hara sat in her usual seat closest to the fireplace where she gently dozed off.

Henry, Sam's oldest son, twenty-five and serious and stable, quietly started a conversation with Glory, her fifteen-year-old daughter. Glory was rebellious, and she and Sam had been butting heads like bighorn sheep for the last six months. Glory was very intelligent and strong willed. Sam quietly admired her for it, but it made mothering her extremely challenging. Now Henry turned to her and asked, "Glory, who was the girl you were with earlier today? I haven't seen her before."

Glory smiled and said, "She's pretty, isn't she? She's my new friend, Ríona. She's an Irish girl who recently moved to the village."

"She's quite the tiny waif of a thing," Henry replied. "Does she have family here?"

"I haven't met any of them," Glory replied, "but the way she talks about her family. There must be a lot of them."

Sam immediately thought of the woman she had seen at the hot springs with Lipson. So she interjected, "I may have seen her this morning. Was she a tiny girl with blonde hair and a green dress?"

"Yes, that would be her," said Glory warily. "Why all the interest?"

"She seemed too young to be alone in the village," said Sam carefully. "You mentioned relatives. Do you know where they're living?"

Glory looked warily at her mother. "She's older than me, Ma," she replied. "No, she only mentioned them offhandedly. She said she's got many cousins here."

Mrs. O'Hara startled, alert and awake in the corner, but the old woman didn't say anything.

Sam looked thoughtfully at her daughter. "Glory, I'd really like to meet this Ríona, before you spend a lot more time with her. Can you bring her by for dinner tomorrow night?"

Glory looked rebellious, but she said sweetly, "Of course, Mother. I'd be happy to invite her."

Sam was suspicious but accepted her word at face value and let the matter drop.

The next evening, Glory missed dinner.

Seamus was preoccupied with making a silver brooch in the shop. So after dinner, he rushed back to finish the commission, leaving it to Sam to locate their daughter. As she asked around the village, Sam was directed towards the trail leading to her cave, a place she had never shared with anyone, a sanctuary she considered solely her own. She was surprised at how jealous of that place she felt, knowing intellectually that anyone else might have found it at any time, but to her, it was her own private cave.

Nearing the top of the trail, Sam heard Glory's fearful voice echoing as if she were inside the cave. Glory's voice was in the midst of an exchange with another female, whose voice had a cajoling and sing-songy tone. Concerned for her daughter, Sam increased her pace.

As she cleared the rise where the entrance to the cave was situated, Sam found herself face to face with another coyote. It was clear that it couldn't be the same one she had seen in her youth. Yet the fact that she'd only seen coyotes in the area twice—and in the same spot—was a surprise to her. Seeing Sam, the coyote yipped and growled, preventing her from reaching the cave entrance. Sam called out for Glory, but Glory didn't respond. Then the coyote lunged, snapping at Sam and biting her hand, drawing blood. She was shocked by how hard it bit her. She felt like she'd been hit in the hand by a hammer.

She stumbled backward over the rise and tumbled down the trail. Sam regained her footing and saw the coyote watching her from above. When it saw that Sam had regained her bearings, it charged again, this time its sharp teeth catching her on the forearm, piercing her clothing and skin. It clamped its jaws tight on her arm and shook its head violently from side to side, twisting her arm, mostly by her shirt. Sam cried out in pain and with great effort yanked her arm free, tearing the cloth of her shirt as well as the flesh on her arm. Once again she tumbled backwards, over the edge of the trail. Sam fell head over heels down the side of the mountain until she came to rest on a lower part of the trail, which switchbacked back and forth up the side of the mountain. Dazed and shaken, Sam shook her head slowly. She peered back up the trail and saw the coyote running down towards the first switchback turn, and her blood ran cold. She turned and fled, glancing back to see it following behind her at a distance. Her arm and hand dripped blood from the bite wounds, as she ran down the trail with every bit of speed she could muster.

When she finally reached the bottom of the trail, she looked back and saw the coyote standing about 100 yards behind her, watching. She turned to run towards Finn's cabin, which was close by but unexpectedly standing before her was Eoinn. She quickly recounted the incident in between gasps for breath, and Eoinn's got more and more angry as she spoke. "Go and fetch Finn, Sean, and Colin!" he commanded. "Tell them to arm themselves, and then meet me at the trailhead!" Without another word, Eoinn stomped off toward the new mine entrance that ran to the crystal cave hot springs down inside the mountain. This new cut was completed just the previous year.

Sam hurried to Finn's cabin, yelling for him. Finn threw open the door and asked what the commotion was all about. As she explained, Finn's face registered total shock. Without allowing Sam to finish her horrible tale, Finn abruptly turned and ran back inside. At that, Sam turned away and ran onwards to Sean and Colin's shared cabin, the one with the lean-to that had been her room growing up. When she arrived, she could barely speak, as she was so winded from her exertions. Without warning, she threw open the door, startling her friends who sat reading. Sean and Colin stood up in alarm. Her words came out in heaving gasps. Sean immediately came over and put his hand on her back to steady her as she caught her breath. While she related her ordeal, Colin cleaned her wounds and wrapped bandages around her arm and hand. After hearing her story, Colin and Sean exchanged glances. Then Colin stepped into the bedroom and returned with two, long spears with bronze blades on the end. In addition, Sam saw that girded around his waist was an intricately decorated scabbard which sheathed a sword with a bronze handle. Wordlessly, Colin handed the second spear to Sean, and they all left the cabin, heading towards the trail.

Finn was waiting for them at the trailhead with a spear of his own. In addition, an oak-handled, two-headed axe hung from his belt. Moments later, Eoinn arrived. He was also carrying a spear, and Sam felt both shocked and relieved. These specific weapons were unfamiliar and even antiquated to her, but they seemed somehow perfect for dealing with a rabid coyote. Realizing she had been bitten, Sam voiced her concern about the possibility of contracting rabies but exhaustion soon caught up with her as they began ascending the trail.

The older men moved with surprising speed and endurance, outpacing Sam. By the time she reached the top of the rise, only Sean awaited her, holding a lit torch. Catching her breath, Sam learned from Sean that the others had driven the coyote away. Sean reassured her that the animal didn't seem rabid, moving as it did with perfect agility and speed. Once she had caught her breath, Sean handed Sam the torch and led her into the cave.

They dashed through the familiar tunnel, Sean navigating the passages with a miner's instinct. Suddenly, they veered into a narrow corridor she hadn't seen before. It was tall enough to run without crouching. The path sloped gently downhill, and soon they entered a vast cavern, the ceiling of which was lost in shadow. Across the expanse, the flicker of torchlight illuminated the scene of a struggle. Colin's sword clashed against metal, voices shouting amidst stalagmites rising up from the cavern's floor and towering far above the combatants.

As Sam and Sean neared, a blinding flash lit the cavern, a burst of light reminiscent of a photographer's phosphorous flash. In that instant, she imagined that she witnessed an incredible tableau, Eoinn, Colin, and Finn stood shoulder to shoulder wielding their weapons. They were resplendent in silver armor, white cloaks, and of all things, Eoinn wore a crown on his head. They were engaged in battle with a group of smaller people, but their forms were fuzzy to Sam at that particular moment. Still dazed by the flash of light and then the abrupt return to near total darkness, Sam lost Sean's grip and fell, sprawling across the gritty, sandy cavern floor. When her vision cleared, she saw Eoinn, Finn, Colin, and Sean surrounding a figure on the ground. They were not wearing the armor and cloaks she thought she'd seen in that split second of brilliant light. Dread filled her as she recognized that it was her daughter Glory who was lying on the ground. Terrified, Sam rushed to her daughter's side, and as she arrived, the men parted to let her through.

To her great relief, Glory was alive and apparently not much the worse for wear. Sam embraced her and helped her sit up. Glory initially gazed at her with confusion, before recognizing her mother. "Ma?" Glory whispered, hugging Sam. Sam inquired about Ríona, but Glory seemed confused, repeatedly asking, "Who?" Even after returning home and tucked safely into bed, Glory claimed no memory of Ríona or entering the cave with anyone.

Relieved but bewildered, Sam hoped Glory would recall more by morning. Pressing Finn, Sean, and Colin for details proved futile. Overhearing a snippet of conversation between Finn and Sean in Irish, Sam overheard Finn uttering the words, "*Tá an draíocht bronntanas ag an gcailín, agus sin tarraingteach do an tsórt mícheart.*" She understood enough to know they spoke of a gift in the girl that attracted the wrong sort.

For now, it was readily apparent that no further answers were forthcoming, but still, Sam was grateful to have her daughter home safe. She would be content counting her blessings, as Mrs. O would say.

I I I I

October 1st, 1909

Elias Dotson and Sinclair Lipson were walking in the remnants of Eagle City, close together but not touching. Lipson was elegant in his white, linen suit and his white hat with the black band as usual. He was smoking a cheroot, holding it in his hand, and gesturing while he talked. As he argued his case, the smoke trailed and made circles and lines beside them. His rust-colored hair, sideburns, and handlebar mustache were long and his eyes were squinting under his wild, bushy, auburn eyebrows. He often watched his companion without turning his head as they moved through the street which was lined with empty, decaying structures.

Elias Dotson was huge. He made Lipson look like a child. He wore a tall, black hat with a wide, flat brim, a long, black duster, split up the back to above his waist, large, black boots, and black gloves. The arms of his duster were wide, and they hung long at the cuff. The tips of his gloves were long, hanging like feathers. Dotson looked bored and disappointed. He had a large, hooked nose under shaggy, black brows, his long, shiny, black hair was pulled back and fell over his shoulders and down his back. He had the complexion and features of a native man. He was a heavy man, his cheeks hanging in jowls, his chin doubled or trebled depending on how he held his head. His eyes were active, always moving and pausing on anything shiny or metal.

Dotson sighed audibly, almost a groan. His voice was deep and rumbled in his chest, almost a bass croak. He said, "Why am I here, you silly dog? I don't understand."

Lipson brandished his cheroot with a flourish, saying, "Don't get your feathers all ruffled. I'm showing you the leftovers of all this excitement. I thought you'd be happy. You won, at least this round."

Dotson looked around at the devastated landscape, the trees had been cut for almost a mile around, the land was covered in tailings from various mining endeavors, and the few remaining buildings along the main street were near collapse. Everywhere old platforms for tents were abandoned and rotting.

He sighed again, and in his rumbling bass voice sounded exhausted as he said, "Look at this mess you've made. How could I be happy with any of this? You're gloating, but you pretend to have lost only because you find this amusing. But the obvious truth is that nobody has won anything here. You've ruined the forest. You've poisoned the streams and rivers, and you've left most of these men penniless and destitute."

Lipson looked at Dotson and said, "This land will heal, and these people have all left—Well, at least most of them. But your friend Seeley and his interlopers are still here. They haven't left, and their village is growing and successful. Surely you must be happy about that."

Dotson looked at Lipson suspiciously. "Despite your best efforts, the village remains. But I must say you keep surprising me at how far you'll go to get rid of them. Why do you hate them so much? For my part, I find Seeley to be interesting. I believe he's got good ideas and is suited to this kind of place."

Lipson growled, "He's a lout, a boor, and has no respect! He took that land without permission. He acts like he's got every right to be there. I tried to work with the man, but he cast me aside, sent me packing! Told me to stay away. So as far as I am concerned, he and his people can suffer the consequences of their actions!"

Dotson stopped walking and looked over at his companion. He waved his hand at the torn and devastated landscape, filled with trash and stumps.

"How far? How long? To what end? You always have to win. You never agree to let things go. How far?"

Lipson stopped as well and a low growl escaped his throat.

"As far as I need to go! As long as it takes! I'll have them out of here. They can burn," said Sinclair Lipson.

Elias Dotson stood staring, his mouth agape as he shook his head in disbelief. "Burn? Playing with fire again? You never learn."

I I I I

June 30th, 1910

The sun hung low over Crystal Village, casting a warm, golden hue across the rooftops as Jeremiah Redding and his family gathered at Mrs. O's Restaurant. Though Mrs. O had long since retired, her legacy lived on in the bustling eatery, now a cornerstone of the community. Tonight, however, the air was heavy with a mix of celebration and sorrow. David, Jeremiah's eldest son, was leaving the village to seek his fortune elsewhere, and the family had come together to bid him farewell.

The small dining room was filled with the aroma of freshly baked bread and roasted meats, but Jeremiah's appetite was nonexistent. His wife, Margaret, sat beside him, her hand resting on his arm. Across the table, David was animatedly discussing his plans with his siblings, his youthful enthusiasm contrasting with the somber mood of his parents.

As the meal progressed, the conversation flowed around Jeremiah like a gentle stream, but his mind was elsewhere. He couldn't shake the feeling that David's departure was more than just a personal loss—it was a symptom of a deeper malaise within the village. For years, he had watched as Eoinn Seeley and the Original Eight made decisions that, while well-intentioned, often left the rest of the community feeling sidelined. The young people of the village, this whole generation really, had grown up safe and comfortable. Now they wanted to go make their own marks in the world.

When the meal finally came to an end, and David had hugged each family member goodbye, Jeremiah felt a mix of pride and heartbreak. He watched as his son disappeared into the night, the weight of the evening settling heavily on his shoulders. Margaret squeezed his hand, her eyes filled with understanding.

"I need to take a walk," Jeremiah murmured, his voice thick with emotion.

Margaret nodded, her expression gentle. "Go. Clear your head."

As Jeremiah stepped out into the cool night air, he felt the familiar pull of anger and frustration welling up inside him. His feet carried him down the quiet streets, past the homes of friends and neighbors. The village was a place of beauty and community, yet it felt as though those in power were blind to the desires of its people.

Before he knew it, Jeremiah found himself standing before Eoinn Seeley's home. The stately brick house loomed in the darkness, its windows aglow with the warm light of a fire within. Without fully realizing what he was doing, Jeremiah walked up the front steps and knocked on the door.

The door swung open, revealing Eoinn, his expression one of mild surprise. "Why, hello, Jeremiah," he said in greeting, his tone cordial. "What brings ye here at this hour?"

Jeremiah hesitated for a moment, his mind racing with a thousand thoughts. But the sight of Eoinn's calm demeanor only fueled his frustration. "My son is leaving, Eoinn," he began, his voice cracking with emotion. "He's leaving because he doesn't see a future here in the village. The miners are grumbling that the mountain has played out, and the village hasn't seen a new building in years. My son doesn't see a path for his future, a place he can make his own mark. And he's not the only one—there are other young people talking about leaving too. They want to see the world, they want to travel, they want more than is available here. And you lot just keep doing the same things, as if all is right with the world."

Eoinn's brow furrowed, genuine confusion etched on his features. "I'm sorry to hear that, Jeremiah. But surely ye understand that we've always had the village's best interests at heart. We're working on new projects, new industries that will secure our future."

Jeremiah's lips curled into a bitter smile. "New industries? Like what, Eoinn? More mining? The veins are drying up, and you know it!"

Eoinn shook his head, his voice earnest. "Not just mining. We're exploring other avenues—manufacturing like furniture making, crafts like glass blowing and ceramics, and of course, silver and gold smithing. If we need more expertise to help train the next generation, we can bring the relevant experts here. We've done it before, we can do it again."

Jeremiah's laughter was sharp and mirthless. "You think people will flock here just to live in a village that is owned lock, stock and barrel by you? And run by a council that doesn't listen to its people? You have no idea what the rest of us want, Eoinn. You're so focused on preserving your vision from fifty years ago that you've lost sight of the present!"

Eoinn's frustration began to show, his voice tinged with defensiveness. "That's not fair, Jeremiah. We've always been open to suggestions. We want what's best for everyone."

Jeremiah's anger flared, his words cutting like a blade. "Open to suggestions? When was the last time you actually listened to us, Eoinn? When was the last time you considered that maybe, just maybe, we want to have a say in our own lives? We're not children, but you treat us like we need to be taken care of! We just want ownership in something and a say in how things are operated. You own everything! If I were to leave here, I'd be starting out from scratch after working here my whole adult life! That wouldn't have been the case if I'd raised my family in San Francisco, or New York, or Chicago. At least we'd own our house. We own nothing in Crystal Village!"

Eoinn opened his mouth to respond, but no words came. He stood there, grappling with the realization that his well-meaning intentions had not been enough. The silence stretched between them.

Jeremiah took a deep breath, his voice softer now, but no less determined. "I know you care about this village, Eoinn. But caring isn't enough. We need change. We need a voice. We need ownership. We can't live our lives hoping that you will take care of us. That can't go on forever. And since Rose died, you've kept more and more to yourself and kept the community at arm's length. You won't live forever, and if this village is to survive you, we need a voice outside the Original Eight."

Eoinn nodded slowly, the weight of Jeremiah's words settling heavily on his shoulders. "I'll think about what you've said, Jeremiah. I promise you that."

Jeremiah nodded, the fire of his anger cooling to embers. "I hope you do, Eoinn. For all our sakes."

With that, Jeremiah turned and walked down the porch steps and away, leaving Eoinn standing in the doorway. He was confronted with the realization that his dreams for Crystal Village might not align with the dreams of its people.

IIII

August 20th, 1910

The air was as dry and hot as a furnace, thought Sam. It was about two o'clock in the afternoon. She could smell smoke. The air was hazed with smoke and had been for weeks. The summer of 1910 had been the driest on record, and the region was a tinderbox. Hundreds of small fires burned across the landscape, sparked by passing trains and dry lightning storms. Most fires were smoldering, nearly out, but the threat of a larger conflagration loomed over the village like a shadow. This had been a dry, hot year, whereas last year had been the opposite, a very wet year filled with torrential rains and marked with mudslides. This year there had been so little rain that any spark could easily ignite a forest fire.

She went up the trail to her cave to take a look beyond their protected valley. Over the years her trips up this trail had cleared the path and made it easier to traverse. She hoped that from the elevated vantage point of the cave she would be able to see out past the village and get a sense of what fires might be out in the range. As she climbed, she noted that there were clouds high in the sky, but not rain clouds, they were clouds of smoke. The higher she climbed, the stronger the mountain winds became. Looking back, she saw winds bending trees as she ascended the trail.

She reached her lookout spot and could see down the valley toward the base of Eagle Creek, where Eagle City had stood for a few short years. Off to the west, she saw lines of smoke coming off of the hillsides but nothing too urgent. Satisfied that things looked safe, she walked over to the cave entrance and went inside.

Once her eyes acclimated the darkness, she could see the intricate drawings and carvings that had been made in the walls of the cave. In the center was a place where a stalagmite had been cut off to serve as a seat. She walked to it and sat down, allowing herself to relax after her strenuous climb. The coolness of the air was a balm after feeling like she was roasting from the heat outside. She had explored the cave and the tunnels behind it many times. The cave system extended into the mountain for hundreds of yards. Her mind flashed back to the last time she'd come up here, the fateful day the coyote had bitten her, and the men had helped her rescue Glory.

As she thought back on it, she realized with confusion that nobody had ever explained who it was that Colin, Finn and Eoinn had been fighting with in the cave. "Now, why haven't I ever pushed them for an explanation?" she asked herself aloud. Her voice echoed in her own ears tinnily. She found it extremely odd and even a bit disturbing that nobody had seen that girl Ríona again. What is more, when she had asked around, nobody knew Ríona or her cousins. All of this was peculiar, but it was wholly unlike her that she hadn't asked Sean for an explanation of the events of that day. She sat and pondered this, confused for a few minutes and then went back outside.

As she emerged from the mouth of the cave, she immediately noticed that in the distance, to the southwest, there was a huge, black cloud that hadn't been there previously. At first, she mistook it for a rain cloud, sighing softly to herself with hope and relief. Her relief faded quickly with a sinking feeling as she realized it was more smoke. At that moment, she felt the first incredible gust of wind. It seemed as if it might lift her off the ground. The heat of the air was dry and scalding. She looked out across the valley and the fires that had been smoldering just minutes previously were now blazing high into the air. She watched as they grew, stoked into raging infernos by the wind. Even at a distance she could hear the pop and sharp snap as new pines caught fire. She knew it was the pitch in the white pines that made them go up like torches. Tree after tree caught fire, sending billowing clouds of smoke up into the sky. She could see smoke gathering on all sides and realized the village was in real danger because of this fire.

She ran down the trail as fast as she could. As she arrived back on Broadway at the main square, smoke had already begun to roll in like a heavy fog and was smothering the village. The thick, black smoke made the square seem as dark as night. Someone had thrown on the street lamps, and people were grabbing up lanterns. In the midst of the growing confusion Sam saw Glory coming down the street toward her. They looked terrified. At the north end of the square, Sam saw that Eoinn and Finn were huddled together near the entrance to the mining company offices. First, Sam signaled to her children to wait for her. Then she ran to Eoinn and Finn and told them what she had seen.

Eoinn looked at Finn and said, "So, this is how it ends."

Turning to Sam he said, "We've got to evacuate the village! I'm going to have the ore train pulled out onto Broadway, and we're going to load the people and belongings into the carts and send them off toward Kellogg. Sam, I want you to go with them. I want you to lead your family and the people of the village to safety."

By now, the winds were howling like a hurricane, blowing small children off their feet, pelting the villagers with grit and gravel and burning embers.

Sam rushed over to Glory, who was sixteen years old. Eyes watering and throat burning from the smoke, Sam told her to run back to the house, to grab Mrs. O'Hara and her brothers and sisters, and to meet her back down on Broadway. She quickly explained that the ore train was going to pull up, and they would all get into the carts there. "Mind you, Glory, I want you back here fast. But please, all of you pick a few important things to bring with you. Grab the small, yellow trunk from my bedroom, and have your brothers carry it down!"

Sam spied Henry, her eldest, coming out of the mining company offices. She rushed to intercept Henry, and sent him off to find Seamus. She also instructed him to send anyone he came across to Broadway to get on the ore train so they could be evacuated. Seeing that the situation was getting progressively worse by the minute, it was now clear to Sam that people wouldn't have time to gather their things. She realized that the townsfolk must drop everything and come to the train as fast as they could.

As villagers began to arrive, Sam took over coordinating the evacuation. As she helped people climb into the ore carts Sean came up to her and said in her ear, "Sam, I'm going to stay here with the others once ye all evacuate. We're going to try to save the village, but if the fire overtakes us, we'll hide in the mine. I'm going to load a bunch of gold and silver bars in the last two train cars. I want ye to take them with ye."

He handed her a satchel with a long strap that she put across her body from her right shoulder across to her left hip, and rotated the bag to her back. "Important papers," he said. She kissed him on the cheek and told him to be careful.

Sam looked up as the train was pulling out of the mine and onto Broadway, moving slowly. She'd never seen it outside with all the carts, and it stretched nearly the whole length of the road, almost to the bridge. To her great relief, she saw Seamus and Henry as they arrived on the other side of the train.

She called to them, "Henry, go find your brothers and sisters. Grab blankets and soak them in water from the horse trough. Pass that word along to others. Then you all hunker down in an ore cart. When we get out of the village, be ready with those wet blankets to cover yourselves. Listen for the bell! Be on the train before the bell rings ten times!"

Henry nodded and took off in the direction of their house. He was twenty-six and as handsome and strong as her husband had been at that age, but he was like her, very even tempered, reliable, and had good instincts, where Seamus had been a bit flighty. She knew he'd keep the others safe.

Seamus looked at her with fear in his eyes and called out to her—asking what he should do. She called back to him, instructing him to help people board the train and have some of the men look for blankets to soak in the horse trough. She saw that several families were taking off in carriages pulled by one or two horses, and some on horseback. She silently wished them well but focused her efforts on helping those with young children and the elderly to board the train. It was so dark that it seemed like midnight, but it was only four in the afternoon. Small bits of ash and burning twigs were raining down on them. They were coated in white, like snow, but it was blazing hot. Here and there, cinders landed on the villagers waiting to board, and she patted at the back of Mrs. Nicholson's shawl, which had started to smolder.

Soon all the people had squeezed into the ore carts. She heard Seamus call her name. He was holding a spot for her in the last car. She saw that Eoinn, Liam, Angus, Egan, Sean, Colin and Finn were all standing near the last car on the train. Eoinn walked over to the bell and started ringing it. Sam looked up at the top of Big Peak, off to the east, and he saw that flames were cresting over the ridge. The fire was converging on the village, coming down from the east as well as from the west. In the sky she could see there was a roiling ball of flame. It confused her, and then suddenly, there was a huge explosion in the sky. Within seconds, a jet of flame reached down from the clouds into their valley, and everywhere that ball of flame touched, things were igniting like torches. Dozens of trees were engulfed in mere seconds. The train very slowly started to move, and then picked up speed. Sam turned to look at the men who'd rescued her and raised her as one of their own children and the village they had all worked so hard to build from mere tents and cabins. Her heart was breaking. Eoinn gave her the thumbs up sign, and she turned to watch the town go by—determined to memorize its every detail—as they moved onward. Sean ran over and held her hand tightly over the back of the cart, and let go as the train moved away, their fingers slipping from each other's grasp. They both had tears in their eyes from more than just the smoke.

The last ore car, in which she and Seamus were seated, was about a block from the bridge when another huge explosion in the sky erupted. A giant finger of flame shot downward, spinning like a fiery tornado, striking the roof of the stables on the left side of the tracks from her. The small orchard of olive trees that had been planted outside the stable exploded in flame. The heat washed over her with a scorching blast in her face. She ducked down for a moment to allow time for the worst of the heat to pass by. She held her breath and felt deeply grateful for the metal ore cart she was sitting in. Seamus reached over with a wet blanket for her. She wiped her face and hair with it and looked out again. They were maybe one hundred feet from the bridge, and the train was now moving fast, faster than she'd ever seen it move. To her horror, she realized that the stone pillars that held up the bridge were cracking and that one of them was slowly starting to rotate in place.

"Seamus! The bridge!" she screamed. Seamus looked at her with initial confusion. Then as he looked where she was gesturing, his face went ashen. He looked at the stone pillars and then at her. She could see that he was considering grabbing her and jumping out. She motioned to him to wait, and they watched as the train cars ahead of them began crossing the bridge. The pillars began to crumble, the steel cables running along each side were twisting and singing in a high pitched scream.

As their ore cart passed the two pillars, they collapsed, and the roadway of the bridge bucked and started to give way. The train tracks pitched and rolled as if a wave on the ocean, lifting the last five ore carts several feet in the air. Horrified, she watched behind her as the bridge gave way. Several buildings at the edge were on fire.

Meanwhile, the train managed to keep going. Against all odds, all the ore carts made it across the bridge. Sam hugged Seamus tightly and let out a sigh of relief. Together, they looked back over the rear of the cart as the stone pillars on the far side of the bridge toppled over into the ravine. She watched with horror as the bridge disintegrated and disappeared down into the ravine. Seconds later, a section of the edge of cliff—about fifty feet long and several feet deep—crumbled and followed the bridge into the ravine below. She heard and felt it through the ore cart as the train tracks on the bridge were ripped away from the rest of the rail line. The rails shrieked, bent off, and then snapped away as they plunged into the ravine following the rest of the bridge.

As the train flew down the mountainside, she worried that in their haste the extended line of carts might accelerate too quickly and derail the train. However, she realized that the forest was on fire on both sides of them. They had little choice but to attempt to get to safety as fast as possible.

Off to the side of the train tracks she saw yet a new terror, a huge, shadowy figure bathed in flames. It was watching the train. Covered in smoke, it looked vaguely like a Nez Perce medicine man she'd seen once. But this figure was not human! It was easily twice the size of a person. Its head was vaguely animal shaped, coyote-like but grotesque, eyes glowing with flames. Flames dripped from its hands, which otherwise were claw-like. As she gaped at it, the figure's head turned unmistakably and watched her pass. She could see that its bushy eyebrows and sideburns were rust colored. The figure only appeared for a few seconds as the train flashed by, but somehow she could tell it was looking specifically at her. It distinctly reminded her of the way that Sinclair Lipson had looked at her in Eoinn's office. Then, another instant passed, and it was gone. Horrified, she shook her head trying to process what she'd just seen. Her heart was pounding in her chest, and she felt an icy chill despite the heat.

Suddenly, she realized that the wet blanket she was holding was steaming. Her hair felt so hot that it seemed as if her whole head might burst into flame. She threw the blanket over herself. Then she huddled with Seamus, and together they ducked down under the lip of the ore cart. Seamus grabbed her hand in a grip that felt like iron. The trip on the ore carts down to their private rail station outside of Kellogg normally would take an hour, but at this rate, it would probably take fifteen minutes—if they didn't crash the train. A few minutes passed, and she peaked over the back of the ore cart for a moment and saw nothing but flames and smoke. She sighed deeply and returned to Seamus' arms.

15

Pilgrimage

The air in Liam's Bar hung heavy with the ghosts of Crystal Village. Smoke still clung to everyone's clothes and hair, and it worked into the creases of their hands. The lamps threw shadows on the beams. Sam sat at the bar, a glass of whiskey untouched near her hand, watching the amber liquid catch lamplight. Around her, conversations ebbed and flowed—plans for tomorrow, memories of yesterday.

The survivors of the fire had gathered first in Kellogg, then moved down the road to Wallace. The latter city was bigger, and it was also where Liam and some others had invested in businesses. Many of the refugees were camping in a brick warehouse owned by the Sullivan brothers. Every day after doing what they could for those devastated by the fire, some of the survivors would meet at Liam's Bar for the solace of friends and family.

The door opened and conversations faltered. Sinclair Lipson walked in, his white, linen suit pristine and gleaming against the soot-stained clothes of the others. His golden eyes scanned the room before settling on Sam.

"Ah, Mrs. O'Connor," he said, voice dripping with false sympathy, "what a pity about your village."

Sam stared at Lipson in the mirror across the bar. Not a flinch. Not a twitch of her fingers.

"Mr. Lipson," she said, glancing at his pristine jacket, "gloating doesn't suit you." Our village may have burned, but our spirit hasn't."

Lipson leaned closer, his smile thin. "Why play games, Samantha? Your village is gone. A memory. I find a certain ... poetry in its end. Now, I suppose you'll all head back to where you came from."

The room was silent. Sam stood and turned to face him, her movements slow and careful but sure and steady. "You mistake grief for weakness, Mr. Lipson. You've underestimated the people of Crystal Village."

Lipson's chuckle was dry. "And yet, here you sit, with a drink, while the mountains still smolder." He flicked ash from his cheroot onto the floor.

Sam's voice was firm. "This fire has forged us. People will hear of what happened here and see heroism, courage, a community rising from the ashes. They'll come to help us rebuild this whole region. They'll see the beauty of this place, the riches of the newly discovered silver deposits, and this place will flourish."

For a moment, doubt crossed Lipson's face. "You trust too much in sentiment, Samantha. Your village was a footnote in the land's story. Forgotten soon enough."

Sam leaned in, her voice low but clear. "And you, Mr. Lipson? What will you be remembered for? Change is coming, and it will sweep you away like the dust you are."

Something flickered in Lipson's eyes. He straightened, adjusting his cuffs. "We shall see, Samantha. We shall see." He turned for the door, his back stiff with anger.

As he reached for the handle, a large hand, callused and black with soot, clapped him firmly between the shoulder blades. Seamus O'Connor stood there, smiling without warmth. The perfect shape of his handprint stood stark against the white linen—like a brand.

Laughter rippled through the bar—hesitant at first, then stronger, a sound not heard since before the fire. Lipson spun, his face contorted with fury. His eyes locked on Seamus and then darted to Sam, who met his gaze levelly. With a low growl, he yanked the door open and vanished into the night.

The laughter lingered, cleansing the air. Talk shifted from whispers of loss to plans for rebuilding lives here in Wallace and nearby Kellogg.

Sam watched them all, these people who had followed Eoinn's dream into the mountains and out again. She knew it wasn't over—not with Lipson, not with any of it. But for now, it was enough to see hope rekindled in the faces around her.

IIII

The next few weeks were horrific. More than half of the city of Wallace was destroyed in the fire, and similarly, more than half of the nascent town of Kellogg was destroyed. Millions of acres had burned across Montana, Idaho and Washington. There were many small camps and stakes on the outskirts of the towns that also were affected, and many needed to be checked. Between checking on the locals, burying the dead, and clearing debris from the town, there was more work than people. Luckily, the trains were running, helping to bring people into the region to help with rescue and cleanup and helping victims escape to family and friends in other parts of the country.

The arrival of the Buffalo Soldiers from the 25th Infantry Regiment brought military order to civilian chaos, and Company I was stationed in Wallace. For most Wallace residents, these soldiers represented their first encounter with Black Americans—indeed, their first encounter with Black people at all. The racial dimension added complexity to an already unprecedented situation. These men operated under scrutiny that white soldiers would never have faced, yet their professionalism and competence systematically dismantled local preconceptions. Company I's methodical evacuation of women and children, their coordination of train departures, and their unflappable execution of emergency protocols earned respect through demonstrated capability. The soldiers' calm effectiveness in the face of catastrophe left lasting impressions that extended far beyond the immediate crisis.

The soldiers worked tirelessly, not only in rescue efforts but also in the arduous tasks of recovering bodies and maintaining order. Their presence was a steadying force, a reminder that despite the destruction, hope and humanity endured. The soldiers' ability to bridge divides and foster a sense of unity in a time of great need left an indelible mark on the community, one that would be remembered long after the last ember had faded.

Survivors of Crystal Village were better off than many. Liam's Bar in Wallace had rooms above it and a warehouse behind it that all emerged unscathed from the fire. People set up camp in the warehouse, and several of the O'Connor families, including Sam and Seamus' families, were able to take over the vacant rooms above the bar. Others were setting up tents nearby, and since Sam had escaped with a fortune in gold bars, they were able to get plenty of credit with local merchants. The banks had all been destroyed in the fire, and it occurred to Sam that the survivors of Crystal village should set up a bank in Wallace to help with the recovery.

Local merchants were extending credit to everyone they knew, but that could only continue so far into the future. Sam also was keen to get back to the village to find out what happened to the rest of the Original Eight and to see if she could salvage anything.

On the 6th of September, Sam, Seamus, and several of the other adult children of the Original Eight were putting together a pack train of mules to head back to Crystal Village. They were lined up outside of Liam's warehouse in Wallace when Sam observed a group of older men at the end of the street walking in their direction.

Sam's heart leapt into her throat when she recognized Sean, Colin, Angus, Egan, and Liam all walking in their direction, gray with soot but walking and whole. They were leading two mules and one horse, all heavily laden.

Sam broke into a run. As she did, she heard the running feet of many others behind her, but she had the head start. She reached the men out of breath and barely able to speak. She threw her arms around Sean's neck and felt the embrace of all the men, who soon were swarmed by their children and grandchildren. She looked over and saw Seamus and Eva both wrapped around Liam.

It took a while before everyone calmed down. When the tumult caused by their arrival subsided, Liam stepped to the front and said, "Listen now, listen now ... The important thing is that we all made it through this catastrophe. That's what matters the most. But we do have some sad news to relay."

The crowd went absolutely silent. Liam began again, "I hate to have to tell ye that we lost both Eoinn and Finn in the fire." At this grim news, wails and lamentations began among the crowd. Sam was absolutely numb for a moment, but then the enormity of this loss hit her like a wave. She looked across at John Seeley, standing with his wife and son. He looked completely stone faced. Like her, he was in shock. Tears were welling in Sam's eyes, and Sean couldn't even meet her gaze.

Angus Sullivan was the only one who kept his head over the next few minutes. Without a word, he began shepherding the group back towards Liam's Bar. When they all were inside, he got to business.

"Friends, I know that this news hits hard. And there's more news to hit ye with, and it's maybe better to get it done all at once. So I'll lay it out fer ye."

Angus took a deep breath. "Crystal Village is gone. The whole village was completely destroyed. It's a pile of rubble and ash. Not a single building still stands. All the trees are gone, the streams and springs are fouled. As many of you saw for yourselves, the bridge was destroyed, and the stables are gone. The fire didn't stop there, it wiped the slate clean." At this news, many in the crowd were completely stunned and many began to weep. In her heart, Sam felt that she had already known.

"Eoinn and Finn were lost trying to save the mine offices. We all tried to get to them, but alas, the fire was too much. Before he perished, Eoinn brought out a few books of financial records, and he went back to save the rest of the records. Finn was with him. The fire in the offices expanded suddening in an explosion that blasted the building apart. There was no way anyone survived. With nothing more to be done, the rest of us ran into the mines and shut the steel doors. We went far enough into the mines that the smoke and heat couldn't get to us. And as you can see, we were able to save a few of the animals too. Those few creatures are now out in Liam's livery stable here in Wallace."

The crowd was a mixture of grief and denial. John Seeley raised his voice,

"We should rebuild! This is crazy! The village can and should be rebuilt!" Sam's son Henry voiced his assent, "Absolutely! There's still plenty we could do up there. We should all go back!"

Egan Sullivan, who rarely spoke, was the voice that pulled them all back to reality. "Listen, we're all heartbroken. But I want to give ye all a bitter dose of medicine here. The mines were mostly played out. There's no sense in going back up there and reopening them, and they're the only thing left! They barely broke even for the last ten years. Eoinn sacrificed himself trying to get to the financial records for money that the Mining Company had stored in banks outside of Crystal Village. He was successful enough that we've got plenty of money to help all the villagers start a new life anywhere they like in comfort. But no, I can't get behind anyone trying to go back up there and rebuild. That's folly."

The room went absolutely silent again. The only sound was the babbling of one babe who fidgeted in his mother's arms.

Finally, Liam stood up. "My heart is broken," he declared. "I've lost my best and oldest friends. And I've lost that damn village that was Eoinn's lifelong dream. But I'm never, ever going back up there. And I hope I can convince the rest of ye to stay away too. A clean break, a clean start, and a happy life going forward are what we all need."

Sam was watching Sean carefully. He wasn't looking at anyone, and he wouldn't meet her eye. He sat next to Colin and stared at the floor.

Angus stood back up. "Friends, it will take me a few days to sort things out, but as Egan said, we've got resources. Real financial resources are at our disposal. Give me a few days, but I think there's plenty we can do to help ye all get settled and decide what you want to do next with your life. Ye will all share in whatever financial wealth is left of Crystal Village. And that should be plenty to get ye all started on a new path."

Colin stood up abruptly, "Does anyone need any medical help? Either here or anywhere in town?"

And with that, the meeting ended, and people broke off into groups. Sam carefully watched Sean and followed him out the door. When they got out on the sidewalk, he turned to her and said, "Where can we talk? There are things ye need to know, things that must stay secret."

I I I I

That night, Sam and Seamus lay in bed. Sam had her head on Seamus' chest, and he held her in his arms. He could tell she wanted to talk about something, but he didn't press.

"Seamus, what do you want in this life?" she asked.

Seamus lay there contemplating that question. "I never really thought about it. I loved my life in the village. I loved making beautiful jewelry."

"But you could do that anywhere, couldn't you?" Sam asked. "If you could go anywhere in the world, where would you go?"

"Europe. Paris, Vienna, and Rome—especially Rome! Oh and Florence, maybe Venice too," replied Seamus without hesitation.

Sam was startled. She rolled over and looked him in the face. "Italy? You've never mentioned Italy before."

Seamus looked at her carefully. "I never thought of it as an option before. But I had long conversations with Finn about Italy. He told me about the architecture and the artisans there who make jewelry. He said if I ever had the chance to visit, I should go to Europe. He talked about the fact that Paris and Vienna were the best places to hone my craft, that the jewelers there are the best in the world. But he knew that my real love was goldsmithing and silversmithing. And in those disciplines, Italy really stands out. If I could do anything I wanted, I'd spend a year traveling throughout Europe, but then I'd spend another just in Italy."

Sam looked at her husband with wonder in her eyes. It was as if he had a secret world that he'd been living in and had just invited her to join him there.

Seamus smiled at her. "What about you?" he asked. "Where would you want to go?"

Sam sighed, then answered, "I don't know. I never even considered leaving the village. It didn't even occur to me to travel around in America other than on village business. Let alone the idea of traveling to Europe.

264

But listening to you talk about it, I am fascinated. I do remember hearing Finn's stories about Venice and wondering what that would be like." She paused for a moment, then continued, "You know, Sean told me today that he was leaving. That he was going to go back to Ireland to see his family. He said that we can go with him. He said it was just a visit, and then after that, he wanted to go back to tour Europe again. He said Colin was on board and ready to go too."

Seamus chuckled. "So when I said basically the same thing, you weren't expecting that."

"No. I wasn't. But now that you have, I think I know what we're going to be doing for the next year or two. And somehow, going to Europe, for you to see the places Finn told you about makes it almost a pilgrimage in his memory. That seems appropriate somehow. Honorable, actually."

The next day Sam and Seamus met with their children and Sean and Colin, and they brought up the idea of traveling to Europe. By lunchtime they all were aligned that this was a good way to heal from the tragedy of the fire. Sam talked with John Seeley over lunch and convinced him to take over the gold that she'd brought down from the village. Her thought was that he should found a bank in Wallace, and that the gold should go toward financing the rebuilding of the region. John suggested that they call it the Crystal Village Memorial Bank and Trust, but after deliberation, they ended up calling it the Northern Idaho Memorial Bank and Trust.

Over the course of the next few weeks, Angus Sullivan met with each family that had been part of Crystal Village. He helped them plan how they would use the money he could provide to get their families started on a stable path forward. That task completed, he told Egan that he and his family were leaving too. Augus explained that he missed the ocean and wanted to live somewhere by the sea. He was considering the prospect of settling in Maine. Egan said that he would come along too. For years, he had wanted to go to Boston to spend time with some of the professors at MIT and Harvard with whom he had been corresponding. He pointed out that Boston was just a short train ride from Maine.

For his part, Liam decided to stay in Wallace. He loved the area and felt like he had something with his bar, the stables, and the shipping business that he'd started with Peirre Lemieux's cousin. Glory decided to stay as well, as she was still taking care of Mrs. O'Hara. She was now well into her 80s and not enjoying the same vigor that the men of the Original Eight were. Glory also had her eye on a boy who she'd met in Wallace. Likewise, Henry also decided to stay behind and work with Liam at the bar and his other businesses. He was good with books and could manage the financial side of the businesses. He also was close friends with John Seeley and promised to help him out with getting the bank started.

In the end, it was Danny Miller and Eva, and their son Ned who joined the trip to Europe. Danny had run into someone who recognized him as Danny Ferguson, and he felt it was expedient to move along. Susanne and the twins were staying as well. They all had families and were more interested in settling in than in the prospect of further upheaval.

With regard to those headed to Europe, it was several months before they got all the arrangements made, and it was January before they left. As they all stood on the train platform in Wallace, ready to leave, there was much embracing and many tears. A light snow was falling, and the air had a sharp tang. Mercifully, a soft blanket of snow covered the devastation from the fire. Sam was sad to leave her friends and family behind, but there was also a sense of excitement that Sam herself had never felt before. It was a feeling that they were about to embark on a grand adventure, an epic journey to wondrous places. A trip to places she'd only heard about but never even dared to consider visiting.

When the train pulled into the platform, Sam hugged Liam, Mrs. O'Hara, and her children who were staying behind. She hugged Egan and Angus. Everything was a whirl of kisses and tears and promises to write. And then, the train was departing, and they all boarded.

16

Revelation

Jack was on his mountain bike riding north. He was miles uphill from the area where Eagle City had been back in the day. There really was nothing left of the original settlement. Today, it was exclusively a loose collection of modern-day homes. On his way up here, Jack had driven up the Eagle Creek road—which became a dirt National Forest Service road—until he got to the Settlers Creek interpretive trails. In taking this path, he had followed the advice of some locals and left the car unlocked as there'd been a rash of break-ins at local hiking spots. There was nothing of value in the rental car anyway, and he'd rather not have to deal with the insurance paperwork that would inevitably be required for a window repair.

He'd parked the SUV in the small parking area and rode his mountain bike up the trail until he found a small cut-off that he followed for several miles. Sometimes the trail was clear, and sometimes it was swallowed up by clumps of underbrush. This part of the ride was fairly dense forest, and he had no signal for his phone. The mountains in these parts were sometimes sparse and dry, but here he'd come across some pretty rugged terrain, densely wooded with tall evergreens. Jack found himself needing to dismount from time to time to get through some tight spots. As he advanced down the trail, he was enthralled by the beauty of a grove of ancient cedar trees. There was a stream that he followed as it flowed alongside the path. The quiet beauty of the area was still and calm, and he felt like he'd entered an outdoor cathedral, the straight trunks of the trees soaring above, and the branches coming together far overhead. Eventually, he came upon a clearing where people clearly regularly picnicked during their hikes.

Jack paused for a moment to catch his breath in this quiet place. It was spiritual, this grove. He propped his bike against a tree trunk and stretched his achilles tendons. The other day's ride to Murray had been a lot more than he bargained for. It was easy to forget that he wasn't in his twenties anymore, which was the last time he'd spent so much time in the area. Jack flexed his back and neck backwards, stretching as much as he could, until he felt a pop in his lower back. He opened his eyes, and there on the tree, about ten feet in the air, was some kind of marking. After straining his eyes for a few moments, he realized it was some kind of symbol that looked like Two X's underlined. This was accompanied by an arrow that pointed up the hill, and what looked like "3 Mi." Jack felt his heart race a little, and he jumped back on his bike and headed off in the direction indicated by the arrow. As he advanced, he realized that there was a very faint trail. It looked like a deer path, but with effort, he was able to follow it well enough.

As he turned around a bend in the trail, he came across a chain link fence blocking the way that was about ten feet high, with a curl of razor wire at the top. The diamond openings in the chain link of the fence were woven with a synthetic fabric that acted as camouflage, and there was a sign that said, "Do Not Enter. Protected Ecosystem. Danger, Health Hazard." In small letters underneath, he saw the inscription: "U.S. Department of the Interior." The fence was fairly new and well maintained. Jack was skeptical. He'd never heard of anything like this out here. Beyond the fence, where the trail would have continued, someone had planted juniper and red cedar to obscure the path, now growing together far more densely than they would in the wild.

So, he followed along the fence for a few hundred feet and managed to locate a gate. It was padlocked, so he looked around for a rock that was heavy enough to use as a hammer. Soon enough, he managed to locate one that fit his needs. After three whacks, the stone broke the lock, and he was through. He pulled his bike through the gate, backtracked to where the trail intersected the fence, and then continued forward.

After another mile, the forest opened up, and suddenly, there was an old road laid out ahead of him. The trail ended at the road, which disappeared off to his left, headed downhill and to his right up into the mountains. The road was unusual. It was well graded, not like a typical mountain logging track in this area. It was a bit wider than one lane, and there were two wheel-tracks like most of the forest service roads in the region. On the near side of the road, heavy-gauge railroad tracks ran off in both directions. This was not normal. Normally, railroad tracks in the mountains were temporary narrow-gauge logging runs that were pulled up once the current job was completed. Of course, this was done with the intention that they be reused elsewhere by the loggers. Or if heavier gauge tracks were laid for mining that usually meant that they had been installed by a more significant settlement. When those towns died off, those tracks often would get pulled as well. He recalled Henry's story of riding the train out of the village during the fire and excitedly followed the road uphill to see where that might lead him.

As he rode, he noticed that the tracks were still in good condition, despite having a patina of rust. Clearly, they were not in use. Grass had grown to about two feet between the railroad ties. To the left of the tracks was a wagon trail. Jack had initially thought that the road was for trucks, but it was obvious that the twin ruts were too narrow to have been made by truck or car tires. As he continued, Jack could sense that there was water nearby. He heard it in the distance and could feel the blush of humidity and smell the dampness in the air. He was still under the evergreen canopy on the right, but the ground to the left of the road rose very steeply, and ultimately became a rocky cliff face.

The road turned to the left and meandered along for some time. Then suddenly, the trees gave way and all was lit up with sunlight. The ground on the right was a wide field, several hundred acres of tall grass and wildflowers stretching out into the distance for about a mile. To the left, a soaring cliff face had been cut through with explosives at some point. The ground to the right now rose up as well, and it was apparent that someone had cut this pass through the rocks some time ago. There were rocks and some small boulders, and lots of sand and rubble filled parts of the cut, but it was easily passable. The road finally straightened out, and he could hear the distant sound of running water. He realized there was a ravine up ahead, and he could see the remnants of a bridgework that had failed. His heart was pounding. This seemed to be it.

As he approached the ravine, he saw that the road turned into a stone and steel bridge, but that the center span and the far side of the bridge had collapsed. At this point, the road was wide enough to accommodate a wagon on the left side and an ore train on the right—about thirty feet across. What remained of the bridge was extremely well made, very sturdy and constructed with tightly fit blocks of stone and steel girders. Two heavy steel cables on each side of the bridge ran to the edge of the ravine and bent over the edge, cutting deeply into the earth and stone. The remaining ten feet of the train tracks were twisted and then broke off jaggedly.

Jack could see that on the other side of the ravine—about 75 feet across— a corresponding tatter of broken bridgeworks was still in place. Yet to his utter shock, there was an intact town on the other side of the ravine! This was no series of dilapidated, ramshackle buildings falling over like the many other ghost towns he'd come across on various hikes. Rather, this was a fully wrought town, made of brick and stone buildings, all with slate roofs! He could see intact windows reflecting the view back, and in the cobblestoned streets, there were the train tracks—still running through the center of town—and old street lamps along the main street.

Jack straddled his bike, taking in the scene for several minutes. None of this showed up on Google Maps. This was beyond anything he'd ever imagined. His breath caught in his throat. Here was a fully intact town from another era, perfectly preserved yet completely hidden from the modern world. The buildings weren't just standing. They looked inhabited, as if the residents had simply stepped away for the afternoon. Jack felt a strange sense of recognition, like he'd been searching for this place his entire life without knowing it.

He saw that to the left side of the remnants of the bridge someone had tied two ropes, one above, the other below. In the middle of these two ropes there was a half-inch thick, stainless steel cable running between the two ropes, as a way of traversing the ravine. They were attached to the very sturdy steel cables of the failed bridge span on each side as their anchors. Then someone had created metal A frames on either side of the ravine's banks with the foot rope ran through the bottom of the A frames. Likewise, the hand rope ran across the tops of the A frames, and the stainless steel cable completed the three-rope system by running through the center. After carefully inspecting the cable, the ropes, the knots, and all the friction points on his side, it was clear to Jack that this rope bridge was sturdy. More than that, it was meticulously maintained. Someone cared deeply about ensuring their continued access to this place. Instinctively, Jack felt a pull toward the town that easily overrode his usual caution. He knew he would have crossed even if the bridge had been rickety—but he was relieved to see that it was so well made.

Jack left his bike leaning against the side of the ruins of the stone bridge and climbed out onto the rope bridge. Ever so carefully, he inched across, sliding his feet along. Jack moved slowly but confidently, allowing his feet to bear the majority of his weight. Of course, he held tightly to the hand rope. Despite several panicky moments, he never really felt as if he were in any danger of falling. He only paused once mid-trip to focus and catch his breath. Otherwise, he kept moving. He figured if he let himself think about where he was and what he was doing, it might actually become dangerous. Once on the other side, he made a quick inspection of the knots and friction points where the ropes were connected on this side of the bridge. On seeing that they were very secure, he felt even better. Now safely across, he turned his attention to the town.

Along the bank of the ravine on this, the town side, there were some buildings that had collapsed as the edge of the ravine had given way, probably due to erosion. There also was evidence that these buildings on the edge of the town had been burned at some point. The two, large stone buildings that flanked the bridge's landing remained intact, though their iron gates hung open and rusted. The building on the west side of the road showed signs on its facade that indicated it had been an armory. Conversely, the building on the east side of the road still bore a weathered sign, designating it as "Stables." Above the entrance, a steel catwalk stretched between the buildings' second floors, its wood and iron gates pulled back against the walls and secured with large, steel hooks.

The cobblestone street on the other side of the bridgeworks was surprisingly still in very good shape, not a blade of grass growing out of the seams, not a stone out of place. The curbstones were made of slate, and the sidewalks were slabs of bluestone. The railroad tracks continued on this side of the ravine, twisted and broken off where the bridge had fallen, but otherwise, they ran unimpeded from the ravine on into town. As for the road itself, it was wide enough for a horse-drawn carriage to the left and a train to the right. Unlike the ruins of the structures close to the ravine, the remaining town seemed to be in remarkably good shape and well maintained.

Just past the armory and stables, Jack reached the first intersection. Street signs marked the cross streets: Cliff Street running west and Stable Road running east, and the main road, the one he was walking on, was designated as Broadway. The buildings here were massive, long brick structures that stood two stories high with a third floor captured within mansard roofs. They were well-appointed with dormers and decorative trim. The facades were equipped with covered porches, the topmost roof of which came out from the soffit at the base of the mansard roof itself. The first and second floors of the buildings on each side of the road mirrored each other. They were set up with gothic pointed arches both for doorways and windows, the dormer windows having caps that followed the same shape.

Where the buildings started, the sidewalks terminated, giving way to the long, covered porches. The porches themselves became the *de facto* sidewalks after three steps up. Clearly this would have been helpful during bad weather, both in rain and snow. These sheltered walkways would have kept this town traversable year-round, even at the peak of winter. The sidewalks had ornate lamps built into them on tall lamp posts, and the porch sidewalks of the buildings incorporated the same style lamps. These lights were attached with heads both outside and inside the structure and drew fuel oil from the same source. The lamp posts were incorporated into the architecture of the pillars supporting the two floors of porches. The whole of the structure was made from cast iron, and the paint on these lamps, while occasionally peeled or bubbled, had been maintained over the years. The effect of these covered porches with decorative ironworks and incorporated lamps evoked for him a bit of the French Quarter of New Orleans, without the sultry Southern feeling or the plants.

Taking all this in, Jack approached the building on his left and slowly climbed the steps to the porch walkway, stopping now and again to peer into the windows and doors. To his amazement, the glass was intact, and the wooden trim on the windows and doors was in remarkably good repair. Of course, the paint was peeling here and there, but nothing was out of sorts. He cupped his fingers around his forehead and peered inside what appeared to be a saloon. Furniture was covered in yellowed, rotting sheets, but all was well-appointed and intact. Dust covered the floor and bar, but not a single footprint was visible anywhere. The walls were all dark wood, with ornately carved mouldings and woodwork. It looked like a seasonal hotel that had been left for a few years after being closed up carefully at the end of a season.

It was about three in the afternoon, leaving Jack plenty of time to explore. In no particular hurry, he walked down the covered sidewalk looking in windows, trying doors, which were without exception all locked. Every space was the same, as if it had been closed up for the season and that downtime had lasted longer than anyone had expected. Not a window was broken. Not a door was unlocked. It was almost disturbingly intact.

As he made his way north along Broadway, he was bewildered at the scope and scale of this abandoned town. The street continued for several more blocks ahead of him. Yet as he gazed left and right down the side streets, they also went on for blocks. There must be hundreds of buildings here, he thought. The side streets were paved as well, with some grass growing from between the cobblestones, the further out, the higher the grass. He reached another intersection marked Clay Street running east and west. The bridge was behind him to the south if he were to retrace his steps along Broadway.

On the northwest corner of Clay Street and Broadway stood a building that clearly had been a police station. It continued the arched theme, but the windows and doors were carefully fitted with barred iron gates. The front entrance of the building was flanked by two, large lamps with blue, stained-glass globes over them. On the northeast corner stood what had been a fire station, with large beautiful wooden doors most likely for a hand-drawn or horse-drawn apparatus with pumps and hoses. The architecture was delightfully gothic.

Jack noticed that not only were the cobblestoned streets well constructed, they had gutters running to regularly positioned, iron-grated storm drains—much like a modern city. As he peered down Broadway he could see that the street continued for several more blocks before the town terminated where the mountain started growing vertically again. There it seemed as if the train tracks disappeared into an ornately decorated tunnel in the mountain. To the west of the tunnel a large, brick gothic structure stood. It was full of sharply peaked roofs, ornate to the point of ostentatiousness. It was made of three different colors of brick, with intricate patterns inlaid. Intrigued, he wandered onward down Broadway toward this building.

As he walked, block after block, Jack realized these buildings were in too good a shape to be abandoned. The brickwork and stonework was all pointed, with no gaps in the mortar. There was no debris on the street and no grass growing through anything. This wasn't a ghost town—it was a town waiting. For what, he couldn't say, but the sense of expectation hung in the air like the scent of rain before a storm.

He passed a general store, a theater, several saloons, and some restaurants. The signs on these buildings were faded to the point that they were barely legible. However, with effort, you could just make out the words. He passed an open lot that had an ornate, wrought-iron archway across it. He guessed that it was an outdoor farmers market of some sort. On the east side of Broadway, between what appeared to be Randall Road and the final cross street, stood a large, beautifully columned building that took up a whole block. It had a carved stone sign, still in perfect shape, that read, "Crystal Village Hot Springs" in large letters, and underneath in smaller letters, "Pool | Public Baths | Steam Rooms | Showers."

As he stood gawking at this ornate building, off to his left he heard a voice in the distance shout, "Halloooo!" Jack turned to look and saw a man walking out of the front doors of the elaborately decorated gothic building he'd been approaching. The sign above the entrance was now visible, and it read, "Seeley Mining Company" in bright, gold letters inscribed on a dark-blue field. The man was tall, just about Jack's height of six feet. He had white hair, a bushy, white mustache. He wore a dark-blue stetson hat with a black band around the base and a flat brim. He was wearing a dark-blue cardigan sweater under a dark canvas jacket and relatively new jeans with black leather boots. Jack walked toward him and met him in the center of the square that had been built at the intersection of Broadway and Spring Street, close to the large building the man was leaving.

The man approached slowly. He looked to be about seventy or eighty years old but walked crisply and clearly had kept himself in good shape. As he got close enough, Jack could see that he was smiling, and his eyes were pale blue, like Paul Newman's.

The man stopped and put out his hand, and in a deep commanding voice with a local accent, he said, "Hello! I'm Ian Seeley. I see you've found Crystal Village."

Jack balked before weakly taking his hand. "Uhm ... Hi. I'm Jack Seeley ..."

The man's eyes widened slightly, then crinkled at the corners. "Jack! Hello, Jack. I've been waiting to meet you for some time now."

A chill ran down Jack's spine despite the warm afternoon sun. "Meet me?

You know who I am?"

The man smiled, a genuine warmth spreading across his weathered face. "Yes, I've known all about you your whole life. It's sort of my job, you might say. I take care of the village, and I make sure it's preserved for the legacy of the family—at least until someone decides to do something with it. Your grandfather found this place when he was in his thirties, but he decided not to take it on. Sadly, your father never made his way here. So I guess that left you. I'm very excited that you've found it.

I I I I

Jack sat at a table in a cafe on the corner of Broadway and Spring Streets in Crystal Village. He had a steaming cup of black tea in front of him. The table was set for two, and across from him a man sat who called himself Ian Seeley. He'd spelled it out, I-A-N, to be clear that it was different from his great-great-grandfather's spelling. Jack had just been told that when Crystal Village was evacuated in 1910, as the ore train pulled out to escape the oncoming firestorm, the bridge collapsed behind the train. For some reason—perhaps some freakish, mountain air currents—the fire split around the town, and only a handful of buildings along its edges caught fire. His great-great-grandfather Eoinn Seeley and his men fought the fires and put them out, preserving the village.

"But if the village survived the fire," Jack asked, "why didn't anyone come back?"

"That's harder to explain," Ian replied. "Things had gone well for the village for more than forty years, but there were problems brewing. The mine was tapping out. Apparently, they'd pulled as much value from it as they could. But truth be told, they didn't need the money any longer, because Eoinn and Angus had done such a great job investing the village's wealth into funds that could preserve it forever, if they wanted. But they had never told anyone about the finances, other than the other founders. Folks in the village just knew that they had everything they needed. He didn't want to start an argument about finances, since he'd never disclosed it before, so he didn't ever bring it up. The other founders understood how much money there was, but wealth was never their motivation in the first place. As the mine was tapping out, the community was experiencing a lot of stress. Eoinn was trying to find other industries the village could engage in, but at the time of the fire, he hadn't sorted that out.

"The first generation of children had grown up, and they were restless. Some didn't want to stay in the village and take on mining jobs or administration jobs at the mine or work in local stores or restaurants. They wanted to go out into the world and find their way. Some wanted to be educated, and others just wanted out. While he'd been able to stave it off for almost forty years, the townspeople were falling into a deeply divisive political cycle. Half the village supported the Seeley's, the founders and their leadership and ownership of the village, but the other half did not. This second group wanted to have explicit shares in ownership and have a say in how things ran. Eoinn's oldest son John was sympathetic to this second group, and he felt like he was caught in the middle. He simply didn't want to inherit the responsibility of running the mining company or the village. He'd told his father this, and it was a source of immense frustration for Eoinn.

"Eoinn was a great man and a great leader, but in this, he was foolish about people's motivations and willingness to be led. His Achilles' heel was that he had a big ego. He felt that the people of the village should be grateful for what they had, that they should be happy to not be bogged down in owning things, and be happy to be taken care of. He had a bit of a "feudal" mentality, perhaps from his European roots. He just didn't understand the idea that people wanted autonomy and ownership in things.

"In the weeks before the fire, he had come to the conclusion that things had to change, but he was bitter and unhappy about it. So when the fire came, and everyone left, and it was just him and the rest of his men, he gave up on his dream. He told the others that they could stay or they could leave, but that Crystal Village was done. He'd preserve it, protect it, but he fully intended to hide it away. His beloved wife Rose had died a few years before, so he had nobody but his sons who had escaped to Kellogg. Finn, his best friend, stayed with him, and the younger founders left and met their families in Wallace. There they spread the story that the village was destroyed, and that Eoinn and Finn had died heroically trying to save it. They told everyone that there was nothing left. Angus distributed a lot of wealth out to the survivors, which helped people accept their changed fate. There was so much chaos following the fire across the whole region that people just focused on settling in and starting over.

"But that wasn't the truth. The village and the rest of the men *had* survived, and while your great-grandfather John had settled down and was satisfied with his life outside the village, his younger brother Ian was not. John and Ian had a contentious relationship. After the fire, the two had come to blows during a heated argument about going back up to the village to see what was left. John was adamant that he didn't want to go. So after their fight, Ian left in secret, telling no one where he was going. He was the only one who went back up into the mountains to see what had happened. He found the village, his father, and Finn. He was initiated into their plan. They would all stay in the village. They would maintain it and the wealth that it had generated. They would keep it secret and keep it safe.

"Ian became the caretaker of the space, as the others were older men. He forged a business agreement with the law firm that had been set up to manage the trust, and on one of his trips into Boise to meet with them, he met a woman. He brought her back to the village, and she had a son, who they also named Ian. This cycle repeated, until I was born in 1945. But sadly, I never found anyone like my mother. After me, there will be nobody left to take care of this place. So as you can see, this all comes back to you."

Jack sat and listened to Ian's story unfold. He was awestruck by the implications. But he was completely taken aback by the idea that his cousin, third cousin once removed according to Ian, now seemed to be saying he was expected to take over the maintenance from him.

"Whoah! Are you saying that I'm supposed to take care of this place? That this is now my responsibility?"

Ian paused and hesitated for a moment, then he replied, "I'm saying that this is all being left to you. The town, the trust, and all that entails. You're the last Seeley, and you can do what you want with it. If you refuse it, and you don't want to take it on, that's okay too. There's enough money to keep this place intact virtually forever, and I've left clear instructions for what is to happen should anything happen to me."

Ian lowered his voice and leaned forward in his chair staring directly into Jack's eyes, "But this place shouldn't be kept a secret. It should pass on to you, and frankly, I think you should do something spectacular with it."

They continued to talk, and Ian explained how the village had maintained its secrecy over the years. All the way back at the beginning it had been established within the territorial legal system as a state secret. This had been set up early on and renewed repeatedly through use of legal loopholes, and he didn't say but implied that Eoinn had made use of outright bribes. Eoinn Seeley had many connections from the Civil War that really paid off. He'd saved the life of the man who would eventually become the second Idaho territorial governor during the First Battle of Bull Run. He'd met and formed a relationship with Ulyses S. Grant during the War. They'd discovered that County Tyrone in Ireland was where Grant's ancestors were from, and Eoinn knew his relatives there. He played on this relationship as well. Once established as a protected space with a special governmental categorization, the location remained unlisted on maps. Over time, this status extended to aerial and satellite imagery, which treated it like a protected military installation, excluding it from publicly available views. Even Google Maps and similar services had no pictures of the village, because of this existing system that had grandfathered into modern times.

"But what about hikers? How have you kept people from finding this place over the years?" Jack asked. "You're not really that far away from some very popular trails."

"So far," Ian replied, "the signs and fences have worked. There's only one place a person is likely to come across the road, and I'm assuming it's right where you found it. You had to climb a fence that was fairly daunting and ignore the hazard signs."

"Well, actually," Jack said sheepishly, "I found a gate and broke the lock. Padlocks are notoriously easy to break."

Ian smiled and chuckled, "Well, there's your first job tomorrow then. There have been a few instances of small airplanes flying over, despite this being restricted airspace. But visits from ambiguously credentialed men who never explicitly claim government affiliation or declare the site a top-secret installation have kept things quiet."

"So how is all this paid for?" Jack asked.

"There's a trust set up that covers all the expenses," Ian answered, "and it is also quietly taking care of the ancestors of the original eight founders of the village. We track them, and when they're experiencing financial hardship, we step in unobtrusively and help them get back on track. Nobody gets rich, but nobody suffers—if they're willing to work. A few of the people over the years have had drug problems or mental illnesses and were unwilling to accept help, but if a nudge back in the right direction works, we take care of them."

Jack stared through and past Ian, for a moment he was lost in thought. Then said, "When I was applying for college, I was sent a notification that I'd received a scholarship that covered my tuition and all my expenses. However, I never applied for that scholarship. Was that you?"

Ian smiled wryly and said, "Yes. Every descendant of the village receives the same scholarship if they apply to college. Each of them receives the money from a different fund that has its own name and a backstory behind how they were selected. But all of the "scholarships" derive from the same place."

"How is this all managed?" asked Jack in awe of the scale of the operations of the village. "It's got to be a logistical nightmare!"

"It's actually part of the way the trust is arranged," Ian explained. "There's an entire spectrum of legal entities and a broad framework in place—shell corporations and foundations hidden from each other. All those entities are managed by the Crystal Village Trust, though that isn't the legal name we use. There are probably five hundred people working full time to manage it. I don't really have to do much other than show up for board meetings once a quarter, and most of those I attend via video."

"Five hundred people?" Jack stammered. "How big is this trust?"

"Oh, last I checked it was more than fifty billion dollars," Ian replied nonchalantly, "more than enough to keep this place maintained and secret. I don't think you realize how much gold, silver, and precious stones were found here. But more importantly, Eoinn saw early on how the finance industry was going to play out, and he invested well."

Jack was stunned. "But to what end? Why keep this place a secret after all these years? Is the main focus of what you've done with this fund limited to keeping this place maintained, paying for college scholarships, helping people get approved for mortgages, and helping with medical expenses?"

"Well, that's the thing," said Ian thoughtfully. "It's been all up to me—what we do with this place. How we manage the funds for ancestors is managed by a trust that was set up well before my time, and I'm not so involved. As far as Crystal Village goes, I don't have any ties to the outside world, and I wouldn't even know what to do with it. I've been waiting for you. This all goes to you."

Jack paused, then asked, "You don't care if it stays a secret? There's no set of rules I'd have to follow? Are you saying that I can do anything I want?"

Ian nodded. "Once you take this on, you can do what you want with it."

IIII

Jack's head was spinning, and he decided to spend the night in Crystal Village. There was no cellular service out here. Like everything else pertaining to Crystal Village, that was apparently intentional. Jack was able to connect his phone to wifi—Ian shocked him by saying the whole main street of the village was online—to call Amy and tell her he was going to be away for the night. He assured her that he was safe. As night fell, Jack was surprised to note that the village had electricity.

"Yes, even before the fire, the village had electricity," Ian had explained. "Eoinn was nothing if not a futurist. He and Egan Sullivan, one of the founders who was an engineer, saw the benefits of electricity on a trip to Ouray, Colorado. After that, Egan had an idea for what it would mean not only for mining, but for day-to-day living. With that in mind, he bought some dynamos and set up hydroelectric power. As a result, all these buildings have electric lights and power, and all the streetlights are electric. The original dynamo was replaced with a modern hydroelectric system about ten years ago, and I've added some battery banks just last year—so this place has power to spare. Of course, the wiring in the buildings is old, knob-and-tube-style wiring. And it should come as no surprise that I don't turn the street lights on at night, because there's nobody here, but also because that would attract unwanted attention. But be assured, they all work. I have a small crew that comes in to do the work of keeping the place up, about ten people. They're all under strict NDAs, and they are only here during the summer, a few weeks a month."

He and Ian talked for hours. Then Ian showed him to a bedroom in one of the village's three hotels, the Hawthorne. It was one of a handful of buildings that were still in use. His head still buzzing, Jack lay in his bed in the hotel and looked at the ceiling. He chuckled to himself, saying to no one in particular, "Well the mattress leaves a lot to be desired. But the room is elegant."

He felt like he'd stepped back in time. He was on the second floor, and his balcony opened out onto a terrace that overlooked the street. He got up carefully, the bed springs creaking like he was in an old cartoon. He walked over to the balcony and opened the doors, which were in fantastic shape. He walked barefoot onto the balcony and looked over the dark town. The moon was rising and was nearly full in the clear night sky.

Jack walked back in and sat on the edge of the hotel bed, the ancient springs creaking beneath him as he pulled out his phone. The wi-fi connection worked perfectly, and soon he was staring at Susanne's contact information. His thumb hovered over the call button for a long moment before he pressed it.

"Jack?" Susanne's voice came through clearly. "Perfect timing. I just got back to my hotel room."

"How did the meetings go? Did Netflix bite?"

"Better than I could have hoped," she replied brightly. He could hear the excitement in her voice, mixed with exhaustion. "They love the series concept. They want to option all five books!"

"Susanne, that's incredible! Congratulations!" Jack felt a surge of genuine happiness for her success. "Do they need you to relocate?"

"Not exactly. It may take more than a year to start development on a show. They want me to stay involved as a consulting producer, but most of the work can be done remotely. They understand that my connection to Idaho is part of what makes the stories authentic." She paused. "They did offer me a development deal for future projects, which is surreal. I'm flying back to Spokane in the morning to process all of this."

"That's amazing!" Jack replied. "I'm so proud of you."

"Thanks. It still doesn't feel real." Her voice softened. "But enough about me. How was your day? Did you make any progress finding Crystal Village?"

Jack took a deep breath, hardly knowing where to begin. "Susanne, I found it. I found Crystal Village."

Silence on the other end of the line. Then Susanne spoke in a hushed tone, "What do you mean you found it?"

"I mean I'm sitting in a hotel room in Crystal Village right now! The Hawthorne Hotel, to be exact. The whole town is here, Susanne. Intact. Preserved. Like someone just stepped away for the afternoon."

"That's impossible." Her voice was barely a whisper. "The fire destroyed everything. Henry's memoir, all the family stories—"

"That's what everyone was told. But it's not true." Jack stood and walked to the balcony doors. "There's a man here, Ian Seeley—spelled I-A-N— differently than the original E-O-I-N-N. He's been taking care of the place for decades. His family has been the caretakers since 1910."

"Jack, are you sure you're not—I mean, are you feeling okay?"

Jack laughed. "I'm not having some kind of breakdown." He opened the balcony doors and stepped outside. "Hold on, let me show you what I'm seeing."

The moon cast silver light across the cobblestone streets below. Jack held up his phone, switching to Facetime. "Can you see this?"

Susanne's face appeared on the screen, her eyes wide with disbelief. She was sitting on a hotel bed, her hair pulled back in a messy ponytail. "Oh my God, Jack! Those are actual buildings! Actual streets!"

"Broadway runs right down the center of town, just like in Henry's memoir. The hot springs building is here, the mining company office—Seeley Mining Company—everything." He turned the phone to show her the view. "There are covered porches connecting all the buildings on the main street, just like we saw in Molly's photographs."

"This is incredible." Susanne's voice was thick with emotion. "I can't believe it's real. I can't believe it survived all these years."

Jack walked to the balcony railing, holding the phone steady so she could see the moonlit town spread out below. "It's more than survived. It's been *maintained*. The electricity works—they had electricity before the fire, can you believe that? The buildings are sound, the streets are clean. Ian told me the whole story—how the fire split around the town, how Eoinn and the others decided to keep it secret."

"Why secret?" Susanne asked in confusion. "Why not let people know it was still here? Think of all the families who grieved for this place."

"Politics. Internal conflicts that were tearing the community apart before the fire." Jack leaned against the railing. "Eoinn was bitter about the way things had been going. He was depressed after his wife died and became paranoid and secretive. The younger generation wanted ownership, wanted democracy. He felt betrayed by the community he'd built, like they were ungrateful for everything he'd provided."

"So he just ... let everyone think it was gone?"

"Him and Finn McEnhill. They stayed behind, fought the fires, preserved what they could. Then the others of the Original Eight spread the story that the town was completely destroyed, and that they'd died heroically trying to save it." Jack's voice carried a note of sadness. "Ian says Eoinn gave up on his dream of community. He decided to hide the village away rather than deal with the conflicts."

"That's heartbreaking. All those families, starting over and grieving the loss of the village, when their home was still there."

"But here's the thing." Jack's voice quickened with excitement. "Ian is the last caretaker. He's in his eighties, never had children. He's been waiting for someone from the founding families to take over."

"Take over what, exactly?"

"The whole thing! The village, the trust that maintains it, everything." Jack turned to look back at the buildings behind him. "And Susanne, there's money. A lot of money. Apparently, the mines produced more wealth than anyone realized, and Eoinn invested it brilliantly. The trust is worth over fifty billion dollars."

"Fifty billion?" Susanne's voice cracked. "That's not possible!"

"It's been funding college scholarships for descendants of the original families, helping with medical expenses, mortgages—they've been quietly taking care of everyone for over a century." Jack ran his free hand through his hair. "Ian showed me records. Remember that scholarship I got for college? The one I never applied for? Remember how your parents found money for your education unexpectedly?"

"That was them?"

"That was them. They've been watching over all of us, all the descendants, making sure we would have opportunities." Jack's voice grew more animated. "And I keep thinking about my work, about theme parks and immersive experiences. This place could be something revolutionary."

"A theme park?" Susanne's voice carried a note of concern. "Jack, this is a piece of history. These were real people's lives."

"Not a typical theme park. Something respectful, something that honors the story and brings it back to life." He gestured toward the town spread out below him. "Imagine if we could recreate Crystal Village at its peak. Limited access, like Yomohiro's parks in Japan. People could experience what life was like here and meet the people who lived here."

"We?" The word came out softly.

Jack felt his cheeks warm. "Of course! I mean ... if you wanted to be involved. This is your family's story too. You understand these people, their lives, their struggles, better than anyone. And with your Netflix deal, you'll have credibility in the entertainment industry."

Susanne was quiet for a long moment. When she spoke, her voice was thoughtful. "You know, they asked me about other projects during the meetings today."

"This could be perfect for that. Your novels all take place here in Idaho, and this could be a straight extension. Real history, real people, but presented in a way that makes it accessible to modern audiences. Yomohiro doesn't have a U.S. distribution partner yet, so Netflix might be the right partner."

"It would have to be done right," Susanne said firmly. "We'd have to honor the families, tell their stories faithfully."

"Absolutely. We could base everything on real historical records—Henry's memoir, Molly's archives, all the letters and photographs. And apparently, there's tons of stuff here, since the fire didn't actually destroy the place." Jack began to pace the small balcony. "We could use technology to recreate the town as it was but also show the tensions, the difficult decisions people faced."

"What does Ian think about all this?"

"He said the place shouldn't be kept secret anymore. In his words, 'He wants someone to do something spectacular with it.'" Jack stopped pacing and gripped the balcony railing. "Susanne, this could change everything. Not just for us, but for how people experience history, how they connect with their past. I like to think of these kinds of things as 'systems,' and from a systems-design perspective, if we make this work here, we could recreate the model in other places."

"It's overwhelming," she admitted. "This morning I was worried about whether Netflix would even be interested in my books. Now you're talking about bringing a lost town back to life."

"I know it's a lot. But think about it—your great-grandmother Sam King, she was just a nine-year-old orphan when the other founders of this village found her. She grew up to become one of the leaders of this community. That's a story worth telling."

"And your great-great-grandfather Eoinn, for all his flaws, built something remarkable there." Susanne's voice grew stronger. "Maybe it's time their stories were told properly, not just hidden away or reduced to family legends."

"So you'd consider it? Working together on this?"

"Jack, after everything that's happened—finding each other again, discovering all this history, and now this opportunity—I think I'd be crazy not to consider it." She paused. "But I need to see it for myself. I need to walk those streets, see the buildings where my ancestors lived."

"Of course. When you get back, we'll come up here together. Ian wants to show me more of the village tomorrow and explain how everything works." Jack hesitated. "... Susanne?"

"Yeah?"

"... I'm glad we found each other again."

"Me too." Her voice was soft. "This feels like destiny, doesn't it? Being drawn back to this place after so many years."

Jack looked out over the moonlit town, imagining it filled with life once again. "I think our ancestors would be amazed to know that their descendants have come back to the village and are considering ways of sharing it with the world."

"Or terrified," Susanne said with a laugh. "Eoinn Seeley was pretty protective of his vision for this place."

"Then we'll have to make sure we do it right. Honor their memory while bringing their story to the world."

"Get some sleep, Jack. We have a lot to figure out when I get back."

"We do. But I doubt there's much sleep in my future." Jack said, smiling. He felt the weight of possibility settling around him. "Good night, Susanne. And congratulations again on Netflix. You deserve all of this success."

"Thank you. And Jack? Thank you for calling me, for including me in this discovery. It means everything."

After they hung up, Jack remained on the balcony for a long time, watching the moonlight play across the cobblestones and imagining the streets filled with life once again. Somewhere in the distance, he could hear the sound of water flowing through the hot springs, the same springs that had drawn the original settlers to this hidden valley over 150 years ago.

In his mind's eye, he started to see this town reinvigorated and full of people. He imagined the streetlights on, the bars full of patrons, and couples walking on the street with children running around playing games. He started to think about the Japanese model that Yomohiro-san had created for his theme parks, where only a limited number of people were allowed in at a time. He remembered how they ran a lottery for access. He thought about the reality television show that followed the winners around in the parks, and the fact that the show was a huge success.

Jack's musings shifted to the massively multiplayer online games created for the Asian market that extended the worlds established in the movies. He thought about the manga comic books, the theme parks, and the related television shows, where people could visit virtually and participate. He thought about how his new job was to come up with an inside-out version of this model, starting with the theme parks, television shows, and extending toward live action and animated feature films, commissioned novels, comics and online games.

He was wide awake, and he walked back into his room and dressed. He went down into the street and started to explore the town. Ian had given him a key that would open any door in the village. He went to the main electrical room that Ian had shown him and threw the huge axe-like switch to turn on all the power in the village. He switched on the street lights. He made use of the master key. With it, he entered stores that still had vintage goods on the shelves, restaurants that had been cleared of food but had pots and pans and cutlery, and dusty homes that could easily be presumed to have been abandoned months ago—were it not for the peeling wallpaper.

He looked at the town with new eyes, the eyes of a Disney imagineer and theme park attraction designer. He wondered what it would take to install a 360-degree-coverage camera system that could cover all angles of the public spaces of the town. He considered the way that the buildings on the main streets were effectively one unified facade with multiple levels of porches. They were all connected in such a way that you could walk the entire length of the street on any floor of the buildings. He noted that even the third floor at the level of the base of the mansard roofs was interconnected and had iron railings running along the front so nobody would fall off.

He wondered at it all as he wandered the town all night. However, the idea had crystalized for him in seconds. It occurred to him while he was standing on the balcony in the moonlight—He was going to turn Crystal Village into a theme park the likes of which the world had never seen!

<h1 style="text-align:center">17</h1>

<h1 style="text-align:center">Insight</h1>

July 2028

Jack knew that Yomohiro-san needed to approve the unique circumstances behind Crystal Village becoming the site of the theme park. He sat at the desk at his grandmother's house in front of his laptop. He pulled images of the village from his phone and incorporated them into his presentation.

Jack waited until it was morning in Tokyo, and then he instant-messaged Yomohiro-san to ask for a quick video conference. Moments later, Jack was on a video call with him. "Yomohiro-san, it's Jack Seeley calling from Idaho in the US."

"Jack! It's great to hear from you," said Yomohiro. "But I thought you were still on your vacation."

"Well, technically," Jack chuckled, "I guess I am—but I wanted to talk to you about something I've discovered. I believe I may have found the location for the park."

"Please," said Yomohiro, "tell me about this location you've found."

Jack explained about Crystal Village, how he'd found the information about the village in an old trunk, how he'd figured out how to find it, and about the fact that it was still in perfect condition. Then he explained that it had been left to him.

"Yomohiro-san," Jack declared, "I believe that this pristinely preserved, Old West mining town is the perfect location for our park! I'd like to show you a quick presentation that I've put together. This place? It's unbelievable."

Jack walked Yomohiro through his presentation, explaining what each building was, and his thoughts about the approach he wanted to take.

"Jack, this is very interesting," Yomohiro said. "I especially love the bits about how you found the village. Very Goonies. And those pictures are stunning! Can you send the whole presentation to me so I can look through it again?"

"Yes, absolutely," Jack said, "I'll send it now ... There ...I just hit send."

There was a long pause while Yomohiro went through the presentation.

"Jack," Yomohiro said with an excited tone in his voice, "I want to come see it for myself. If you just were to pitch this to the team, I fear they would think you were self-serving, since you own the property. But I think I understand the appeal this has for you, and I would like to come see it in person. I will bring two of my trusted executives and one who I believe will be the troublemaker. We shall see if we can convince her." Yomohiro took a deep breath, trying to calm his own excitement. "So, Jack, when can we come?"

Jack paused and thought about it. "If you give me three weeks, I can have a bit more work done to prepare for your arrival."

"I will have my assistant reach out to you with details on our availability, and she will coordinate with you on how to get us there," said Yomohiro.

"Hai, Yomohiro-san," said Jack.

"Sayonara, Jack."

Jack ended the meeting and thought about what he needed to do in order to convince the board that this was the right place to build their park. Jack picked up his phone and texted Susanne.

Jack: *"Hey. Want to go up to Crystal Village with me in the morning?"*
Susanne: *"Hell yes!"*
Jack: *"Great, I'll pick you up at 8 a.m. with coffee and food."*

Susanne: *"Fantastic! I'm going through my father's things. I found some interesting stuff. More tomorrow."*

Jack called the phone number Ian had given him, telling him he'd be up in the morning. He asked Ian if he had any old photographs or papers that Jack could see. Ian affirmed that he did, and Jack asked him to please have them available when he came. Then Jack went down to join his grandmother for dinner.

I I I I

The next morning Jack arrived at Susanne's house with coffee, pastries, breakfast sandwiches, and an additional supply of sandwiches and drinks for lunch. In their conversation via satellite phone the day before, Ian had told Jack that he'd have a helicopter meet him at the Shoshone County Airport a few miles out of town. So Jack and Suzanne drove there. As they exited I-90 and drove down the dirt road toward the airport, they saw a helicopter coming in for a landing. They drove to the parking area and parked where Ian had suggested. Then they walked over to the new helipad that had been installed just a few months before. A man was waiting, leaning up against another car in the parking lot. He walked up to them and explained he was going to escort them onto the helicopter. He got them settled in the back seat and showed them how to buckle in and get their headphones on. Once they had their headphones with microphones on, they could hear the pilot.

"Hi, Jack, I'm Skip. Ian asked me to come get you. You must be Susanne?"

"Yes, I'm Jack, great to meet you, Skip."

"Hi, yes I'm Susanne," Susanne replied, smiling at Jack.

"Have either of you been on a helicopter before?" asked Skip.

Jack said that he had, and Susanne laughed and admitted that she had not.

"Okay," Skip replied, "so I'm going to be flying you up to Crystal Village today. This is kind of exciting for me. I've been flying Ian and workers up to the village for about fifteen years. But I understand, Jack, that you're

Ian's cousin and might be taking a more active role in the village?"

Jack affirmed that this was the plan, and Skip continued, "That's really fantastic! It's kind of hard not being able to tell anyone about this place. I hope you're planning to do something really wonderful up there. So let's get flying. And, Suzanne, I promise I'll try to keep things as smooth as possible."

Jack grabbed Susanne by the hand and squeezed it tightly, expecting to let go, but she latched on hard. She'd told him in the car that her father's things included a couple of intriguing artifacts that she assumed came from Crystal Village, and that her great-aunt called and said another cousin had a box of things in his attic that might also prove interesting. She explained that she had made plans to meet with her cousin in a few weeks.

The helicopter ride turned out to be very quick. In fifteen minutes, they were setting down in the main square of Crystal Village, near the old mine entrance and the mining company offices. They thanked Skip and quickly stepped off the helicopter, which took off again once they were safely out of the way. Having been awaiting their arrival, Ian stepped out of the corner cafe where he'd enjoyed meals with Jack previously.

Ian approached Susanne and gave her a big hug, saying, "Susanne, I'm so happy to finally meet you! I was truly sorry to hear about your mother's passing last year."

Susanne gave him an awkward smile and thanked him. After dropping their bags in the cafe, they walked through the village. Ian gave them a more deeply involved tour than even Jack had gotten the first time he'd visited.

Together, they walked all the way down Broadway to what remained of the old bridge, occasionally stopping to peer into or enter one of the buildings. They saw that the shelves in the Monsieur Lemieux Mercantile & General Store were still stocked with dusty items. Ian was a good tour guide, pointing down Clay Street. He explained that at the end of this street was the brickyard, where all the bricks used by the town had been fabricated.

Susanne was enthralled. She was as awed walking these streets as Jack had been. Thoroughly enjoying his charges' sense of wonder, Ian showed them the townhouse where Sam King O'Connor and Seamus O'Connor had lived. It was situated next to the Hawthorne hotel where Jack had stayed last time he'd been here. Upon leaving the O'Connor residence, they crossed the street and backtracked half a block, then went into the Hot Springs and Pool building. There Ian showed them the beautifully tiled spaces. The walls of the pool area were all made up of mosaics depicting scenes from the town's history. The images included the first miner who discovered the plateau, the other miners joining him, the arrival of the Original Eight, and the building of the village. There was a scene where a group of men on horses were riding through the village and shooting guns in the air. Finally, there was a scene where the whole village was depicted in winter with Christmas decorations.

Ian said, "The best part of the way that Egan designed and constructed the pool, soaking tubs, and showers is that he took advantage of the fact that the water from the hot springs is naturally antiseptic. You see, there are trace amounts of minerals that naturally form a kind of mild solution that has most of the characteristics of iodine, although not enough to discolor the water. Also, the pools naturally fill and drain, so the water is always fresh and warm.

"Of course, we do have to make sure that the walls are cleaned every so often. To that end, I have a crew that comes in regularly. Otherwise, we'd have a serious mold problem. Yet, despite these minor difficulties, this space has been able to operate for more than one hundred years without any major changes. Luckily, the pipes were all much larger than needed, because at some point they'll get blocked with mineral deposits. That said, they probably have another fifty years before that happens. A while back, I did have to replace some of the pipes near the source of both this hot spring and the spring that feeds the heating systems. That spring has much lower mineral content than this one, but it is also slightly acidic, which leads to some of the pipes rotting out over the years. With that in mind, we did put a new system onto that plumbing that neutralizes the PH."

They returned to the mining company offices, and Ian had laid out a large set of photographs, some in folders, some framed. They were laid out on a long set of tables in the main office room. There were hundreds of them. Jack and Susanne looked through all of them, amazed at the thoroughness of the documentation. Ian explained that several of the people in the village had been photographers, most notably one of the Original Eight, Sean. He had taken up the hobby and was responsible for a large percentage of the pictures. Among the photos, there was a very large, printed and framed image of the "Roebling Bridge" where the detail was incredible.

Susanne said, "These were printed from very large negatives. I'm guessing at least 8x10 plates. This is such a wonderful collection to work from."

"Well," Ian said, "there's a darkroom at the back of the office where Sean and the other photographers worked to make these. A lot of their original equipment is still there, and there's a storage closet with glass-plate negatives that might also be interesting."

After finishing their initial explorations of the mining offices, they walked back over to the cafe to have lunch. Once they were eating Jack told Ian more about his idea to turn the village into a destination and park. He had to start and stop several times, because Ian didn't have any context for Yomohiro Corporation or any of the movies. Jack told him he'd get Ian some DVDs to watch to see some of the movies Yomohiro-san had made. However, as he explained the gist of the kind of work he made and how the theme parks in Japan worked, he saw Ian start to nod his head and smile.

I I I I

The next day Jack and Susanne decided to go explore the family home of Sam King O'Connor and Seamus O'Connor. They'd discussed the natural reticence they were feeling about entering these preserved homes of people who left in such a hurry and under such circumstances. It felt a little disrespectful, but in reality, there was nobody alive from that time. At some point, these places needed to be opened up. Jack wondered what they'd find.

Jack and Suzanne walked in the front door and recognized immediately that things were cleaned and well preserved. There were coats hanging in the front entry closet and boots on the floor. The coats and boots were made of animal fur, and the craftsmanship was outstanding. Of course, Ian had previously explained to them that there were two furriers in the village at its peak. Beyond that, many living here were hunters and trappers part-time. While the fur looked beautiful, the leather hide had become extremely brittle and would need to be preserved professionally.

As they walked further into the townhouse, Susanne said she'd like to go upstairs and explore the bedrooms, but Jack was more interested in going through the room behind the kitchen. He'd discovered that this room was where Mrs. O'Hara had been living in the final days of the village. So giving each other permission to pursue their own interests, they bid each other good searching. Once they parted, Jack went past the parlor, through the living room. He was impressed with its beautiful Persian rugs and ornate furniture, including velvet upholstered chairs, a leather sofa with dark hand carved wood, and a piano on one wall. The room was very dusty but the furniture was covered in decaying sheets that Finn and Eoinn had draped after the village was evacuated. When he lifted up the sheet covering a chair, the upholstery was in remarkably good condition. The wallpaper was peeling in several places, but even that was in much better shape than he'd expected.

Leaving the living room, Jack walked into the hallway heading toward the kitchen. He skipped the dining room. Upon entering the kitchen, he saw that there were blue china plates and cups in a glass-fronted cupboard and a huge, cast-iron kitchen stove. Beyond that, there was a row of counters with a large, enameled, cast-iron sink with hot and cold running water.

Moving on, he stepped into the bathroom off the kitchen and saw a giant, claw-footed tub, a wall mounted sink, and an old-fashioned toilet. The toilet's tank was suspended high above with a pull chain descending. Ian had explained that the very first winter after the fire, Finn and Eoinn had winterized the village, draining all the plumbing fixtures and turning off the water supply. Ian went on to explain that Finn and Eoinn had left the heating systems active so that things wouldn't freeze in the winter. He described how every fall he spent time turning on the heat and wandering from building to building making sure all was well.

From the bathroom, Jack went into the rear bedroom, which Mrs. O'Hara had stayed in for the last decade of the village's occupation. The room was dusty, and again, like the living room, it had suffered some decay with the wallpaper peeling away in sheets. But otherwise, the furnishings and rug on the floor were in great shape. Of course, the O'Connors had only lived in this house for about ten years before the fire.

Here the furniture wasn't covered. There was a desk with a standing mirror and about a dozen bottles of various types aligned to the back in descending size. The chair had been old—even when it had been brought here. It had a worn and threadbare, velvet cushion on a relatively plain, wooden seat. On the wall, framed and behind glass, was a beautiful piece of hand-work made of knotted thread. The bed was sagging in the center, and the covers were quite dusty, yellowed, tattered and decaying.

Next to the bed—which was roughly about a full-size mattress—was a nightstand. Curious, Jack walked over to the nightstand and slid the top drawer open. Inside there was a leather bound book. When Jack opened the first page, he found an inscription that read: *Journal of Mary Margaret Maguire, 1849*. Underneath this inscription, in different ink was written, *Journal of Mrs. John O'Hara*. Jack knew from the records that the foundation kept that Mrs. OHara had died in Wallace in 1919, at eight-seven years old. That meant that she'd been seventeen when she first started keeping this diary. He could see that the first entry had been penned on a ship called the *Emma Pearl* from Belfast to New York. He flipped through the diary, came to the end, and saw that the last entry was made in 1909. He flipped back and realized that she'd stopped writing in the journal for several stretches, but had begun again when she left New York to come West.

I I I I

Journal of Mrs. O'Hara

Friday, 23rd of March, 1849

Yesterday was my last day on land for what feels like the rest of my life. My name is Mary Margaret Maguire, and I am seventeen years old. My brother Thomas Matthew Maguire gave me this journal to keep a record of my new life in America. Yesterday, we boarded the good ship Emma Pearl. The sailors call her a brig, and she is an older ship that the captain and his wife live aboard, as well as a crew of twelve sailors plus a cook and the ship's boy. She's a beautiful ship, with two masts and big railings all around. There are about fifty passengers aboard. Not so big as the clipper ships but more friendly.

I'm sad to be leaving Ireland, but I'm excited for our future. My brother is seven years my senior, and he is my only family left. My mother, also Mary, and my father, James, died of typhoid fever two years ago. It was a terrible disease that killed so many friends and family, especially those hit by the famine.

My family had been lucky. My father was a merchant with a very successful grocery and supply store in the town of Bangor, and we had enough money saved to weather the famine well. We were educated and had a lovely home. But even that didn't save us when this disease ran rampant through our town. My brother had taken over the business, but when I turned seventeen, we had a rather sober conversation about the future and decided that we'd like to move to America to start over.

Thomas sold the family business and home perhaps for less than he could have, but we were anxious to sell and dearly wanted to be ready to leave in the spring. He used the money from the sale to rent us rooms at the local inn, and we packaged the things we wanted to keep for use in America in large sea chests we purchased.

I bought a little book with advice on how to prepare for a sea voyage, and we feel well outfitted for the trip. I have seen that some of the passengers are not so well sorted. We brought our own mattresses for the bunks and plenty of warm clothes and extra food. Our passage includes meals, but many of the families and travelers are relegated to cooking their own meals on the small stove provided for them.

The ship is small, and the accommodations are smaller. Thomas and I are sharing a tiny cabin, which is better than many on the ship can say. It has two bunks facing fore and aft, our heads toward the stern. There is a nice, little scuttle from which we get breaths of fresh air and light during the day. There are twenty private cabins and several larger cabins for the bigger families.

There are several families—I've already spent some time with Cecilly Bannon, who is traveling with her parents and brothers and sisters. She's just about my age and very sweet. They are heading to Pennsylvania where their uncles have already established a farm.

Poor Mr. Donaghy is traveling with his two boys. His wife Eva died in childbirth giving birth to baby John. Having a toddler and an infant is a lot to handle for a man traveling on his own. Some of the older girls have sort of adopted little Michael, taking turns holding him.

Mr. Donaghy brought a wet nurse along, a young woman Rachel Hogg, who is traveling with the family to keep the baby fed and healthy. Mr. Donaghy is paying her passage.

Rachel seems nice but sad. Her baby boy passed on when he was just a month old, a few days before Mrs. Donaghy died. Rachel's husband had already moved to New York to get established before they found out that she was expecting. He never had the chance to meet the baby. It is a sad story, but the timing is fortunate for Mr. Donaghy and little Michael, who would have died without a wet nurse. And silver lining for Rachel, who is now on her way to join her husband in America.

We all boarded yesterday afternoon on the Albert quay and spent the night onboard at anchor. The ship caught the morning tide and headed to sea. I stood on the deck watching as we passed the little town of Bangor, which had been my whole life. The crying of the gulls and mist falling hid my own sadness, I thought. But Thomas could tell how I was feeling and put his arm around me.

Sunday, 8th of April, 1849

As I've mentioned, some of the passengers have to cook their own meals on the little stove outside on the aft deck. That cooking area is where many people gather during the day, as it's sheltered from the wind, and the stove throws off a bit of warmth.

The various passengers are broken out into messes, meaning a group of six to eight passengers who eat together or as needed, cook together. The small cooking area precludes all the passengers staying there at once, but it does have room for about twenty people to congregate. So even when not part of the mess currently cooking, there's always a small group there.

A few days ago I sat and helped Mrs. McKnight with her cooking. She's been feeling unwell at sea, suffering from sea sickness caused by the rolling waves. So I helped her make dinner for the mess her family shares with a few others.

As she finished preparing the food, she made up a small plate with fancy bits and set it aside. I asked her why, and she explained it was for the little folk. She meant fairies. I thought at first she was kidding, but she was very serious. She explained that she always kept a small bit of the nicest food aside for them. At home, she would set the food on the windowsill and here at sea she leaves it on a shelf above the stove. Everyone has soon come to understand that the plate she set aside is not to be touched. No matter how many times the little boys and girls tried, they could never figure out how the food was taken overnight. One group of boys stayed up all night watching, but they fell asleep in deck chairs, and while they slept, the food went missing.

Last evening, I was having trouble sleeping and quietly wrapped up in my coat, shawl and mittens, and went up on deck. The night air was much warmer than it had been, and the wind was light but steady. The sea was calm, and a full moon lit everything up brightly.

The small night crew were spread about doing their work, mostly I suspect, they were just trying to stay awake. I walked back to see who was steering the ship, and it was the first mate. He motioned me over and showed me how the ship's wheel works with its ropes—he corrected me to call them "lines"—going back to a long, wooden arm called a tiller. He let me carefully step over the different lines to look over the back of the boat, called the transom. Hanging from wooden arms there was a small rowboat that he called the "Captain's Gig," and underneath this, I could see the rudder that turns the ship when the wheel is turned and pulls on the tiller from the ropes.

I thanked the mate and went down to sit near the cooking fire. By the time I returned, it was just coals but still warm. I hunkered down near the stove, squeezed between one of the odd pieces of the ship and a sack filled with straw and wood shavings used to light the fire. I was under the little lean-to roof used to shelter the stove.

After a few minutes, I must have fallen asleep, because I was suddenly aware that a girl, smaller and younger-looking than me— but wearing woolen pants and a coat like a boy—was taking the fairy food from the shelf above the stove. She took a little nibble and smiled with delight. She had short, blonde hair, a pretty face, and she was small-boned with fine features. Her cheeks were rosy, and her eyes were large and sparkling.

I had been fairy mad as a young girl, hunting for them all through our garden and with my girlfriends on walks in the woods. My father had brought me a book of fairies that was like an encyclopedia. It listed the different kinds of fairies and talked about how to talk to a fairy if you ever met one. It emphasized things like never saying "Thank you" if a fairy did something nice for you. It also stressed the importance of not using the word fairy—ever. Instead, it urged its reader to refer to them as "the little cousins" or "our neighbors." As I grew out of that phase, I determined that this had all been a girlish whimsy, and when I met adults who seemed really to believe in them, I was always a little baffled.

But here was something beyond my experience! I knew each person on this ship. I knew their names, and I had spoken with all of them, even most of the crew. This wasn't a passenger or a member of the crew. There was definitely something about her, something "other" that seemed to make me be careful. The hairs on the back of my neck were prickling, and I was frozen still. My hands were tucked under my sides, and I gave my hip a sharp pinch to make sure I was awake, and I was.

The girl quickly made short work of the little sweet cake Mrs. McKnight had left for her, and she picked up the plate and licked the last few crumbs clean. She put the plate back, rubbed her belly, and began to turn away. As she turned, she noticed me scrunched away to the side, and she froze, her eyes going wide. She looked like she was going to die of fright, and she took a step back. I said, in a tiny small voice, "Oh ... it's all right. I'm a friend." She startled and stepped out of the little hut, swinging up into the rigging, delicate and light as a dancer.

I jumped to my feet and looked after where she'd disappeared but couldn't find her. I rubbed my eyes and looked back at the plate of missing food and wondered. I said up to the sails, "I'm sorry to have startled you. I'll make sure you have more treats tomorrow." I went below and back to bed.

Tuesday, 10th of April, 1849

We have settled into the shipboard life and are enjoying things as we can. The weather has been a little wintery still and walking on deck often requires a warm coat, hat, and mittens. Still, the brisk, ocean air has been refreshing as it can be quite stuffy below decks.

Thomas and I have been most fortunate in our experience. We both felt a bit queasy for the first few days but have settled into travel without upset. The same can't be said for all of our fellow travelers. Poor, old Mrs. McKnight has been quite sick the whole time.

Yesterday was the first day where the weather was more like spring, and this afternoon the winds were light, and the children were playing on deck. In the morning, I walked by a group of sailors who were on their rest. They sat in the sun singing to themselves. Meanwhile, two of them worked on beautiful pieces of what looked like lace but were made of twine and thread tied in tiny knots. When I expressed my appreciation, having spent years learning how to do needlework and crochet, the sailors smiled and showed me how they did it. One of the men, his name was Jed, a man of about forty, was making a piece that was particularly beautiful. They called these their bits of fancy.

After lunch I was walking back to our cabin when something exciting happened. I saw Mrs. McKnight. She was standing outside of her cabin looking very upset. When she saw me coming, she looked hopeful. She told me that her brooch had gone missing, and she was frantic as she tried to find it. She thought it might have been stolen.

I went into her cabin with her and tried to help her search for it, but it was quite dark and the cabin was very full of belongings. As we searched, we kept the door open, latched in the open position. Suddenly, the whole ship lurched over to starboard, and the deck tilted horizontally, becoming very steep. I grabbed onto the bunk, but poor Mrs. McKnight went sliding down the deck and right out the door of her cabin.

She slid out onto the companionway and was picking up speed when the sailor Jed, who I'd been talking to earlier, saw her sliding. He jumped across and caught her, holding onto one of the take holds on the wall. As he caught her, Mrs. McKnight was confused and began wailing. And as he held her there, suddenly her brooch broke loose from wherever it had fallen in the cabin and slid out onto the companionway as well.

I yelled to Jed, and he saw it coming and caught that as well before the ship finally began to settle down. Mrs. McKnight continued to howl and wail with dismay, not understanding that Jed was just trying to help.

It was at that moment that the first mate turned the corner and ran over, pinning Jed to the deck and forcing him to release Mrs. McKnight. Jed tried to explain what had happened, and he even reached out to show Mrs. McKnight that he had saved her brooch, but she misunderstood and claimed he had stolen it. Things were getting very heated when I stepped out of the cabin and explained the whole thing.

Mrs. McKnight was mortified, both because she'd seemed so weak and frightened, and because she'd blamed Jed, who was the hero in all this, as if he were a criminal. The mate apologized to Jed, and to his credit, helped him up and straightened his uniform. Jed was grateful to me for helping clear his reputation.

This evening at dinner, Jed brought me a piece of knotted fancy as a gift to thank me for standing up for him. Jed had tied tiny knots and loops to turn them into flowers and vines and all sorts of things. Jed's knotted fancy is about a foot across in both directions, absolutely huge compared to most of the ones I'd seen! It's absolutely gorgeous, and I'll cherish it forever.

I haven't seen my little fairy friend again, but I've been making sure that extra treats are left out for her. I've even started making little cookies shaped like roses, which the children love. I make sure that the prettiest of them are kept in reserve for my friend. I've noticed since I've started doing this that our cabin smells fresher, and it s often clean when I haven't had time to pick it up. I've noticed that when I go looking for things I've misplaced that they somehow are always on top of the pile—even if I know they weren't there when I last checked.

Friday, 4th of May, 1849

Thomas squeezed my hand this morning as the fog parted, and we saw the land of America for the first time. The watch had yelled down from above, that call we'd been longing to hear, "Land Ho!" And as a result, the deck quickly became crowded. In the distance there was a blur of land, and we could see the sails of several ships as well. As I started looking, I realized that as the fog gave way, there were ships ahead, behind, and on both sides. Some were far in the distance, but a few were closer.

The air had smelled of land last night as I stood on deck before going to sleep in our cramped berth. Throughout the day yesterday things had started to change. First was the wildlife. We saw whales breaching and dolphins swimming near the bow. There were sea birds following the ship, gulls like we had at home, but also in the air, I saw V lines of large geese flying north. These geese were not white but black and grey geese, unlike the ones at home. They honked happily at each other as they flew.

That we should find ourselves coming to America today shouldn't have been a surprise after all that, but it was. I left an extra special fairy treat for my friend last night, a little flower made of sugar. So maybe that helped us find our way here.

The breeze was picking up, and before we knew it, we could see the shore clearly. We saw some islands, a few with houses on them, as we were coming in. The ship turned to the south, and we began moving faster toward our destination. The first view I had of New York sent chills down my spine. I saw a church steeple, white in the distance, and I saw smoke coming from stovepipes.

The captain came on deck and announced that we would be arriving in New York later in the day. He gave instructions that we should begin to pack our cabins. That tonight we would be on shore for the first time in America. The air was positively charged with excitement. I've just taken the time to write this all down, as I expect I won't have time to write much for the next bit of time. I'm so excited to find my way in this new land!

I I I I

Susanne walked up the stairs to the second floor. She saw that there were four bedrooms, the largest being the Master that was located at the front of the building. There were also stairs that led up to the third floor, but she avoided them for the moment.

She went first into the front bedroom, hoping to find some memories or keepsakes of her great-grandmother. She was not disappointed. The room was covered in a layer of dust, and the wallpaper was peeling off the walls in sheets. Still, the plaster was all intact, and the woodwork was varnished but dusty. The ceiling had the dull sheen she associated with whitewash, having done a few renovations in her parents' and grandparents' homes in Kellogg. Luckily, in this case nobody had tried to paint over the whitewash, which notoriously wouldn't hold paint.

Suzanne was pleased to see that there was a beautifully carved sideboard desk and mirror that was covered with small pictures and tiny bottles of medicines and cosmetics. They had that wonderful, old-timey feel of collectibles that she'd come across in various shops over the years. The labels on the bottles were in perfect condition, and she loved the one called "Dr. Thomas' Eclectic Oil, containing Spirits of Turpentine, Camphor, Oil of Tar, Red Thyme and Fish Oil, specially prepared. A household remedy for external and internal use. Common Sore Throat, Muscle Soreness, Superficial Burns and Abrasions." She couldn't imagine taking a swallow of that.

In the drawer of the desk she discovered hair brushes, scissors, and a jewelry box with necklaces, rings, bracelets, and earrings. There was a binder of old letters and postcards that she set aside. There was a thick, leather-bound journal, which she opened to find neat, small lettering.

She dusted off the chair, sat down, and started reading.

IIII

Journal of Samantha King

September 19th, 1875

Yesterday I went back to the cave above the hot springs with a lantern. As I said in my last entry, the cave had beautiful wall decorations, and it looked like it went back for some ways, but I didn't have a lantern. Plus, the coyote ran me off and gave me quite a scare. This time I was ready for him, I brought a slingshot and a walking stick with me. But he never showed up, much to my relief.

I entered the cave just after breakfast, it was a Saturday, and I had carved out time to go off by myself. I didn't tell anyone where I was headed, but I left a note on my bed, just in case I ran into trouble. I also brought with me a lantern, a long spool of string, a sandwich and jug of water, chalk, and a small bag of tiny, smooth stones in case I ran out of string and needed to mark my way back. I also brought some paper and a pencil to copy some of the drawings.

As I reached the ledge outside the cave, and checked for the coyote, I was a little out of breath. I sat on a rock near the edge and looked down on the village. It was so amazing to be able to look at all my friends going about their daily missions, unaware that I was above observing them. It felt a little godlike, and I thought of Nathaniel Hawthorne's A Wonder-book for Girls and Boys that I had read a few years ago. I thought about how he retold those ancient Greek myths. I felt especially like Icarus and Daedalus flying above the Earth, as long as I didn't become Icarus flying too close to the sun!

After resting for a few minutes, I turned and went to the opening of the cave. I paused to light my lantern and then went inside. The walls were covered in detailed carvings. There were decorations cut into the stone walls, and both the carved lines and the surface of the cave were painted with pigments of contrasting colors. They were absolutely stunning.

On the right side of the cave there were numerous depictions of a large bird. The first grouping of images showed the bird at the top of the cave, about a foot across, with people and animals below it. The drawings were both beautiful and intricate, cut into the stone and decorated with paint. The people were grouped below the bird, with what looked like goats, bighorn sheep, and deer mixed together. Some of the people looked like they were holding spears. I realized that the bird was a raven, thinking back to the day I had first come here when the raven and the coyote were "talking" to each other.

I wandered the edge of the cave, the floor was packed with smooth earth and gravel. More drawings of the raven followed the first, one with the raven flying over a mountain, and jagged streaks that I soon recognized as lightning following behind it. There was another drawing of a large group of people with a big man standing in the middle of them.

There was an opening at the back of the cave that was about five feet tall and three feet wide. I poked my head in and held the light out, and I saw that this was a tunnel going further into the mountain. I continued on the other side, but the depictions on this side of the cave featured a coyote. At first, I thought it was a dog or a wolf, but then I suddenly thought about the raven and the coyote outside this cave, and it made sense.

On this side of the cave there were many carvings where the coyote was doing things. In one, it held a long stick with streamers on the ends, in its mouth. After looking carefully at it, I suddenly realized it was fire—a stick on fire, the "streamers" were even painted with reds. In another, the coyote was digging into the side of a hill. The artist really captured the essence of what a dog looks like when digging. From the hole in the hill sprang a river, painted in a wonderful blue color, and fish jumped from the river, and the river ran all the way to the sea or maybe to Lake Coeur d'Alene.

I wandered the cave, looking at the carvings, and then over the entrance to the tunnel, I saw that Coyote and Raven came together. Coyote was depicted with his mouth holding his fire stick, and Raven was drawn spreading his wings with lightning shooting from behind. I don't exaggerate when I say that I shuddered when I saw that.

After a little while I found a rock and tied the end of my string to it. I started walking down the tunnel, letting the string play out behind me. The tunnel went forward for about twenty feet until it opened into a large cave. This one was about thirty feet high and about twenty feet around. The ceiling of the cave had stalactites and the floor had stalagmites pointing upwards. I remembered the trick that C is for ceiling and G is for ground to be sure I used the right words.

There was a flat area in the center of this cave where someone had cleared away a stalagmite, and there they had created a spot for a fire. The ceiling was covered in soot, and after my eyes got used to the dimness, I saw that there was a place above with a hole, where smoke could escape. At the back of this cave there were three openings. The one in the center was tall, about eight feet high. The other two were smaller, about five feet each in height.

This cave was simpler, despite being bigger. There were places on the wall with flat spots that looked like shelves, and some were even big enough that someone could sleep there. At one point or another, some of the smaller shelves probably had been used to store things. In a small nook on the wall I found an old woven basket and a small carved box. There was nothing in them, and the basket was very fragile, so I didn't do more than look inside. But the box was in good shape and had a little lid on it. It seemed to be carved from a single piece of wood.

I wandered the caves for a long while, tunnels leading to more caves, each seemed to have less evidence of human habitation or usage. Finally, I came to a spot where as I entered the cave, the fire on my lantern began to sputter, and I noticed it was hard to breathe. Sean had explained that when they dug tunnels in the mines sometimes they would come across pockets of gas that needed to be cleared out. So fearing the worst, I got a little nervous and decided to make my way back out.

When I got to the entrance of the cave I stood outside and just breathed in the fresh air. What a relief! The cave hadn't felt too bad. It was damp and smelled a bit like a wet cat. Sometimes there were bats, which I'm not afraid of, but I will admit that they would startle me from time to time. I stood breathing in the fresh air, looking out at the village and off into the distance. My little adventure had been fun, so I decided to leave my supplies in the cave and to head back home. I'll go back sometime when I can break away.

I I I I

September 12th, 2028

Jack, Susanne, and Ian all stood on the corner of Broadway and Spring Street, watching as Skip piloted the helicopter down in the center of the square. They had been working on getting the village ready for this meeting for more than a week. They had spent long days and nights working with a crew that at times grew to thirty people. But they were satisfied that the village was ready for their esteemed guests.

Five people stepped off the helicopter. The first was Kisho Yomohiro, who walked arm in arm with his daughter Taki Yomohiro. She was in her late twenties, and she was his protege and an aspiring animator herself. She often served as eyes and ears for her father on assessing projects. Next came Mr. Itsuki Tanaka, head of the Yomohiro Corporation parks in Japan, sixty years old, tall and enthusiastic. He walked next to his associate, Mr. Riku Hamada, head of the studio business of Yomohiro Corporation. He was fifty-eight and compactly built. Finally, the last to emerge was Ms. Akari Ito, fifty-five, elegant, and meticulously dressed in a black suit. She was the head of legal, licensing, and partnerships. Jack had met all of them during his interviews, with the exception of Ms. Ito. He'd been told to address her that way, not as Ito-san.

As Skip took off from the square to return to pick up the guests' luggage and additional supplies, there were numerous greetings, bows, hand shakes, and introductions. Jack carefully introduced his cousin Ian Seeley, and then Susanne, who he explained was both a childhood friend and ancestor of one of the original founders, as well as a successful author of young adult fiction with a Netflix production deal.

Jack presented each of the visitors with a jeweled pendant, each containing a cut crystal, one of several different types. Each pendant was offered to its recipient in an elegant, wooden presentation box and covered in a

Japanese silk gift cover. Jack made this a sort of semi-formal presentation, as if passing them a gift. Jack asked them all to please put these on and to wear them at all times while in the village. He explained that the pendant contained a GPS tracker that would help them to be found if they got separated. The guests each slipped the pendant over their heads. Any sense that Ms. Ito would push back—which her initial reaction implied—was quashed by her delight at the quality of the charm on the necklace, hers being a polished star garnet the size of a grape.

They had opened up the whole town. The crew had gone through and cleaned all first floors of the buildings on Broadway, as well as cleaning, painting, and setting up guest rooms in the Hawthorne. Jack had insisted that they bring in new linens, mattresses, plus box springs and pillows for all the rooms being used. His last experience sleeping on the old mattresses at the village left him a bit nonplussed. He also brought in a small crew to cook for them, working out of the kitchen at the Hawthorne. They'd had to upgrade the facilities to ensure that the chefs would be happy. Over the course of their visit, they and their guests would enjoy food both Japanese and American, focusing on flavors of the American West.

They'd spent time working on the town as well. Jack had large prints of many photographs made and mounted behind plexiglass, and then he had these photos put on stands around the town in the location that the photographer would have stood when the pictures were taken. The photos included numerous busy street scenes from various points of time, some of the town decorated for Christmas, some showing a celebration when Idaho became a state on July 3rd, 1890, and some that were just everyday street scenes.

As they took a tour of the village, Jack could see that Ms. Ito was going to take some convincing. Yomohiro-san had warned him in advance that she was always the hardest to convince when it came to new efforts, but he had assured Jack that she could be won over. On the other hand, it was clear that Yomohiro-san was enthralled. He walked about the town with wide eyes, excitedly commenting to his daughter, Taki. Tanaka and Hamada were both having a good time and seemed very interested in the experience.

When they'd finished one full circuit of Broadway, with several stops to look into buildings, they ended back at the lobby of the Hawthorne. There Jack explained they'd all be staying that night. They served themselves from a buffet that has been set up at the side of the room, and were all seated. While they ate, Jack sat between Ms. Ito and Tanaka-san.

"What did you think of the tour of the village, Ms. Ito?" asked Jack.

"It certainly is well-preserved. I am not a big fan of Western movies, so much of the historical reference is not of my liking. But I suppose for those who like such things, it is interesting. I did like the bath house. I look forward to using them later. You know, in Japan, we have some famous hot springs like these that also have an iodine smell."

"I didn't know that," Jack replied, "how interesting."

"Ah, Akari," Tanaka said, "you must be joking. The Wild West is one of the great iconic periods of world history. It's like our Edo period. It's one of the things most associated with America."

Ms. Ito answered, "Tanaka-san, we each have our interests. I do understand how some could find it appealing. I do like the landscape here, and the air is very clean and fresh."

Jack had been thinking the whole time about what could win over Ms. Ito. He said, "If you like hot springs, perhaps you would find the Crystal Cave of interest. We didn't talk much yet about the mines, but there's a beautiful cave that was found deep under the mountain. It has natural hot spring pools, and the walls are all covered in giant quartz crystals. They're quite beautiful. If you like, you could go there during our break this afternoon."

At the mention of this, Ms. Ito perked up and smiled politely, bowing her head. "Hai, that sounds wonderful, actually."

Jack sensed that this was finally something she was interested in, and he added, "There are also some beautiful outdoor, natural, hot spring pools and some cool pools of water on some of the creeks. We call them "swimming holes" in this part of the country, where you can bathe as well. And of course, there is the Crystal Village Baths that you mentioned already, which Finn McEnhill modeled after various Roman baths he had visited in Europe."

Jack had done some research on Japanese *onsen*, which are traditional, hot spring spas that are quite popular in Japan. Based on Ms. Ito's reaction, he finally had found some common ground.

As lunch was ending, Jack stood and went over to a case that had been set up on a sideboard, opened it, and took out ten beautifully wrapped gifts, each about five by five inches. Susanne joined him, and they walked around the table presenting each member of the Yomohiro Corporation team with two gifts each. There was much ritual refusal of the gifts and finally acceptance of them. Jack knew that nobody would open them immediately, but inside each box was a gemstone that had been taken from the mine and cut and polished to perfection. Each person got a rare star garnet, as well as one other gem. Jack made sure to include a rare blue diamond for Ms. Ito.

After lunch, Skip returned with the luggage, and everyone was shown to their rooms. Jack and Susanne got people settled into their rooms, and Susanne took Ms. Ito a robe and sandals. Together, they went off to try the hot pools of Crystal Cave.

In 1905, the miners had cut a direct tunnel to the cave. The passage exited the mountain a few hundred yards east of the main mine entrance, not too far from the dining hall on Spring Street. This tunnel had inset electric lights, was a much shorter route than the other one, had dressing rooms carved into the walls near the cave, and offered warm showers. The tunnels and dressing rooms were ornately carved and had beautiful examples of veins of precious metals and stones. These metals and stones were exposed, highlighted, and lit for effect.

While the ladies went off for their soak in the Crystal Cave, Tanaka and Hamada both enjoyed the Crystal Village Baths in the village with Ian. Meanwhile, Jack took a walk with Yomohiro-san and his daughter Taki. They walked every street in the village, opened doors into homes and stores, admired the craftsmanship of the buildings, and discussed the idiosyncrasies of the layout of the town. Jack showed them the outdoor hot spring pools, the swimming holes, and the site where various placer mines had been before the village started cutting shafts. He showed them that one could pan for gold and stones using a sluice that was still in place. Of course, the sluice had been put back in place over the last week, but all involved appreciated the theatrics.

When they all reassembled for dinner in the dining room of the Hawthorne, it was clear that the group was greatly appreciative of what Crystal Village offered. However, these were also very seasoned and hardheaded business people. After dinner was served, Jack had a presentation to give.

"My friends," Jack began, "I'm so happy that you've come, and I'm pleased that we have had an opportunity to share Crystal Village with you. At this time, I'd like to show you a little about my thinking for how all this could come together as an American Yomohiro Corporation theme park."

He turned on a projector and brought up a map of the village. He showed the buildings that were set up already for guests, such as hotels, and the commercial spaces for stores all highlighted. Then he showed them the residences that were available, which included a large number of the buildings. He explained that they would need an on-site staff of actors to portray the people living in the village and to set the tone for the guests. He highlighted the locations they would have those actors live, which he had sprinkled throughout the village. He also overlaid a series of tunnels that would be cut beneath the village, linking to a "basement" door in each of the "cast" homes. The idea was that the actors could access park spaces that way, and these passages could also be used for emergency services and other park staff.

"Our preliminary analysis says that if we go through with what I've just shown you," Jack explained, "we'd need a staff of about five hundred people, four hundred of them actors. In addition, we'll need one hundred to run operations. That would leave us room for between one thousand and 1,500 guests at any given time."

Then Jack brought up a new map that showed where more hotels could be developed on the plateau, should they decide they needed more guests to make the economics work. "Should we want to expand to a larger group of guests, or if we wanted overflow housing for special events, we could accommodate that by adding hotel space at the end of Long Street."

Ms. Ito raised her hand and asked, "What is the expectation for televising the activities in the park? We have found we need about a one-hundred-person crew each week, with about twenty of those people involved in shooting and another fifty involved with editing, the remainder in supporting roles."

Jack smiled, then exchanged the map with a fully aligned aerial image of the village. After a moment, it was clear that this wasn't an image but rather a video capture. The first clue was seeing three people exit the cafe on the square, and then footage of the helicopter coming in to land. This was obviously drone footage taken of the arrival of the guests this morning. Then the footage changed to a ground camera view of the executives disembarking from the helicopter, the camera angle kept changing to different views.

Next the cameras showed the tour that the group had taken, the images jumping from tight close-ups of the faces of people in the group to other angles. These various shots included everyone but Ian, who only showed up in the distance shots or in the periphery of the main shots. Interestingly enough, each time his face was very slightly blurred. The audio of the conversations was crisp and clear and had been edited and overlaid to form one, cohesive narrative. In typical reality TV form, Jack and Susanne were interviewed in cutaways, telling the audience what they had been thinking at the time of the various events and conversations.

Several clips included shots of the executives going into the mines and hot springs, but these were edited tastefully to ensure no violations of privacy made it through the end. Finally, they were shown a live view of the room they were in currently. These shots were captured with excellent, dim-light cameras and included close-ups of each person's face, and a narrator's voiceover that humorously described their reactions live.

The video ended, and Jack brought up the lights. Then he paused, not saying anything to the room. He let the silence continue until it began to be uncomfortable. He could see that his Japanese guests were both intrigued and uncomfortable. Nobody said anything for at least a full minute, which felt like an eternity, when quietly Miss Taki Yomohiro began slowly clapping. Yomohiro-san broke out in a huge smile and quietly began to laugh. Tanaka-san was shaking with what Jack had assumed was anger, but he too began laughing out loud. Hamada-san and Ms. Ito both began to smile, and Jack let out a quiet sigh of relief.

Yomohiro said, "That may have been the most astonishing thing I've ever experienced. I assume you're going to tell us all how you did it, but I must say, Jack—this was incredibly well executed! I know you've only had a few weeks to prepare for our arrival, so that makes it doubly impressive!"

"Thank you, Yomohiro-san," said Jack, "What you've all just seen is a preliminary test of a new camera system that is called a hybrid mesh approach to capturing video. Much like we've seen with hybrid mesh approaches to wifi signals, a criss-crossing pattern of cameras is put in place to ensure that every likely angle and location is visible. These new, micro-telephoto lenses are pretty incredible and can be hidden easily. We blanketed the street and various rooms with cameras, and we augmented those cameras with micro-drones. The mesh system is both video and an active, real-time, three-dimensional mapping of all public areas of the park."

Jack held out his hand, and a tiny drone the size of a fly landed on it. The screen behind him showed live video from the drone, pointed at Jack's face.

Hamada-san signaled that he had a question. "How did you capture the video and audio with such accuracy and quality? In our other parks, we have film crews that follow the subjects around, and it is quite intrusive. Is there a control room somewhere that had a director switching cameras all the time? Or are you capturing video from every camera all the time and then going back and editing it?" It was obvious that he thought this was how it had been done and was skeptical of the approach.

Jack kept his face very neutral, but he noticed that Hamada-san had just subtly included Crystal Village as one of the Yomohiro Corporation's group of parks, revealing that he'd unconsciously transitioned to assuming this was going to happen.

"The necklaces we put on you when you landed," Jack replied, "not only contain a highly accurate positioning system so we know where you are in the village, they also contain very sensitive microphones to record conversation. These pendants help the camera mesh to determine where each visitor is in reference to the other. Then the AI systems use a three-dimensional map of all the visitors plus facial recognition to frame shots much like a human camera operator would. It also enables automated switching and activates only the cameras that are in position to capture the relevant images. Anyone not wearing a necklace is inherently obscured to the cameras, and the system automatically blurs their faces—which you may have noticed was the case with Ian. He showed up in shots but only in relation to those wearing trackers, and he was blurred. That's because we don't want to have people's faces captured if they are not part of the public viewability of the park. This may be important for special guests and visitors. The final edit was done with a crew of three people working from our offices in Oakland, as was the voiceover we just heard."

Jack looked toward the ceiling and said, "Thanks, guys, you can call it a night. I appreciate all the hard work today."

The narrator's voice from the control room said, "You got it, Jack. Thank you, everyone, for being such good sports! We hope the rest of your weekend goes as smoothly as this day did."

The Japanese guests were nodding and smiling toward the ceiling. Yomohiro looked at Jack and winked, something he was famous for in Japan. At the end of each Yomohiro special on Japanese TV, he would say a few words to the audience, then wink. "Jack," he said, "I think I speak for the rest of the team when I say that this has exceeded our expectations. I look forward to seeing what you've got in store for us for the rest of the weekend."

Jack smiled, bowed his head, and said, "Thank you, your appreciation for our efforts is gratifying. We kind of used up our bag of tricks today. It's been a huge amount of effort to get ready, and I hoped that we could take the rest of the weekend to let you all explore the village and relax. We've unlocked all the doors to all the buildings. Only the first floors on Broadway have been cleaned and set to rights. If you go into any other structures, they're still as they were left by the previous occupants on August 29th of 1910. The only exception is that after the fire, Eoinn Seeley and Finn McEnhill removed all the food and anything that might rot or spoil from each building. I encourage you to explore. Everything has been maintained and is safe."

Ms. Ito spoke up and said, "I feel an obligation to admit that I was skeptical before coming here, and I have found the day, the location, and the video to be delightful. I must say that the Crystal Cave and hot spring pools were magical. But it is important that we discuss the fact that this village is owned by your family, Jack. We need to be able to go back and report to our board of directors and employees that you are not self-dealing, and that there are no improprieties."

Jack smiled, having expected this issue to come up earlier in the day. "I'm glad you brought this up," he replied. "This place is important, and I believe it should be shown to the world. I have full control—thanks to my cousin Ian—of the foundation that has been set up to manage it. I've had a team of lawyers working on the implications of making it public, and they have also been sorting out mechanisms we can use to ensure that we pass any scrutiny from any party without any question of ethical issues or wrongdoing. The lawyers assure me that they have several different approaches we could take that will work. They say it's just a question of the two groups' legal teams engaging to find common ground. As far as the financial implications go, we simply will not charge Yomohiro Corporation for usage of the land or facilities. We'll only charge for park-specific improvements such as the tunnels, and we'll do that at cost. Yomohiro Corporation can pay us a share of profits, to be negotiated, from the content filmed here and the content derived from the use of the village. This greatly reduces the up-front cost. Further, it incentivizes the village and all the descendants of the Original Eight founders to participate, and it encourages the foundation that controls it to continue to make improvements."

Ms. Ito smiled and nodded her head. All of the Japanese guests bowed slightly, and Jack signaled for dessert. The wait staff brought out small dishes of pudding sprinkled with locally harvested, mountain huckleberries.

Jack said, "My mother's family was from the coast of Maine, and as a child, we would go there sometimes in August. Her family had a recipe for a pudding made from a seaweed that the locals call sea moss. It's a very simple pudding that to me has always felt like the perfect blend between America and Japan. This sea moss pudding has been flavored with vanilla bean, and we've placed some local huckleberries picked right on the slopes of these mountains on top to tie it together. I hope you enjoy it."

The guests all smiled and carefully tasted their pudding, which was very lightly sweetened, maintained a slight bit of oceanic essence, and was very fresh tasting. Jack knew that the story behind the pudding, plus tying them all together with the local fruit would be appreciated by this audience. Yomohiro was savoring each mouthful of the pudding with his eyes closed, a distant smile on his face. Jack looked over at Susanne and she met his eyes, smiling.

I I I I

Journal of Mary Elizabeth Maguire O'Hara

Wednesday, 18th of November, 1863

The air is sharp with the onset of winter. John's absence is a hollow ache. His letters are infrequent, but when I receive them, they are a short reprieve. I cling to Rose's company. Our shared laughter staves off the solitude that encroaches with each passing day. She misses Eoinn just as much as I miss my John.

In the quiet hours in the still after midnight, a soft tapping at my window beckoned to me. She was there again, my little cousin from across the sea who followed me from our shared shipborne travel. I found her seated upon the outer sill, her small feet swinging with a carefree rhythm. In the early days of our friendship, she would scarcely reveal herself. But over the years, she has become more comfortable with me.

I still leave her treats and offerings in the kitchen each night, and the food that I make has a bit of extra sparkle and taste as a result. The apartment I share with Rose is uncommonly clean and free of dust and the grime of the city. While my little friend doesn't talk with me, she does abide by my presence as long as I don't approach her directly.

Thursday, 19th of November, 1863

Today brought an unexpected turn, a twist of our intertwined fates. Just after sunset, my little cousin appeared at my window, her usual mirth dampened by a shadow of concern. Rather than her normal aloofness, she was looking directly at me. She beckoned me to follow with an urgency that set my heart racing.

I grabbed my shawl and ran out the door after her. She ran on her small feet staying just in sight, waiting at each turn so I could find her. In a forgotten corner of a large lot was a trap set to capture animals, perhaps raccoons or stray dogs. My friend was standing next to it in a commotion. Inside was one of her kind, perhaps a companion, who had found himself ensnared—a cage meant for lesser creatures now a trap for one of noble blood.

The iron frame of the trap, cold and unyielding, held him fast, its presence anathema to their kind. My hands worked quickly to open the cage. As he emerged, his form more akin to a child than the sprites of lore, he regarded me with an ancient wisdom in his gaze. A nod, a gesture, a silent acknowledgment of a bond between a human and the fair folk. They disappeared quickly, but I could feel their presence as I wandered back home.

Friday, 20th of November, 1863

Tonight my window became a gateway to secrets untold. My little cousin, her spirit restored, almost danced with a joy that filled the room. Her companion, who I'd never seen before last night, joined in her revelry. They sat on the sill of my open bedroom window, telling me stories. While they wouldn't come in, not a breath of cold air entered the room.

She spoke, in hushed tones, of leaving a crowded kingdom in the old world, and how in this new world, she could birth a new kingdom in which she could lead her people. A place where the little cousins might reign, their magic unfettered by the iron grip of man. They both talked about living in the underworld, and how humans had come and carved into their world by digging mines. They talked about how the walls and ceilings and floors of their underworld were decorated with artwork and drawings that told the story of their people, and how they longed for a place to do this in a new kingdom, a new underworld in the new world of America.

I listened, my soul alight with the promise of their words. In my heart, I vowed to be their guardian, their confidante in a world that didn't even acknowledge their existence. As I pen these words, the echo of their laughter lingers.

I I I I

Susanne stood on the outcropping outside of the cave site next to Jessie Blackwell, cultural liaison for the Coeur D'Alene tribe. Jack was making his way up the last section of the trail behind them. Jessie was an old friend of Susanne's, and when she and Jack came across mention of this cave in the journal of Sam King, they decided that before they did anything they should bring a Coeur D'Alene tribal representative out to look at the cave with them.

Susanne had reached out to Jessie, who was intrigued when they read her the description of the cave. Jessie asked if they'd gone up to the cave yet, and Suzanne explained that they wanted to have someone from the tribe come with them so nothing inappropriate was done. Jessie had been gratified. "This is a first for me," she chuckled, "usually someone finds something, and we hear about it on the news,"

Jack finally arrived and handed the two of them flashlights. Jessie had a professional camera rig with two flash units on a frame to either side of the camera so that she could document the find. After they all caught their breath and appreciatively looked out over the village and surrounding mountains, they entered the cave.

Jessie let out a loud gasp as she looked at the walls. She had warned them not to touch the walls in any way before they entered. As they wandered around the space, which was about fifteen feet across and about nine feet high, they murmured appreciatively.

"Wow!" said Susanne.

"This is amazing," said Jack.

"Holy crap!" exclaimed Jessie.

Sure enough, Sam's description of the pictographs-petroglyphs on the wall were accurate. Jessie had explained that a pictograph is a painting on a cave, and a petroglyph is a carving into rock. This was sort of both, as Jessie educated them in their advance conversations, which didn't really exist in their tribal history. Jessie walked around the space taking pictures. Jessie explained that she wanted to document every square inch of the cave. Meanwhile, Susanne was preparing to use a 3D mapping app on her phone that automatically creates an interactive model of a room, or in this case, a cave.

The walls were absolutely covered in carvings made directly into the stone of the walls. Every square inch of the surface of the cave, including the ceiling, was covered in intricate carvings ranging anywhere from a half-inch to an inch deep into the rock. The carving was intricate and exact. All surfaces of the cave were covered in lines and grooves in interlocking geometric patterns. There was a background pattern that was made of lighter, thinner, and shallower carvings. These were either there as background texture or used to emphasize the depictions of animals and even human figures on the surface of the cave. The figures were carved more deeply into the rock, with thicker outlines. And after the rock had been carved, it had been covered in pigments to accentuate the carvings.

The background pattern carvings on the walls of the cave tended to be darker, sometimes a deep rusty red and sometimes black, and the surface of the cave walls was painted with lighter colors, sometimes with white, sometimes with lighter browns or oranges.

The ceiling of the cave was split into scenes of daytime and nighttime, with one half of the ceiling being a brilliant blue with wispy clouds. The intricate, carved lines were painted with white, and the surface was painted blue. There was a brilliant sun that looked like it might be covered in gold leaf carved in the area above the cave's entrance. And around the center of the cave's ceiling there was a demarcation line that transitioned from daytime blue to nighttime black. The transition moved from blue to yellow to orange to red to purple, then black. On the nighttime side of the cave the carving lines were painted with white, and there were stars, and the moon was highlighted. These seemed to be coated in silver leaf.

"Whoah, what the hell? This is unbelievable! The intricacy of these carvings and the use of pigments ... And I've never seen images of Coyote and Raven in the same space in such an explicit way ..." Jessie simply stopped talking.

Jack turned to her and asked, "What is it?" He walked over to see what she was looking at. There—in the same style as the rest of the carvings but closer to the back of the cave—was an image of a man on a horse. He was drawn with the obvious outlines of a cowboy hat, and the color of his hair was red. They looked around and saw that in this area of the cave there were images of wagons and of a man holding a pickaxe. Upon closer inspection, they realized that these drawings were sprinkled throughout the room. This demonstrated that the artwork in the cave not only captured the seemingly ancient images of native Americans and native figures that Sam King O'Connor described in her journal, but it also included images that reflected more modern times. In one area of the cave there was something high up on the ceiling that could only have been a helicopter.

"What the actual ...?" said Jessie, her voice trailing off. "Are you guys screwing with me?"

Jack and Susanne looked at each other sheepishly, and Jack said, "Jessie, we've never come up here before. All we were going off was the journal.

But seriously, who the hell would have made these images?"

Jessie grunted in exasperation. "This is obviously a hoax. I believe you that you haven't been up here, but come on, this is actually insulting. Someone created this recently. The story it seems to tell is much more linear than anything I've ever seen in pictographs or petroglyphs. This is very Western, more like Celtic artwork. Like something made recently pretending to be an archaeological find."

"But who would have done this?" Suzanne asked. "Nobody has been up here for the last 150 years."

Jessie looked at her and said, "Listen, I'm not sure what to make of this. But I'm going to make the call that this is definitely not a tribal site. I'd be laughed out of the room if I tried to authenticate this." She paused thoughtfully. "Well, I guess it's good news for you guys, because if this had been a real archaeological site, you'd have been tied up with years of red tape as we sorted out ownership and visitation rights and all that."

Jack looked frustrated. "Jessie, listen, I'm not sure what the heck is going on here, but if this is a cultural site, or if it was, I'd be more than happy to have it tied up for as long as it took. You're sure you don't want to take more time here?"

Jessie looked at him for a few heartbeats. "No. I appreciate that the two of you had good intentions. But this isn't historical. I've never heard of a Coeur D'Alene or a Nez Perce cave site like this. In fact, I can't think of any regional tribe that has caves with walls carved this intricately and painted with pigment or gold or silver leaf. This is much more like some of the ancient Celtic sites scattered across Ireland and France. Those sites have petroglyphs somewhat like these ones, although without any pigments. There has been speculation that those ancient Celtic carvings may have been painted with pigments that didn't hold up over the years. But none of that is part of the regional tradition here. Obviously, someone has been working on this recently—there's a freaking helicopter on the wall! No, this is not something we're going to take an interest in as a tribe. But like I said, the good news is you can proceed forward with whatever plans you've had. This cave is not a preservable site."

After listening to Jessie's ruling, they did spend a little time walking back into the second chamber and looking around, but there was nothing left in it. Sam's journal had mentioned a box and a basket, but neither of these were present. The carvings on the walls slowly diminished as they moved further into the cave. They decided not to go any further into the tunnels at this point and headed back to the village.

While they walked, Jack talked to Jessie about the project in general. She had signed an NDA before the helicopter flew them up here. He asked if she would be interested in coming on board as a consultant, to make sure that any storylines or approaches they took to native culture was accurate and not offensive. She expressed interest but said she'd need to take it back to the tribal council for discussion. She explained that a few of the elders were more likely to get involved.

After the helicopter took Jessie back to the Coeur D'Alene reservation down in Plummer, Jack and Suzanne sat down for lunch. They were quiet. After a little while, Jack said, "I think something weird is going on here. I can't figure it out, but when you read Mrs. O's and Sam's journals, they are constantly talking about encounters with fairies and strange people meeting with Eoinn around the hot springs in the middle of winter. I asked Ian about the cave, and he said he never heard anything about it."

"I know," said Susanne, "it's a bit freaky actually. When I first read Mrs. O'Hara's journal, I thought she was taking poetic license, just making things up. But as I got further in, I wasn't so sure. Sam seems so concrete in her personality, not prone to whimsy. But all these descriptions of interactions with the coyote and raven and the fairy girl in the village—I don't get it."

"Well," Jack said, "we're not going to figure it out until we do, so let's roll with it. Let's incorporate these ideas into the story of Crystal Village. I mean, Native American legends and Irish fairy tales overlaid on the Old West? How can you beat that? Let's bring it all together."

I I I I

Alameda, California, October 2028

Jack stood across from Diana Rollins and Bill McKenna next to a giant table. A detailed, scale model of Crystal Village sat on the table. The three were wrapping their heads around the scope of the project they had taken on.

The room they stood in was an old aircraft hanger in Alameda, California, a community based on an island next to Oakland. An old U.S. Navy air base there had been commercialized, and some of the old aircraft hangers were used by movie studios and other businesses. Yomohiro Corporation had leased two of these hangers that stood right next to each other to support the needs of the Crystal Village project. Covid-19 had created a bit of a wasteland among the old Alameda Navy yard. Since then, it had been seeing success by catering to businesses that needed large spaces. Of course, it hadn't fully recovered, but that left an opportunity now. While it was easy to use VR headgear to jump into a high-resolution model of the village, sometimes this physical model helped with conversations.

Jack pointed out that the buildings on Broadway—with their three-tier porches running the length of the street and all interconnected—must offer some unique opportunities for storytelling. He imagined the third-floor windows of townhouses and hotel rooms allowing children to escape into the night air for J.M. Barrie-inspired, Peter Pan-like adventures, led by Elven actors. They discussed the implications of this from a safety perspective, and how they would ensure full camera coverage.

Bill was enthusiastic, but Diana expressed concern about the risks of children falling from the roof. Jack waved her aside with frustration saying, "We're not at the stage where we should be poo-pooing ideas." However, Bill took her concerns as a challenge. He talked about set design from Mary Poppins, and how the roofs of London turned into a set for dancing and music. He offered some preliminary suggestions as to how the chimney sweeps' domain could be turned into a playground for children that was safe enough to allow them some freedom and "safe risk taking."

Bill walked over to a whiteboard and started sketching modifications to both the buildings themselves and the design of the railings to ensure they could be safely traversed, even at night by fairly young children.

"What I'd really love to figure out," Bill said thoughtfully, "is how to make the kids fly."

Jack clapped his hands together, "Yes!" He shouted, "That's what I'm talking about! This needs to be an incredibly magical experience for kids! They. Must. FLY!"

Reluctantly, Diana started to play along. "I was on a vacation in Belize a few years ago, and there was a pretty remarkable zipline adventure I went on. I had actually wondered if it was possible to incorporate something like that into the parks when we were at Disney."

Jack nodded thoughtfully and said, "We researched it at one point, but the throughput was too slow. Lines would be backed up for hours—even with Fastpass or reservations. You wouldn't be able to handle large volumes. Guests would need too much help to get geared up and hooked in. Cast members would need specialized training. But for something like this, it could work ..." He paused, thinking.

Bill handed them some mixed-reality glasses. They all turned theirs on. This allowed the physical model to be extended digitally into a sort of mixed-reality "hologram" that included the mountains surrounding the village. The mountains remained translucent, so it wasn't "photo-real" mixed-reality, but it gave a sense of the dimensionality of the village in the real world.

"Jack, I have an idea," Bill began. "There's enough vertical rise between the peaks on three sides of the village that we could literally run zip lines all around. There's no reason we have to be limited by gravity—with small electric motors, we could zip uphill even. We could run one to the mouth of the Indian Caves. We could run others in other directions. I bet we could even interconnect them to incorporate turns. Frankly, we could just put a mesh across the whole valley and computer control the movement of the zipline, you know, have it go anywhere we want! The person attached would be on a long tether, so changes in direction would be buffered anyway— might really feel like flying." He sketched his idea on the whiteboard.

Jack's mouth slowly dropped open. "Bill, this mesh system idea is really fascinating! Where we want direct movement from fixed points we could interconnect the "sky mesh" to local connections. Like a spiderweb. Hell, we could connect all of the main buildings on Broadway, even across the various intersections. We could connect those to an entire web of lines running all over the town. I love this idea of powered ziplines, almost like a little ski lift. So you could zipline up and down."

Diana was taking notes furiously. "Guys, wouldn't that mean the town would look like it had a wire grid or mesh above it? Think about it, this may not look very good."

Bill smiled. "We've been playing with camouflage techniques for electrical wires. Some municipalities have been playing with masking cell phone towers, water towers, and fuel tanks. We could mask some of the wires using smart paint, or we could use projectors that would hide them. But the best way is probably the smart paint. It's basically paint that functions as a low-resolution video screen, and it can get quite brightly luminous, so you could match the luminosity of the sky.

The sky image would either be dumb, meaning a static image, but luminosity would match the backlight of the sky. Or it could be broadcast. By this, I mean it shows a video image taken from a camera nearby, in this case pointed at the sky. There's a tradeoff in smart paints, luminosity versus pixel resolution, power consumption, durability, and some other factors. Some applications use smart paint on walls for video walls, but to get to any kind of resolution, you can't have the screen be very bright. But at very low resolutions, you can be blindingly bright. To mask an object against a bright sky, we mostly need to ensure the luminosity matches the sky, with a minor bit of pattern like clouds. We'll have to play around. The bigger issue is helicopters, drones, and planes. I think we can do something from above that might be just as valuable at accentuating visibility for aircraft, maybe even blink the whole grid red on and off from above. We'll need a path for helicopters to come in and out of the village, both for our own needs and for emergency extraction if someone has an accident or health emergency. But we can work through all that."

For parts of the gridwork where we can't mask it against the sky, we could incorporate lines into a "faux" electrical grid. If the timeframe you're tapping into is post-Edison, you could have these heavy Victorian, almost steampunk brackets with thick electrical wires and struts." He drew a few rough sketches that showcased his idea, and Jack and Diana broke into huge smiles. "You wouldn't run full voltage electricity through them. They would be just for show."

Bill paused thoughtfully, then said, "You know, I wasn't going to go down this line of thinking, but the newest smart glasses in development are getting to the point where we might consider them as part of the experience in Crystal Village. They're expensive, like a few thousand bucks a pair right now, with costs dropping as production ramps up. It's not like we'd need millions of pairs of them, probably we can get away with one to two thousand. We could incorporate them into the visitors' experience and enhance a lot of things visually. Like the wire mesh, we could erase them from view in the glasses. Or if we wanted to add visual effects to some of the characters—or even insert objects that aren't there—we could do quite a lot. Then we wouldn't need smart paint. We'd simply need to map the physical grid and "erase" it like it was on a green screen. But if you took off the goggles, you'd see everything ... so maybe we do both."

Jack said, "I'm open to the idea. We just need to make sure the goggles aren't intrusive into the experience, and that they work reliably. Budget's always a concern, but like you said, it's not necessarily a deal-breaker. Maybe we just use them for specific experiences. I don't imagine anyone walking around town with bug-eyes. Even if we tried to make them "period-looking" or steampunk-adjacent, I can't imagine a whole village walking around with them on."

Jack looked down at the model of the town, then at the space behind the whiteboards. They were in a room that was the size of a football field. The giant table with the scale model was about 100 feet long by 100 feet wide and was on wheels that enabled it to be broken apart to let people walk into the center of it. It was surrounded by a sea of whiteboards, also on wheels. Behind the whiteboards was a giant, empty space.

Jack waved his hand and said, "Let's build an "at scale" model a few feet off the ground of the rooftops and mock up some of these motorized ziplines. Then we can see what it feels like." Diana nodded, then picked up her phone and made a call.

I I I I

Susanne stepped out of her Uber in front of the giant aircraft hanger in Alameda, California. She'd never been to Oakland before and was thrilled with the warm weather. She was pleased to see that flowers were in bloom everywhere. More importantly, she was excited to catch up with Jack, who had hired her onto the project's writing team. Jack had given her a bunch of reading to do before she flew out. As a result, she was learning a lot about writing scripts for interactive environments. She had eight novels to her name, and she loved writing, but it was hard to make a living without a hit book.

She walked into the little reception area and said hello to the young, African American woman behind the reception desk. She was very stylish in a hip sort of way, dressed in some kind of sleek athletic wear that was all black but had interesting textures.

"Hi, I'm Susanne O'Connor. I'm here to meet Jack Seeley."

"Hi, Susanne, I'm Kiara. Jack has you on the list. I just need to see your ID, and I have a badge all made up for you. Then I'll take you back."

After viewing Suzanna's ID, Kiara handed her the badge, which Susanne clipped to a belt loop on her pants. Then the two of them walked through the door and into the hangar. It was huge, and the whole space was made up of *rooftops*—not the whole building. Rather, it was just as if someone had sliced the rooftops off of the intersection of a street and laid them on the floor of the hangar. She recognized the rooftops of buildings from Main Street, with mansard roofs and the porches on the front. She marvelled, seeing that the whole thing was built to scale, a whole intersection, all four corners. Above the rooftops there was a gridwork at the ceiling level that was painted sky blue. The ceiling above that was brightly lit in an attempt to simulate the brightness of the sky outside.

Kiara brought her over to an observation area marked off by tape, with the word "observation area" stenciled on the floor. It had several stools to sit on, and she took a seat.

"Jack will be with you in a few minutes. He's finishing a meeting, but he thought you'd get a kick out of the trapeze."

"Thanks so much, Kiara," Susanne replied. "I appreciate it." *Trapeze,* she *thought ... What in hell?*

She watched as a man and woman climbed up onto the rooftops, which were only about six feet off the ground. They stretched, warmed up a bit, and then they started checking each other's harnesses. The individual harnesses attached at the back to very thin wires running about fifty feet up to the gridwork above the rooftops. They both were wearing gloves, knee, elbow, and shin pads, and what looked like skateboard helmets. After checking their harnesses thoroughly, they both stood up and began running towards the intersection.

Susanne assumed they were going to jump down into the space between the buildings, but they didn't. As they approached the intersection, they leapt into the air. To Susanne's shock, they flew through the air, spanning the gap of the intersection lightly and easily, landing on the building on the other side. The woman turned hard right and leapt from the corner of the building toward the opposite side of the intersection, kitty-corner to the building she stood on. She soared into the air on a tall arc, and at the apex of the arc, she executed a 360-degree flip before landing on the other building. In the meantime, her partner had taken a less acute right turn and jumped to the building on the other corner of the intersection.

Susanne was delighted. Jack had tried to explain to her that they'd come up with some mechanisms to support aerobatics, but it hadn't sounded nearly as exciting as this. Kiara came back with a pair of glasses for her to try on. They were surprisingly heavy in her hands, but not uncomfortably so, when she put them on. They had adjustable hooks that went behind her ears, and when she finished adjusting them, they were both comfortable and very "attached." As a result, she had no concern that they'd slip or fall off. They were more goggles than glasses, covering her entire eyes, but without the bulk she associated with VR or mixed-reality glasses. Kiara reached over and pressed a button on the frame of the glasses and held it on for three seconds.

Suddenly, the world around her changed. The lighting became much more sophisticated. The grid work near the ceiling and the ceiling itself disappeared and became daytime sky. She turned her attention to the two people running across the rooftops and was delighted to see that the cables attaching them to the gridwork also disappeared. They now appeared to be truly floating and flying around the rooftops. The entire buildings were now filled in below the rooftops and the streets below them. The lighting in the hangar was very different with the glasses on, things seemed to be stage-lit theatrically. She seemed to be sitting on a platform that was hovering in the air, a trick of the glasses that was defined by the taped-off "observation area."

A few minutes later, Dianna arrived, suddenly appearing on the hovering platform. "Hi, Susanne, nice to see you again, and welcome to the Alameda workshop! Really great to have you here. What do you think of the flight grid?"

"Oh, Dianna, it's really amazing! It's only been a few weeks, how did you pull this off?"

Dianna said, "Oh, well, we're used to rapid prototyping for theme park design and also for film sets. It was pretty busy in here for a few days but nothing too out of the ordinary. The bigger trick will be getting this to work on-site in the village. The grid will be much higher in the air, and some of the routes will be really complicated. But we'll work it out."

Dianna waited patiently for a few minutes while Susanne watched the team work out on the rooftops. Diana reached over and clicked a button on the glasses a few times. Each click changed what Suzanne saw. On the third click, the room reverted to normal, but in the upper right corner of her vision she saw the words "Mixed Reality." Dianna ushered her through a door on the side into another hanger just as big as the first. She saw clusters of whiteboards and tables. A large model of the whole village was laid out on tables with wheels. There was a giant projection of Crystal Village's immediate physical surroundings, including all the neighboring mountains, overlaying the model. The projection showed up as semi-transparent, which she knew must be coming from her glasses.

Jack was standing with a team of people, deeply engaged in a conversation. They were all wearing glasses similar to the ones Susanne was wearing. Jack was facing away from them as Dianna and Susanne walked in, so they politely paused at the doorway. The group was made up of six people and was led by a woman who was quite animated.

Jack raised his hand and got her attention, saying, "Monica, I get it. But I don't think the rest of the team is following you. Can you just walk us through it one more time?"

Monica let out a deep breath and began again. "The writers are pulling together the outlines for all the different storylines. For instance, we have one storyline that focuses on the village citizens and their struggle against the miners from outside the village. We have another storyline about the Fairies who followed Mrs. O over from Ireland. We have another storyline about Coyote and Raven, who are mythological Native characters.

"Each of these storylines needs to be fleshed out into very comprehensive stories. Some of them will be hundreds of pages long, like a novella. Then these will be fed into the custom AI. Each character who is part of the village has its own custom AI model that defines their personality. Some of these are quite extensive and very rich, with a whole history and backstory. Simply stated, the AI is given a set of constraints based on what that character's capabilities are, what their personality is, and what their motivations are. The writers pull together daily, weekly, and monthly outlines to lay out the rough sketch of what is going to happen in each storyline, but the AI effectively pulls the detailed story together and then writes a script for each character. Since there are hundreds of characters in the village—each of them with a human actor who needs to be able to improvise against the overall stories with our visitors—we need to make sure everyone understands enough about those characters to be able to act out their parts effectively."

A chubby man in his forties with wire-rimmed glasses raised his hand,

"But Monica, why are we using the AI to do this—why not just get the writers on it? I don't like disintermediating our writing team. This has been a major issue for the last few years. Why would we just dive right into a situation where we are handing the reins over to an AI?"

Monica paused thoughtfully and said, "Mitch, I understand your concern. But there's a bunch of reasons we have to involve the AI in this so deeply. First, we are pushing this through really fast. There are so many characters and so many people to hire and get trained that we really can't afford to take the time for the writers to cover every aspect of every story and every character. It would take a year or more. Second, the AI models for each character serve a secondary purpose.

"Only a few dozen guests at a time are able to go into the village in the beginning and at our peak, maybe fifteen hundred or so. Our most aggressive model gets us up to twenty-five hundred visitors at any given time. A theme park like Disney World has between fifty thousand and 150 thousand visitors a day. In order for us to make money on this, we need the immersive, online video game and the television show to take off. The AI models in the game for each character need to behave just like the players would expect the characters to behave in the village, display the same characteristics, and attitudes. And we'd need every character to have dialogue written in every language we support. The storylines online and in the park will interweave with each other and constantly evolve.

"This can't be fully scripted—it has to be interactive. If a player interacts with one of the characters, we have to have dialogue that is informed by events that are happening in the park and across the video game universe and vice versa. Keeping all of that in sync in real time is impossible without using the AI. Plus, the actors in the park have autonomy and will be able to adlib lines. Those interactions need to be fed back into the overarching AI models so that the gameplay is informed in real time by activity happening in the park.

"But as we've discussed before, we're going to compensate writers fairly for this. Each writer assigned to crafting the model around a character will be credited and compensated for each time that a character speaks in any of the environments. Each writer who works on the overall script will be compensated more highly than the standard WGA rules for writer compensation, plus will have a variable bonus based on the success of the stories they're involved in. AIs are great at the tactical stuff but not creative enough to craft the broader story arcs or to flesh out the model for each character fully. That's the work the writing team will be focused on for the foreseeable future."

Mitch seemed appeased by Monica's explanation and nodded his head. The rest of the group seemed to have gotten over the hump.

"Okay," said Jack, "Any more concerns or questions?" He paused. When nobody responded he said, "Great, then let's get at it."

The group exited past Dianna and Susanne, and Jack saw them and broke into a huge smile.

"Susanne! You're here! Excellent!" He walked over and gave her an enveloping hug.

Dianna smirked and looked away for a moment, then looked back, "I'll leave you two to it then." As she walked away, she gave Jack a rather pointedly confused and somewhat impressed look. She'd only met Susanne over video conferencing previously, and Jack notoriously was not a player when it came to relationships.

"Thanks, Dianna," said Jack, blushing. "Okay Susanne, you've gotten to see a bit of the operation here. What do you think?"

Susanne smiled and said, "Super impressive and I have to admit, a little intimidating. But holy crap—you're a big wig here!"

Jack smiled sheepishly, "Heh. It's always a little weird when different worlds in my life collide."

Susanne reached over, squeezed his hand, and smiled kindly at him. Jack took a deep breath and shook his head lightly, as if shaking off his emotions.

"Actually, it's good that you were here for that conversation," said Jack. "Mitch is the head writer on the project, and you'll actually be reporting to him for your part on the project."

Susanne looked a little nervous, "Oh. Yeah, I guess I should have realized that I'd be working with someone other than you and Dianna. Is he okay with me working on his team? I don't want to feel like I'm swooping in just because we're friends."

Jack paused and looked directly into her eyes. "Susanne, let's get that out of the way right now. Yes, we are friends. Yes, you are part of the Legacy of Crystal Village, and you're directly a descendant of two of the founders of the village. So you'd have a part to play here regardless of whether your profession happened to be writing. At the very least, you'd be a producer on the project—which you are, by the way—if that hasn't been made clear yet.

"But I passed your books around to Mitch and his team before I told them about your connection with the project, to have them see if you might be a fit. Mitch was super excited about you. His daughter is a huge fan of your work, she has all your books. He admitted that he'd secretly been reading your stuff for years, because he likes to keep tabs on what she's reading. You were "in" before I even explained your unique relationship to the village. That only made him more excited."

"Oh!" said Susanne, suddenly embarrassed.

"So, if that leaves you ready to dive in, let me take you over to the writers' room and get you connected with the team. Then tonight, let me take you out for a good dinner."

18

Duality

March 2029

The setting sun painted the sky in orange and lilac as the writing team gathered in the main bar of the Hawthorne Hotel. They had all flown in that afternoon by helicopter. They were the first group to use the new helipad on the other side of the bridge, which had been installed to accommodate the flight grid over the village. It was on the farm site that originally included animal pens and fields where a series of crops were rotated.

The team was enjoying the warmth of the giant fireplace in the front sitting room. The hotel was one of the first restored buildings, its wood polished to a honey glow, and its brass fixtures shining like new. The gathering was an initial meeting between the Crystal Village creative team and two tribal elders who represented both the Coeur d'Alene and Nez Perce tribes.

Jack sat beside Diana Rollins. The writers were a diverse group of ten people marked by the combinations of open laptops and notepads. Among them was Susanne O'Connor and Mitch, the head writer.

At the head of the table sat the two tribal elders. Calvin Whitebird was a Nez Perce elder with a lined face and long steel-gray hair. Beside him sat

Sarah Stensgar, a Coeur d'Alene elder with long dark hair that was streaked with silver. Earlier, the team had learned about the collaborative efforts underway with both tribes to develop culturally authentic experiences within the park. Led by the Coeur d'Alene Tribe, the annual Spring Root Feast would be a celebration of traditional root gathering and preparation, as well as featuring an indigenous food festival, basically an indigenous "taste of" event. The park would also host, in partnership with both tribes, annual powwows and a Nez Perce *Tamkaliks* Celebration, providing opportunities for cultural exchange and education. These events would also be integrated into the game world, allowing Native players to participate in and even lead these virtual celebrations.

Jack cleared his throat, and the room fell silent. "Thank you, Elders Whitebird and Stensgar, for joining us today," he began. "We recognize that this conversation, held here on the ancestral lands of your people, is a crucial step in our journey to create a story that honors both the past and the present. We understand that these stories are not just filled with characters and plot points but include references to living traditions that carry deep cultural and spiritual significance for your people. We are truly honored to have your guidance and participation in shaping these stories and ensuring their authenticity."

He paused, then added, "I want to take the opportunity to announce to the team that we will be hiring a cultural liaison who will work with us throughout the project. This person will be an active member of both the Crystal Village leadership team and a representative of one of the tribes. We're also working to find a few additional members of the writing and production team to bring on as part of this initiative. We're specifically looking for representation from both tribes if we can find the right people. If you know anyone, please alert Mitch. We also look forward to the upcoming celebrations led by your tribes, which will enrich the experience of Crystal Village for all who visit, both physically and virtually. We're here not only to learn from your wisdom about the stories of Raven and Coyote—which we hope to incorporate respectfully into our narrative—but also to seek your ongoing guidance as members of our Cultural Advisory Board."

Calvin nodded back. "These beings, *ínpin* and *Qáac*—Coyote and Raven—are teachers and guides. They're not just characters in *titwáatit*, in stories," he began. "They are part of our culture, they are real beings to us. We have an oral tradition going back to the beginnings of our people." Calvin added, "Remember that my people, the *Nimíipuu*, may tell these stories differently than Sarah's people or other tribes. Each nation has its own relationship with these beings."

Sarah nodded and leaned forward. "Coyote is often misunderstood," she said. "He is a trickster, yes, but not evil. He's not all good, and he's not all bad. He is chaotic, and he can be callous, and he can be aggressive. He can also behave in a boorish way. He can be jealous, and he can be prone to anger, and he can hold a grudge. But at the same time, he also can be fun and creative and has a spirit of adventure. Overall, he is more often than not a force for good, a force for change."

Calvin nodded his agreement and added, "Raven is also a bit of a trickster but more ordered and less chaotic. He is slower to act. He is less impetuous than Coyote. But he still can behave in ways that we'd call "bad" today. I think it's important that we honor the totality of their personalities."

One of the writers, a man named Tom chimed in. "I've really felt a pull towards these stories, maybe because I've got a hint of Cherokee in my family tree according to 23 and Me." Mitch looked pained and took a deep breath.

"Tom, there's more to it than genetics. You weren't raised in these traditions. We're here to listen and learn," Mitch said.

Sarah leaned forward to engage with Tom. "It's a good thing to learn about your family history. Mitch is correct to suggest that the experience of our people, our traditions and our culture are much more than genetics. Perhaps this is the opportunity to learn more about native people and cultures in general. Maybe someday you will find an opportunity to look into your Cherokee roots and reengage with that part of your own history."

Tom grimaced, nodded his head, and said, "Sorry, you're right." Then he sank back into his chair as Calvin continued.

"These beings, Raven and Coyote, are teachers and guides," Calvin continued. "They're not just characters in stories. They're part of our world and our history. Approach them with respect. They are not your characters to command. Respect them, and they will lend you their strength."

Jack nodded, "Thank you for meeting with us and agreeing to share your stories and your culture. We want to learn from you, and we need to understand what these stories mean to you, so we can honor them," he said.

Jack had prepared for this meeting for weeks. He was concerned about approaching this the wrong way—the wrong approach could lead to cultural appropriation that would do real damage to these people. He also wanted the experience of Crystal Village to be powerful and moving for the visitors and virtual participants, and the kind of authenticity that came from this collaboration would be valuable.

Calvin said, "The Nez Perce, or *Nimiipuu*, have lived with the rivers, the forests, and the mountains since time immemorial. We followed the seasons and the game and lived by the waters that wound their paths through the land."

Sarah added, "My people are the *Schitsu'umsh*, or the Coeur d'Alene, as we were named by French traders for the sharpness of our trading acumen. But our name for ourselves speaks of something greater—we call ourselves the Discovered People. Some interpretations are more like "Those who are found here." It refers to the deep, ongoing connection we have to the land, and the unbroken lineage going back many generations."

Tom raised his hand. At a nod from Calvin, he said, "I think I understand the importance of getting this right. These stories, they're part of who you are as a people."

Calvin nodded. "That they are. When you tell a story, you breathe life into it. You give it power, even as you take power from it."

"Our legends of Raven and Coyote are not fables or fairy tales," Sarah explained. "They are the lessons we carry with us each day. Raven and Coyote are real to us, as real to us today as they were to our ancestors."

Susanna looked around the room, trying to catch everyone's eye. "As storytellers, we have a responsibility to honor your culture and learn from it without trying to change the meaning of the stories, without trying to take ownership of them."

Sarah said, "I am grateful for the respect you show our stories, but remember that for us, stories are medicine. They carry a power, a spirit that can heal or harm. When we tell a story, we invoke its power. In our culture, the story is a ceremony. Narrating the journey of a sick person who finds healing isn't just a tale—it's the medicine that wraps itself around the one who needs it, aiding in their recovery. I also have found that one cannot tell a story without inherently changing the story. Stories have a way of taking ownership of you, as much as the other way around."

Calvin nodded. "As you amplify these stories through your mediums—your games, movies, shows, and this park—you must be mindful of the consequences. These aren't just characters. Telling their stories could have unintended consequences."

Jack said, "We'd like to ask you both to be actively part of the ongoing editorial review of this work. We want to navigate this appropriately. It's important that we look at the bigger picture. This isn't just a theme park we're creating. We're not building "Native Land" and "Fairy Land." If we're going to tap into the power of your culture, we want to be thoughtful about the implications."

"You must tread carefully," Calvin agreed, "for each time a story is told, it is reborn. With each retelling, you must ask—does it honor the source? Does it change the meaning? Your Crystal Village has the potential to be a place of profound connection, but it must be built upon a foundation of reverence and truth."

As the group settled in, and trays of drinks were circulated by the serving staff, the group slowly quieted down to listen to the stories of their guests.

"Traditionally," Calvin began, "these stories would only be told during the winter months when the snakes are sleeping. We've been given special permission to share these stories with you as part of our cultural outreach efforts and for education. There are protocols in our traditions about when and how these stories can be shared. Our willingness to share these as broadly as we are is unusual, and we ask for your understanding and respect.

There are other stories we have decided not to share."

Before beginning his story, Calvin paused, taking a moment of silence. "*Hipáayin*—listen well," he said softly in Nez Perce, creating a ceremonial space before sharing the ancient story. "This is not our story of Raven," he clarified, "but one that has traveled far from the northern coasts to reach us. Yet it carries wisdom we can share." The room was silent, listening to the masterful storytelling of Raven tricking Sky Chief, transforming into his grandson, and the core message of Raven as a bringer of light was clear.

Calvin let his voice fade out for a moment, then he explained, "This story reminds us of the transformative power of light and wisdom. It celebrates cleverness, courage, and the responsibility we have to bring good things to our people."

The room had the feel of a sacred space as the writers listened carefully. Sarah listened to the story, gently nodding her head, her eyes closed reverently. When Calvin finished, she said, "In our Coeur d'Alene tradition, we know *Skwest*—Coyote—as the one who prepared the world for the human beings who would come later. He shaped our rivers and mountains, our homeland. He was both wise teacher and foolish trickster, showing us how to live and how not to live."

Then she began her story.

Coyote Steals Fire

In the time before humans walked the Earth, when the animals were the only inhabitants, the world was a cold and dark place. The Sun would rise and set, but its warmth did not reach the ground, and the nights were filled with an icy chill that cut to the bone. The animals shivered in the cold, their fur and feathers providing little comfort.

On top of a distant mountain lived the three Fire Beings. They were mighty and fearsome entities who guarded their fire with a relentless vigilance. They never slept, their eyes were as sharp as the eagle's, and any creature that dared to try and steal their fire was met with a swift and terrible punishment.

Coyote, with his sharp eyes and cunning mind, saw the despair of his fellow creatures. He felt a deep compassion for them, and a resolve stirred within him. He would steal the fire from the Fire Beings and bring it back to warm the world.

But Coyote knew he could not do it alone. So, he called upon his friend, a small bird known as First Helper. Together, they devised a plan. First Helper, with his bright feathers and loud call, would create a diversion. While the Fire Beings were distracted, Coyote would seize the opportunity to steal the fire.

The journey to the mountain was long and perilous, but Coyote and First Helper pressed on, driven by the hope of a warm world. When they finally arrived, Coyote snuck to the outskirts of the Fire Being's camp to watch from afar. He saw that the Fire Beings took two rocks that they would bang together, creating sparks. Those sparks would land and create a fire.

Coyote ran back to First Helper with a plan. First Helper took to the air. He flew high and flapped his wings mightily, sending feathers whirling in the air and his call echoed through the mountains.

The Fire Beings, startled by the sudden commotion, looked skyward. Their attention was fully captured by the strange spectacle, and they failed to notice the sly Coyote creeping towards their sacred fire.

With a swift movement, Coyote snatched a glowing ember from the fire. Without wasting a moment, he turned and ran down the mountain, the stolen fire clutched tightly in his mouth. As soon as the Fire Beings realized their fire had been taken, they gave chase. But Coyote was swift, and the mountain was steep. Despite their might and speed, the Fire Beings could not catch him.

Coyote returned to the waiting animals, the stolen fire still glowing brightly. The creatures of the Earth rejoiced, their joyous cries filling the once cold and silent night. But their celebration was cut short as the fire began to spread, threatening to consume the world in its hungry flames.

Seeing the danger, Coyote acted quickly. He diverted water from the river, which flowed over the burning land, putting out the fires. Then he picked up two stones and struck them together as he had seen the Fire Beings do, creating sparks that ignited the flames again. He showed the animals how to control the fire, how to nurture its warmth and keep its hunger at bay.

From that day forth, the world was no longer a place of darkness and cold. Fire belonged to the animals and later, to the humans. It provided them with warmth, light, and a means to cook their food. Every time they sat around a fire, they would remember the brave and clever Coyote who risked everything to steal the fire from the mighty Fire Beings.

The room was silent as the writers gathered their thoughts. Tom hesitantly raised his hand. "Elders, if I may," he began. "The story of Coyote stealing fire paints him as a hero, yet I've heard other tales where his actions bring about destruction. How do we reconcile this duality?"

Calvin nodded thoughtfully, having fully expected the question. "That is the very nature of Coyote," he explained. "He is a complex being, capable of great deeds and great follies. Like us, he is multifaceted, neither wholly good nor wholly evil. His stories are lessons in balance, teaching us about the consequences of our actions."

Mitch shifted in his seat, raising his hand, and Calvin pointed to him. "Elders," he said, "how do we ensure we're capturing the essence of Coyote, especially in light of all his complexity? I have to admit, when we first started discussing the script, we saw Coyote as the perfect villain."

Sarah nodded appreciatively. "Balance," she said. "Coyote teaches us about balance. He is neither a villain to be conquered nor a hero to be idolized. He is a being of nature, embodying both creation and chaos. Raven too has many sides to him. I think it would be helpful for you if you hear more stories about Coyote that explore Coyote's chaotic and impetuous nature."

Calvin shared a knowing glance with Sarah before saying. "This is the story of Coyote and the Salmon Chief."

The room fell silent, the writers hanging on Calvin's every word, pens poised.

Coyote and the Salmon Chief

In the time when the world was still learning its shape, when the great Columbia River carved its path through the mountains and valleys, there lived the Salmon Chief at the thundering falls of Celilo. He was a being of great power and wisdom, keeper of all the salmon people who brought life to the tribes along the river.

The Salmon Chief was not like other beings. His lodge was built from the mist of the falls themselves, and his robes shimmered like the scales of countless fish. He understood the sacred cycles—when the salmon should run, how many could be taken, and the ceremonies that must be performed to honor their sacrifice.

Coyote, in his wanderings, came upon the falls during the salmon runs. He saw the abundance of fish leaping up the cascades, their silver bodies flashing in the sunlight like scattered coins. His mouth watered at the sight, and his stomach growled with hunger.

"Salmon Chief!" Coyote called out boldly. "I am hungry, and I see you have plenty. Share your salmon with me!"

The Salmon Chief emerged from his misty lodge, his ancient eyes studying the trickster. "Welcome, Coyote," he said with measured words. "The salmon people are generous, but they require respect. You must fast for four days, purify yourself in the sweat lodge, and offer prayers of gratitude. Only then may you take what you need."

Coyote's ears flattened against his head. Four days? Prayers? Ceremonies? His belly ached with immediate hunger, and the salmon were right there, practically throwing themselves onto the rocks.

"That seems like a lot of trouble for some fish," Coyote said dismissively. "Surely you can make an exception for me. I'm Coyote! I've done great things for the people."

The Salmon Chief's expression grew stern. "The salmon are not '*some fish,*' *Coyote. They are people, like you and me. They choose to give their lives so others may live. This gift requires proper acknowledgment.*"

But Coyote was already eyeing the rushing waters, calculating how he might snatch the salmon without all this ceremony. "I understand, I understand," he said, waving a paw dismissively. "But I'm really quite hungry right now."

That night, while the Salmon Chief slept, Coyote crept to the water's edge. He had fashioned a crude net from willow branches and began scooping up salmon after salmon, stuffing them into baskets with greedy haste. He took far more than he could eat, thinking he would smoke them and have food for many days.

But as soon as Coyote's net touched the first salmon without proper ceremony, the Salmon Chief awakened. His eyes blazed with the power of the rushing water, and his voice boomed like thunder over the falls.

"Coyote! You have broken the sacred trust! You take without asking, without gratitude, without respect for the salmon people's sacrifice!"

The Salmon Chief raised his arms, and immediately every salmon in the river turned and began swimming back toward the ocean. The fish Coyote had caught dissolved into mist in his baskets. Within moments, the Columbia River was empty of salmon for the first time since the world began.

"Wait!" Coyote cried, realizing what he had done. "I was just hungry! Bring them back!"

"The salmon people have withdrawn their gift," the Salmon Chief said solemnly. "They will not return until you learn the proper way to ask for their help."

Days passed, then weeks. The tribes along the river began to suffer as their most important food source disappeared. Children cried with hunger. Elders grew weak. The people sent messengers to Coyote, pleading with him to make things right.

Coyote's heart grew heavy as he saw the suffering his impatience had caused. He returned to Celilo Falls and found the Salmon Chief sitting in meditation beside the now-quiet waters.

"Salmon Chief," Coyote said, his voice humble for perhaps the first time in his life. "I have been foolish. I thought only of my own hunger and ignored the wisdom you offered. Please, teach me the proper way. I will fast, I will purify myself, I will offer the prayers. The people are suffering because of my selfishness."

The Salmon Chief studied Coyote's face and saw genuine remorse there. "Very well," he said. "But you must do more than learn the ceremonies, Coyote. You must teach them to the people, so they will always remember the proper relationship with the salmon people."

And so Coyote fasted for four days, purified himself in the sweat lodge, and learned the prayers and songs that honored the salmon people's sacrifice. He learned to take only what was needed, to use every part of the fish, and to offer thanks for their gift of life.

When the ceremonies were complete, the Salmon Chief called to his people. Slowly, like silver threads being rewoven into the river, the salmon began to return. First a few, then hundreds, then thousands, until the Columbia ran thick with their abundance once more.

Coyote kept his promise. He traveled to every village along the river, teaching the people the proper ceremonies for honoring the salmon. And to this day, when the salmon run, the people remember Coyote's lesson about respect, gratitude, and the sacred relationship between all living beings.

The salmon still give their lives so others may live, but they do so knowing they are honored, respected, and remembered in the proper way.

Calvin let his voice fade out for a moment, then he explained, "This story reminds us that all relationships—whether with the salmon people, the land, or each other—require respect and proper protocols. Coyote's hunger was real, his need was genuine, but his impatience and disrespect nearly cost everyone their most important source of life. The salmon people are not just food—they are relatives who choose to give their lives so we may live. This story teaches us that when we ignore the proper way of asking, of showing gratitude, we risk losing the very gifts that sustain us."

He paused, looking around the room at the writers. "Notice too that Coyote's mistake didn't just affect him—it affected all the people along the river. This is why we say Coyote is a teacher. His failures become lessons for everyone. And when he finally learned humility and proper respect, he didn't keep that knowledge to himself. He shared it with all the tribes, ensuring the salmon people would always be honored correctly."

Calvin glanced at Sarah, who nodded approvingly. "This is the kind of story that shows Coyote's complexity—his selfishness nearly caused disaster, but his ability to learn and change turned him into a teacher who helped establish the proper relationship between our people and the salmon that continues to this day."

Susanne had been quiet throughout this session.

"Calvin, Sarah," Susanne began, "thank you for the stories you've shared about Coyote. I think we're all seeing the complexity you've mentioned. Sometimes he can seem petty, and sometimes he can seem playful like a child, and sometimes he can seem impetuous like a child. Does he grow over time? Is the Coyote talked about in these stories immutable, or does he evolve?"

Calvin looked from Susanne to the other writers, his expression serious. He had shared stories of Coyote's foolishness and his impetuous nature, but he could see they were still grappling with the creature's heroic side. He leaned forward, his hands resting on the table.

"You ask if Coyote evolves," Calvin said, his voice lowering into the cadence of a storyteller. "In our stories, Coyote is the one who prepares the world for the coming of the human beings. To do this, he had to be more than a trickster. He had to be a warrior. He had to be a savior. To truly understand this, you must hear of his greatest battle, here in this very land."

The room grew quiet again, the writers leaning in.

"This is the story of the Swallowing Monster of the Kamiah Valley."

Coyote and the Swallowing Monster

In the age before this one, when the world was not yet finished, the land was filled with 'ilap'ílap cicy'a'á—great monsters who preyed upon the animal people. The most terrible of all was a monster whose body was a mountain and whose mouth was a cave that breathed a mighty wind. This monster lay in the valley of the Clearwater River, and for days on end, it would inhale.

One by one, the animal people were drawn into its gut. Deer, Bear, Elk, Fox—all were pulled from the trails and forests by the monster's relentless breath. Soon, the land grew quiet. The forests were empty. The trails were bare.

Only Coyote was left. He had been far away, and when he returned, he found the world silent and empty. He called for his friends, but only the echo answered. He followed the tracks, all leading to the Kamiah Valley, and there he saw it: the great Swallowing Monster, its massive body filling the canyon.

Coyote knew what he had to do. The world would not be safe for the new people, the humans who were coming, until this monster was gone.

But he could not fight it from the outside. He had to be clever. He went to the mountains and gathered five flint knives, sharp and strong. He took pitch from the pine trees and braided a long, strong rope from serviceberry branches. He tied the knives to his wrists, his waist, and his head, hiding them in his fur. He tied one end of his rope to the peaks of the mountains and the other around his waist.

Then, he walked to the edge of the canyon and called out, "Monster! I am Coyote! I am here!"

The great monster opened its eyes, which were like deep pools of water, and began to inhale. The wind rushed past Coyote, pulling at his fur. But Coyote held fast to his rope, digging his heels into the earth.

"You cannot swallow me!" he taunted. "I am too strong for you!"

The monster inhaled harder. The wind became a gale. Trees

bent and rocks skittered across the ground. Coyote held on, his rope straining. He was showing the monster his strength, making it angry.

Finally, the monster grew furious. It opened its mouth wider than ever before and gave a great, world-shaking gasp. The wind was so powerful it snapped Coyote's rope. He flew through the air, right into the monster's gaping throat.

Inside, it was a vast and crowded place. In the dim light, Coyote saw them all: the animal people, huddled together, weak and afraid. Bear was there, and Deer, and Rabbit, and all the others. They had given up hope.

"Coyote!" they cried. "You are here too! Now we are all doomed."

But Coyote just grinned his sharp-toothed grin. "Did you think I came here by accident? I came to get you out. Now, build me a fire. We need light."

The people were confused, but they did as he asked. They gathered what dry wood they could find inside the monster's belly and soon a small fire flickered to life. By its light, Coyote began to explore. He saw the great ribs of the monster arching above them like the timbers of a massive lodge. And far in the distance, he could hear a rhythmic booming.

THUMP-THUMP. THUMP-THUMP.

"What is that sound?" he asked.

"That is the monster's heart," said Bear. "We stay away from it. Its power is too great."

"That is where we must go," Coyote said, pulling out his flint knives.

He led the people toward the sound. As they got closer, the beating grew louder, shaking the very floor of the monster's gut. There it was: a heart as big as a hill, pulsing with dark energy.

"Now listen to me," Coyote said. "I am going to cut the heart. When I do, the monster will die. Its mouth will open. You must all run out as fast as you can. Do not look back. Just run!"

With a great yell, Coyote leaped onto the heart and began to slash at it with his flint knives. One knife broke, then another. The monster roared in pain, its whole body shaking. The people inside were thrown from their feet.

Coyote kept cutting. He used his third knife, then his fourth. Finally, with his last and sharpest knife, he made a deep gash. The heart gave one last, mighty beat, and then was still.

A great darkness fell. The monster's body shuddered and then lay quiet. Far in the distance, a sliver of light appeared as the monster's mouth fell open.

"Go! Now!" Coyote shouted.

The animal people scrambled toward the light, pouring out of the monster's mouth and back into the world. They ran to the hills and the forests, free once more.

Only Coyote was left inside. He was covered in the monster's blood and fat, and he was tired. He was so busy making sure everyone else got out that he almost forgot himself. By the time he reached the mouth, the jaws were beginning to close. He had to squeeze through a small gap, which is why Coyote is so flat and sleek today.

When he was outside, he looked upon the massive body of the dead monster. He knew he had one last job to do. He took his knife and began to carve up the great beast.

He took a piece of the liver and threw it to the east, saying, "You will be the Blackfeet people. You will be strong and fierce."

He took a piece of the heart and threw it to the south, saying, "You will be the Ute people. You will be swift and have great endurance."

He threw pieces to the west, creating the coastal tribes. He threw pieces to the north, creating the peoples of the cold lands. He populated the entire land with different tribes, giving each a gift from the monster's body.

When he was finished, all that was left was the blood and the water he had used to wash his hands. His friend, Fox, came to him and said, "Coyote, you have given a body and a home to all the other people. What about this valley? Will there be no one here?"

Coyote looked at the blood-mixed water in his hands. He sprinkled it on the ground right there, at the foot of the monster's body.

"You are right," he said. "From this blood, a new people will be born. They will be small in number, but they will be strong of heart and spirit. They will live here, in this beautiful valley, forever. They will be the Nimiipuu—the Real People."

And that is how the world was made safe. That is how the tribes were created. And that is why, to this day, the heart of that great monster can still be seen in the hills near Kamiah, a reminder of the time when Coyote was not just a trickster, but a savior.

Calvin fell silent, letting the weight of the story settle in the room. "So you see," he said softly, "Coyote is not simple. He can be a fool, yes. But he is also the one who made the world safe for the people."

Something fundamental shifted inside Susanne as she listened to the elders. The gears of her creativity felt like they'd latched onto a much bigger sprocket than she was used to. She was excited by this opportunity, and her mind was awash in ideas.

This challenge was immense, she'd never attempted anything of this scale. She suddenly felt a fierce determination to honor these stories with the authenticity and depth they deserved. She was tapping into something that spanned across eras, across generations, that tied all the way back to her great-great-grandmother and her great-great-great-grandfather. It was like that for the Native timelines as well.

Looking around the room she saw something similar in Jack's eyes and an echo of it in all the writers. She said, "As we shape the narrative of Crystal Village, we have a chance to bring these stories to life, to offer visitors more than just entertainment. We are crafting an experience that resonates with more fundamental touchstones, generational touchstones, that tie us all back to the very beginnings of humanity. This feels profound."

The room was still under the spell of Calvin's story. The writers looked at Coyote not as a simple trickster, but as a shaper of worlds, a hero who had faced down primordial chaos. Jack felt the weight of that responsibility settle deeper.

"You have seen Coyote the Savior," Sarah said, her eyes sweeping across the room. "You have heard how his courage made the world safe for the Nimiipuu. But for every story of him making the world right, there is another of him making it wrong. His actions have consequences that last forever, for good *and* for ill. Calvin's story tells why his people are here. I will share a story that tells you why something important is gone from all of our lands."

She paused, letting them absorb the thought. "This is a story you will hear told in different ways all along the rivers, from my people to Calvin's people. It belongs to the land itself, and to all who felt the great emptiness when the buffalo left. This is the story of Coyote and the Buffalo Bull."

She paused, letting them absorb the thought.

Coyote and the Buffalo Bull

In that same time, after the monsters were slain but before the world was settled, Coyote was wandering. And as he so often was, he was hungry. His stomach growled so loudly that the birds in the trees flew away. He had traveled for days across the plains of the great Columbia Plateau, and the land was rich, but he could find nothing to fill his belly.

At last, he came upon an old Buffalo Bull, sitting alone by a creek. This was no ordinary bull. He was old and scarred, but his eyes held the wisdom of the mountains. He was the keeper of all the buffalo.

"Grandfather," Coyote said, for he knew to be respectful when he was truly desperate. "I am starving. Can you help me?"

The old Buffalo Bull looked at Coyote with his calm, deep eyes. "You are always hungry, Coyote," he said, his voice like the rumbling of distant thunder. "But I will help you. Watch closely."

The Bull walked over to a large buffalo skull lying in the grass. He lowered his head and tapped the skull with his horns three times. Then he began to sing a low, powerful song. As he sang, a young, fat buffalo cow rose up from the skull, shook herself as if waking from a dream, and stood ready.

"Take this one," the Buffalo Bull said. "It is enough for you. Cook it and eat your fill. But you must follow one rule, and it is the most important rule: When you are done, you must gather all the bones and return them here. And you must never, under any circumstances, break the skull. For the skull is where the life of my people is kept."

Coyote's eyes were wide with amazement and hunger. He promised he would obey. He took the buffalo, cooked it, and had a great feast. True to his word, he carefully gathered the bones and the unbroken skull and returned them to the old Bull.

The next day, Coyote was hungry again. He returned to the Bull, who once more performed the ceremony and gave him another buffalo. For many days, this continued. Coyote would come, the Bull would provide, and Coyote would feast.

But Coyote, being Coyote, grew lazy. And with laziness came arrogance. He began to think, "Why should I have to ask this old Bull every day? I have watched him. I know the song. I am Coyote! I am clever enough to do this magic myself."

So one day, after he had eaten, he did not return the bones. Instead, he waited until the old Bull was sleeping, and he crept back and stole the sacred buffalo skull. He carried it far away to his own camp, feeling very proud and clever.

The next morning, he woke up hungry. He placed the skull before him and tried to imitate the old Bull. He lowered his head and tapped the skull with a stick. He began to sing, but his voice was not deep and powerful like the Bull's; it was a yipping, impatient sound.

Still, the magic was strong in the skull. A young buffalo cow appeared. Coyote was overjoyed! He had done it!

He cooked the buffalo and ate, but as he was finishing, a greedy thought entered his mind. "Why only have one? I could have a whole herd! I could be the richest of all the people, with meat for every day!"

He ran back to the skull. He wanted more buffalo, and he wanted them now. He picked up a heavy rock. "Come out, buffalo!" he shouted, and he struck the skull with all his might.

Instead of a buffalo appearing, a terrible cracking sound echoed through the valley. The sacred skull shattered into a hundred tiny pieces.

At that exact moment, a great silence fell over the land. The buffalo cow that Coyote had been eating vanished into thin air. Far across the plains, every buffalo that grazed stopped, lifted its head, and turned. As one, they began to walk eastward, away from the Plateau. A great river of brown fur and thundering hooves flowed toward the rising sun, never to return.

The old Buffalo Bull appeared before Coyote, his eyes not angry, but filled with a deep and ancient sadness.

"You foolish creature," the Bull said, his voice a low moan. "I gave you a gift. I taught you the proper way. I warned you. The skull held the life of my people in this land, and in your greed, you have broken it. Now, they are gone."

Coyote looked at the empty plains and the shattered pieces of the skull. For the first time, he understood the weight of what he had done. His hunger was gone, replaced by a cold, empty feeling in his gut that was far worse. He had wanted everything, and now he had nothing. The people would have nothing.

And so it is. The buffalo left our lands and never came back. You can travel from the great falls of the Columbia to the Bitterroot Mountains and you will not find the vast herds that once were. They are gone because Coyote, in his greed and impatience, broke the sacred trust and shattered the life that held them here.

Sarah let her hands rest in her lap, her story finished. "Coyote is a creator, yes," she concluded, looking at each of the writers. "But he is also a destroyer. His greatest lesson is that power without wisdom, and action without respect for the rules, leads to permanent loss. What he breaks, sometimes, can never be fixed. You must remember this when you tell his stories. You must show both the hero and the fool."

Monica, the writer who also served as a liaison with the technology teams, raised a hand. "Calvin, Sarah, the stories of Coyote are so compelling, and they speak to the human experience in such profound ways," she said. "But I can't help but wonder, are there more stories of Raven we could hear? It feels like we've focused so much on Coyote's chaos that we might be missing Raven's role."

Calvin glanced at Sarah and gave a slow, deep nod. "You are wise to ask," he said. "It is easy to be distracted by Coyote's noise. Raven works in quieter, more cunning ways. His power is not always in the thunder, but in the seed that breaks the rock."

Sarah added, her eyes reflecting the glow of the room's lanterns, "Raven is a great transformer. Where Coyote often breaks things by accident or greed, Raven often breaks things on purpose, to free what has been trapped. This next story teaches us that even in the face of what seems like an unstoppable blockage, one small, clever act can bring life back to the entire world."

Calvin's voice dropped into the familiar, resonant tone of the storyteller. "This story tells of a time when the world faced a different kind of fire—the slow, cold fire of starvation. This is the story of how Raven freed the salmon."

Raven Frees the Salmon

In the time before, the great rivers ran full and strong, but they were empty. The people who lived along their banks grew hungry. Their children grew thin. They would look to the water day after day, but the salmon, the lifeblood of the people, never came.

Far downriver, near where the water met the great salt sea, lived two powerful and greedy sisters. They had woven a weir, a great fish-dam, all the way across the river. It was so tightly woven with cedar roots and magic that not a single drop of water could pass without their permission, and certainly not a single salmon. All the fish that swam up from the ocean were trapped in their basket, and they feasted while the people upstream starved.

Raven saw this. His heart grew heavy seeing the suffering of the people. He flew to the great weir and saw the two sisters guarding it, their faces hard with greed. He tried to reason with them.

"Sisters," he called. "The people upstream are hungry. You have more fish than you can ever eat. You must let the salmon go."

The sisters just laughed. "The salmon are ours," they said. "If the people are hungry, let them learn to be as clever as we are."

Raven knew that words would not work. He would have to use his cunning.

He perched on a high branch, and watched. He saw that they were not just greedy for fish, but for all beautiful things. Their lodge was filled with shiny shells, smooth stones, and the iridescent feathers of birds. They were proud and vain. He also saw that they loved to gamble, to prove they were smarter and luckier than anyone else.

He flew away and changed himself. He became a tall, handsome chief from a far-off, unknown tribe. His cloak was not of raven feathers, but was woven from the golden light of the afternoon sun. In his hair were combs of gleaming abalone, and around his neck were strings of shells that no one had ever seen before. He was beautiful and dazzling, and he walked with the confidence of one who owned the world.

He came to the sisters' lodge and called out a greeting. When they saw him, their eyes grew wide with desire. They had never seen such finery. They invited him in, hoping to trade for some of his treasures.

"I do not trade," said the beautiful chief, who was Raven. "But I do play games of chance. I have heard you are the most clever women on this river. I will wager all of my finery,"—and he swept his shining cloak wide—"against all the salmon in your weir."

The sisters looked at each other. Their greed was a sharp hook in their hearts. To have all this beauty? To prove their cleverness? They could not resist. "We accept!" they said.

They decided to play slahal, the bone game. One sister would hold the two bones, one marked, one not, and the visiting chief would have to guess which hand held the unmarked bone.

They sat across from each other. The sister began to sing her power song, swaying and moving her hands to confuse him. The drums beat. The people from the starving villages gathered silently outside the lodge, watching, hoping.

Raven, in his disguise, sat perfectly still. He did not watch her hands. He watched her eyes. He saw the tiny flicker of pride in her left eye just before she settled her hands. He knew.

"It is in your right hand," he said calmly.

She opened her hands. He was right. The unmarked bone was in her right hand. She had lost.

A great silence fell in the lodge. Then the sisters began to shout. "You cheated! It is dark magic! We will not honor the bet!"

The handsome chief began to laugh. It was not a man's laugh. It was the rough, knowing caw-caw-caw of a raven. His beautiful cloak dissolved into a swirl of black feathers. The shining shells turned to smoke. Before them stood Raven in his true form, his eyes like chips of obsidian.

"Greed does not understand honor," he croaked. "So it must be taught with tricks."

While the sisters were still staring, stunned by the transformation, Raven leaped past them. With his great, strong beak, he grabbed the main locking pin of the weir, the one carved with their magic. He pulled and twisted, and with a sound like a great tree splitting in a storm, the pin snapped.

The magic was broken. The river, held back for so long, surged forward with a mighty roar. The whole weir was torn apart and washed away. And on the crest of that wave, a silver tide of salmon poured upstream, their bodies flashing in the sun.

The people heard the roar of the breaking dam and ran to the riverbanks. They saw the fish returning, and a great shout of joy went up that echoed from the mountains. They would have life again.

Raven had broken the dam. He had freed the life-giving salmon, not with force, but with patience and a clever plan. Raven circled

once in the sky above them, his work done, and then flew on, looking
for more trouble to fix, or perhaps, more trouble to start.

Calvin let the story settle. "And so," he finished, "Raven teaches us that power is not always about being the strongest. Sometimes, it is about being the smartest. He shows us that when greed creates a blockage that harms the community, it is a sacred duty to break it, to release the life that belongs to all. That is his kind of healing. That is his kind of renewal."

Jack looked around the table at his team and saw by the expression on their faces that they'd begun to see what he saw. The stories they were to tell would be bridges that could create a through line between ancient cultures and the modern world.

The writers began to stir.

Diana Rollins gave voice to the collective sentiment. "This has truly been a gift," she said.

The room came alive with the scratching of pens on paper, the clicking of keyboards on laptops, the murmur of voices discussing plot points, character arcs, and thematic resonance. The air was electric with creative energy, each writer keenly aware that they were not just spinning tales but preserving a legacy. The small hotel staff brought out rolling whiteboards, large sticky pads of paper set on stands, and trays of sandwiches.

Jack stood, ready to guide the session. "Let's begin," he announced, "by honoring the roots of these stories. Let's spot-weld them into the framework of Crystal Village. Each visitor should feel the power of Raven and Coyote as symbols that transcend time."

And with that, they set to work, the dance of creation began anew under the watchful gaze of the elders who had shared their most precious narratives. The writers embarked on the sacred task of storytelling, where each word, each line, each scene would be a homage to the enduring spirit of the Native people and the land from which they sprang.

At one point, Sarah Stensgar approached Susanne and asked to speak to her privately. "I am glad to be included in this project for many reasons. I thought you should know that my grandmother knew this place and one who I believe might be your ancestor, Sam King O'Connor. She told me many stories about meeting her, and how this place was somewhere she felt welcome."

Susanne was awed by this. "Sarah, this is such a gift. We have Sam's journals, and she wrote extensively on a friendship with a young Coeur d'Alene woman named Stelkupmi. Was she your grandmother?"

Sarah smiled broadly, "Yes, she was my grandmother! She went on to be a great leader of our people. It would be so nice to learn more of their friendship. Would it be appropriate for you to share these journal entries with me?"

Susanne replied earnestly, "I would be so honored to share her journals with you! What a wonderful gift this is for both of us. Sam was my great-great-grandmother." Then, with tears in her eyes, she said, "I would be honored to continue the friendships between our families."

Sarah reached out and grasped Susanne's hand and pulled her into an embrace.

As the evening turned to night, the elders were whisked off to rooms in the hotel for some rest and relaxation. Meanwhile, the writers were drinking coffee and gearing up for a long creative session. Jack knew well enough not to break the spell. They'd get more done in the next few hours than in the next few weeks.

IIII

Hours later, Susanne snuggled under the covers of her bed and couldn't sleep. She wasn't sure how much of it was due to the sheer volume of coffee she'd consumed in the last twenty hours or the ideas bouncing around in her head. Eventually, she couldn't stay still any longer, and she crawled out of the bed, taking the comforter with her. She slipped on her boots and walked to the large French doors that opened up onto the balcony.

She was on the second floor of the Hawthorne Hotel, which meant the deck outside her doors was the roof of the first floor balcony, and the roof of her deck was the floor to the third floor balcony. She wrapped the comforter around her tightly, opened the doors, and went out into the frigid March air.

The village was silent and dark, all the street lights were still in the process of being refurbished. The sky was dark, and a light snow was falling. There was no wind, and the streets below were wet as the snow instantly melted. She thought about the careful planning of Egan Sullivan and Finn McEnhill all those years ago leading to a street clear of snow tonight. She walked to the balcony, her feet making prints in a fine dusting of snow that trickled in as it fell.

She gazed down the street to the left and right and saw that to her right was a custom metal screen. It was this screen that blocked the path between the hotel balcony and the balcony of the home that Sam King and Seamus O'Connor had shared with their children and Mrs. O'Hara. The beautiful screen was made of bronze, copper, and silver, creating the illusion of a lattice with vines and flowers growing on it.

She walked over to it and traced her fingers over the pathways of vines, and she wondered if Sam had done the same in the past. Susanne felt another of her periodic flashes of connection to Sam King. She peeked through the screen to see the recently refinished floor of the balcony that would have been right outside of Sam and Seamus' bedroom. She wondered how often Sam had stood out on this balcony looking at the village.

Behind her, she heard a quiet clearing of a throat, which startled her. She spun around and saw that on a wooden bench, also bundled in his bed's comforter was a man sitting on the balcony outside of the room next to hers. The balcony was a shared space across four bedrooms.

"Hey, Susanne, sorry to scare you," said Jack from underneath his self-made hood, the comforter enveloping his face in shadow.

"Oh, Jack! It's okay, but what a start you gave me!" Suzanne laughed.

Susanne walked over to Jack, and he scooted over to one side of the bench, making room for her. He opened his comforter and she sat down and snuggled against him. It was cozy and warm and comfortable. Jack tightened his arm around her, and she leaned her head on his chest.

"How long have you been out here?" she asked.

"Just a little longer than you. I love coming out on these balconies at night, especially with the lights all off. With the clouds tonight it's really dark. The first time I came out here at night the stars were out, and I could see the Milky Way so clearly."

Susanne shivered slightly, and Jack rearranged himself on the bench, then rearranging the comforters to maximize warmth. She curled up against him, and he put his arms around her. To her surprise he wasn't wearing a shirt, and she was just in a tank top and bottoms. Their skin to skin contact was electric.

She turned her head upwards, put her hands around his neck, and pulled him down into a kiss. He kissed her back with vigor, and they sat there for some time, kissing. After a few minutes, Jack reached down and scooped her up, carrying her inside.

I I I I

Jack woke to the buzzing of his phone on silent. The room was dark in the pre-dawn, and he struggled to find his phone on the nightstand. "... Hello?"

"Jack, it's Amy ... ... I'm calling with some bad news."

Oh, no, thought Jack. "Hi, Amy. What's going on?"

"Jack, your grandmother died in her sleep last night. She went peacefully. I'm so, so sorry."

Jack paused and took a deep breath, almost a sob. He took another breath and said, "Oh, Amy. I'm so sorry you had to find her. Are you doing okay?"

Susanne rustled in the bed next to him, and sat up, wrapping her arms around him gently from behind. He reached up and took her hand.

Amy paused herself for a deep breath. "I'm ... I'm ... okay. We knew it was coming but not how soon. I guess I'm just glad that she passed in her sleep, and that she didn't have a decline of any kind. It could have been so much worse."

"I know," said Jack. "Oh, man. Amy, let me make some calls, and I'll come down to meet you at the house. Not to get into the details of things, I want you to know that she had told me in no uncertain terms that she wanted you to have the house and her nest egg. So I don't want you to be worried about anything while we sort all this out."

He heard Amy sob. "Oh, Jack. Really? I hate to admit that my mind had gone there already, but what a kind thing. I loved her. That's so kind."

"I'll be down in a few hours, and I have someone who can make all the arrangements. Gran and I had discussed it at length, and she had everything planned out in detail. I'll be there by lunch."

He and Amy finished their call, and he lay back on the bed, Susanne curling up against him. Tears were running down his face. He was sad but strangely buoyant, like the world had changed orbit on its axis, and gravity was suddenly different.

The next few days were a blur, with papers to sign, funeral arrangements to approve. Amy was extremely gracious about the whole thing, and he had all the things of his grandparents that he wanted to keep transferred up to the village and put into storage.

On the day of the wake and funeral, Ian came down off the mountain for the first time in years. In preparation for the event, he and Jack went through the list of people from the area who were attending, and they identified which of them were descendants of the Original Eight. This was the impetus to set up a meeting of the descendants sometime in the next few months so he could open up about the village, the Trust, and invite them to come to one of the open house weekends before the park opened.

During this conversation, Ian disclosed something else to him. Jack knew that his great-grandfather John had married one of Angus Sullivan's daughters. It turned out that his mother was also a descendant of Angus Sullivan, which he never had put together, despite his mother being a Sullivan. One of Angus' children had moved to Bar Harbor, Maine and had a big family there. The odds seemed long on this. Apparently, the Foundation's relationships with colleges led to a higher likelihood of descendants ending up in the same schools, and his parents had met in college.

None of his mother's Sullivan relatives were making the trip for the funeral, but Jack had spent some time as a kid with those relatives and was looking forward to reconnecting in the weeks following his grandmother's funeral.

I I I I

May 2029

The auditions for Crystal Village's cast were well underway in Oakland. Dianna had assembled a team of casting directors and the producers, including Jack, Susanne and Ian, to find the right actors to bring the village's rich history to life. Many of the smaller roles were filled already. Today was the day they were focusing on someone to portray Finn McEnhill, one of the Original Eight founders. This was a role that required gravitas, gruffness, humor, and a touch of the mystical.

Ian had asked to be there for the casting call, which struck Jack as unusual, but it gave him a chance to bring his cousin to Oakland and to take him out for some nice meals while they were in town. That day, a dozen actors auditioned, each bringing their own interpretation of Finn to the stage. All of them were talented, but none seemed to capture the essence of the "Finn" that Jack and Susanne knew from the journals.

Late in the afternoon, when the team was about to call it a day, a man who could have been anywhere between sixty and eighty years old walked into the audition room. He wore a worn tweed jacket, which was a bit frayed at the edges, and an Irish flat cap. He moved briskly despite his age.

He introduced himself in a gravelly voice with a thick Irish brogue. "Name's Finnegan McEnhill, but ye can call me Finn. I'm here to audition for ... well, m'self, I suppose."

The room fell silent. Jack exchanged a look with Susanne, who shrugged and widened her eyes. Ian, who had been observing the auditions, leaned forward with interest. None of the other actors had gone down the "method acting" path, and this approach certainly got the attention of the room.

"All right, *Mr. McEnhill*," Jack said with a smile, "Let's see what you've got."

Finn nodded, took a deep breath, and began to recite lines from the script. The scene portrayed Finn working out the architecture of the village. He spoke with absolute authority and wandered off and on script, ad-libbing points of history and architecture and engineering. He talked about the hot springs, the bridges, and the mines easily, and as if from personal memory.

When he finished, the room erupted in applause. Finn bowed his head modestly, a wry smile playing on his lips.

"That was really great," Jack said. "It's like you've lived the character."

Finn's eyes twinkled. "Aye, ye might say that I've got a bit of experience with the man."

As the team discussed the next steps, Ian approached the old actor. "Finnegan," he said quietly in a hushed tone, his voice uncharacteristically exposing a bit of an Irish accent. "Might I have a word with ye in private?"

The two men stepped aside out of easy eavesdropping range, and Ian looked into Finn's eyes, searching for a sign, a confirmation of his suspicions. "It's been a long time," Ian said in a voice just above a whisper.

Finn's smile deepened, and he placed a hand on Ian's shoulder. "Aye, Eoinn, it has."

Ian felt a warm comfortable feeling spread through him. Here was Finn, his old friend coming back to the village.

While the rest of the team was focused on the discussion about Finn's audition, Susanne had been watching Ian and "Finn" with some interest.

19

Flight

July 2029

The newly constructed Crystal Village Visitors Center just outside Kellogg on Route 90 had all the finishing touches completed. The new parking lot was full of cars, and a minibus sat off to one side. The architecture of the main hall felt almost church-like, with a soaring ceiling of wood paneling and post and beam construction.

The room was overflowing, with about three hundred people in attendance. Jack stood at the raised podium, preparing to give a speech to the living descendants of the Original Eight founders of Crystal Village. On the projection screen behind him was the photograph of the Original Eight founders he had discovered in his grandfather's trunk. The design team had taken the handwritten letters naming each of them from the back, transferred them to the front and made the text light yellow against the black and white image. Each founder was named: Eoinn Seeley, Finn McEnhill, Liam O'Connor, Sam King, Angus and Egan Sullivan, Sean O'Neil, and Colin O'Shea.

Jack stepped up to the microphone and kicked off the discussion. "Hi, everyone," Jack began. "Thank you for coming. I know some of you have traveled a great distance to be here. Thanks to the handful of folks on the online meeting, I understand why each of you were unable to make the trip, and I hope we can give you as good a virtual experience of this as possible.

"Either Susanne or I have spoken with each of you and given you the high level story of what has happened here and the history of Crystal Village. But let me address you all and make sure we're super clear …

"The people in this room are the legacy of Crystal Village. All of us are descendants of the Original Eight founders of the village. Some of us are descended from more than one of the founders, like myself and one branch of the Millers." Jack clicked the controller on the podium, and the slide switched behind him to a family tree showing the eight founders, their lines, and where a few of them interconnected.

"As I've told you all, the village and the responsibility for the manage-ment of the foundations and investments coming to me was a huge surprise. But rather than bog down on how we've gotten here, I'd prefer to focus on what things will look like going forward." Jack moved to the next slide. It showed the total assets of the Crystal Village Foundations to be $51 billion. The room gasped.

"I want to get this out of the way immediately. This money is not ours. Meaning, the people in this room cannot receive a cash payout based on the assets stored in these foundations. The structure of all this was set up more than a century ago. The bulk of the money is set aside to cover the future expenses of maintaining the village. In addition, there are smaller portions of this total number that are assigned in various trusts and foundations. These legal entities are responsible for handling things like: ensuring that all of us who attended college received scholarships, or that our health insurance payments are covered in the event of your healthcare being cut off, or if necessary, that we are taken care of in old age or infirmity. Or maybe upon the death of someone's parents, the children found out that their parents had a much bigger life insurance policy than anyone expected. These functions are all carried out by the arm of our foundation that is designed to ensure some basic level of financial security for all of us. When I found out about it, I was both grateful and angry. I was grateful that someone out there had been looking out for me my whole life, and that when my parents died, I was taken care of financially. But I was also angry that this was done in secret, that it was done behind my back.

"That ends today. I now lead the board of the overarching foundation that has a view into all the interconnected finances. Now, it's complex. There isn't really a thing called the Crystal Village Foundation. But for our purposes, let's just use that as a placeholder for all the different funds that are part of that very large number.

"I have instructed the foundation to stop acting in secret. From this point forward, all of your interactions with Crystal Village will be open and transparent. That said, you've all signed documents before coming here that guarantee confidentiality, that you will not disclose any of this publicly, and that you will not disclose this to any of your children until they are eighteen years old. I hope you're all okay with this, and that you see the wisdom of it.

"I also have asked the foundation to set up an individual case manager for each family here. That way you will have someone you can call and talk to should you need financial help or financial advice. There's no reason that we can't make this money work for us as a group. There are ways to open up low interest loans or to receive mortgage assistance or other similar sources of financial assistance.

"Now, onto the Crystal Village plans that we're enacting in collaboration with the Yomohiro Corporation, and what that means not only to the legacy of your families but also to you individually today. Yomohiro Corporation has agreed to a profit-sharing agreement that will push revenue received from Crystal Village into a trust that directly benefits the descendants of the founders. This is Crystal Village in all its forms—the village itself, the licensing agreements, the video games, the movies, the television shows, and all content deals forever—all of these will push into a specific trust. That trust is for the families of Crystal Village, which is how I think of us. Any success that this project has will pay out to the people in this meeting, our children, and their children going forward, as long as there is money coming in. That money will be made directly available to all of us, split evenly across the entire group." The room let out another gasp, and there was a scattering of applause.

"I'm not sure how much this will be. It could be a few hundred dollars a month. Or it could be a lot of money. It really depends on how successful Crystal Village is. So I don't want to set anyone's expectations too high. It will be at least eighteen months before those payments start coming in, because it's a profit-sharing model, meaning the expenses of the operation must be paid off before there are profits. But I will tell you all that I am bullish on this. I believe we're going to be very successful. To prove that out, I'd like to invite all of you to please come up to the village for the day, and see what we're doing there. You'll get a tour, you'll get demos of the technology we're building there, and a nice sit down with some of the actors we've already hired. All this is intended to give you a sense of what we're pulling together. Then, I'd like to invite all of you back here for an entire week in the month or so before we open to the public. You're all going to be treated to the guest experience we're going to open up to the whole world, via lottery."

The whole room erupted in cheers. After it died down, Jack said, "Great! Please come with me to the train that has pulled up outside of this building. It will take us right up to the village. For those of you online, stay tuned, and you'll see that you'll be taken with us on this voyage, specially hosted by the lovely Susanne O'Connor."

I I I I

Jack surveyed the bustling hangar in the Alameda campus of Yomohiro Corporation. Nearby, Bill McKenna discussed the finer points of special effects with his team, and Dianna reviewed safety protocols. Meanwhile, the writers huddled in the corner, debating the latest script revisions. He caught the eye of Susanne, who sat with them. They both smiled and each turned away.

The day's focus was the beta test of the augmented reality technology that was going to be used in some experiences within the park. This was an important step in the development of the park. Before opening Crystal

369

Village to the public, this had to work correctly. Done right, Crystal Village could be the most immersive experience in theme park history. But they had to get the augmented reality technology working properly, and it had to be very convincing to be acceptable to the audience.

The problem was not dissimilar to those from the beginnings of 3D animation. There was a period in history where the animation was very good but not quite good enough. Buildings and inanimate objects were believable, but animals and human bodies didn't move correctly. When they conquered that hurdle, expressions and movements of human faces were just not quite right. Over millions of years, humans have evolved to become experts at reading faces. So much of our brain is wired for this that we can detect the smallest twitch of a smile or flicker of doubt—and in an instant, know whether to trust, fear, or comfort the person in front of us. Animation doesn't always get the subtle nuances correct, leading people to be very uncomfortable with animation that looks very close to real but is subtly not real. This problem is described as "The Uncanny Valley." It is that subtle difference between something natural and unnatural, a computer-generated, still image of a face might look perfectly fine. But take that image and turn it into an animation without the subtle shifts in emotion and nuances of movement, and you get "The Uncanny Valley." Humans find it deeply unsettling.

There's a similar problem with the augmented reality environment. There are visual cues, shortcuts, that the brain uses to assess for threats and to grab our attention when things are "not right." Augmented reality struggles with minor misalignments and small visual glitches that shatter the illusion and reveal that the digital item is not physically present. Small nuances in lighting or integration to the whole with what the person is seeing are critical components of this issue. And minor issues have major impacts.

Jack cleared his throat, drawing the room's attention. "Let's remember why we're here," he said, his voice steady. "We're creating a world for our audiences. It has to trick their brains into believing what they see. Every detail matters."

Bill nodded, "We've got this, Jack. The effects will be seamless. The visitors won't even see the cameras or mics. They'll be too caught up in the magic."

The writers, led by Mitch, looked up from their discussions. "The scripts are solid," Mitch said. "We've woven the legends of Raven and Coyote and the fairies into almost every storyline, every character. They'll be having a blast without realizing we nudged them in the right direction."

The first group of beta visitors, a mix of friends, family, and industry insiders, arrived. They were enthusiastic and curious. Each visitor was fitted with augmented reality glasses and walked into the stage set that recreated a section of Broadway that included several of the buildings. Once everyone was in place, Bill McKenna picked up a microphone and counted down from five to one. Then the augmented reality system was engaged. Gasps and murmurs of awe filled the hangar.

Jack watched from the control room as the visitors explored this slice of Crystal Village. The virtual characters, including a lifelike Coyote, interacted with the guests. The virtual characters' movements were guided by the AI, based on repeated sessions with actors in motion-capture suits.

As the day wore on, glitches emerged. A guest's glasses failed to register an approaching virtual horse properly, and the horse seemed to be floating six inches off the ground. Another guest's audio cut out, requiring a change-out of their headset. Coyote began acting out of turn, his AI struggled to sync with the live input.

Jack watched the monitors and data readouts from each person on a huge screen projected on the wall of the control room. "Terry, talk to me," he said. "What's going on?"

Terry, the tech lead, was a flurry of motion as he tapped at his tablet. "We've got a couple of pathfinding errors in the rendering engine. It's not accounting for the physical environment properly."

Jack took a deep breath. "It's fine, Terry. Just let us know what we need to get this fixed. This obviously can't happen when we open to the public. And this group will get bored if we don't give them something that works."

The tech team were eminently professional and were constantly and quickly troubleshooting the errors as the beta test continued. Jack paced, uncharacteristically moody.

As the test concluded and the visitors departed, Jack's team regrouped. They were determined to iron out the issues. They worked long into the night making fixes and re-running simulations, with staff members standing in the set with AR headsets on while they drank coffee.

At around 3 a.m., they watched as Coyote's character finally moved smoothly through the virtual village. His antics were now a source of delight rather than disruption. Jack allowed himself a small smile.

As the team settled into the rhythm of their work, Jack's thoughts turned to the legends of Coyote. There was something about the character's rebellious spirit that resonated with him. Coyote was a disruptor, a being who challenged the *status quo*. That's how Jack saw himself and his work.

Jack mulled over the idea that perhaps Coyote's essence had seeped into the project itself, infusing it with a touch of chaos, a spark of the unexpected. It was a fanciful thought, but it was jammed in his brain sideways, an idea he couldn't push aside.

The glitches they'd faced, those bugs had already been resolved weeks before they set up this test. Could it be sabotage? Or was it the legacy of Coyote, playfully poking at their creation?

Jack shook his head, pushing the whimsical notion aside. They had a park to build, stories to tell, and magic to weave. Coyote's spirit, whether myth or mischief, would be a part of it all, a reminder that even in the most high-tech of worlds, the ancient tales still held power.

As the team rallied to address the challenge, Jack's leadership shone through. He inspired them with the promise of creating something truly extraordinary. Together, they would bring Crystal Village to life.

IIII

High above the bustling construction of Crystal Village, two figures stood in the fading light of dusk. Sinclair Lipson stood in his pristine, white-linen suit that seemed untouched by the dirt and grime of the world below. His constantly smoldering cheroot added a sweet, acrid tang to the air.

Beside him, Elias Dotson loomed—a black-hatted, black-haired mono-lith wrapped in a black duster. It was as if he were a fragment of the night sky, torn free and given form.

They gazed down at the park taking shape below, a world of wires and technology bonded to the bones of this historical town and infused with the tales of the American West. Sinclair Lipson watched with a mix of fascination and disdain. He began, his voice alive with a mischievous energy, "Do you feel it? The pulse of creation—it's invigorating! We could sweep it all away, you and I. Bring it crashing down around their ears."

Dotson, sighed—a sound like the rustle of dry leaves. "Dog," he replied, his bass voice rumbling in his chest, his words clawing their way from his throat in a croak, "you see chaos where I see the foundations being laid for something powerful. These stories they're telling are *our* stories. By retelling them, they're giving us life anew! The power of our stories is being celebrated, not squandered." His normally ponderous nature was shifted. He was, for the first time in an age, showing interest and curiosity.

Lipson scoffed, the ember of his cheroot momentarily flared, sending out sparks as he waved his hand to encompass the village below. "Celebrated? They're trapping us in their narratives, binding us to their whims. We are not theirs to command."

Dotson's gaze drifted down to the workers. "Yet in their telling, we are *remembered.* In each retelling, we *live.* Is it not better to be a tale on the lips than a forgotten whisper in the winds of time?"

Lipson folded his arms, his golden eyes narrowed as he considered Dotson's words. "Perhaps," Lipson conceded, "but we'll see if their stories do us justice. If they falter, if they fail to honor the essence of what we are ..." His voice trailed off, heavy with the threat of retribution.

Dotson's eyes seemed to flicker with a newfound interest—a spark that hinted at the possibility of change. "Then we will guide them," he declared, a firmness creeping into his tone for the first time in ages. "We will ensure our stories are told as they should be."

Lipson's mouth curled into a half-smile, a plan already forming in the depths of his cunning mind.

I I I I

The game design team was assembling in a conference room in the Oakland offices of Yomohiro Corporation. Today's agenda was the Crystal Village video game. Jack settled into his chair at the head of the table. The room had screens lining the walls and a holographic virtual reality interface at the center of the table for giving demos.

Susanne sat in the middle of the table. She was focused on her leather-bound notebook as she prepped for the meeting. Mitch, the lead writer, took his place beside her. His yellow notepad was filled with scribbled notes and crossed-out lines. The rest of the team took their seats.

"Susanne, Mitch, the floor is yours," Jack said, leaning back in his chair.

Susanne cleared her throat, "Crystal Village, the game, is a portal to another time, to a place where the figures of Raven and Coyote walk the streets and trails. Where fairies live under the mountain. Where the cowboy culture of the Old West comes to life, infused with Native stories as well as the fairy tales of Europe."

Mitch picked up seamlessly, "We're telling a story of order and chaos, of learning and entertainment. Players will navigate a village where the mundane meets the magical, where a chance encounter with a trickster spirit might change their fate."

Jack was so happy that they'd brought Susanne into this project, both personally and increasingly, professionally. She was incredibly creative and found solutions to complex problems with slick, narrative solutions. There was a depth to her understanding of the village's lore that brought authenticity to the presentation. It was as if she were channeling the spirits of her ancestors.

"When you step into Crystal Village, you step into a *living* story. Each character you meet, each secret you uncover, each action you take impacts the stories that everyone else experiences. Every version of this world is interlinked in real time."

Mitch leaned forward, his hands spread wide. "The park is the heart of the game. It's where the virtual and the real collide, and players can see the impact of their actions ripple through both worlds."

Susanne nodded, her eyes flicking briefly to meet Jack's. "It's like dance or jazz. Every step, every note played pushes the story in a new direction, and every story is constantly evolving and being rewritten."

Susanne masterfully spun the tale of Crystal Village for the game design team. Then she walked them through how it would play out in the physical park. She explained how all of these narrative elements would come together to craft multiple stories and experiences that needed to be expanded on in the video game reality, and that this in turn expanded the world of Crystal Village in every way. She talked about the integrations of the live actors with AI counterparts in the game. She explained how game play would inform the story in the park, and how interactions in the park would inform the gameplay. Gamers who watched the television show highlighting the experiences of the park visitors would see the impact of their gameplay. Events that took place in both worlds were a shared reality.

She talked about Eagle City, the once ephemeral, canvas tent town. She talked about how it would provide a robust, mature counterpart to the sober history of Crystal Village. They'd positioned "new" Eagle City only half a mile from Crystal Village, but with some skillful and well-considered landscape architecture and path design, the voyage between the two for park visitors felt like a much longer distance. There were underground access tunnels for cast members and support staff who could take the direct route.

The White Elephant Saloon was now a solid timber structure. Eagle City beckoned adults to partake in the wilder side of frontier life—a place where the clink of poker chips and the clomp of cowboy boots on wooden floors promised escapades and liberations from the constraints of the real world. Was tonight the night to kiss a dancing lady, or was it the night a drunk and angry miner challenged you to draw down in a showdown? In the world of the game, other ghost towns were made real, and these locales featured all sorts of adventures of varying complexity. Long term, they'd even build cities out in the vastness of the nineteenth century United States.

Crystal Village was not merely a playground for world-weary adults looking for a distraction. It was also a nurturing playground for the curious and creative, both adults and children. In the compassionate hands of characters inspired by Mrs. O'Hara and the village's hands-on educators, young explorers of the park would have many learning adventures available to them.

In one whole sequence of adventures, kids (or adults) could learn the alchemy of cooking. Park visitors would have their senses delighted by the fragrant spices and recipes passed down from the villagers, from the various immigrant cultures of Europe who formed the beginnings of the village, and from the Chinese settlers who blended their culinary heritage into the mix of foods in the village. In the game, virtual cooking lessons would be paired with augmented reality in players' own kitchens, enabling participants to cook along with the lessons.

In the park and in the game, younger children would hone their skills in plant and wildlife identification and wilderness survival skills, such as hunting and archery. Older children visiting the park would go on expeditions to find treasure or to hunt for game (using AR, not actually killing animals) or gather food to keep the village fed. All of this would be guided by the magic of augmented reality and promised a safe and enchanting experience.

The game version of Crystal Village went much further, with adventures in the wilderness, in the mines, and in the caves of the fairy kingdom. Players could travel down the trails of the mountains, could paddle canoes through the rivers and lakes of the region. They would find children lost in the woods, who turned out to be fairies. They would meet other players in the virtual world who were from all over the world. There were adventures with the Coeur d'Alene and Nez Perce tribes. These experiences were designed to teach children how to live in harmony with the land but also to educate them about the mysteries of Coyote and Raven and many other figures from their stories. Likewise, Mrs. O'Hara would tell them stories of the "Little Cousins." Her stories would initiate mysteries that would lead to discovery of the fairy world.

In the physical park, the only traditional attraction planned was the mine flume ride, which offered physical thrills for the riders and provided them with a glimpse into the fairy realm under the mountain. It was a roaring, water-splashed narrative. The ride promised tales spun from the lives of the miners who had once chased fortune deep beneath the mountain. But in the game world, the mines entwined with the land of the underworld, where the fairies lived under the mountain, and the adventures there were epic and complex.

Back in Crystal Village, both in the park and in the game, as dusk fell and the stars came out, the fairies of the mountain realm would emerge. This was intended to tap into the same sense of wonder that had once inspired Barrie's tales of Neverland. The fairies would call to the children, their hands outstretched to lead them on nocturnal journeys that took advantage of the flight grid hidden in plain sight above the Village.

The game designers were as enthralled as everyone hoped they would be. There was an enthusiastic discussion full of ideas for storylines. And this was when Susanne hit them with a hard problem.

She said, "Okay, so you're all clear on how this will work. We have the game engine from the Japanese parks that we can use to build our world in. But we have a difficult problem to solve. We're going to have players from all over the world coming to play. And hopefully, we're going to have millions of players joining the game. But they're all supposed to be from this tiny village in the wilderness. We need to find a way to recreate that experience—where each player has a house in the village to call their own. But where they feel the intimacy of this small village in the wilderness that park visitors will feel."

One of the game designers named Peter said, "They've solved the problem in Japan the same way online games solved the early problems of concurrency—with different instances of the game—each limited to a small set of visitors."

Susanne interrupted, "Peter, for those of us who don't speak technology, can you explain that?"

"Sorry," Peter said, "Rather than letting every single user log into one instance of the game, we create thousands of versions of the game all running independently. Each of these instances is limited to a small number of users, generally less than 10,000."

Jack responded, "Yes, and we're going to need to come up with a version of that. But we want, of course, to take things to another level. If a group of real-world friends wants to play together, we need to make it easy to do that. Otherwise, you're going to have people lost in different instances. And also, we want the magic of letting the virtual players see the impact of their gameplay in the park. Ideally, this won't just be big, scripted storylines in which centrally scripted storylines in both the game and the park reflect each other. We want small, personal things to play out too. For example, what if a player left a cart in the woods, or what if a character did something that became notorious in the game? How cool would it be if that showed up on the television show, or if their character in the game was referenced in the story on the show?"

Peter said, "I think if we get large audiences in the game, we're going to find that there will be some commonality in approaches and outcomes that we can look for with data science. Once we see similar outcomes on a large scale, even if they seem individual to the player, we can work to incorporate those outcomes into the park and therefore into the show."

This led to a lengthy debate and collaboration among the whole team. As the meeting drew to a close, Jack knew that they were on the cusp of something extraordinary. With Susanne and Mitch at the helm of the narrative, he felt confident that Crystal Village would come alive for both physical and virtual visitors.

As the team dispersed, Jack lingered, his eyes following Susanne as she gathered her notes. She looked up, caught his eye, and blushed deep red. He smiled and told her what a great job she'd done.

IIII

Jack got ready to host a video conference with the team in Japan who had designed the lottery dynamics for selecting who would win tickets to visit the park. The lottery model used in Japan was very simple, it was a random model. The chance of someone winning was completely randomized. Tickets were given away in bundles of three. But typically in the Japanese parks, visitors would come from anywhere from one to three days. And because the lottery was random, there were no rules about selling them after a user was selected. It had become so lucrative to sell won tickets on a secondary market, that over time, the visitors to the parks were devolving into only those wealthy enough to afford it. This was very counter to the intent of Kisho Yomohiro, who wanted all people to have an equal opportunity to visit.

The model in Japan also led to many situations where larger families could only send three representatives, and couples would end up bringing a friend. Jack was confident that this was a problem that technology could solve, not only for Crystal Village but also for the existing Japanese parks.

Also joining the video conference was his old friend Tarmo Saarholm, who was currently a professor of mathematics and computer science at MIT, but who had done his undergraduate work with Jack at Brown University. Tarmo was originally from Finland, and he and Jack roomed together for all four years. When Jack's parents died, Jack went back to Finland with Tarmo for the summer of his junior year. They'd roomed together again when Tarmo did his postdoctoral work at CalTech, and Jack was working at Disney. Tarmo was one of the world's experts in designing expressive auctions and combinatorial optimization.

At Jack's request, Tarmo put his lab at MIT onto the problem of ensuring that the auction was fair for disparately sized groups of people. Jack also asked Tarmo's team to optimize the lottery for other characteristics that would match the mix of visitors for any given cohort, since visitors would come up to the village from Saturday to Friday every week. It was imperative that they find a way to match families and individuals to have a compatible mix.

Jack's screen split into squares: Jack in his office in Oakland, Itsuki Tanaka and the Japanese engineers at a conference table in their Tokyo office, Tarmo's book-lined office at MIT. Tarmo, sleeves rolled up, leaned forward and began.

"So, here's the problem," Tarmo said, his voice level and clear, a hint of his Finnish accent coming through. "If you use a basic lottery, you get chaos. Some people win multiple times, some never win at all. Families get split up, and pretty soon, only the wealthiest are going to come—because they can buy up the winning tickets on the resale market."

Jack nodded. "It's like tossing everyone's names into a hat, pulling out a handful of slips of paper, and hoping it works out. But it never really does."

Tarmo smiled. "Right. But your village isn't just about random chance. It's about community. So we need a system that actually understands the attributes of people. Who they are, what they want, and how they might connect."

One of the Tokyo engineers glanced up from his notes. "But isn't that too complicated? There are thousands of possible groups, combinations …"

"Millions," Tarmo corrected gently. "Actually, with enough applicants, the number of combinations is so huge you'd need more paper than exists on Earth just to write them down. But that's the beauty of the math. We don't have to check every possibility—we use smart algorithms to search for the best ones."

Jack leaned in, eager for Tarmo's favorite analogy. "Explain it like you did for my board."

"Imagine," Tarmo said, "hosting the world's biggest dinner party. You have so many guests, and each one comes with their own hopes. Families want to sit together. Singles want to meet other singles or maybe join a group of friends. Kids need other kids to play with. Some people want quiet, some want a party. Your job is to arrange the tables so that everyone feels at home—and maybe leaves with new friends. If you just assign seats randomly, you'll get awkward silences and empty chairs. But if you match people thoughtfully, you create magic."

A murmur of understanding rippled through the call.

"That's what combinatorial optimization does," Tarmo continued.

"We take everyone's application—not just names but their group size, preferences, connections, personalities, interests. Maybe this single mom wants her kids to meet others their age. Maybe these two friends want to come together but are open to meeting new people. We build a giant map, a "graph" in mathematical terms, that connects all the possible groupings."

Jack jumped in. "And we go further. If you've never been to the village before, you get a boost. If you've tried many times and never got in, your odds go up. If you're a family, we try to make sure there are other families the same week, so your kids have friends. If you're single, you won't be alone unless you want to be. You'll have a chance to meet people who might become friends—or maybe more."

Tarmo nodded, his eyes twinkling. "We even let people express preferences. If you want to come with another group, or you're open to meeting strangers, you can say so. Our algorithms take it all in, and find the best possible mix—maximizing fairness, diversity, and the chance for real connections."

The Tokyo lead engineer frowned. "But couldn't people try to cheat? Say, they might pretend to be single just to get better odds?"

Tarmo shook his head. "We design the rules so that telling the truth is always best. That's called incentive compatibility. If you game the system, it won't help you. The math is built to reward honesty and openness."

Jack grinned. "So every week, when the new village cohort arrives, it won't just be a random crowd. It'll be a carefully balanced community—families, friends, singles, kids—all with the best chance to have the time of their lives."

Tarmo summed it up, "It's what happens when you replace luck with mathematics and randomness with meaning. Instead of just doling out tickets, we're building a new kind of social fabric—one week at a time."

Tarmo leaned back in his chair, and Jack recognized the look—his old roommate was about to make one of his leaps.

"You know what this reminds me of?" Tarmo asked. "That summer in Lahti, after your parents died ... Remember how my grandmother just seemed to know exactly who to invite to dinner each night? The widow from next door when the young family was visiting. The teenager who was struggling when the older couple was there with their stories. She was doing combinatorial optimization without knowing it."

Jack felt something catch in his throat. "She was building community."

"Exactly. And now we're trying to teach a computer to do what she did by instinct." Tarmo's fingers moved across his keyboard. "The math isn't magic. But maybe it can help us remember how to be human."

Jack felt a wave of gratitude. "And for the record," he said, "I still think the math is magic. Even if Tarmo swears it's just algorithms."

Tarmo laughed, "Math is just another kind of story, Jack. This one just happens to build villages."

Itsuki Tanaka was smiling. "Jack, I love this! And once you've got this working at Crystal Village, we can retool the lottery at our Japanese parks."

The Japanese team all said goodbye and dropped off the call, leaving just Jack and Tarmo on the line.

"Thanks so much for helping out on this project, Tarmo!" Jack said. "It's always fun when we get to work together!"

"I agree, this was really fun!" Tarmo chuckled. "And such a perfect application of my lab's work. I can't wait to publish the results of this project. I've been trying to find business applications for this approach. We've successfully used it to do natural resources auctions, and we're running several organ matching programs that compare the characteristics of the organ donor with the characteristics and level of illness and need of the recipient. But this is something else altogether, it feels very wholesome."

"It really is," said Jack, "and I can't wait to see the result."

I I I I

The air conditioning hummed softly in the conference room at Yomohiro Corporation's Oakland offices. Jack sat at the conference table and reviewed his notes for what he knew would be a difficult conversation. Diana sat across from him, her tablet open to a lengthy email that had arrived the night before. The message had been forwarded through different tribal council members before reaching them, and its contents had kept Jack awake until nearly dawn.

The door opened, and a woman in her early thirties entered with the confident stride of someone accustomed to walking into rooms where she wasn't entirely welcome. She wore a navy blazer over dark jeans and silver earrings that caught the light as she moved. Her long black hair was pulled back in a professional bun. Her expression was serious but not hostile—the look of someone prepared for a challenging conversation but willing to engage in good faith.

"Mr. Seeley, Ms. Rollins," she said, extending her hand. "I'm Dr. Aiyana Stensgar. Thank you for agreeing to meet with me on such short notice."

Jack stood and shook her hand, noting the firmness of her grip. "Dr. Stensgar, thank you for coming. Please, call me Jack. I understand you have some concerns about our project."

Aiyana took a seat and placed a leather portfolio on the table. "I do, and I appreciate your willingness to listen. I should begin by saying that I've been following the Crystal Village project since the first rumors began circulating in our community. My initial reaction was ... skeptical, to put it mildly."

Diana leaned forward. "We've been working closely with Elders Whitebird and Stensgar. Are you related to Sarah?"

"Sarah is my aunt," Aiyana replied. "And while I have tremendous respect for her wisdom and her decision to collaborate with you, I represent a different perspective within our community. I'm a cultural anthropologist by training, but I also work as a tribal liaison for several organizations. I've seen too many well-intentioned projects that end up perpetuating harmful stereotypes or appropriating our culture and stories without understanding their deeper significance."

Jack felt his stomach tighten. "I appreciate your directness. What specific concerns do you have?"

Aiyana opened her portfolio and pulled out a thick folder. "I've been reviewing the materials your team has shared with the tribal councils, as well as some leaked script excerpts that have been circulating online. There are several issues I'd like to address."

She spread out several printed pages. "First, the characterization of Coyote and Raven. While your writers have clearly done research, there's a tendency to simplify these figures into Western narrative archetypes. Coyote isn't just a 'trickster'—he's a complex cultural figure whose stories carry specific teachings about balance, consequence, and our relationship with the natural world. When you flatten him into a mischievous character for entertainment purposes, you lose the cultural context that gives these stories their power."

Diana made notes as Aiyana spoke. "We've been working with the elders to ensure authenticity ..." she offered.

"The elders are wonderful resources," Aiyana interrupted gently, "but they represent one generation's perspective. There are younger voices in our community who have different concerns about how our stories are being used. We've grown up seeing our culture commodified and misrepresented in television, film and literature. Theme parks are a particularly concerning trope. There were numerous "Wild West shows" all over the country that perpetuated harmful stereotypes. Disneyland and Disneyworld had Frontierland and the "Indian Village" from the 1950s through the 1970s that staged "Indian" dances and encampments with actors from non-Native backgrounds and used "pan-Indian" themes that blended elements from numerous cultures. They romanticized and statically portrayed various tribes lumped together as exotic curiosities for white people who saw them as "primitives." We're naturally wary of any project that promises to 'honor' our traditions while ultimately profiting from them."

Jack shifted in his chair, feeling the weight of her words. "I understand your concern, but we've made significant efforts to ensure cultural sensitivity. We're not just using these stories as entertainment—we're trying to educate people about their deeper meanings."

"With respect," Aiyana said, her tone remaining professional but firm, "that's what every project claims. The road to cultural appropriation is paved with good intentions. The question isn't whether you intend to honor our culture—it's whether you have the systems in place to ensure that you actually do."

Diana looked up from her notes. "What would those systems look like?"

Aiyana pulled out another document. "I'm glad you asked. I've prepared a detailed analysis of what authentic collaboration would require. First, you need Indigenous writers on your team—not just consultants but full creative partners with decision-making authority."

Jack frowned. "We've been trying to find Indigenous writers to join the team, but it's been challenging. The writers we've approached either weren't available or weren't interested in the project."

"That might tell you something about how the project is being perceived in our community," Aiyana replied. "When Indigenous writers decline to work on a project, it's often because they don't see genuine partnership being offered. They see tokenism."

"That's not what we're offering," Diana said defensively. "We want authentic voices involved."

"Then you need to be willing to give those voices real power," Aiyana countered. "Not just the ability to suggest changes, but the authority to make them. Would you be willing to give an Indigenous writer veto power over storylines that misrepresent our culture?"

Jack hesitated. "That's ... that's a significant level of creative control to hand over to someone who isn't familiar with the broader vision of the project."

Aiyana leaned back in her chair. "And there's the problem. You're asking us to trust you with our most sacred stories, but you're not willing to trust us with creative authority over how those stories are told. You want our blessing, not our partnership."

The room fell silent for a moment. Jack could feel the tension building, but he also recognized the validity of her point.

"You're right," he said finally. "That was a defensive response, and it proves your point. If we're serious about authentic collaboration, we need to be willing to share real authority."

Aiyana's expression softened slightly. "I appreciate that acknowledgement. It gives me hope that this conversation might actually lead somewhere productive."

She pulled out another set of documents. "The second issue is representation on your oversight committees. You need Indigenous voices at every level of decision-making, not just in advisory roles."

Diana nodded. "We could establish a cultural oversight committee ..."

"With real authority," Aiyana emphasized. "Not just the ability to make recommendations that can be ignored when they are inconvenient. This committee would need the power to halt production if cultural protocols are being violated."

Jack felt his business instincts kicking in. "That level of oversight could significantly impact our timeline and budget. What if there are disagreements about what constitutes a violation?"

"Then you work through them," Aiyana said simply. "The same way you work through any other creative disagreement. The difference is that you'd be treating cultural authenticity as a non-negotiable requirement, not an optional nice-to-have."

"But what if the committee's vision conflicts with the broader creative vision of the project?" Diana asked.

Aiyana fixed her with a steady gaze. "Then maybe the broader creative vision needs to change. If your vision can't accommodate authentic representation of our culture, then perhaps you shouldn't be using Indigenous stories at all."

Jack felt a flash of frustration. "Dr. Stensgar, we're trying to create something that celebrates multiple cultures, including yours. We're not trying to exploit anyone."

"I believe your intentions are good," Aiyana replied. "But intentions aren't enough. The entertainment industry is littered with projects that had good intentions but caused real harm to Indigenous communities. What matters is the impact, not the intent."

Jack steepled his fingers over his brow and closed his eyes for a moment. "I have to admit, at this point I'm wondering about whether it even makes sense to include Native storylines. I'm not even sure we can pull this off in a way that is collaborative, appropriate, doesn't involve cultural appropriation, and celebrates what Indigenous culture brings to the broader world. I wanted to include these stories, this content, because I truly believe that representing your culture is the right thing to do, that leaving your people out would do harm, would ignore contributions of your people to history. Now I'm struggling. Do you believe we can do this?"

"Just because something is hard doesn't mean we should avoid doing it," Aiyana said. "I know I'm pushing on you. I know this is all a lot. But I agree with your sentiment that ignoring the contributions of Indigenous people to history is not the outcome that makes sense."

She pulled out another folder. "Which brings me to the third issue—economic equity. Let me explain something that I suspect you don't know."

"Economic equity?" Jack asked.

"When I started researching the Crystal Village project, I became curious about the historical connections between our people and your ancestors. My aunt talked me through how your foundation had put an economic safety net beneath the descendants of the Original Eight. This got me thinking. I spent weeks in tribal archives and genealogical records."

She pulled out a genealogical chart. "What I discovered is that there are several families in our community who are direct descendants of the Original Eight founders of Crystal Village. Over the generations, there were intermarriages between settlers and tribal members. These families have been part of our community for over a century, but they were never contacted by your foundation."

Jack stared at the chart, his mind racing. "I ... we had no idea."

"Of course you didn't," Aiyana said, though not unkindly. "Your foundation tracked descendants through official records. But many of these mixed-heritage families weren't documented in the same way, especially the women who married into tribal communities. They've been living here, part of our nation, while their cousins received college scholarships and financial support."

Diana looked up from her notes. "How many families are we talking about?"

"At least six that I've identified so far, possibly more. Some are descendants of Seamus O'Connor through his son Albert, who had a daughter named Catherine who married a Coeur d'Alene man in 1932. Others trace back to the Sullivan line—one of Angus Sullivan's grandsons married into our community in the 1920s, and their descendants have been part of our nation ever since. These families have as much claim to the Crystal Village legacy as anyone else in your foundation, but they've been completely overlooked."

Jack felt a wave of shame wash over him. "This is ... this is a serious oversight."

"It's more than an oversight," Aiyana said firmly. "It's a pattern that reflects how Indigenous people are often erased from historical narratives, even when we're integral to them. Your foundation has been operating for over a century, helping descendants build wealth and opportunity, while our related families struggled with the same challenges facing many Native communities—poverty, limited educational opportunities, health disparities."

Diana set down her pen. "But surely the foundation couldn't have known about these connections if they weren't documented in the official records."

"That's exactly the problem," Aiyana replied. "The 'official records' were created by systems that systematically excluded Indigenous people. When Indigenous women married white men, they often lost their tribal status. When Indigenous men married white women, their children were often not recognized by either community. The absence of documentation doesn't mean these connections didn't exist—it means the systems weren't designed to track them."

Jack leaned forward. "What would you recommend we do about this?"

"The newly identified families should be included in the foundation's support systems retroactively," Aiyana said. "That means educational assistance for current students, healthcare support, and inclusion in the profit-sharing arrangement you've established for Crystal Village."

"That could be quite expensive," Diana said carefully. "We'd need to understand the full scope before making any commitments."

Aiyana's expression hardened. "So you're saying that correcting a century of exclusion is too expensive?"

"That's not what I said," Diana replied quickly. "I'm saying we need to understand what we're committing to so we can do it properly."

Jack held up a hand. "Diana's right that we need to understand the scope, but Dr. Stensgar is also right that we have a moral obligation to address this. The cost shouldn't be the determining factor—the question is how we can make this right. We're also treading into a delicate area, which continues to be difficult to navigate. The Crystal Village Foundations are not part of the Yomohiro Corporation. Diana's comments are helpful, but ultimately this is something we must resolve through the foundation, not as part of the conversations about the Crystal Village Project that we're embarking on with the Yomohiro Corporation. Luckily, I have full authority to address the foundation issues, and I have full authority to ensure that the Yomohiro project engages with your people and culture in a way that can address your concerns."

Aiyana nodded approvingly. "That's a better response. I can provide you with detailed genealogical documentation for each family. Some may not be interested in reconnecting with the Crystal Village legacy, but they should have the choice."

"Agreed," Jack said. "What else?"

"I'd like to propose the establishment of a Cultural Authenticity Board that includes both tribal elders and younger community members. This board would review all content related to Indigenous stories and characters before it's finalized."

"How would this board be structured?" Diana asked. "Who would appoint the members?"

"The tribal councils would nominate members, but the board would operate independently," Aiyana explained. "We'd want representation from multiple generations and different areas of expertise—historians, storytellers, artists, educators. The goal isn't to create another bureaucratic layer, but to ensure that authentic voices are heard throughout the creative process."

Jack rubbed his chin thoughtfully. "How would this board interact with our existing creative team? Would they review everything, or just content specifically related to Indigenous stories?"

"Initially, just Indigenous content," Aiyana said. "But I'd argue that in a project like Crystal Village, where different cultural traditions are meant to intersect, the lines aren't always clear. A scene between Coyote and one of the Irish fairy characters, for example—that would need input from both cultural perspectives."

Diana looked up from her notes. "What about timeline concerns? If the board needs to review content before it's finalized, that could significantly slow down production."

"Good storytelling takes time," Aiyana replied. "If you're rushing through cultural content without proper review, you're more likely to make mistakes that could damage relationships with our community. The cost of getting it wrong is much higher than the cost of taking time to get it right."

Jack nodded slowly. "That's a fair point. But we also have contractual obligations to our partners and investors. We need to find a way to balance cultural authenticity with practical production needs."

"I understand that," Aiyana said. "Which is why I'd recommend bringing Indigenous voices into the process from the beginning, not just at the review stage. If you have Indigenous writers as full creative partners from day one, you won't need as much back-and-forth review later."

She pulled out another document. "Which brings me back to my earlier point about hiring Indigenous writers. You'll need to hire someone who can represent the Nez Perce tribe, but I may be able to help with the Coeur d'Alene representation. I happen to know someone who would be perfect— my cousin, Valerie Stensgar. She just completed her MFA at The Institute for American Indian Arts in Santa Fe, and she's been working on a collection of stories that reimagine traditional narratives for contemporary audiences."

Diana perked up. "What's her background?"

"She has a degree in Indigenous Studies from UC Berkeley and an MFA in Creative Writing from IAIA. She's published short fiction in several literary journals and has been commissioned to write for a couple of documentary projects. More importantly, she understands both the cultural significance of these stories and how to adapt them for modern media without losing their essence."

Jack leaned forward. "Would she be interested in joining our team? And what would she expect in terms of creative authority?"

"That depends on whether you're serious about giving Indigenous voices real power in this project," Aiyana said. "Valerie won't be interested in being a token hire or a cultural rubber stamp. She'd want to be a full creative partner with meaningful input into storylines, character development, and narrative direction."

"Define 'meaningful input,'" Diana said carefully.

Aiyana smiled slightly. "The same level of input that any other senior writer on your team would have. The ability to propose storylines, develop characters, and yes—veto content that misrepresents our culture. Whoever you hire from the Nez Perce is going to need similar veto rights."

Jack exchanged a glance with Diana. "We'd need to meet with her to discuss the specifics, but in principle, I think we could work with that arrangement. It may require that these writers be given a producer credit."

"Good," Aiyana said. "I should mention that Valerie has some conditions of her own. She'd want her name prominently credited on any content she works on. She'd want the right to speak publicly about the project. And she'd want assurance that Indigenous storylines won't be cut if budget pressures arise."

Diana frowned. "She'll need to agree to constraints on what she can talk about publicly, just like every other writer. And the last point could be problematic. All content is subject to budget constraints."

"Then maybe you need to prioritize differently," Aiyana replied. "If Indigenous stories are integral to your vision of Crystal Village, they shouldn't be the first thing cut when money gets tight."

Jack held up a hand. "Let's not get ahead of ourselves. We're committed to including Indigenous stories—the question is how to structure the collaboration in a way that works for everyone. And while budget constraints are real, the stories also have to work. The more common scenario is we create content that doesn't resonate with the audience, and therefore we discontinue it."

"I appreciate that," Aiyana said. "But I hope you understand why we're cautious. We've seen projects where Indigenous content gets marginalized when commercial pressures increase."

She pulled out a final document. "I'd also like to see a commitment to ongoing cultural education for your entire creative team. This isn't something you can learn in a weekend workshop. Understanding Indigenous cultures requires deep, sustained engagement."

"What would that look like practically?" Diana asked.

"Quarterly workshops with tribal historians, storytellers, and cultural practitioners. Field trips to cultural sites. Participation in appropriate community events. The goal would be to help your team understand not just the stories themselves, but the cultural context that gives them meaning."

Jack considered this. "That sounds reasonable, but it would need to be voluntary. We can't mandate that our team members participate in cultural education outside of work hours."

"Then make it part of work hours," Aiyana said simply. "If cultural authenticity is truly a priority, invest the time and resources to do it properly."

Diana made more notes. "How would this education be structured? Would it be the same for everyone or tailored to different roles?"

"It would depend on each person's responsibilities," Aiyana explained. "Writers working on Indigenous storylines would need deeper cultural knowledge than, say, someone working on technical aspects. But everyone should have at least basic cultural competency."

"And how would this be evaluated?" Jack asked. "How would we know if the educational offerings are effective?"

Aiyana paused thoughtfully. "That's where the Cultural Authenticity Board would come in. They'd assess whether the team's cultural understanding is reflected in the actual content being produced."

The room fell silent for a moment as Jack and Diana absorbed everything they'd discussed.

"Dr. Stensgar," Jack said finally, "these are all significant changes to how we've been approaching this project. I want to be clear that we're committed to doing this right, but implementing everything you've outlined would require substantial restructuring of our creative process."

"I understand that," Aiyana replied. "But consider the alternative. If you proceed without making these changes, you risk creating content that offends our community and damages your own reputation. The short-term costs of restructuring are much lower than the long-term costs of getting it wrong."

Diana looked up from her notes. "What would convince you that we're serious about these changes?"

"Actions, not words," Aiyana said firmly. "Hire Valerie or someone similarly credentialed as a full creative partner, not just a consultant. Establish the Cultural Authenticity Board with real authority. Include the newly identified families in your foundation's support systems immediately, not after months of bureaucratic delays. And create a formal paid cultural liaison role with the authority to raise concerns directly with leadership."

Jack studied her face carefully. "Dr. Stensgar, would you be willing to take on that liaison role?"

Aiyana was quiet for a long moment. "I would consider it but with conditions. I'd want a written agreement that outlines my authority and responsibilities. I'd want regular access to all creative materials related to Indigenous content. And I'd want the right to speak publicly about this project, both its successes and its failures."

"The last point could be challenging," Diana said. "We typically require confidentiality agreements from all team members."

"Then we have a fundamental disagreement about transparency," Aiyana replied. "I won't be silenced if this project goes off track. Our community needs to know what's happening with their stories."

Jack leaned back in his chair, weighing the implications. "What if we structured it so that you could speak publicly about cultural issues, but with some limitations around proprietary business information?"

"I could work with that," Aiyana said, "as long as the limitations are clearly defined and don't prevent me from raising legitimate cultural concerns."

"Fair enough," Jack said. "When could you start?"

Aiyana smiled for the first time since entering the room. "I already have, in a way. I've been documenting everything since I first heard about this project. I have files on every public statement, every leaked script, every interview your team has given. I came into this meeting prepared to be your strongest critic. Instead, I'm cautiously optimistic that you might actually get this right."

She stood and gathered her materials. "I'll send you Valerie's contact information tonight. I'd also like to arrange for you to meet with some of the newly identified families. They deserve to hear about this directly from you, not through intermediaries."

Jack stood as well. "Dr. Stensgar—thank you for bringing these issues to our attention. I know this conversation wasn't easy, but it was necessary."

"Call me Aiyana," she said, extending her hand again. "And you're right—it wasn't easy. But I've learned that the difficult conversations are usually the most important ones. The fact that you were willing to have this conversation, and that you didn't get defensive when I challenged your assumptions, gives me hope."

Diana gathered her notes. "What's our next step?"

"I'll draft a formal proposal outlining everything we've discussed," Aiyana said. "You can review it with your team and let me know which elements you're willing to commit to. Then we can move forward with introducing Valerie and setting up meetings with the families."

After she left, Jack and Diana sat in silence for several moments.

"That was intense," Diana said finally.

"It was necessary," Jack replied. "And she was right about everything. We've been approaching this from a position of privilege, assuming that good intentions were enough."

Diana nodded slowly. "There could be financial implications for the foundation."

"There could be," Jack agreed. "But she's also right that we have a moral obligation to address this. And frankly, the foundation has significant resources. The Crystal Village story was always about bringing different communities together. If we can't do that authentically in our own project, we have no business telling that story."

He stood and walked to the window, looking out at the San Francisco skyline across the bay. "Besides, if we get this right, it could be a model for how other projects approach cultural collaboration. That alone would be worth the investment."

Diana closed her tablet. "So we're moving forward with her recommendations?"

"All of them," Jack said firmly. "It's time to put our money where our mouth is."

I I I I

Sinclair Lipson awaited the arrival of Ríona in a forest clearing surrounded by ancient cedars that soared above like a cathedral. The grass and leaves of ferns and flowers were kissed by the silver light of a crescent moon. He waited with the impatience of one who is accustomed to having his way. The forest seemed to hold its breath waiting for the meeting.

With a rustle like the whisper of silk, Ríona appeared. Her presence was like a breeze that carried the scent of wildflowers. She was no longer the naive sprite who had once hung on Lipson's every word. Time had given strength to her bearing, her eyes now sharp as flint, her posture regal and unyielding.

Lipson, in his usual white, linen suit, now seemed out of place against the ancient backdrop of the forest—like a man who had wandered too far from his own story into one where he was not welcome. Smoke drifted from his hand.

"Ríona, my dear," Lipson began, his voice smooth as honey, "it has been far too long."

Her lips curled into a smile that did not reach her eyes. "Sinclair Lipson, or should I say it like the Okanogan people, *Sinkalip*? That's their word for

Coyote, isn't it? Always games and masks with you. Whichever mask you wear today matters little. What brings you to my forest?"

He shifted, a flicker of discomfort crossing his features. *Her forest?* He had walked these mountains for eons before she was even born. But he set aside his annoyance at her presumptuous assertions. "Seeley and his ancestors are back in the mountains," he said, "they're building again at Crystal Village. It's … troublesome."

Ríona's laugh was like the tinkling of bells but with an icy edge. "Troublesome? It is an offense. Their noise disrupts the song of the night."

Lipson leaned in, his cheroot casting its glow and causing shadows to dance across his face. "Then let us join forces once more. Together, we can ensure this "village" never sees the light of day."

Ríona regarded him with a cool detachment, the moonlight casting her features in shadow. "Why would I help you, *Sinkalip*? You, who toyed with my heart as a child toys with a butterfly—capturing it, admiring it, then tearing of its wings."

He winced as if struck, the memories of a century ago still painful. "I was … unkind," he admitted, his usual bravado faltering. Then he moved forward, slyly, convincingly. "But time has passed, and I have changed."

She stepped closer, her gaze piercing. "Time has indeed passed, but some wounds do not heal, Coyote. Your words are as empty as a bird's nest in winter."

Lipson's jaw clenched, his composure slipping. "Then think of the forest, Ríona. Think of your kin, the dances in the moonlight that would be overshadowed by the clamor of humans. Help me, and we can rid ourselves of them."

Ríona's expression softened, not with forgiveness but with calculation. "Perhaps," she conceded, "but anything we do will be on my terms. I will not be a pawn in your game again."

Lipson nodded, a begrudging respect in his eyes. "Your terms, then. What do you propose?"

She circled him, her steps light upon the mossy floor. "We will cause mischief, many little problems that will gradually heat up and boil over into chaos. But know this, Coyote—I do this for my kingdom, for the stillness of the forest. When the time is right, I will have my revenge on you for the heartache you caused."

Lipson swallowed, the taste of fear unfamiliar on his tongue. He had sought an ally in Ríona, but he had found a formidable adversary with a score to settle.

"Agreed," he said, his voice a mere whisper among the ancient trees. "Let us begin."

As the moon climbed higher, casting its silver gaze upon the world below, Coyote and the Fairy Princess set their plan in motion.

I I I I

In a new building constructed to look original, sat a local datacenter that had been used to store files locally. This was a node in the overall cloud infrastructure that ran the games, the local networks, and the systems that ran the park. This space was not kept particularly secure, since the village hadn't opened yet. And only the Yomohiro team was working here right now.

Inside the datacenter there were several workstations for people to connect directly into all the overarching systems. This included software development tools and source code management environments.

It was late on a Tuesday, and Ríona and three of her lieutenants stood outside behind the large juniper bush. They waited for the last of the workers to leave for the night. The door opened and revealed a portly man with a mustache and wearing a mesh-backed baseball hat. He shut the lights off inside as he closed the door behind him, heading home for the evening.

Ríona waved her team forward, and they went into the room. They closed the door behind themselves.

I I I I

The sun had barely kissed the horizon when the first of the beta testers arrived at the gates of Crystal Village aboard the newly crafted but completely authentic steam train. The Roebling bridge had been fully restored and properly reinforced along the edges of the ravine. And the train was able to pull all the way onto Broadway, the locomotive, a coal car, and two passenger cars. The crew had expanded and restored the turntable to turn the train around as well, hidden just inside the opening to the mine.

Among these guests were some of the descendants of Crystal Village, friends and family of the crew, and a handful of journalists under strict press embargo until closer to the park's launch date. The guests were in costume already, as were the crew. They were fitted with their necklaces, and some of the guests were testing out the AR goggles as well.

They kicked off the testing just after breakfast. The first glitch emerged as a tester named Brian strolled down Broadway with a virtual Coyote at his side. The AI-driven character was supposed to amuse Brian with tales of the village's past, a cunning guide through the cobblestone streets. Instead, Coyote's form flickered, his fur changing colors as if he were a chameleon caught in a disco light. Brian's laughter rang out.

Jack, watching from a control room, couldn't help but chuckle at the sight. "Well, that's one way to interpret a trickster spirit," he mused, making a note for the tech team.

The day progressed, and the glitches continued, each more absurd than the last. In the saloon, a virtual actor portraying a grizzled miner was telling stories to testers. At the climax of a tale of a harrowing cave-in his voice suddenly shifted, becoming operatic and soaring. His rugged face contorted in surprise as he belted out an aria befitting of the grandest stages, much to the delight of the guests who erupted in applause, convinced it was all part of the show.

Susanne, witnessing the spectacle, leaned over to Jack. "You know, there's something oddly fitting about a gruff miner with the voice of a tenor. It's like Coyote himself is directing the show."

Jack nodded, his eyes twinkling with the seed of an idea. "Maybe we should let Coyote "direct" more often. Could make for some entertaining gameplay."

The glitches seemed to multiply as the day wore on—a virtual prospector whose pickaxe strikes rang out as church bells, street lamps that pulsed like living hearts, a horse that galloped backwards through solid walls. Each malfunction sent ripples of laughter through the beta testers, who in their mirth began anticipating the next impossible moment.

By evening, the team's notebooks overflowed not with bug reports but with story possibilities. Jack and Susanne convened with the writers in the restored saloon, their faces lit by the warm glow of oil lamps that, mercifully, behaved exactly as oil lamps should.

"All right, team," Jack said, spreading the day's chaos across the table in sketches and scribbled notes. "Let's not see these glitches as setbacks but as Coyote's way of contributing to the narrative. We'll embrace the chaos and turn it into something players will love."

Susanne leaned forward, her eyes bright with possibility. "Think of it as Coyote leaving his paw prints all over our work. It's unexpected, it's challenging, and above all, it's fun!"

In the weeks that followed after the launch of the game, Coyote's glitches took on a life of their own, the glitches becoming features, the unexpected becoming the expected. Beta players learned to anticipate Coyote's interventions, to laugh at the absurdity, and to revel in the unpredictability.

And through it all, Jack and Susanne couldn't shake the feeling that Coyote was out there somewhere, watching over their shoulders, a wry smile on his lips as he watched his legend grow in a new world of his own making.

20

Success

Jack stood on the weathered porch of the Monsieur Lemieux Mercantile & General Store, surveying the faint lines of the flight grid criss-crossing high above the rooftops. The smart paint had not been activated yet, so the grid was faintly visible. These lines, the veins of Bill McKenna's ambitious flight system, promised a new kind of freedom—a chance to glide through the air with the grace of a bird. It was an innovation that defied gravity, inviting visitors to step off the solid ground and into a story that unfolded in the skies.

The sounds of construction filled the air. Jack watched as his dream materialized with each passing day. Across the street, Jack saw Susanne walking with some other writers. Jack paused, captivated by the familiar grace in her movements. He thought of the summers of their childhood—and all the time they were spending now on reviving Crystal Village.

Jack stepped off the wooden porch of the general store and called out, "Susanne! Care to join me for dinner tonight?"

She turned, her face lighting up at the sound of his voice, a fondness in her eyes. "I'd love to, Jack!"

As evening settled over Crystal Village, Jack and Susanne found themselves seated at a corner table in the Hawthorne Hotel's dining room, the gentle clink of silverware and the murmur of conversation enveloping them in warmth.

"Do you remember the fort we built in the woods behind your grandparents' house?" Susanne asked, a playful glint in her eye.

Jack chuckled, the memory vivid in his mind. "How could I forget? We were convinced it was impregnable—until Pete and Danny decided to test our defenses with a barrage of pine cones and puff ball mushrooms."

They laughed, the sound of their merriment mingling with the soft music that filled the room. Jack felt the years peel away, revealing the continued presence of the boy who had once harbored dreams as vast as the sky.

Susanne leaned forward, her voice softening. "You always had such grand plans, even then. Remember how you were going to turn that fort into a castle, with towers and a moat?"

Jack's eyes met hers. "I suppose I've always been a dreamer," he replied with a smile playing at the corners of his lips. "It's what led me to this career, envisioning a dream, making that dream real for myself, and then expanding that reality for the whole world to experience. You do the same thing with your writing. I have noticed that more than one of our adventures as kids ended up in your books."

Susanne blushed slightly. "You mentioned before that you'd read a few of my books, which of the books did you read?"

Jack smiled. "All of them. I didn't tell you before because I didn't want to act like a fanboy. By the way, I couldn't help but notice that Skylar always had unrequited feelings for Jake." Jack was referring to the two central characters of her series, who were fairly obviously based on the Jack and Susanne of their childhood.

Susanne laughed and blushed again, "Oh ... wow. You're not in my target demographic, Jack. That's really something."

The conversation flowed naturally, carrying them through recollections of secret trails and hidden meadows, whispered confidences and shared aspirations. As the meal progressed, Jack felt a sense of contentment in Susanne's presence—a connection that had matured into something enduring, something lasting.

The last of the evening light faded, and the stars now filled the sky. Jack offered his hand. "Let's take a walk," he said.

Together, they strolled through the quiet streets of Crystal Village, guided by the soft luminescence of the lamps. The only people in the village were the construction crews and support staff who were present to make sure they were comfortable and had their needs met. As they walked along, Jack looked back down Broadway and saw a few lone figures and a single cluster of workers standing under one of the street lamps. They turned onto Spring Street, walking past the original cabin homes of the eight founders, until they reached the hot springs. The air was cooler now, the night sky filled with a dense blanket of stars.

They followed the trail to the hot springs, then shed their clothes, as villagers had been doing since its founding. They stepped into the steaming waters of the large pool, the heat of the water enveloping them in its familiar embrace. Around them, the village lay silent.

In the seclusion of the hot springs, Jack and Susanne drew together with a quiet confidence. Their hands met beneath the surface of the water, fingers entwining as they shared stories—their hopes, their challenges, and the paths that had led them back to each other.

As they soaked in the healing waters, they found solace in each other's company, the barriers between them dissolving with each breath. Jack suddenly knew in his bones that his connection with Susanne was not a fleeting infatuation. His feelings for her had transitioned into a permanence that he'd never before experienced in a relationship. One forged out of shared values, history and mutual respect.

The night deepened, and the stars seemed to grow in brightness, as if drawing closer to witness the unfolding of a love that had been nurtured over time. Jack and Susanne shared a quiet moment of utter contentment, holding each other and floating beneath the stars.

IIII

In the dim glow of a gaming lounge in Spokane, Sinclair Lipson and Elias Dotson sat side by side. The hum of computers and the soft click-clack of keyboards formed a backdrop to the vibrant world of gaming. In his impeccable white suit, Lipson stood out in the sea of casual gamers. His cheroot left a trail of sweet smoke that was quickly dispersed by the cafe's ventilation system.

Dotson sat alert in his chair, every fiber of his being exhibiting enthusiasm and rapt attention. His black duster draped over him like a shadow. His hat was set aside on the counter next to him. His complexion was ruddy, almost gray amidst the room's dim ambient blue-hued light. His eyes were active, watching everything around them.

Before them, a group of children and teenagers, VR headsets strapped on, delved into the virtual world of Crystal Village. They navigated the cobblestone streets, interacted with virtual villagers, ran through forests and caves, and unraveled the tales of Raven and Coyote. The game brought the legends to life with a vivid reality. Their game play was broadcast to a series of screens mounted on the walls. Most of the players were actually playing the game, but a few sat and watched, like Lipson and Dotson did.

Lipson watched the game play with a mix of fascination and irritation as the glitches he had so carefully orchestrated became celebrated features within the game. Players delighted in Coyote's unexpected appearances, his pranks that disrupted their quests, and the sudden, whimsical challenges they presented.

"Look at them," Lipson muttered bitterly, taking another puff of his cheroot, only to be met with a stern glance from a teenage girl at the front desk. "No smoking in here, sir," she said firmly, pointing to the "No Smoking" sign by the entrance.

Lipson rolled his eyes, extinguishing the cheroot with a flick of his fingers, pinching the burning end between his fingertips, the ember dying with reluctance. "These children find joy in my mischief," he continued, turning to Dotson. "They laugh at the chaos I bring. I will begrudgingly admit that it feeds my ego, yet it does not satiate my desire for vengeance on the Seeleys."

Dotson, his gaze fixed on the screen displaying the game, let out a sigh that seemed to carry the weight of centuries. "You see, Dog, your tricks have taken on a life of their own. They've become lore within this digital realm, and the players revel in it. Perhaps this is the power you sought but not the battleground you expected."

Lipson's mouth twisted into a wry smile. The irony wasn't lost on him. "Indeed," he conceded. "But the real park, the flesh and bone of Crystal Village, it remains untarnished by my hand. That is where I must strike, where the impact will be felt beyond these glowing screens."

Dotson's interest was piqued by how obtuse Lipson was. *How has he missed so obvious a truth?* He leaned forward. "Look closer. See how the tales of Raven and Coyote are spreading, how the stories gain strength with each retelling. This game gives us access to more power, more influence! It binds our essence into the hearts of a new generation, one that is vastly larger than any group that has ever believed in us. This technology is fascinating, something sparks anew in my mind. For the first time in an age, I see new possibilities! And it all comes from the *physical place*, the village as Jack Seeley has reinvisioned it. Don't you see? If you manage to succeed in your foolish quest for vengeance, you will destroy the opportunity that is blossoming in front of our eyes!"

A spark of realization flickered in Lipson's eyes as he watched the enthusiasm and dedication of the players before him. "Perhaps you are right," he murmured as he considered the possibilities. "Perhaps there is merit in this unexpected turn of events. But on the other hand, that Eoinn Seeley has gotten so deeply embedded in my skin, he's like a tick that I can't quite chew loose. Maybe, with his ancestor Jack, I can find a path forward."

The room buzzed with the energy of the game's launch event. The excitement of the players was obvious as they navigated the virtual village and the forests around it. Players were communicating, coordinating by their voices as they traveled in packs. Lipson and Dotson found themselves on the verge of a potential alliance, united by the power of their own legends being reborn in the hearts and minds of those who played.

As the night wore on and the cyber cafe' began to empty, the two figures remained, a silent accord forming between them. Coyote's tricks brought delight to thousands in the virtual world.

Dotson looked at Lipson and thought, *Perhaps, just perhaps, this newfound appreciation will lead to a resolution of this feud between Lipson and the Seeleys. A resolution that is not yet upon them, but its seeds have been planted, waiting for the right moment to bloom.*

I I I I

The conference room at Yomohiro's Alameda office hummed with tension. Jack pushed through the glass doors to find Valerie Stensgar sitting at the head of the table, her laptop open, jaw set in a line that brooked no argument. Around the table sat the writing team—Mitch, Tom, Monica, and three junior writers whose names Jack was still learning. Dr. Aiyana Stensgar occupied a chair near the window.

"Jack, thank God." Mitch rose from his seat, relief evident in his voice. "We've got a situation here."

Valerie's dark eyes flicked to Jack, then back to her screen. "Not a situation. A process violation."

"Look, I understand cultural sensitivity," Tom began, his hands spread in what he probably thought was a reasonable gesture. "But we're talking about one story segment. It's already integrated into the AI system, and pulling it now would—"

"Would what?" Valerie interrupted. "Cost money? Inconvenience the timeline?"

Jack settled into the chair at the foot of the table. "Someone want to fill me in?"

Monica cleared her throat. "Tom found a collection of Raven stories on an ethnographic website. He pulled one for a sequence where people meet Raven. It's already been processed through the AI, integrated into both the park experience and the game."

"It's a beautiful story," Tom insisted. "We use it to have Raven teach people to see through deception. Perfect for our themes."

Aiyana spoke for the first time. "That particular story is restricted. It's part of our winter ceremonial cycle, shared only within the community during specific times and contexts."

"But it was on a public website," one of the junior writers protested.

Valerie laughed humorlessly. "So was the Coca-Cola formula at one point. Doesn't mean you get to bottle it and sell it."

Jack studied the faces around the table. Tom's jaw worked as if he were chewing something bitter. Since his original transformational experience during the initial review with the tribal elders, he'd reverted to his old adversarial tactics. The junior writers looked confused, caught between competing authorities. Monica tapped her stylus against her tablet, calculating the technical implications.

"How did this get past our review process?" Jack asked.

Mitch shifted uncomfortably. "Tom found it over the weekend. He was excited about the thematic fit, so he fast-tracked it through the AI integration. We were going to present it to the cultural board today."

"After it was already locked into the system," Aiyana observed dryly.

"I was being proactive," Tom said. "We're behind on content delivery, and this filled a gap perfectly."

Valerie closed her laptop with deliberate precision. "This is exactly why Indigenous communities don't trust collaboration projects. You make decisions about our stories without us, then ask for forgiveness instead of permission."

"That's not fair," Tom replied. "We've been bending over backward to include your perspectives."

"Including our perspectives?" Valerie raised her left eyebrow. "Tom, I'm not a consultant you bring in to rubber-stamp your decisions. I'm a writer on this team. You're actually supposed to coordinate with me on issues related to Native storylines."

Jack had navigated similar tensions at Disney, though never with stakes quite like these. The room waited for his judgment.

"Monica, what's involved in pulling the story from the AI?"

She consulted her tablet. "Once the learning is integrated, disentangling it is quite hard. Maybe two weeks of work."

"Two weeks we don't have," Mitch added. "The beta launch is ..."

"The beta launch will happen when it's ready," Jack interrupted. "Not before."

Tom leaned forward. "Jack, be reasonable. It's one story. How is this different from using any other public domain folklore?"

"Because it's *not* public domain," Valerie said. "Just because someone posted it online doesn't make it free for commercial use. Would you take a copyrighted song just because you found it on YouTube?"

"That's different. That's intellectual property law."

"This *is* intellectual property!" Aiyana interjected. "Cultural intellectual property. The fact that your legal system doesn't recognize it doesn't make it less real."

Jack watched the interplay, recognizing the deeper currents beneath the surface argument. This wasn't just about one story. It was about power, respect, and the fundamental question of who got to make decisions about Indigenous narratives.

"Valerie," he said, "what would you need to feel confident this won't happen again?"

She studied him for a long moment. "Editorial authority over all Indigenous content. Not consultation. Authority."

The room erupted in murmurs. Tom's face flushed red. "You can't give one person veto power over entire storylines!"

"Why not?" Susanne's voice came from the doorway. She entered carrying two coffee cups, handing one to Jack. "We give Monica technical authority over AI integration. We give Bill authority over attraction safety. Why is cultural authority different?"

"Because it affects everyone's work," Mitch said. "If Valerie can kill any story she doesn't like—"

"Any story that appropriates sacred traditions," Valerie corrected. "This isn't about what I like and don't like. I'm not here to censor your creativity! I'm here to protect my people's spiritual heritage. And I'm also a writer, Tom. I value your creativity and contributions. But not when you just copy a random story you found online and drop it directly into the AI systems that drive audience interactions."

Jack sipped his coffee. The solution felt obvious, but he needed to present it in a way that preserved everyone's dignity.

"Valerie, I need to disclose something to the team." He set down his cup. "You're not just a writer on this project. Yomohiro has also given you producer credit under explicit contract terms."

The room went silent. Tom's mouth opened, then closed.

"Her producer credit comes with certain rights," Jack said to the room. He looked at Valerie and continued. "Including editorial authority over content within your domain of expertise. I want to be clear that this isn't me giving you special treatment. It's me recognizing the authority you already have."

"Since when?" Tom demanded.

Jack looked directly at Tom and paused for ten full seconds before continuing. The room shifted uncomfortably as they waited. "Since Kisho Yomohiro decided he wanted authentic Indigenous voices as creative partners, not just consultants," Jack said. "It was signed off in the original contract negotiations."

Monica looked up from her tablet. "That actually makes the technical integration cleaner. If Valerie has producer authority, I can set the system up so she can approve or reject story changes without full committee review. I can actually require her approval before the system allows content integration on specific storylines."

"This is ridiculous," Tom muttered. "We're letting political correctness derail the creative process."

Aiyana's voice cut through the room like a blast of cold air. "Political correctness? Tom, we're talking about respecting the spiritual traditions of living people. If that's too politically correct for you, perhaps you should consider whether this is the right project for your talents. There are multiple other storylines the writing team is working on, why do you feel obligated to force these issues when it comes to Indigenous stories?"

The junior writers exchanged glances. One of them raised her hand tentatively. "I have a question. If we want to use Indigenous stories, what's the right process?"

Valerie's expression softened slightly. "You ask. You explain the context, the intended use, the audience. You listen to the answer, even if it's no. And you understand that some stories aren't for sharing outside the community, no matter how beautiful or thematically perfect they might be."

"But how do we know which stories are restricted?" Sarah asked.

"Simple. You ask," Aiyana repeated. "Every time. That's what cultural review means."

Jack nodded. "From now on, all Indigenous content goes through Valerie before AI integration. No exceptions."

Tom pushed back from the table. "Fine. But don't blame me when we're behind schedule because every story needs committee approval."

"Tom." Jack's voice carried enough authority to stop the other man at the door. "It isn't lost on me that you created this situation by skipping through the previously acknowledged process. Any delays caused by this aren't Valerie's fault, they come directly back to your feet. So we're updating the process as a result of its failure, of your failure to follow the established process. This isn't a committee. Valerie is the producer for Indigenous content. Her decisions are final, just like Monica's decisions on AI integration are final. Valerie's producer title isn't just for a name in the credits. Her contract spells out her right to approve, revise, or reject scripts and storylines involving Indigenous content, period. If you can't work within that structure, we need to discuss your role on the team."

Tom's face cycled through several expressions before settling on grudging acceptance. "I can work with it."

After he left, the room felt lighter. Monica was already pulling up the AI integration interface. "Valerie, I can show you the interfaces into the AI system and walk you through the back end flows so you can see how stories get processed. Might help you understand the technical constraints."

"I'd appreciate that."

Susanne moved to the window looking out over the bay. "You know, this reminds me of something Sam King wrote in her journals. She talked about learning to gather camas and other native crops from Stelkupmi and showing her how Colin had used some herbs in ways that differed from how the Coeur d'Alene people used them. Sam said the key in these conversations was knowing when to lead and when to follow."

"Stelkupmi was my great-grandmother," Aiyana said quietly. "She would have appreciated that observation."

"And Sam was my great-great-grandmother," Susanne said, smiling. "If they could find a way to work together in those times, we can certainly make this work today."

Jack felt something shift in the room's atmosphere. The tension hadn't disappeared, but it had transformed into something more productive. "Valerie, I know this wasn't the smoothest introduction to your expanded role. But I'm glad you pushed back. The project is stronger for it."

She nodded, then opened her laptop again. "I'll need to review all the Indigenous content currently in development, and previously approved. And I want to establish clear protocols for future submissions."

"Whatever you need, this is your domain," Jack said.

As the meeting dispersed, Jack lingered with Susanne.

"Think Tom will be a problem?" Susanne asked.

"Tom *is* a problem. I don't like anyone skirting the process, regardless of the type of content being integrated. And I don't like his attitude. He's blaming Valerie for a two-week delay that is fundamentally his fault. I don't like his lack of accountability. I'll let Mitch deal with that situation. The bigger problem is a system that's trained people to think consultation means asking permission to do what they were already planning to do, even after they've done it." Jack finished his coffee. "But systems can change."

"Speaking of change," Susanne said, "Aiyana mentioned something interesting. Apparently, several Coeur d'Alene families have Crystal Village connections we never knew about. Descendants of the Original Eight who married into the tribe."

Jack smiled. "Yes, she and I discussed it a few weeks ago. I have the team at the foundation looking into it. Aiyana is going to facilitate a group meeting with all the impacted people and families, so we can have a transparent conversation about it."

"It's kind of heartbreaking. How did the foundation miss this?" asked

Susanne.

"Because they were looking for the wrong names in the wrong places. Cultural bias."

"Exactly." Susanne gathered her things. "Makes you wonder what other connections we've missed. What other stories we don't know."

As Jack walked back to his office, he thought about the morning's confrontation. It hadn't been comfortable. Change is hard, but the new approach had caught the issue. Crystal Village had always been about bringing different worlds together, finding ways for diverse communities to thrive alongside each other.

His phone buzzed with a Slack message from Valerie: *Beginning review of existing Indigenous content. Thank you for backing me up.*

Jack smiled and typed back: *Thank you for holding the line. That's what producers do.*

IIII

Crystal Village brimmed with anticipation as the final dress rehearsal kicked off. Jack and Susanne walked the cobblestone streets in their period garb. The day was beautiful, a warm early spring day. The weather forecast was for more of the same for the next week.

The general store's windows were adorned with replicas of historically accurate goods. The streets were full of actors in full kit. Men dressed as miners and tradesmen, hats tipped at jaunty angles. Women in gingham dresses and petticoats chatted animatedly, their scripted lines flowing like natural conversation. It was as if each character was breathing life into the village.

Actors fine-tuned their roles as individuals and as a cast, their voices carrying snatches of scripted dialogue as they learned the roles. The goal was for them to embrace their backstory so deeply that they could adlib "in-character" as easily as rattle off prewritten script. The actors practiced this in-character adlibbing as well. As they did, set builders were putting final touches on the facades of the general store and the saloon. The steady beat of hammers resounded down the street like competing heartbeats.

An actor who had been cast as Egan Sullivan practiced his monologue beside the recreated structure of the Roebling Bridge. The actor's voice was rich with an Irish accent that brought the character to life. He was telling a story about the way the bridge had been constructed, and how he'd designed the road and sidewalks of Broadway to stay warm enough to melt snow during the height of winter.

The sound of electric saws and nail guns floated on the breeze from the direction of Eagle City. Its White Elephant Saloon was rebuilt and redesigned, now a solid-timber, post and beam structure. The idea was that Crystal Village represented safety and family friendly adventure, but nearby Eagle City was where adults could go to experience the steamier, riskier side of the era.

Susanne turned to Jack, smiling as she took in the completed scenes of the village. Her eyes sparkled with joy.

"We did a good thing here," Susanne said. "I keep thinking about the stories we used to invent when we were kids. But I never thought we'd be part of one as amazing as this!"

Jack smiled, "We always did know how to dream big."

The rehearsal for the opening day unfolded with delight. The guests arrived, including all the members of the descendants of Crystal Village. Children wandered wide-eyed and eager. They followed fairies under the mountain. Their giggles echoed through the tunnels as augmented reality brought the fantasy to life. The archery range rang with the twang of bows and the thud of arrows finding their marks.

As dusk settled over the village, Jack and Susanne found themselves near the hot springs. Susanne drew him forward with a gentle tug. They shed their costumes, following the pattern of their ancestors and the habit they'd been forming for months, and they slipped into the water.

Jack and Susanne shared a quiet moment of connection. The village, with its demands and deadlines, fell away, leaving only the two of them. Jack and Susanne floated in each other's arms and shared a kiss.

"This has been one of the best parts of being up here," said Jack.

Susanne said, "In Sam O'Connor's journal, she talked about this being a nightly ritual with Seamus before they had kids. And then at some point, when she was older, she began coming here early in the morning before sunrise, by herself. It feels universal, the act of bathing in warm water under the stars. I hope we can do it for the rest of our lives."

Jack smiled and slowly dunked his head under the water.

I I I I

After his afternoon briefing about the various glitches and problems plaguing the park, Jack had a thought spark in his mind. He began to consider that the man the state had assigned to review operations at the park seemed always to be around when things went wacky. Sinclair Lipson was his name, and Jack had run into him a few too many times for him to believe it was a coincidence. He remembered the chance encounter they'd had on that flight from Los Angeles to Spokane. He'd been surprised the first time Lipson had arrived in the village waving his credentials from the state of Idaho to whomever would pay attention.

Jack had always been one to confront his problems head-on. He imagined it was a trait inherited from generations of Seeleys who'd tamed the American West. But nothing in his past had prepared him for the enigmatic Sinclair Lipson—a man who seemed to have stepped out of the pages of Crystal Village's history and into the present day.

Jack's research revealed the troubling figure of Lipson lurking in the shadows of his great-great-grandfather's time, a man with a cheroot perpetually smoldering between his fingers and a vendetta against Eoinn and all the Seeleys that spanned over a century. He saw pictures of Lipson sprinkled throughout the period of Crystal Village's first life. There were references in various journals to Sinclair Lipson as well.

Must be his ancestor, thought Jack. Jack recalled the man introducing himself on the plane as Sinclair Lipson, "the third." Lipson's presence was an enigma. The man was a living anachronism.

As Jack walked through the village, the weight of this mystery pressing upon him, he spotted Lipson leaning against the general store's facade. Lipson was smoking one of his damnable brown cigarettes, his white suit somehow unstained. Lipson's eyes, sharp and cunning, followed Jack's approach.

"Mr. Lipson," Jack said, "We need to talk."

Lipson's smile was slow and calculating, a predator's grin that sent a shiver down Jack's spine. "Jack Seeley," he drawled, "the man of the hour. To what do I owe this confrontation?"

Jack squared his shoulders, meeting Lipson's gaze. "I've been watching you. It seems to me that wherever you've gone in our park, trouble seems to follow."

Lipson chuckled, a sound absolutely devoid of humor. "Trouble? I've done not a thing to your park. I'm simply here ensuring that Crystal Village is safe for the good people of Idaho and the many visitors you plan to entertain here. My thoughts go to the stories this park is built upon. Why, you and I are cut from the same cloth, Jack. We both understand the value of a good story, even if those stories are a bit ... chaotic."

Jack paused for a moment before he replied. "We're trying to do something important, something meaningful, here. Ever since we met I've had the sense that there is something else going on with you. I get the distinct sense that you're trying to break things, that you either want to control or destroy this place."

"That sounds like an accusation, Jack." Lipson's eyes narrowed, a flicker of something—anger, admiration—crossing his features. "Ah, but what is control but a story we tell ourselves? And destruction ... it can be quite the catalyst for creation, don't you think?"

Jack felt the conversation slipping into a realm of philosophy and rhetoric that offered no solid ground. He needed answers, not riddles. "What is it that you want, Lipson? Why are you haunting this place?"

Lipson pushed away from the wall, his movements languid yet deliberate. "Seeley, your ancestors—they wronged me ... my ancestors, and I intend to balance the scales. Your park will never see the light of day if I have anything to say about it."

The threat hung in the air, a threat that seemed to leach the warmth from the setting sun. Jack's fists clenched at his sides. "That was before either of us was even born! But no matter, Lipson. We'll stand against whatever chaos you throw our way, and we'll come out the other side stronger for it. We've faced worse, and we'll stand our ground."

Lipson looked a little surprised at Jack's choice of words, which Eoinn had said almost exactly to him more than a century ago, but then his smirk returned, a serpentine twist of his lips that made Jack's blood boil. "We shall see, Mr. Seeley. We shall see."

With that, Lipson turned and strolled away, his white suit making him seem like a specter in the gathering dusk. The peculiar little man left a trail of tobacco smoke, but he also left Jack with a renewed determination to protect Crystal Village.

IIII

Sinclair Lipson stood in a glade in the densest part of the forest awaiting the arrival of Ríona. He stewed on his encounter with Jack. He had intended to reach out to Jack with an olive branch, to find a way to align their causes. Yet somehow, that Seeley arrogance had just made him so angry. He saw now that this was spinning beyond his control. He'd come to the village today expecting to leave as an ally to Jack Seeley, not further entrenched as an enemy. He felt a pang of genuine regret.

The shadows were growing long, and the air had turned crisp with the approach of evening. Lipson's usual overly confident demeanor was tinged with a rare sense of apprehension. At that moment, Ríona stepped into the glade, radiating a barely restrained fury, her delicate features hardened by a resolve that spoke of imminent reckoning.

"Ríona," Lipson began, "our play has been entertaining to say the least. But I sense a fervor within you that goes beyond mere mischief. This park … it demands a response befitting our stature. You are taking things too far."

Her sharp voice cut through the gathering dusk. "You are correct,

415

Sinclair. These petty pranks no longer suffice. This park, this affront to our sovereignty—it must feel the full extent of our ire."

"I'm uncertain about this, Ríona. The stories being created in this Village, and in their games, they are not the simpering venality we had feared. The stories are strong and powerful. They ... honor us," said Lipson.

Their scheming was brought to an abrupt halt by the arrival of another—a presence preceded and surrounded by a stillness among the trees, almost like a spell. Ríona's mother stepped forward, her aura of regal authority irrefutable. Nobody needed to address her as "Queen."

"Daughter," she addressed Ríona, "you tread a dangerous path—one that leads not to liberation but to a place from which there is no return. We are blood and honor bound to the Seeleys and to the descendants of the ones who brought us here. You were born here, so you do not remember, but our kingdom would never have come to us without the people of this village."

Turning her gaze to Lipson, she continued with a calm that belied the gravity of her words. "You, harbinger of chaos, once you were a creature of mirth, now you stand on the brink of darkness. Beware, for the abyss also gazes into you."

Lipson, caught off balance by her sudden appearance and the resonance of her counsel with his own emerging impulses, hesitated. "Your majesty," he ventured, a note of uncertainty creeping into his voice, "the park encroaches upon that which is sacred to us. Are we to stand as idle spectators? Are you not worried about this place diminishing us?"

"Your arguments certainly seem focused on encroachment and violation of the sacred. But you forget that I was here this whole time. I saw what you wrought back in those early days, with the forests cut down, the earth and rivers poisoned and ravaged with pollution from the swarm of men covering the forests like ants and "mining" for riches. You could care less about the village encroaching on our land. You are angry with the Seeleys. You want to defeat Eoinn. We are all of one blood, foolish dog. Just as you are blood bound to us, we are equally all blood bound to them. We are all kin."

Lipson looked at her through his bushy auburn eyebrows, feeling his resentment for Eoinn Seeley flare in his heart. He said, "I hear your words, your majesty, but I have not forgiven Seeley for his slights. This village project should not stand."

Her eyes held the stillness of the deep forest, unshaken by his entreaty. "The cedar stands tall not by resisting the wind but by bending with it. You must learn this dance, Coyote, the delicate balance between resistance and surrender. Open your heart, and you will find the path that leads to harmony."

Ríona, a creature of passion and pride, felt the boundaries of her mother's words like the confines of a cage. "Yet, mother, they have stolen our essence and mixed it into their narrative, twisted our legacy for their gain. To remain silent is to consent to our own binding."

The mother looked at her daughter with pity. "I feel no binding. I feel enhancement, growth, and renewal. We must help them navigate through these stories. We must influence, but we do not obliterate."

Ríona turned to Lipson, looking for his support. But Lipson, his vision of mischief suddenly clouded by the wisdom of the queen, withdrew into the sanctuary of his thoughts.

Ríona turned her back on them both. "Then I shall tread my own path through this affront," she declared.

She disappeared into the forest, a force of nature herself. The queen vanished into the night with a parting glance, leaving Lipson to confront the unexpected road ahead. This was a path that called for a subtlety and finesse he had long forsaken.

21

Wonder

The Granger family from Minneapolis won their tickets to Crystal Village in the very first lottery. They found themselves at the beginning of a new kind of adventure.

Bill Granger was a high school history teacher with a penchant for the Old West. For years, he had constantly told his family tales of frontier life. He'd read them the Laura Ingalls Wilder "Little House" books, and they'd gone on road trips to follow the route they took across the country. His wife Sharon was a librarian with a love for Westerns and historical novels.

Michael Granger was a spirited eight year old with a mop of untamed hair. He clutched his asthma inhaler with a mixture of awe and excitement. Lucy, their thirteen-year-old daughter, gazed out the window of the Crystal Village Welcome Center outside of Kellogg with a sense of wonder. She had often lost herself in the worlds of fantasy and fiction, and she was eager to embrace the reality of this place.

The family and two other eager groups were ushered into the changing rooms. They replaced their modern attire with period clothing, tailored to fit as if they had stepped out of a daguerreotype. Bill's blood pressure pills were now nestled within an ornate, brass pill container and took on the guise of a remedy that wouldn't seem out of place in a 19th-century apothecary. Michael's inhaler was now encased in a steampunk-influenced case that made it look timeless. Lucy wore a dress that swished around her ankles and a necklace that held a garnet crystal that held the light like a captured star. She felt the edges of her reality blur.

The steam train to Crystal Village awaited them. Its cars harkened back to an era when travel was as much about the journey as the destination. The train whistle pierced the air in a long scream as the Granger family and their fellow travelers settled into the plush seats.

Lucy watched the world transform as she peered through the window, and the train chugged along the tracks. The landscape of the Idaho mountains rolled by and shifted with each mile. The rhythmic clatter of the wheels on the tracks became the heartbeat of their trip, a steady pulse that carried them ever closer to Crystal Village.

Michael's eyes were wide with excitement as they passed through the mountains. His imagination was alight with the possibility of bandits and outlaws lurking behind every tree. Sharon looked at her children and leaned into Bill, her hand resting lightly on his arm.

As the train emerged from the wilderness, the restored Roebling Bridge came into view and then the village itself. The train pulled alongside the new platform at the Crystal Village station and came to a stop with huge plumes of steam blooming from the engine. There were only three passenger cars behind the coal car, followed by the obligatory kaboose.

Lucy stepped off the train and onto the platform and felt a shiver of anticipation. Michael ran up behind her and slid his hand into hers, which he'd not done since he started second grade last year. She looked down at him and smiled.

The Granger family made their way into Crystal Village. The streets were filled with characters as rich and vibrant as those on the pages of Lucy's beloved books.

IIII

Lucy gazed out the window of the nursery room on the third floor of the townhouse that her family had been given for the week. She gazed across at Michael, who had settled into bed for the night.

Their parents had retired to their room downstairs, entrusting their children to the care of the village for the evening's surprise and secret special event. Sharon hadn't been able to resist teasing that some kind of surprise might be in store, which had been required to get the children to go to bed so early. Lucy, in her flannel nightgown, watched as figures appeared outside the window, silhouetted against the nighttime sky. They were fairies, dressed in iridescent costumes that shimmered with an otherworldly glow, their delicate wings shimmering as they beckoned to her. Lucy unlatched the windows and the fairies pushed them open.

The first of the two fairies stepped forward. "I'm Kori, and this is Timka. We're here to take you and Michael on an adventure."

Lucy went to Michael's bed and woke him. Michael stared at the visitors, who were coming inside the balcony doors, his eyes wide with wonder. He clutched Lucy's hand as the fairies—actors in disguise—fitted them with what they called "magic helmets." These helmets were fitted over their heads and were reminiscent of the leather caps worn by World War One fighter pilots, but more steampunk and delightful in their design with integrated "magic goggles".

There was a flutter of excitement as the fairies attached "magic wings" to the children's backs with clasps that went around their shoulders to a belt at the waist. A second belt connected between their legs to a large buckle on the chest that was fitted with an ornate, silver flower. "These wings are powered by our magic and only work when we sprinkle you with the dust of flight. Please understand that they won't work if we aren't with you, and they will only work when we say it's safe, should you try to fly," Timka explained.

All four of them stepped out onto the balcony outside the window, where the new magic goggles subtly changed everything about the world around them. Some things were brighter and easier to see, others were darker and harder to see. The fairies gave off a sparkling magical glow, and in the distance, they could see other children being helped out of their bedrooms by other fairies.

The harnesses hidden in the "wings" were attached to invisible lines that snapped into the invisible grid network that had been woven above the city. The illusion was maintained because the inconvenient reality of the harness and associated gear was erased by the magic goggles. Lucy felt a tingle of anticipation run down her spine as the fairies led her and her brother to the edge of the balcony. "Are you ready to fly?" Timka whispered in her ear. Lucy and Michael affirmed that they were. Then Kori reached into a leather bag on her belt and threw a handful of sparking, glowing fairy dust over their heads. The magic wings began to hum and vibrate, and they could see each other's bodies begin to glow and sparkle. "Fly, fly, my friends!" Kori whispered excitedly.

Lucy and Michael stepped towards the edge of the balcony with their hearts pounding. The harnesses engaged with a gentle hum. To their amazement, they soared into the air, bounding across the streets and out over the village below. They flew from rooftop to rooftop, the fairies guiding them with graceful ease. Their laughter mingled and carried with the night breeze.

The adventure took a turn as they approached the edge of the village, where the "fairy caves'" beckoned. They took one last leap into the air, and they flew all the way there, arcing smoothly towards the jutting outcropping high above the village. The entrance was a stone facade of carved intertwining roots and sparkling crystals. Timka reached into her own belt pouch and extracted a handful of dust that was pitch black. It absorbed all light and color. She sprinkled it over them, and their bodies ceased glowing. She took the opportunity to unclip their invisible flight cables. "Okay, remember that you aren't able to fly anymore—at least until we sprinkle more flight dust on you."

Michael sighed, "Oh, but that was the best thing ever."

"I think you'll have just as much fun with this next adventure," said Timka reassuringly.

Michael agreed that the caves did look exciting, and the little group walked into the fairy caves. The entrance was carved in extensive Celtic patterns, and painted in beautiful contrasting colors. Together, they followed a path deep into the mountain. Eventually, it opened into a soaring cave. On the far side of the cave a beautifully carved, silver and gold, filigreed archway opened to reveal a flume-style ride that dipped into the heart of the mountain. The magic goggles decorated and reconstituted the ride such that it seemed completely magical and not part of an amusement park ride.

Lucy and Michael boarded their boat that seemed to be hewn from an ancient tree. The fairies joined them, their luminescence casting a soft glow on the walls of the tunnel. The ride began, the boat gliding through underground rivers and caverns aglow with virtual wonders displayed by their goggles.

They passed scenes of fairy life, from artisans crafting dewdrop jewelry to dancers twirling in an underground meadow of starflowers, all rendered in breathtaking detail by the AR technology. Lucy felt as if she had stepped into a storybook, the narrative unfolding around her with each twist and turn of the ride.

At one point, they "accidentally" took a wrong turn, and Timka and Kori helped them fend off an attack by a mountain troll who was very territorial. The special effects made this entire journey feel completely real, and it was far and away more magical than anything they'd ever experienced.

Eventually, the journey came to an end. The fairies sprinkled them with more flight dust and escorted them back through the air all the way to their room. Lucy and Michael, their minds brimming with the night's enchantment, were tucked into their beds by their fairy guides. As the fairies took away their magic goggles and departed, Lucy caught a glimpse of their true faces—kind and human, yet touched by the magic they had helped create.

In the quiet that followed, Lucy lay awake, her thoughts adrift in the wonder of their flight. As she finally drifted to sleep, her dreams were filled with the laughter of fairies and the freedom of the skies.

IIII

Kisho Yomohiro stood outside the terminal of the Spokane airport. His eyes squinted against the bright sunlight, and he was greeted by a driver holding a sign with his name on it. The man wore a sharp, white, linen suit that immediately set him apart from the others. "Sinclair Lipson, at your service, Mr. Yomohiro," he introduced himself with a slight bow. Yomohiro couldn't help but feel a twinge of unease.

Once they had pulled out of the airport, the driver struck up a conversation. "You know, sir, I'm glad I have a moment of your time on this ride. I understand that your helicopter had some unexpected difficulties."

"*Hai*," replied Yomohiro, nodding curtly, trying to avoid engaging with the man.

The drive to Crystal Village was filled with Lipson's murmured stories of local discontent and technical issues plaguing the park's attractions. *For this to be true, my entire US team would have to be hiding things*, thought Yomohiro. Despite his skepticism, Yomohiro listened intently, his mind churning with the implications of Lipson's words.

Upon arriving at Crystal Village, Yomohiro's unease grew as he met with Jack. Jack's warm welcome did little to quell the doubts Lipson had sown. Yomohiro quietly but forcefully demanded to experience the attractions firsthand, his insistence brooking no argument. When Jack hesitated over the flying grid, citing concerns for Yomohiro's age, the comment stung his ego, fueling his determination to prove his vitality.

Strapped into the harness of the flying grid, Yomohiro's heart pounded with a mix of adrenaline and trepidation. As he soared above the village, any lingering doubts evaporated in the thrill of flight. The wind rushed past him, and the landscape unfolded below with breathtaking clarity. It was a moment of pure elation, a triumph that turned Lipson's dark tales into mere shadows.

Emboldened by his flight, Yomohiro ventured next into the depths of the flume ride. As before, he insisted that he be allowed to go alone, with no accompaniment. The ride, a journey into the heart of the mountain, began with the rush of water and the excitement of adventure. But as the ride progressed, a sudden bump brought everything to a halt. The power failed, plunging Yomohiro into darkness. His AR goggles, the window to the park's augmented reality, went dead, leaving him alone in the silent bowels of the earth.

In the stillness, Yomohiro's breath steadied, and he found himself enveloped by the raw power of the mountain's interior. Slowly, his eyes seemingly becoming accustomed to the dark, a faint glow began to surround the tunnel his flume boat sat in. It was then that the fairies found him—beings of grace and light affiliated with the Mountain Queen. They approached with curiosity, drawn to the artistic soul that had crafted worlds of wonder over a long life.

The fairies led Yomohiro on an unplanned tour of the underworld realm. They showed him the secrets of their kingdom, the hidden beauty that lay beyond the reach of technology. When the fairies returned him to the flume ride, they whispered enchantments that reawakened the power and restored the ride's technology-based magic.

As Yomohiro emerged from the tunnels, he was met with a flurry of concern. The team expected complaints and frustration, but instead, Yomohiro spoke of an experience that transcended expectation. He recounted his encounter with the fairies with an artist's passion, convinced it was the pinnacle of the ride's design.

Jack listened intently and captured every detail of Yomohiro's story. He was baffled as to what the man had experienced, but he loved the richness of this twist. The fairies' tour, an unintended interlude, became the seed of inspiration that would bloom within the virtual world of the game. It was a narrative twist that would enrich the lore of Crystal Village, an easter egg for players to discover and cherish.

As Yomohiro basked in the afterglow of his adventure, Jack and the team realized that sometimes the most profound experiences come from the unscripted moments, from the magic that dwells in the unexpected.

I I I I

Sinclair Lipson paced the streets of Crystal Village. With each step his cheroot left a jerking trail of smoke that mirrored his simmering frustration.

He had hoped to sway Kisho Yomohiro to see the folly of this endeavor. He had hoped to disrupt Jack Seeley and the Seeleys in general. But Yomohiro's unexpected adventure with the fairies of the mountain had only deepened his commitment to the park.

Lipson's thoughts had been a whirlwind of schemes and regrets for months. All of his plans had unraveled, and the root cause was a vendetta that felt increasingly hollow. He was beginning to realize that he was a coyote who was caught in a trap of his own making.

As he brooded, he heard a tinkle of laughter and chatter from around the corner. A swarm of children of varying ages ran into view. Their eyes were wide with the thrill of freedom and discovery that children rarely get in the world today, unsupervised exploration in a place their parents considered inherently safe. They spotted Lipson and rushed toward him with the enthusiasm and guilelessness of the young.

"Look, it's Coyote!" said a small girl. She pointed at Lipson with a mix of awe and delight. The children's perception didn't surprise Lipson in the least. Little ones often saw through his disguises. But normally, their reaction was one of fear, not delight.

The other children chimed in with effervescent excitement. "Please, Coyote, tell us a story!" "Did you really steal fire for us?" "Can you play a trick on Raven?" "Are you really married to a star?"

Lipson was taken aback, his anger momentarily forgotten as he was swept up in the children's innocent adoration. They didn't see an angry, frustrated man. They saw his true self, a mythic figure whose stories had played out for them in the virtual realm of the video game version of the park. Of course, they would expect to see him here.

For a moment, Lipson stood frozen, the reality that the park had generated was beginning to dawn on him. Then, as if a dam within him broke, he found himself softening. His heart warmed to the children who looked up at him with such earnest expectation.

"Well now," Lipson began, his voice taking on the sly, playful tone of the Coyote they knew him to be. "Did I steal fire? Oh, indeed I did. But not for mischief, my young friends! It was to bring warmth and light to the world—to help those who shivered in the cold and dark."

The children listened, spellbound, as Lipson told tales of adventure that showcased his cunning, his brave deeds and narrow escapes. He spoke of his encounters with Raven, of their rivalry and their grudging respect for one another, of their relationship that had become a kind of friendship over the centuries. It was a realization that was surprising to him in the moment he said the words. As he told the story, he felt the weight of animosity toward the Seeleys lessen, the desire for revenge blunted by the children's innocent joy in their conversation with him.

In that moment, Lipson realized that the park, with its intertwining of legend and reality, had given him a gift—a chance to remember who he was, and to be what was needed by the world. He had the opportunity to be remembered not as the embodiment of chaos, not as an immature and impetuous trickster, but as a figure of lore and lessons learned. The children's belief in him, in the character he had inspired in their game, offered a path to forgiveness and growth and change. It offered him a way of letting go of the bitterness that had clouded his existence for so long. But most importantly, it allowed him the space to see himself from the outside for the very first time in his very long existence and to understand what he could truly grow into.

As Coyote's stories came to an end, the children erupted in cheers and applause. They swarmed around Lipson, their earlier questions now transformed into expressions of gratitude and wonder. Coyote found himself basking in the warmth of their attention and joy.

With a newfound sense of purpose, Lipson decided to align himself with Jack and Susanne, with the vision of Crystal Village as a place where stories bridged the gap between past and present and the seen and unseen worlds. He even began to forgive Eoinn, to see the park not as a battleground for old grudges, but as a blank slate where new stories could be written.

The children rushed off like a flock of birds, and their laughter and happy shouts echoed through the streets of the village. Once again, Lipson stood alone, a wry smile on his lips—but this time as a trickster reborn, ready to embrace a new role for an old Coyote.

22

Legacy

The late afternoon sun cast shadows upon a clearing that surrounded one of the cave entrances to the realm under the mountain. Ríona and her mother stood facing one another. The regal mother regarded her daughter with compassion, but Ríona stared back defiantly.

The flutter of huge wings was heard above them, and Raven swooped down and landed in the clearing. His dark feathers glittered with iridescence in the setting sun. Before their eyes he transformed into his Elias Dotson form, his wings became gloved hands that emerged from the sleeves of a black duster. His head was ensconced in a tall, wide-brimmed, black hat. His body was huge, a mixture of rolls of fat encasing muscles. He was close to seven feet tall, his hat adding even more height.

"Your Majesties," Raven began, "I come to you as an arbiter, I seek balance and an end to this conflict." His voice was deep and resonant, and his former weariness was replaced with a renewed sense of purpose.

The Mountain Queen nodded. "Raven, your counsel is most welcome. The Princess has let her passions guide her actions. She is risking the harmony of our realm."

Ríona trembled with barely contained anger. "Mother, it is our legacy that is at stake! The humans, their machines, their technology, their stories—this park—it's changing everything!"

Raven tilted his head, oddly birdlike. He regarded the Princess with ancient eyes. "Princess, the humans do indeed spin their stories, and this invites change, and change is frightening and difficult. But remember that our stories are the bedrock upon which theirs are built. They give voice to our stories, ensuring we are remembered, ensuring we endure. This brings with it a kind of leavening that is renewing and powerful. Do not let your fear of change cause you to throw away the opportunities it brings."

A rustling in the underbrush announced the arrival of Coyote. He leapt over a log as he entered the clearing, and transformed midair into his Sinclair Lipson form. He fluidly pulled a long, brown cheroot from a bag at his hip and lit it by striking a match on his belt. He puffed smoke a few times before speaking.

Coyote said, "My friends, I have had a realization, an epiphany. I was wrong about this place. It is not a bad thing, this Crystal Village. It is a renewal of our relationship with the world around us. It strengthens what and who we are. It does not wrest control away from us, and it does not insult our role in the world. I have seen the positive change it can bring with my own eyes."

Ríona spun to face Coyote, her eyes were blazing with anger. "Betrayal! You would have us believe that our stories are safe in their hands? That they honor us and do not ensnare us?!"

Coyote met her gaze coolly. "Princess, I once sought to stop them. I had been denied and thwarted by Eoinn Seeley, who I did not trust, who I felt didn't offer me respect. I let my pride and anger build into a flaming inferno that threatened to destroy the land. And I could have gone on to destroy the entire world if Seeley hadn't stopped me. I was wrong to react that way, and it has taken me until now to understand that. I have repeated the same negative cycle over and over for hundreds of years. I have seen the joy, the reverence held for our stories. They're not binding us to some outside notion of who we are, they're freeing us to change, to grow, to become something new, something better."

The Queen let out a sigh. "Daughter, we must consider the possibility of coexistence, of a symbiosis that strengthens both our stories and theirs.

We would not be here without them."

The Princess looked panic stricken and felt her conviction wavering. She turned her gaze to the cave entrance, then to the forest. "I cannot abide by this. They diminish our sovereignty! They bind us to their stories in a way that binds us to them! They force change upon that which never changes, which never should change!"

Raven spread his arms in a gesture that caused his duster to flow outward like wings. "Our sovereignty is not diminished by sharing our stories. The more our stories are shared, the greater our connection to the world. The greater our strength. The method is as important as the message. Their approach is inherently dynamic. It is always changing, shifting, and retelling our tales in a way that reflects the way the seasons change, the way the world itself changes over time. To not change, to resist change, to be always the same is a trap. Do you not feel the strength of these small changes flow through you? It is empowering! It is invigorating!"

The Princess felt her resolve hardening, her uncertainty turning back to anger. She looked from her mother to Raven and finally to Coyote, whose words echoed in her mind. A plan took root there. She closed her eyes and let out a guttural growl. With a swift motion, she turned and fled into the forest.

The Mountain Queen spoke. "Raven, Coyote, our task remains unchanged. We guide, we influence, we watch. But we do not destroy that which seeks to honor us."

Coyote nodded and bowed his head. Raven gave a solemn nod. "So it shall be."

I I I I

Eoinn walked alone through the quiet streets, his footsteps echoing softly against the stones of Broadway. The village slept peacefully around him, guests and staff alike unaware of the restless energy that had drawn him from his bed. It was approaching two in the morning.

He followed the familiar route past the mining offices, up the gentle slope past the community meal hall. The air grew warmer as he approached, carrying the faint medicinal tang of the hot springs. Steam rose from the natural pools like ghostly fingers. This place had always been sacred to him—a meeting ground between worlds, where the boundaries grew thin and ancient powers could gather.

She was waiting for him beside the largest pool, her long, blonde hair flowing like liquid starlight. The Queen stood with her back to him, her presence commanding even in stillness. In the steam-hazed air, her voice carried differently. Somehow it was more intimate, as if the mist itself conspired to keep their words secret.

"Ye felt it too," he said quietly, his Irish accent thickening as it always did in her presence.

She turned, her ageless face marked with worry. "The disturbance in the deep places. Aye, old friend. The mountain itself cries out in pain."

Eoinn moved to stand beside her at the pool's edge. The warm water rippled with each breath of steam that whisked from its surface. "How bad is it, then?" he asked.

"Worse than ye know," she replied. Her voice carried the weight of centuries, but now it trembled. "My daughter has found the old paths. She means to draw power from sources that should never be tapped." She wrapped her arms around herself, as if fighting off a chill despite the warm air.

"Ríona." The name tasted bitter on his tongue. "I had hoped she would find peace after ... after what happened with Glory."

The Queen's laugh held no humor, and she turned away from him to stare into the steaming water. "Peace? She burns with *rage*, Eoinn. The stories your descendant tells, the games they play—she sees them as chains binding our kind to human whims." She gestured toward the village below, her hand shaking slightly. "She believes the only way to break free is to destroy what ye have built here."

Steam swirled between them as Eoinn absorbed this news. He had known this day might come, had prepared for it in his way. But hearing the threat spoken aloud made it real in a way that mere possibility never could.

"Fire," he said. It wasn't a question.

"Aye." The Queen stepped closer to the pool's edge, and the water began to darken, showing images that made Eoinn's breath catch. Flames racing through forests, mountains glowing like coals, the village reduced to ash and memory. "She has studied the old texts, learned the words that can wake the sleeping anger of the mountains. If she succeeds in her working ..."

"The entire region burns." Eoinn watched the visions play out in the water, his heart heavy. "Not just Crystal Village. Everything from here to—"

"Everything," she confirmed, and the images dissolved back into clear water. "And she will not listen to reason. Not from me, not from anyone. The corruption has already begun to touch her mind, Eoinn. I've lost her."

Her shoulders sagged with the weight of a mother's grief. Eoinn reached out instinctively, his hand settling gently on her shoulder, offering what comfort he could.

"What would ye have me do?" he asked, though he already knew the answer.

"Tell them." Her voice was firm despite her distress. "Your great-great-grandson and the O'Connor girl. They have the blood, the connection to the old ways. They can help ye stand against what's coming."

"They don't know what they are. Jack thinks he's merely human, and Susanne—"

"Has been having dreams," the Queen interrupted. The Queen's eyes glittered with ancient knowledge. "I've been watching her sleep, watching her dream. Dreams of fairies and ravens, of caves filled with light. I feel a strong connection to this one. The strongest since Mary, the first human I ever loved. The awakening has already begun in her. It needs only guidance to bloom into true power."

Eoinn felt the familiar weight of leadership settling on his shoulders, heavier now after a century of quiet caretaking. The role of protector, of teacher, of the one who must burden others with terrible knowledge—it felt like putting on armor that no longer fit.

"How long do we have?"

"Days at most, perhaps hours. She gathers power with each passing minute, and the corruption spreads through her like poison." The Queen stepped closer to him, her hand briefly touching his arm. The contact sent warmth through him, a reminder of older, gentler times. "There is something else ye must know. An old rival walks among you."

"Coyote." Eoinn's voice hardened. "I've been watching him, waiting for him to come for me—"

"He is not what he once was." Her interruption was gentle but firm. "The years have changed him, as they have changed us all. There may be hope … for alliance rather than enmity."

"After what he did to the village?! To the whole region? After he nearly—"

"After what we *all* did. The old feuds serve no purpose now, Eoinn. If Ríona succeeds, there will be nothing left to fight over! Nothing left to protect."

The truth of her words settled into his bones. The luxury of old grudges was one they could no longer afford.

"I'll speak to Jack and Susanne tonight," he said finally, dreading the words even as he spoke them. "They deserve to know what's coming." He paused, looking down at the peaceful village. "Gods help me, once I tell them, their innocence dies forever."

The Queen nodded, her face etched with understanding. "Be gentle with the revelation, old friend. The truth of what they are will be burden enough without the weight of our fears added to it."

She began to walk back toward the forest path, her footsteps silent on the heated stones. As she reached the edge of the clearing, she paused and looked back at him. "Remember, Eoinn—they are stronger than they know. As are you."

Then she disappeared into the shadows between the trees, leaving only the scent of mountain flowers and the soft sound of water lapping at stone. Eoinn remained by the hot springs, looking up at the stars, at the peaceful village spread below. He steeled himself for the conversation that would forever change two lives and remake them into something far more dangerous.

The armor of leadership settled fully onto his shoulders. After a century of hiding, Eoinn Seeley was about to step back into the light.

I I I I

The balcony of the Hawthorne Hotel offered a perfect view of Crystal Village under moonlight. Jack and Susanne sat together on the bench outside their room. The other rooms on this floor were reserved for employees of Yomohiro Corporation but were vacant tonight. They'd both woken up from a deep sleep filled with nightmares and came outside together to process and let the adrenaline wear off.

"I still can't believe this is real sometimes," Susanne said softly, her hand finding Jack's.

Jack squeezed her fingers gently and laughed. "Which part feels most impossible?"

"All of it. The fact that our families built this place, that we found each other again, that we're actually making it work." She leaned back against him. "Sometimes I feel like I'm living inside one of the fairy tales in Mrs. O'Hara's journal."

"Maybe you are." The voice came from the doorway of the room next to theirs, and they turned to see Ian stepping onto the balcony. But something was different about him—he moved with more purpose, his shoulders straighter despite his age.

"Ian," Jack said, gesturing to an empty chair. "Couldn't sleep either?"

"No, lad. And it's not Ian ye should be calling me." Eoinn settled into the chair, his eyes reflecting the starlight in a way that seemed almost otherworldly. "There are things ye need to know, both of ye. Things I should have told ye long ago."

Susanne felt a chill that had nothing to do with the mountain air. "What kind of things?" she asked hesitantly.

Eoinn was quiet for a long moment, as if choosing his words carefully.

When he spoke, his voice carried a faint Irish accent that neither of them had heard before.

"My name is not Ian Seeley, your distant cousin. I am Eoinn Seeley, the founder of Crystal Village, your great-great-grandfather, Jack. And I've been here for more than a century, watching over this place, waiting for the day when I would be needed again."

Jack stuttered, "That's impossible. You'd have to be—"

"Quite old, yes." Eoinn's smile was sad. "Impossible for a human, perhaps. But I was never exactly human, Jack. None of my men were."

Susanne leaned forward, her mind already connecting pieces of a puzzle she hadn't known existed. "The stories. Mrs. O'Hara's journal entries … about fairies. The way certain people seemed to live longer than they should have."

"Aye, lass. Ye've always been quick to see the truth hiding behind the tales." Eoinn's accent grew stronger as he shed the pretense of being merely human. "We called ourselves *Tuath Dúchais*—the exiled nobility. Cast out from the fairy courts for choosing human bonds over pure blood."

"Fairy courts." Jack's voice was flat with disbelief. "You're telling us that fairies are real—and that we're descended from them? Seriously?"

"Not fairies as the children's stories paint them. We are beings of earth and light, of deep magic and older wisdom. Some humans called us elves, others dwarves, some knew us as the fair folk or the hidden people. Some thought of us as angels, others as demons. All names for the same truth— we were the first children of this world, before humanity learned to dream of us in diminished forms."

Eoinn reached out and placed a hand on each of their shoulders. The touch sent a jolt through them both, like lightning contained in flesh.

"The exile made us stronger, not weaker. When we chose love over law, connection over isolation, we gained something our pure-blooded kin never possessed—the ability to grow, to change, to become more than we were born to be."

Susanne felt something stirring within her. "The dreams I've been having. The way I sometimes know things I shouldn't know."

"Your gift awakening," Eoinn confirmed with a wry smile. "Through Liam's line, ye carry the sight—the ability to perceive what others cannot, to speak to those who dwell between worlds. Mrs. O'Hara had a similar gift, but hers came from living alongside the hidden folk and her friendship to them. Yours runs deeper, carried in your very blood. And a more mystical connection; Mary O'Hara became a member of the O'Connor family when she moved in with Sam and Seamus. There's a straight through-line from her friendship with the Mountain Queen and you as a descendant of her chosen family."

Jack's skepticism warred with a growing sense of innate recognition. The connection he'd always felt to this place, the way the mountain seemed to respond to his presence, the dreams of golden light flowing through stone ...

"And me?" he asked quietly.

"Ye are the sole heir to my line and a member of the lineage of Angus Sullivan. The mountain knows your blood, Jack. The hot springs, the caves, the veins of gold and silver—they recognize ye as kin. Ye can speak to the bones of the earth itself, feel the heartbeat of the mountain, ask it to remember winter's cold or summer's warmth."

As if summoned by his words, Jack felt something shift in his perception. He got a flickering sense of the network of caves beneath the village, the flow of underground streams, and the slow pulse of the mountain's ancient heart. It was overwhelming ... and exhilarating in equal measure. And then ... it was gone before he was able to explore its full dimensions.

"Why tell us now?" Susanne asked, though part of her already knew the answer.

Eoinn's expression grew grave. "Because danger is coming. The Mountain Queen came to me tonight with a warning. Her daughter Ríona means to destroy Crystal Village, to burn it and everything around it with fires drawn from the earth's molten core."

"The same Ríona from Sam's journal?" Jack's mind raced, trying to process the implications. "She's still *alive*?"

"Aye! Alive and consumed with rage. She sees the stories you tell, the games you've created, as chains binding her kind to human whims. She believes the only way to break free is through destruction. And she hates you in particular, Susanne. She had an infatuation with Glory O'Connor and tried to take her into the mountain kingdom. I intervened, doing battle with those who tried to take her. It led to a feud with her mother and the rest of the hidden folk under the mountain for many years. She has resented the O'Connors ever since and frequently was a bane to Liam after the great fire. She means to burn this all."

Susanne's enhanced perception suddenly flared, showing her glimpses of the future—walls of flame racing through the forest, the village consumed by heat that could melt stone, and the mountain itself turned into a volcanic weapon of devastation.

"When?" she gasped.

"Soon. Days, perhaps hours. She's already begun the working, drawing power from sources that should never be touched." Eoinn said, sadly. "The corruption spreads through her like poison, and with each passing moment, she grows more dangerous—to us, to herself, to everything within a few hundred miles."

The three sat in silence for a moment, the peaceful village below them suddenly feeling terribly fragile, its future existence tenuous at best. A light breeze stirred the air, carrying the scent of pine.

"What do we do?" Jack asked finally.

Eoinn stood, his posture straighter than it had been in decades. "We prepare. We learn. We remember what we are." He looked down at them both with something like an apology in his eyes. "The awakening won't be gentle, I'm afraid. Your heritage has been dormant too long. But you have strength ye don't yet know, connections to this land that run deep."

Susanne felt the truth of his words resonating in her bones. "Will it be enough?"

"It will have to be." Eoinn moved toward the door, then paused. "Get what rest you can. Tomorrow we begin your true education. And tomorrow …" He looked out over the village one last time. "Tomorrow, everything changes."

As he disappeared into the doorway of the room next to theirs, Jack and Susanne remained on the balcony, hands clasped, staring out at the village that had become their home. The stars above seemed brighter now, as if responding to the awakening magic in their blood.

"Are you afraid?" Susanne whispered.

Jack considered the question. "Terrified!" he admitted. "But also ... alive. For the first time in my life, everything makes sense."

She squeezed his hand. "Then we face it together."

Below them, Crystal Village slept on, unaware of the danger that loomed.

I I I I

The cathedral of ancient cedars stood like a natural temple, their massive trunks rising hundreds of feet into a canopy so thick it filtered the morning light into green-gold streams. The air here felt different—older, charged with an energy that made the hair on Jack's arms stand on end. A small stream bubbled nearby, its voice the only sound besides their footsteps on the soft ground.

Eoinn led them deeper into the grove, his movements graceful and strong. The transformation that had begun the night before continued—his white hair had darkened to steel gray, and the lines on his face seemed less pronounced. He moved like a man decades younger, with purpose that spoke of authority long dormant.

"This place has always been sacred," he said, his Irish accent now permanent. "The trees remember when the world was young. The barriers between realms is thin here."

Susanne felt it immediately—a tingling in her fingertips, a sense of presence just beyond the edge of vision. "Something's watching us."

"Someone," Eoinn corrected with a slight smile. "Finn, ye can stop lurking. They need to see ye as ye truly are."

A figure stepped out from behind one of the massive cedars. It was Finn McEnhill, but like Eoinn, he seemed transformed. Gone was the quiet demeanor of the actor they'd hired. This Finn moved with predatory grace, his eyes reflecting depths that spoke of centuries lived rather than decades.

"Jack, Susanne," Finn said, his voice carrying tones that seemed to resonate with the trees themselves. "Time we met properly."

Jack stared. "You're not the actor we hired … but you are."

"I am Finn McEnhill," he replied, stepping fully into the filtered sunlight. "The original. When ye began casting for the role, I couldn't resist the irony of auditioning to play myself."

Susanne's enhanced perception showed her the truth—this man carried the same otherworldly energy as Eoinn, the same connection to forces beyond mortal understanding. "You're *Tuath Dúchais* too."

"Aye, lass. Exiled for the same crime as the rest—choosing human bonds over pure blood." Finn smiled. "Though in my case, the choice involved a certain fondness for architecture, mechanical things, and frankly, for battle, that my pure-blooded kin found … distasteful."

Eoinn gestured for them all to sit on a fallen log that formed a natural bench. "Finn has a gift for working with elemental forces. His specialty is fire, primarily, though he can coax cooperation from earth and air when needed."

"And you're going to teach us," Jack said. It wasn't a question.

"We're going to try," Finn replied. "Though I'll warn ye—awakening dormant heritage isn't gentle. It's like learning to use muscles ye never knew ye had. And you'll never be the same again."

Eoinn placed his hands on the ground, and immediately the earth around them began to glow with faint green light. "Jack, place your palms on the earth. Feel for the mountain's heartbeat."

Jack knelt and pressed his hands to the needle-covered ground. At first, nothing happened. Then, gradually, he began to sense something—a vast, slow pulse that seemed to come from deep within the mountain itself. "I feel a pulse!" Jack exclaimed in awe.

"Good," Eoinn murmured. "Now ask it to show ye the network beneath us. The caves, the streams, the veins of precious metal."

Jack closed his eyes and reached out with senses he'd never known he possessed. Suddenly, his perception exploded outward. He could feel the vast network of caves beneath Crystal Village, and throughout the mountains, he felt the flow of underground rivers and the deposits of gold and silver that had first drawn his ancestors here. It was like suddenly being able to see in all directions at once. He gasped and sat up, shaking his hands.

"Overwhelming, isn't it?" Eoinn's voice seemed to come from very far away. "The mountain wants to share everything with ye at once. Learn to ask for small pieces at a time."

Jack put his hands back on the ground and closed his eyes, concentrating. Golden light was flowing from his hands into the ground, racing outward like veins of precious metal. Where it touched, the forest floor began to glow with the same warm radiance.

"Remarkable," Finn breathed. "I've never seen such a strong connection on first awakening."

Eoinn turned to Susanne. "Your turn, lass. But your gift works differently. Close your eyes, and tell me what ye see beyond sight."

Susanne obeyed, closing her eyes, but she did not see or feel anything. Finn reached over and placed his hand gently on her head, and immediately her perception shifted. The physical world became transparent, revealing layers of reality she'd never imagined. She could see the life force of the trees, the ancient spirits that dwelt within the grove, and something else— threads of silver light connecting all living things.

"I can see ... connections," she whispered. "Lines of light between everything. They're beautiful."

"Those are the bonds that tie all life together," Eoinn explained. "Through Liam's line and your connection to Mrs. O'Hara's friendship with the Mountain Queen, ye can perceive them, even influence them. Try reaching out to one of the trees."

Susanne extended her awareness toward the nearest cedar. The ancient tree's consciousness was vast and slow, filled with memories of centuries. She felt its welcome, its recognition of her heritage. When she opened her eyes, silver light was flowing from her fingertips, creating patterns in the air that seemed to write themselves across the morning mist.

"Both of ye are stronger than I dared hope," Eoinn said, pride evident in his voice. "But strength without *control* is dangerous. Finn will teach ye to harness these gifts, to use them with precision rather than raw force."

Finn stood, his hands beginning to glow with controlled flame. "The first lesson is always the same—respect the power, don't try to dominate it. Work with the elements as partners, not tools."

Jack felt the mountain's presence still thrumming through his connection to the earth. "How long do we have to learn this?"

"Not long enough," Eoinn admitted. "But ye have advantages your ancestors didn't. Ye've got Finn, and ye've got me. The village itself will help—it was built on sacred ground, with respect for the old ways. The stones remember, the springs know their purpose. When the time comes, Crystal Village will fight alongside us."

Susanne looked between the two ancient beings who had become their teachers. "And Ríona? What happens when she comes?"

Finn's expression grew grim. "We remind her that some fires burn too hot for any single being to control. And if that fails ..." He let controlled flame dance between his fingers. "We show her the power of old blood."

The morning light shifted through the canopy, and somewhere in the distance, a raven called—a sound that seemed to carry both warning and promise in the mountain air.

I I I I

In the pre-dawn gloom, Ríona stood in a forest clearing deep in a valley of the Idaho mountains. It was a place where multiple ley lines intersected, creating a steady source of power for her to draw upon. Her delicate features were twisted in a snarl of determination.

The air around her wavered and crackled with arcane power as she cast her spell. Her voice rose and fell in an ancient incantation in an unknown language. Her hands moved with precision. She drew symbols in the air with her fingers that hovered and glowed with a baleful light. She called forth a fire that would cleanse the land.

As the final words of the spell left her lips, the ground trembled. Deep within the earth a rumble began, and the forest floor cracked open, unleashing a roaring fire. It grew quickly and fed on Ríona's rage until a wall of flame erupted out into the trees on the edge of the clearing. The fire surged and raced through the underbrush, leaping from tree to tree, moving through the valley and up towards Crystal Village.

Ríona watched with a mixture of triumph and horror as the eldritch fire she had birthed spread across the mountains. It created a conflagration that devoured everything in its path. The flames roared in the direction of Crystal Village, the heat so intense that it seemed to warp the very air.

I I I I

The first hints of smoke arrived in the village just as Jack and Susanne stirred awake. They emerged from their room onto the balcony to see the sky turning a sickly orange, the smell of burning wood growing stronger by the second. Jack called the command center on his cell phone and warned them that fire was coming. A loud alarm rang out, calling the village to action.

Jack and Susanne rallied the villagers and organized a desperate defense against the approaching inferno. The fire brigade was summoned, and they deployed the hidden fire suppression systems that were charged with fire retardant foam. But there was no pressure in the system. No amount of tinkering could force the system to pressurize, and ultimately, they gave up.

The decision was made to load the train and evacuate the village. Once again, alarms rang out, and the voice of the command center called to guests and staff telling them to leave their belongings and to proceed immediately to the train. The training of the team paid off, and less than twenty minutes after the call went out, the train was loaded with guests and team members and was ready to leave the station headed back down to Kellogg.

As the train was being loaded, Eoinn approached Jack and Susanne. "The time has come," Eoinn said. "Once everyone is safely away, we will go and make our stand."

Jack and Susanne nodded, indicating that they understood. Yet both of them felt the cold grip of fear in the pit of their stomach. The train slowly began to pull away. Jack and Susanne looked at each other, knowing that their last chance to run was leaving with the others. The train began to speed up and moved away from them. Jack sighed. At least all of the guests and employees had been successfully evacuated.

As the fire raged closer, Eoinn walked towards the edge of the village, heading west on Spring Street, past the Seeley Mining Company office building, and up behind it into the forest. Jack and Susanne followed. They paused on a slight rise overlooking the village on the edge of the forest. It was near where the mountain rose at the edge of the cove of land on which the village stood, to the northwest of the town square, behind the mining company offices. In the distance, the mountains gave way to valleys and the Montana border. The fire was approaching from this direction, stampeding towards them like a runaway herd of buffalo.

The wind began swirling and intermittently blowing in the direction of the fire, feeding the flames. The air was beginning to fill with smoke and floating embers. In the distance, a chorus of crackling flames could be heard—and was growing in intensity.

Susanne reached out and grasped Jack's hand. There was a strength in her grip.

Eoinn's gaze was steady as he looked out over the mountains and the village. This fire reminded him of the great fire that had signaled the end of Crystal Village the first time. He was adamant that this time there would be a different ending to the story.

Susanne looked at Jack with a quiet confidence, as if she knew some secret plan that would save them all. He was afraid. Yet somehow, seeing the look in Susanne's eyes, he felt a sense of calm begin to grow from within his chest.

The air grew tense, electric with the anticipation of the looming con-frontation. The fire raged while they waited, a monstrous entity that sought to devour all in its path. Jack, Susanne, and Eoinn stood watching the forest, the tension growing as the fire approached. The smoke was growing thicker, and embers and ashes rained down like hail.

A figure emerged from the shadows. It was Sinclair Lipson, his white suit still immaculate in the dim light. His arrival was both unexpected and unsettling, yet he approached the trio with an air of sincerity that gave them pause.

"Lipson," Jack addressed him, his voice laced with skepticism, "what are you doing here?"

Lipson's eyes, normally angry and condescending, held a look that Jack had never seen on him before. He looked repentant.

"Jack, I've come to realize that the path of destruction is not the way. Ríona threatens all we hold dear! I have come to help you save the village because I cannot stand by and watch our stories turn to ash!"

Jack stared at him in confusion. He turned to Susanne, then to Eoinn, hoping for answers.

Eoinn watched the newcomer closely. "You speak of saving the village, Coyote. How can we trust you? Hell man, you were responsible for the first fire that threatened this village a century ago! I was the one who had to save it! It wouldn't even be here if it was up to you! Why the change of heart now?"

Jack's head snapped up when Eoinn referred to Lipson as Coyote, and his mouth dropped open. Susanne somehow seemed to have already known, her expression thoughtful rather than surprised. Jack met Susanne's eyes and mouthed, *Coyote?!* Susanne made her eyes big, and shrugged her shoulders.

Coyote's gaze shifted to the ground, as if searching for the words to explain his transformation. "Eoinn, you know that I've walked this land for eons. Sometimes reveling in the chaos I created. In the past, I would do something stupid and obstinate, but always I would learn from those mistakes and change my ways. Somehow in the last few hundred years, I've been just as obstinate, just as selfish, but somewhere along the way, I lost my ability to learn, to change. But watching the village come to life again, hearing and watching my stories retold and renewed, seeing the joy and wonder that they bring ... It has awakened something within me. I want to protect that, not destroy it."

As he spoke, Coyote's own form began to shift subtly. His edges seemed to blur slightly, and there was something in his movements that suggested barely contained wildness, as if his human appearance was a costume he wore rather than his true nature.

Jack gaped at Lipson, and looked at the others to see if they were reacting to what Jack was seeing. They weren't.

Susanne turned to Lipson. "How do we stop Ríona?"

Coyote's expression hardened. "She is the daughter of the Mountain Queen. Ríona was born here in the mountain kingdom of her mother. Together, we can stop her. Let me join you, and work together with you instead of against you."

At that moment, Finn McEnhill stepped out of the forest. He moved with the grace of someone who had never truly aged, whose body remembered battles fought with more than mortal weapons.

"You need someone who knows how to fight fire with fire!" Finn said, confidently.

"Finn," Eoinn breathed, relief evident in the tone of his voice. "I was getting worried—"

"You knew good and well that I'd show up when things got interesting." Finn's smile was sharp as a blade. "When have I ever let you face the dangerous ones alone?"

Eoinn nodded his recognition that Finn had a valid point.

With a crackling sound, the flames began cresting the rise ahead of them. The heat distorted the air like a desert mirage, and the roar grew deafening. Eoinn turned back to Lipson and nodded to acknowledge that he'd heard him and accepted his offer of help. "We'll take all the help we can get, Coyote!" he yelled above the fire's roar.

The fire ahead of them leapt higher, and within the flames, they could see a figure taking shape. Ríona emerged from the inferno, her delicate features twisted with rage, her hair streaming out in all directions like liquid flame.

"SEELEYS!" her voice boomed across the valley. "YOU HAVE TAKEN OUR STORIES AND MADE THEM YOUR PLAYTHINGS! YOU HAVE BOUND US TO YOUR NARRATIVES LIKE PETS IN A CAGE!"

Eoinn stepped forward, his voice carrying clearly despite the roar of flames. "Ríona! You were welcomed here once! Your mother and I made peace long ago! Why do you break that covenant now?"

"Because you have forgotten what you are!" she screamed back. "You hide behind human faces and pretend to be mortal! You let them turn our sacred tales into entertainment! You allow them to bind me and my people with their tales. Where is your pride? Where is your power?"

The fire surged forward like a living thing. Eoinn raised his hands, and a barrier of cool, green light sprang up between them and the flames. "Jack," Eoinn yelled out as he strained to maintain the magical barrier, "place your hand on the ground, lad! Feel what lies beneath!"

Jack knelt and pressed his palm to the earth. The sensation was immediate and utterly overwhelming—he could feel the mountain's slow heartbeat, the network of caves and streams, and the deposits of precious metals that had drawn his ancestors here. He could see in all directions at once.

"Good!" Eoinn cried out, sweat beading on his forehead as he maintained the barrier. "Now speak to it! Ask the mountain to remember the cold of its depths!"

Jack closed his eyes and reached out with senses he'd never known he possessed. He felt the village's foundations, built on bedrock that had stood for millennia. He asked the stone to remember winter, to recall the ice that had filled these valleys in winters past. Golden light began to flow from his hands into the ground.

Susanne watched in amazement as the light raced beneath the village like veins of golden fire. Where it touched, the advancing flames slowed and cooled.

"Susanne!" Eoinn shouted, his voice strained. "Look with more than your eyes! See what drives this fire!"

Susanne didn't know how she did it, but something shifted in her perception. The flames became transparent, and she could see the rage that fueled them—Ríona's fury made manifest but also something else. Pain. Loneliness. The fear that she and her kind were being controlled, chained by the power created by the storytelling across the village and the game worlds.

"She's not just angry," Susanne said. "She's afraid."

"Fear can be more dangerous than rage," Coyote observed, his own form continuing to blur at the edges as his true nature wrestled to assert itself. "It makes creatures do things they would never consider in their right minds."

The fire pressed hard against Eoinn's barrier, testing its strength, searching for a way through. Cracks of orange light began to appear in the green shield.

"This is just the first wave," Eoinn warned with a grunt, his body taxed with the exertion of his power. "She's measuring our strength, seeing how we respond. The real attack—"

His words were cut off as the flames suddenly intensified, roaring up toward the sky in a column that dwarfed the trees. Ríona's body rose up within the fire, no longer fully solid, her form flickering between that of a woman and a living flame.

"You think your little magic can stop me?" she taunted. "I draw power from the mountain's heart, from the same sources that feed your precious hot springs!"

His energy almost overwhelmed, Eoinn's barrier flickered and began to fail. "Jack! Susanne, Finn—you need to link with me! Join your power to mine."

Jack, Susanne and Finn each lay their hands on Eoinn. The moment their skin touched Eoinn's, energy flowed between them like lightning seeking ground. Jack's golden light merged with Susanne's emerging silver radiance and Eoinn's deep, green glow. From Finn poured another energy, a fire that vibrated at a different frequency than the one attacking them. Coyote stepped closer, placed his hands on Eoinn's back, and from him flowed an auburn sheen that merged with their combined power, creating a wall of force that pushed back against the flames.

The effort was tremendous—and exhausting! Jack could feel Eoinn's strength flowing out of him like water through a broken dam.

"How long can we hold this?" Susanne gasped, feeling the tremendous drain as their combined energies fought against Ríona's assault.

"Not long enough," Eoinn admitted through gritted teeth, sweat streaming down his face. "We need ..."

The fire suddenly exploded outward, splitting into multiple streams of destruction. Each tendril moved with deadly intelligence, probing for weaknesses in their defense. One serpent-like tendril of flame coiled around their barrier and struck at the village's edge. Another rose high into the air, preparing to rain fire down from above.

Jack felt the mountain's confusion as two forces pulled at its power simultaneously. Through his connection to the bedrock, he could sense Ríona's violent demands, her attempts to tear energy from the earth's deep places. But he could also feel the mountain's resistance, its desire to protect what had been built with love and respect.

"She's fighting me for the mountain itself," Jack gasped, golden light flickering as he struggled to maintain his connection. "We're both drawing from the same source."

"The mountain will choose," Eoinn said, his voice strained but certain. "It knows the difference between taking and asking, between violation and partnership."

Jack pressed deeper into his connection with the bedrock, not demanding power but requesting aid. The response was immediate—the cobblestones of Broadway began to glow with warm golden light. The hot springs sent up clouds of cooling mist that rose to meet the flames. From the mine entrances came blessed, cold air that flowed through the village like a protective breath.

Crystal Village was fighting back.

Ríona felt the mountain's rejection of her methods immediately. Her flames flickered as the land itself began to resist her violent attempts to extract its power.

"Impossible!" she snarled. "The mountain cannot choose sides!"

"It already chose—long ago!" Eoinn called back. "When my men and I bound our essence to this place! When we built in harmony with the land, instead of seeking dominance over it!"

The fire around Ríona began to waver, but instead of retreating, her expression hardened with desperate fury. She dropped to the ground and plunged her hands deep into the earth, her scream of effort echoing across the valley.

"Then I will take what it will not give!" she cried out. "I will tear the power from its very core!"

The ground beneath her cracked and began to glow with an ugly, red light. She was no longer asking the mountain for its strength—she was violating it, ripping energy from sources never meant to be touched by living beings.

"She's going for the deep fire!" Finn called out, his face pale as he watched the spreading fissures. "The molten heart of the earth itself!"

Jack felt the mountain's agony through their connection. Ríona's assault was like daggers driven into living flesh, and the pain was overwhelming. But worse than the pain was what Jack could sense spreading through the underground networks—corruption racing toward populated areas throughout the region.

"She's not just threatening the village," he gasped. "The whole Coeur d'Alene region—maybe beyond. The corruption is spreading through every underground channel."

The temperature climbed noticeably as cracks spread outward from Ríona's position. Steam began to rise from the fissures, but this wasn't the clean mist of the hot springs—this was superheated vapor carrying the stench of sulfur and burning rock.

Ríona's transformation accelerated. Her hair became literal flame, her skin took on the appearance of molten rock, and her eyes blazed with stolen fire. But there was something wrong with the power she'd claimed—it fought against her even as it consumed her.

"Help me," she whispered, and for a moment, her true self was visible through the elemental fury. "I can't ... I can't stop it."

Then the corruption surged back, and she was lost again in forces beyond her control.

"Too late," she said, her voice now carrying the rumble of earthquakes. "I am become fire itself! Let us see how your pathetic magics fare against the power that forged the mountains!"

She raised her transformed hands, and the earth erupted. Geysers of corrupted steam shot up around them. The cracks raced outward toward the village like fingers of destruction, and Jack could feel the mountain screaming in agony as its deep places were violated.

This was no longer a battle they could win through coordination or clever tactics. This was raw, stolen power unleashed without wisdom or restraint—the kind of force that could turn the entire region into a wasteland of ash and molten rock.

Eoinn looked at his companions—Jack struggling desperately to maintain his connection to the wounded mountain, Susanne backing away from the expanding zone of corruption, Finn preparing for what might be his final stand, and Coyote now fully in animal form, circling like a predator seeking an opening that might not exist.

The old guardian made his decision.

"Get back!" he commanded, stepping forward toward the expanding inferno. "All of you, get back now!"

"Eoinn, no!" Finn called out, understanding immediately what his friend intended. "There has to be another way!"

"There is no other way!" Eoinn bellowed, his voice carrying calm certainty. "She's beyond reasoning now. The corruption has taken hold. If I don't stop her, she'll burn everything from here to the ocean!"

He began to walk toward Ríona, each step taking him deeper into the zone of impossible heat. The disguise of mortality began to fall away—his white hair darkened to a dark brown, his lined face smoothed, and his eyes blazed with the green fire of growing things.

"Ríona!" he called out, his voice somehow carrying clearly through the roar of flames. "This isn't what you wanted!"

For a moment, the flames around her flickered, and something almost human looked out through the elemental fury.

"It's too late," she said, tears of liquid fire streaming down her transformed face. "The power won't let me go."

Eoinn raised his hands, and his voice rang out with the authority of centuries. "I call upon the compact made between the *Tuath Dúchais* and this land! The agreement sealed in blood and starlight! I offer my life force to restore the balance!"

The mountain responded immediately. Through Jack's connection, he felt the land's deep gratitude, its recognition of an ancient oath being fulfilled. Power flowed up from the earth's heart—not the corrupted fire Ríona had stolen but the clean, green energy of the earth itself.

Eoinn became a conduit for that power. Emerald light erupted from him like a dam bursting, washing over the valley in waves of healing energy. Where his light touched the corrupted fissures, they sealed. A beam of green light shot from Eoinn, directly into Ríona, who was hovering fifty feet in the air. She flew backwards, out of view. They heard her crash into the trees on the other side of the clearing.

The mountain's mist rose higher, carrying the scent of pine and growing things. Cool air flowed from every cave and mine shaft, turning the superheated air breathable again. The village itself began to glow—not just the cobblestones, but every building, every street, every carefully tended garden.

Crystal Village was alive, and it was fighting for its survival.

The fire met Eoinn's power and screamed. Steam rose in towering billows as corruption battled purity, as violation met healing, as the earth's wounded depths were offered restoration instead of further harm. For a moment that stretched like eternity, the two forces were perfectly matched.

Then Eoinn's light began to overwhelm the flames. The emerald radiance spread outward in waves, each pulse driving back the fire, cooling the superheated air, sealing the cracks that had opened in the earth. The corruption racing through the underground networks slowed, stopped, and began to reverse itself.

But the cost was everything. Everything Eoinn had, everything he was.

As the last of the corrupted flames sputtered out, Eoinn collapsed. The transformation that had revealed his true nature reversed itself with brutal swiftness—his hair turned white as winter snow, deep lines carved themselves across his face, and his hands and body became frail, those of a man who had lived far beyond his allotted years.

Jack reached him first, catching the old man before he could topple over. The change was heartbreaking to witness—all the vitality that had returned to Eoinn during their training was gone, burned away in that single, desperate act of protection.

"Did we save it?" Eoinn whispered, his voice barely audible.

Jack looked around at the village below them. The buildings still stood, their golden glow fading but intact. The hot springs sent up gentle wisps of clean steam. The mountain itself felt peaceful again, its deep places healed rather than violated. Through his connection to the bedrock, he could sense the corruption retreating along every underground channel, the threat to the wider region dissolving like mist before the sun.

"Yes," Jack said, his voice thick with emotion. "The village is safe."

Eoinn smiled, and for a moment, something of his true self shone through the aged features. "Good. That's ... that's all that ever mattered." His eyes found Jack's face with effort. "You understand now, don't you? What you are? What this place means?"

"I understand," Jack promised, tears streaming down his face. "I'll protect it. I'll honor what you built here. I'll make sure the stories continue."

Susanne knelt beside them, her own face wet with tears. She leaned down and kissed Eoinn's forehead gently.

"Thank you," she whispered. "For everything. For waiting for us. For teaching us. For showing us what it means to sacrifice for something greater than ourselves."

Eoinn's gaze moved to encompass them all—Jack and Susanne, Finn who knelt nearby with grief etched across his ancient features, even Coyote who stood at the edge of their circle with uncharacteristic solemnity.

"The stories," Eoinn said, his voice growing fainter. "Keep telling the stories."

His eyes closed, and his breathing grew shallow. But there was peace in his expression, the contentment of a guardian who had fulfilled his deepest purpose.

"The village will remember," Jack said softly. "We'll make sure of it."

Eoinn's last breath was barely a whisper, but it seemed to carry with it all the love he'd held for this place, all the hope he'd invested in the future he would not see.

Finn collapsed beside his oldest friend, his shoulders shaking with grief of losing a relationship that spanned centuries, as he sobbed quietly. In the sudden silence that followed, they could hear something else—the distant roar of flames still raging through the forest beyond the village, the natural fire that Ríona's corruption had spawned, racing toward populated areas with unstoppable hunger.

The immediate threat to Crystal Village was over, but the fires were spreading. Flames raged through the forest, spawned by Ríona's initial assault, but the fire now burned with its own hungry life. The flames flowed through the mountains, leaping from tree to tree, racing toward valleys where people lived and worked, unaware of the destruction bearing down on them.

Jack could feel it through his connection to the mountain—thousands of acres burning, the fire spreading faster than any human effort could contain. Wildlife fled in panic, and the smoke was beginning to drift toward populated areas.

"The forest," Susanne said, her enhanced perception showing her the scope of the devastation. "It's still burning. All of it."

Finn looked up from his grief, his eyes tracking the orange glow on the horizon. "Ríona's corruption may be stopped, but the fire she started ..." He shook his head. "It'll burn for days, maybe weeks."

Coyote, still in his animal form, lifted his muzzle to the wind. He transformed back into his Sinclair Lipson persona. His amber eyes reflected the distant flames. "I can smell it reaching toward the valleys. Toward towns."

The weight of it settled over them like a shroud. They had saved Crystal

Village, but at what cost? The fire racing through the wilderness would consume everything in its path.

A great shadow passed over them. With a mighty, croaking caw that echoed through the valley, Raven appeared. His wings were vast, covering the sky like storm clouds. The ancient being had felt the disturbance in the natural order and come to restore balance.

Raven circled above, his keen eyes taking in the scope of the destruction. He called out, and from the depths of the forest, a host of fairies emerged, their forms shimmering with an ethereal light. They were from the realm under the mountain, and they had answered Raven's call to save the forests they cherished.

With a voice that resonated with the authority of the ages, Raven called to the fairies. The fairies began to weave their magic, their delicate hands casting forth a mist that rose to meet the flames. The mist, imbued with the healing power of the fairies, spread through the mountains, blanketing the fire with a cool embrace.

Coyote, seeing the efforts of the fairies and understanding his role in this ancient dance of elements, reverted once again to his animal self and ran through the forest, leaping from place to place with impossible grace and speed. Wherever he stepped, the flames would diminish, his very nature turning destruction back upon itself. His auburn power flowed through the forest floor, creating firebreaks and safe passages for the fleeing wildlife.

High above, Raven beat his wings and let out another great caw. Lightning bolts flew out from under his wings. Clouds gathered around him, dark and heavy with the promise of rain. With a cry that seemed to split the sky, Raven summoned the waters, calling forth a deluge that poured down upon the flames.

The fire met its match in the combined magic of Raven, Coyote, and the fairies. Steam rose in great billows as the rain fell, and bit by bit, the fire was extinguished. The fairies' mist and Raven's rain worked in harmony, and a faint song floated on the breeze seeming to call for hope and renewal. The forest was scarred by the fire, but the song of the fairies seemed to promise life would return, green and vibrant, in the fullness of time.

Raven, his task with the forest fire complete, soared high above the village once more. With a final, triumphant call, he disappeared into the expanse of the sky, but his presence lingered like a blessing over the land.

The rain continued to fall, gentle but persistent. The fairy lights moved through the forest like fireflies, each one a point of healing in the darkness. And gradually, impossibly, the massive fire died down. The fairies began to fade back into the forest, their work complete, leaving behind only the gentle rain and the soft glow of renewed life.

Jack walked over to Susanne and hugged her. They stood watching with satisfaction and near disbelief at the threat finally diminishing. Jack looked over at the fallen form of Eoinn and felt his heart catch.

The rain continued to fall, washing the smoke from the air and cooling the scorched earth. But even as they watched the last of the forest fires die under Raven's storm, movement at the edge of the clearing caught their attention. Ríona was rising from the place where Eoinn's power had cast her into the trees. They were horrified to see that the corruption that had been consuming her was still there, still eating away at her essence from within. Eoinn's sacrifice had broken her connection to the mountain's power, but the corruption she had absorbed in her fury continued to burn through her.

She stood slowly, her form wavering between fairy and elemental force. The sickly green energy still flowed around her—a chaotic mix of her anger, her own power, and the corruption she couldn't purge, fighting against each other within her body. She screamed in fury, her voice distorted by the forces warring within her. She turned her gaze on them, and Jack could see the truth—this wasn't just anger and fear anymore. This was a being literally being consumed by power she could no longer control.

"You think his sacrifice saved you?!" Ríona screamed, her form flickering as the corruption fought against her attempts to maintain coherence. "I am still here! I am still burning! And if I cannot stop this fire, then I will take you all with me!"

The air around her began to crackle with unstable energy. This wasn't the focused assault of before—this was raw, chaotic power seeking any outlet, any target for the pain that was consuming her.

Finn stepped forward, his face grim. "The corruption is still spreading through her. She's fighting it, but it's too strong."

"She's dying," Susanne said, her enhanced perception showing her the truth. "The deep fires are burning away everything that makes her who she is."

Coyote circled their position, his form blurring between human and animal as he sensed the dangerous instability of Ríona's power. "Corruption like that doesn't just fade. It has to be purged, or it consumes everything."

Jack felt the mountain's unease through his connection to the bedrock. Even with its deep places healed, the land could sense the wrongness radiating from Ríona. "How do we help her?" he asked.

"I don't know if we can," Finn admitted. "The corruption has been building in her for too long. It may be too late to—"

"It's never too late!" The voice came from the forest edge, and they turned to see the Mountain Queen emerging from the shadows. Her face was etched with sorrow as she watched her daughter's pain.

"Mother," Ríona whispered, and for a moment, the corruption flickered as her true self fought to the surface. "I can't ... I can't stop it. Help me."

The Queen stepped closer, her own power radiating calm and healing. "My daughter, you must learn that some burdens are too heavy to carry alone."

She turned to Susanne, her eyes holding depths of ancient wisdom. "Child of two worlds, you have the gift to reach her. Through the connection you hold to Mrs. O'Hara's line, I bless you."

Susanne felt a surge of energy, the Queen's gift stirring within her, responding to the crisis. But this wasn't just about power—it was about connection, about reaching through the corruption to find the frightened girl beneath.

"Ríona!" she called out, stepping forward despite the dangerous energy crackling around the fairy princess. "I know you're in there! I know you're fighting this!"

"I can't fight it anymore," Ríona replied, her voice breaking. "It's too strong. It wants to burn everything, destroy everything I've ever cared about."

"Then don't fight it alone," Susanne said, moving closer. "Let us help you."

The corruption flared, sending waves of searing energy toward Susanne. But the Queen's gift protected her, turning the chaotic force aside with walls of silver light.

"You think your borrowed power can stop this?" the corruption spoke through Ríona, her voice now altered and horrific. "I will burn until there is nothing left!"

But Susanne could see through her enhanced perception that this wasn't Ríona speaking—it was the corruption itself, using her voice, her form, her pain as a weapon against everything she had once loved.

"That's not you talking," Susanne said firmly. "That's the poison you absorbed, trying to use your voice. But I can see the real you, Ríona. You're still in there, still fighting."

Finn stepped up beside Susanne, his flames dancing in patterns that somehow harmonized with the chaotic energy rather than opposing it. "The corruption feeds on isolation, on the belief that you have to face this alone. But you don't."

Coyote moved closer as well, his Sinclair Lipson form solidifying as he drew upon his own experience of redemption. "I know what it's like to be consumed by forces you can't control. The anger, the need to lash out—I've been there. But there's another way."

"The stories don't trap us," Jack added, understanding flooding through him. "They connect us. Every tale told with love, every wonder shared—it creates bonds stronger than any corruption."

The corruption fought back, sending tendrils of chaotic energy toward all of them. But now they were working together, their combined power creating a shield of protection around Ríona rather than a barrier against her.

"You're afraid," Susanne said, looking directly at Ríona through the swirling chaos. "You're afraid that caring means being controlled, that love means losing yourself. But look what isolation has brought you instead."

For a moment, Ríona's true self broke through the corruption's hold. "I just wanted to be free," she whispered. "Free to choose my own path, to love without being owned."

"Then choose now," the Mountain Queen said, stepping closer to her daughter. "Choose connection over isolation. Choose love over fear."

Susanne felt the Queen's gift reaching its full power, and she knew what she had to do. She ran forward, directly into the aura of chaotic energy that surrounded Ríona, her silver light flaring to protect her from the worst of the corruption.

She reached Ríona just as the fairy princess collapsed, her form wavering between flesh and elemental chaos. Up close, Susanne could see the true extent of the damage—the corruption was literally eating away at Ríona's essence, consuming everything that made her who she was.

"I can't stop it," Ríona gasped. "It won't let me go."

"You don't have to stop it alone," Susanne said, holding Ríona embraced in her lap, laying her hands on Ríona's chest. The contact sent jolts of agony through both of them as the corruption fought against the healing touch, but she held on.

She reached out with the Queen's gift, not to fight the corruption directly, but to offer Ríona an alternative source of strength. Through that connection, Ríona could feel her mother's love, the concern of her people, even the genuine desire of these strangers to help her find her way back.

"I can feel them," Ríona whispered in wonder. "They don't hate me."

"They never did," Susanne assured her. "They were just waiting for you to come home."

The corruption made one final, desperate assault, sending waves of pain through both women. But now Ríona was fighting against it rather than being consumed by it, and that made all the difference.

Jack, still connected to the mountain, helped ground the excess chaotic energy, sending it into the deep network beneath them to dissipate. Finn and Coyote added their own power to the effort, creating a circle of support around the two women.

With a sound like distant thunder, the corruption finally broke. The chaotic energies that had been consuming Ríona from within suddenly released her, leaving her collapsed in Susanne's arms. Her skin was pale, marked with shining silver scars from her battle with forces too powerful for any single being to control, and the sickly light was gone from her eyes.

Ríona looked up at Susanne with eyes that were once again her own—frightened, exhausted but clear.

"I'm sorry," she whispered. "I was so afraid of losing myself that I nearly destroyed everything. Including myself."

The Mountain Queen knelt beside them, gathering her daughter into her arms with infinite tenderness.

"My child," she said softly, "you have learned what I could not teach you—that strength shared is strength multiplied, not divided."

She looked up at Susanne with gratitude shining in her ancient eyes. "And you have shown us all what it means to choose connection over isolation."

As the magical energies settled into new patterns, the mountain itself seemed to sigh with relief. Jack could feel it through his connection to the bedrock—Crystal Village was not just saved, but somehow strengthened by what they had endured together.

The bonds between the realms, between old magic and new stories, had been tested in fire and proven unbreakable.

I I I I

Signs of renewed life were everywhere, the charred earth already sprouted delicate, green shoots that pushed through the blackened soil. Locals had never seen the mountains recover from a fire faster. Everything was wreathed in green. Crystal Village was quiet, its cobblestone streets awaiting the return of laughter and footsteps.

Months had passed since the fire, and the village had been a hive of activity. Jack and Susanne, along with the dedicated team, had worked tirelessly to restore the park to its former glory. The scars of the fire had been healed with care and attention, the buildings on the edge of town had been refurbished, and the stories of Raven and Coyote and the Fairies were embedded even deeper into the bones of the village. They recreated the fire within the game world, and a very similar version to what had played out in real life was recreated as fantasy for millions of gamers. Ríona was seen as a great "boss level" villain, and the redemption of Coyote and the intervention of Raven loomed large across the metaverse. Ríona's own redemption arc was powerful and the players in the game loved it. They couldn't beat her by dominating, they had to do it as a team, collaboratively, and by winning her over.

Now, as the park prepared to reopen, there was a sense of anticipation in the air, a collective breath held before the plunge into a new chapter. Jack and Susanne walked hand in hand through the village, their steps echoing on the empty streets. They had chosen to make Crystal Village their home, to be the custodians of its legacy and the shepherds of its future. They buried Eoinn in the graveyard up at the base of big peak, alongside his beloved Rose.

As the sun set on the day of the grand reopening, Jack and Susanne stood on the balcony of their home, watching the village come alive. They had decided to take over the townhouse of Sam and Seamus O'Connor. The street lamps glowed warmly, illuminating the faces of the guests as they explored the wonders of Crystal Village. The sound of music and laughter drifted up to them, a melody of joy and celebration.

There, in the quiet moment between dusk and nightfall, Susanne turned to Jack, her eyes shining with a secret. "Jack," she whispered, her voice barely audible above the din of the village, "I have something to tell you."

Jack looked at her, his heart skipping a beat at the seriousness in her tone. "What is it?"

She took his hand, gently guiding it to her belly. "We're going to have a baby, Jack."

Jack's eyes widened, a surge of emotion flooded through him. He pulled Susanne into an embrace with the realization that they were about to embark on the greatest adventure of their lives.

Below them, Crystal Village pulsed with life. Street lamps cast pools of amber light across the cobblestones, and music drifted up from the saloon. A group of children chased each other through the streets, their laughter echoing off the brick buildings. Jack watched a raven circle overhead, its wings black against the purple dusk. The bird landed on a nearby roof peak and fixed them with knowing eyes. Susanne squeezed Jack's hand, and he felt the weight of generations flow through him—all those who had come before, who had built this place, who had protected its magic. Their child would be born into this legacy of stories and wonder, where the boundary between reality and legend blurred, where ancient powers still moved in the shadows of the mountains. The raven spread its wings and took flight, disappearing into the gathering night.

Epilogue

The morning air was crisp with the beginnings of fall. Finn McEnhill strolled down the cobblestone street of Crystal Village with an easy gait that belied his age. He had a meeting with two of the newest additions to the village's cast, a couple who would breathe life into roles that held a special place in Finn's heart.

As Finn approached the house, nestled among the others that lined Spring Street, the door swung open. Standing there were Sean and Colin, who greeted him with warm smiles and a familiarity that seemed to stretch beyond the mere roles they were about to inhabit. Both men seemed to be in their late sixties, their faces lined with the kind of laughter and joy that only a life well-lived could etch. They had come to Crystal Village to take on the roles of two of the original founders. It felt like they were returning home.

"Aye, Finn," Sean said with a strong Irish lilt. "It's good to see ye, old friend."

Colin nodded in agreement, his eyes twinkling with a mischief that seemed to dance just below the surface. "We've been looking forward to this, to bringing the story of Sean and Colin to life once more."

Finn chuckled, "Lads, I can't tell you how much it means to have ye here."

The couple invited Finn inside, and as he crossed the threshold, a sense of déjà vu washed over him. He found himself in a living room that was the very image of the one that had once been. Sean and Colin moved through the house with an ease that spoke of a deep connection to the space. They shared stories of their life together over the last one hundred years, of the stages they had graced, and the audiences they had enchanted. Their love for each other was as tangible as the love they held for the theater, for music, and for the craft of bringing characters to life.

The afternoon waned, and Finn rose to take his leave, his heart full of the stories shared and the promise of the performances to come. As he stepped outside, he turned to the couple, who stood at the door, their hands clasped together.

Finn said, "Sean, Colin, welcome home."

The couple smiled, and as Finn walked away, he heard their laughter, a sound that was both new and achingly familiar. It was the laughter of friends long gone but never forgotten, the laughter of a village that had endured through fire and time.

Postscript

The forest was alive with the sounds of nature—a rhythm of rustling leaves, the soft murmur of a nearby brook, and the occasional chitter of a red squirrel. The air was rich with the scent of pine and the musky undertones of damp earth.

Amidst this woodland wonderland, two little girls, twins with locks of golden hair and eyes bright with the boundless curiosity of youth, frolicked under towering trees. Their names were Sienna and Skye Seeley.

Sienna climbed over logs and flipped over rocks to find bugs and worms. Skye gathered wildflowers, her small hands cradling delicate petals as she hummed a tune of her own making.

The game they played today was simple—tag in the shadows, chasing each other in the patches of darkness that flitted across the forest floor. Feet never touching the sunlight, only the shadows. Their joy was infectious.

Suddenly, Sienna's foot caught on a hidden root, and she tumbled to the ground with a startled cry. The fallen leaves cushioned her fall, but a sharp stone nicked her knee, drawing a thin line of crimson that stood out against her fair skin.

Skye rushed to her sister's side, her concern etched in the furrow of her brow. "Sienna, are you okay?" she asked, her voice tinged with urgency.

Before Sienna could respond, a figure stepped out from the embrace of the trees. He knelt beside Sienna, his white suit impossibly clean against the wild tangle of the forest.

"There now, little one," he said with a wink. "Let's have a look at that knee."

The girls' initial surprise gave way to delight. They clambered over him, their small arms wrapping around his neck in a tangle of hugs and giggles.

Sinclair Lipson's laughter joined theirs, a sound that seemed to belong to the forest as much as the rustle of leaves and the call of birds.

Sienna, her knee forgotten in the joy of the moment, looked up with adoration. "Uncle Sinclair, you always know when we need you," she said, her words spoken with the earnest belief that only children possess.

Lipson's eyes twinkled as he helped Sienna to her feet. "Well, I have a bit of a knack for being in the right place at the right time," he replied, a hint of the old trickster still playing at the edges of his smile.

The twins' laughter filled the forest, mingling with the songs of birds and the murmur of the brook.

Character Lists

First Stakeholders in Northern Idaho

- **Hank Randall**: Former Union Lieutenant, younger brother to Barney. A steady, cautious man haunted by war memories.
- **Barney Randall**: Former Union Corporal, older brother to Hank. Enthusiastic and optimistic miner who relies on his brother's judgment.
- **Madeleine (Maddy) Randall**: Barney's wife who convinces Hank to accompany her husband on the mining venture, she stays back in Chicago.
- **Joe Welch**: Former platoon member and childhood friend of Barney and Hank, who discovered the mining claim. Large, bearded man with a bear-like grip who invites the Randall brothers to join his venture.
- **Tom**: Miner already established at the claim site who seems reserved about the mining prospects, friend of Joe's.
- **Rick**: Another established miner at the claim site who appears cautious about the opportunity, friend of Joe's.

The Original 8 Founders of Crystal Village

- **Eoinn Seeley**: Leader of the Irish group, tall with dark hair and mustache. Former Captain in the Irish Brigade who commands natural authority and respect. Founder and visionary behind Crystal Village, husband to Rose.
- **Sam King**: Nine-year-old orphaned girl initially mistaken for a boy, found at her family's cabin after her parents and sister died.

Shows remarkable resilience and adaptability. Later marries Seamus O'Connor and becomes Sam King O'Connor, a respected village leader.

- **Finn McEnhill**: The oldest of the original group, with white and red streaked hair. Master architect with remarkable ability to visualize structures, constantly grumbling but hardworking and dependable.
- **Liam O'Connor**: The tallest of the group, with wild auburn hair and sideburns. Charming and strategic diplomat, often sent on recruitment and reconnaissance missions. Father to Seamus, Joshua, and Eva.
- **Sean O'Neil**: The youngest and shortest of the Irish men, with reddish-brown hair and green eyes. Kind-hearted, musical, and often tells jokes and stories. Skilled photographer who documents village life.
- **Colin O'Shea**: A blond doctor who wears spectacles, clean-shaven and close friends with Sean. Served as their military medic and continues as village doctor with knowledge of herbal medicine.
- **Angus Sullivan**: One of two brothers, with dark curly hair and reddish-brown beard. Skilled with throwing knives and business negotiations. Financial steward of Crystal Village who manages village wealth and investments.
- **Egan Sullivan**: Angus's brother, quiet but brilliant engineering genius. Known for his dry wit and intelligence, designs geothermal systems for the village and mines.

Old West Characters (through 1910)

Crystal Village Residents:

- **Rose Seeley**: Eoinn's wife who helps establish Crystal Village. Dark-haired, elegant woman who supports her husband's vision.
- **Mrs. O'Hara (Mary Margaret Maguire)**: Irish matron who runs Crystal Village's operations, central kitchen and dining hall. Later owns a restaurant. A commanding presence who maintains strict standards and is highly respected in the community.
- **Pierre Sylvestre Lutinel de Lemieux**: French Canadian merchant

who manages village logistics and supply chains, organizes hunting parties, and maintains mule trains. He's got broad North American and international contacts.

- **Stanley Finch**: Crystal Village Constable, friendly middle-aged police officer.
- **Danny Ferguson/Miller**: 23-year-old newcomer to Crystal Village, fleeing unjust prosecution in Eagle City. Later marries Eva O'Connor.
- **Cheng Wu**: Elder Wu brother who runs the laundry with his brother and helps import Chinese goods.
- **Jian Wu**: Younger Wu brother who works in the laundry with his brother and imports Chinese goods.
- **Mei Wu**: Cheng Wu's wife who teaches villagers tai chi and shares Chinese cuisine.
- **Zhong-Ling Wu**: Jian Wu's wife who teaches tai chi and cooking alongside Mei.
- **Mrs. Semanski:** Maker of Pierogies
- **Mrs. Lombardi:** Maker of Pasta
- **Mrs. Russo:** Maker of Italian sausages
- **Mrs. Stein:** Maker of German sausage
- **Mrs. Rosenberg:** Maker of challah bread and matso and chicken soup

The O'Connor Family:

- **Elizabeth O'Connor:** Married to Liam, mother of the O'Connor children.
- **Seamus O'Connor**: Liam & Elizabeth's son who marries Sam King. Strong, kind man, sometimes speaks without thinking. Skilled jewelry maker and metalsmith who works with precious metals.
- **Eva O'Connor**: Liam & Elizabeth's daughter, eventually marries Danny Ferguson/Miller.
- **Susanne O'Connor:** Liam & Elizabeth's daughter, modern day Susanne is named after her.
- **Joshua O'Connor:** Liam & Elizabeth's son who defends the village

leadership structure during political disputes.
- **Ned Miller**: Danny and Eva's son.

Sam and Seamus' Family:

- **Henry O'Connor**: Sam and Seamus's oldest child, reliable son who stays in Wallace to work with Liam after the fire.
- **Susanne O'Connor**: Sam and Seamus's daughter.
- **Albert O'Connor**: One of Sam and Seamus's twin sons.
- **Andrew O'Connor**: One of Sam and Seamus's twin sons.
- **Glory O'Connor**: Sam and Seamus's youngest child.

Seeley Family:

- **John Seeley**: Eoinn's son who becomes caught between village politics and his father's leadership style. Jack's great-grandfather.
- **Mary Seeley**: John Seeley's wife, daughter of Angus Sullivan. Jack's great-grandmother.
- **John Seeley Jr.**: Young son of John and Mary Seeley. Jack's grandfather.

Contentious Residents:

- **Jeremiah Redding**: Village carpenter skilled in balloon framing and timber framing. Frustrated by resistance to new building methods, later challenges village governance.
- **Margaret Redding**: Jeremiah's supportive wife with sharp mind and quick wit.
- **Tom Whitaker**: Miner who challenges Eoinn about village governance and mine ownership, desires more representation for villagers.
- **Mary Whitaker**: Tom's wife who shares his concerns about village governance.

Mysterious Strangers:

- **Sinclair Lipson**: Mysterious figure in a white linen suit with handlebar mustache and auburn hair. Antagonistic toward Crystal Village and its founders, particularly Eoinn Seeley and Sam King.
- **Elias Dotson**: Massive man in black clothing who accompanies and argues with Sinclair Lipson.
- **Ríona**: Mysterious young woman who befriends Glory O'Connor.
- **Ríona's mother**: Leader of a group within the mountains.

Native Visitors:

- **Stelkupmi**: Young Native American woman studying to become a healer for her tribe, forms friendship with Sam and shares knowledge about native traditions.
- **Sanhamin**: Stelkupmi's grandmother, a tribal elder and healer who shares knowledge with the villagers.
- **Hustalk**: Stelkupmi's uncle who breaks his arm and receives treatment in Crystal Village.

Residents of Eagle City:

- **Wyatt Earp**: Famous lawman serving as Deputy Sheriff of Kootenai county, runs White Elephant Saloon in Eagle City.
- **Jim Earp**: Wyatt's brother, helps run White Elephant Saloon.
- **Josie Earp**: Wyatt's wife, bartender at White Elephant Saloon.
- **Jack Enright**: Member of Earp's syndicate, hotheaded but brave man involved in lot dispute.
- **William Buzzard**: Determined settler who builds cabin and attempts hotel construction on disputed lot.
- **Deputy Sheriff Hunt**: Shoshone County law officer who arrives late to handle lot disputes.
- **Calamity Jane:** Famous western character, runs a western show that

travels the country.

Other Important Historical Characters (Real Historical Figures):

- **Jonas Brown**: President of Idaho County Bank who handles the Seeley Mining Company's gold deposits.
- **A.J. Prichard**: Prospector with white beard and dark mustache, member of National Liberal League seeking to establish a secular society. Responsible for finding the initial gold in the region.
- **John Roebling:** Famous bridge engineer, designer of the Brooklyn Bridge and enthusiast of intentional communities.
- **Washington Roebling:** Son of John Roebling, takes over the Brooklyn Bridge project after his father's death. Former comrade of Eoinn's from the Civil War.
- **Frank & Lu Worden:** Proprietors of Worden Mercantile, and founding citizens of Missoula Montana, all the way back to when it was called Hell's Gate, and then Missoula Mills.

Modern Day Descendants of Crystal Village

- **Jack Seeley**: Former Disney Imagineer in his early forties, discovers Crystal Village while researching his family history. Great-great-grandson of Eoinn Seeley. Employed by the Yomohiro Corporation to build their parks business in the U.S. He is a creative and visionary theme park designer who inherits Crystal Village.
- **Audrey Seeley**: Jack's elderly grandmother, bedridden but sharp-minded, living in a house built by her father-in-law in 1910.
- **Susanne O'Connor**: Jack's childhood friend and successful novelist, descendant of Sam King and Seamus O'Connor. Lives in her family home in Kellogg and becomes involved in the Crystal Village project.
- **Ian Seeley**: Elderly caretaker of Crystal Village. Wears a dark blue Stetson hat and maintains the abandoned town, he's a descendant of Eionn and Rose and cousin to Jack.

- **Molly O'Connor Flood** - Susanne's great-aunt, retired elementary school teacher and family historian for the O'Connors.

Modern Day Employees of Yomohiro Corporation

- **Kisho Yomohiro**: Legendary Japanese animator and filmmaker in his 60s, founder of Yomohiro Corporation. Wears tweed jackets and bow ties, has a modern-day Walt Disney-like persona, but his aesthetic vision is more modern, darker and visionary. He is known for his creativity, and for creating immersive experiences.
- **Taki Yomohiro**: Kisho's daughter who accompanies him to visit Crystal Village.
- **Mr. Itsuki Tanaka**: Japanese executive leader from Yomohiro Corporation who heads the parks division, and visits Crystal Village.
- **Mr. Riku Hamada**: Studio head at Yomohiro Corporation who visits Crystal Village.
- **Ms. Akari Ito**: Legal and partnerships executive at Yomohiro Corporation, particularly interested in hot springs.
- **Diana Rollins**: Jack's former right-hand person from Disney who joins his team at Yomohiro Corporation and leads the Crystal Village project under Jack. Highly organized project coordinator who helps develop the theme park concept.
- **Bill McKenna**: Head of film and attraction gadget shop at Yomohiro, veteran of motion picture industry and theme park visual effects. Designs the flight system for Crystal Village.
- **Mitch**: Head writer for Crystal Village project.
- **Monica**: Lead AI and story integration expert who develops the system for generating character interactions in both the physical park and online game.
- **Tom**: Writer who inappropriately claims Cherokee ancestry based on DNA testing.
- **Tarmo Saarholm**: MIT professor and Jack's college friend, expert in combinatorial optimization who designs the visitor lottery system.

- **Terry**: Technical lead working on AR implementation for the park.
- **Peter**: Game designer working on the virtual world mechanics.
- **Kiara**: Receptionist at the Alameda workshop where park features are developed.
- **Kori**: Character Actor playing a fairy who helps lead the Granger children on their nighttime adventure in Crystal Village.
- **Timka**: Character Actor playing a fairy who assists in the Granger children's magical journey.
- **Finnegan McEnhill** - Mysterious older actor who auditions to play "himself" in the Crystal Village productions.
- **Dr. Aiyana Stensgar** - Cultural anthropologist and tribal liaison in her early thirties. Professional, direct, and uncompromising in her advocacy for authentic Indigenous representation. Carries herself with the confidence of someone accustomed to challenging authority. Aiyana is the great-granddaughter of Stelkupmi, the young Native American woman who befriended Sam King and the Crystal Village founders in 1870.
- **Valerie Stensgar** - Aiyana's cousin, recent MFA graduate from The Institute for American Indian Arts in Santa Fe. Indigenous writer specializing in contemporary adaptations of traditional narratives. Hired to lead Indiginous storyline integration for the Crystal Village project.

Modern Characters

- **Sinclair Lipson III**: Grandson of the original Sinclair Lipson. A mysterious man in a white linen suit with auburn hair and handlebar mustache, encountered by Jack at LAX and on the flight to Spokane, and then works for the state of Idaho inspecting Crystal Village.
- **Amy**: Caretaker for Jack's grandmother in Kellogg, Idaho.
- **Jessie Blackwell**: Cultural liaison for the Coeur d'Alene tribe who helps evaluate the authenticity of cave findings.
- **Calvin Whitebird**: Nez Perce tribal elder who provides cultural guid-

ance for the Crystal Village project, explaining the significance of Raven and Coyote stories.

- **Sarah Stensgar**: Coeur d'Alene tribal elder who works with the writing team to ensure respectful representation of native traditions. Granddaughter of Stelkupmi.
- **Skip**: Helicopter pilot who has transported workers to Crystal Village for 15 years.
- **Bill Granger**: History teacher and Western enthusiast, father of Lucy and Michael, wins lottery tickets to visit Crystal Village.
- **Sharon Granger**: Librarian and mother of Lucy and Michael, accompanies family on Crystal Village visit.
- **Michael Granger**: Eight-year-old boy with asthma, full of spirit and imagination, experiences magical adventure in Crystal Village.
- **Lucy Granger**: Thirteen-year-old dreamer who embraces the magic of Crystal Village and accompanies her brother on nighttime adventures.

O'Connor Family Tree

First Generation (Ireland → Crystal Village)

Liam O'Connor (b. ~?) ∞ **Elizabeth Finnegan** (m. 1858, County Tyrone, Ireland)

Second Generation (The Crystal Village Children)

Children of Liam & Elizabeth:

1. **Joshua O'Connor** - Village mediator, defended leadership structure
2. **Eva O'Connor** → **Eva Miller** (m. Danny Ferguson/Miller, 1885)

   - Son: **Ned Miller** (joined European trip post-1910)

1. **Seamus O'Connor** (m. Sam King, 1884) - Metalsmith/jeweler
2. **Susanne O'Connor** (original namesake) → **Susanne McBride** (m. Patrick McBride, 1912, Wallace) lived to age 83 (d. San Francisco, CA)

Third Generation (Sam & Seamus's Children)

Children of Sam King & Seamus O'Connor:

1. **Henry O'Connor** (b. 1884, eldest) - Founded bank with John Seeley, wrote memoir (1952)

2. **Susanne O'Connor** (b. 1887) – Named after aunt, stayed in region post–1910
3. **Albert O'Connor** (b. 1890, twin) – Ancestor line continues
4. **Andrew O'Connor** (b. 1890, twin) – Ancestor line continues
5. **Glory O'Connor** (b. 1894, youngest) – Stayed in Wallace, cared for Mrs. O'Hara

Fourth Generation (Henry's Line - Molly's Branch)

Henry O'Connor had three sons:

1. **James O'Connor** – Continued main O'Connor name line
2. **Thomas O'Connor – Molly's father**
3. **Michael O'Connor** – Moved around the country

Albert O'Connor (twin) had:

- **Catherine O'Connor** → married Coeur d'Alene man (1932)
- *This created a "lost" Indigenous connection to Crystal Village legacy*

Fifth Generation

Thomas O'Connor (Henry's son) had:

- **Molly O'Connor** → **Molly O'Connor Flood** (retired teacher, family historian)

Modern Generation (Susanne's Line)

Through **James O'Connor** (Henry's Son) had:

1. **Jimmy O'Connor** (m. Sally Frost, 1975) had:

- Daughter: **Susanne O'Connor** (modern day) - Novelist, great-great-granddaughter of Sam King & Seamus O'Connor

477

- Daughter: **Susanne O'Connor** (modern day) - Novelist, great-great-granddaughter of Sam King & Seamus O'Connor

Author's Notes

This book began as a spark of imagination in the early 2000s. I had a dream one night about finding an abandoned village in the mountains, and that it was completely intact. It was the kind of dream that sticks with you. I couldn't get it out of my head. I was out for a walk, and I imagined that a town like this would make for a great theme park.

Gary Hebert may remember several random phone calls during his time at Disney to bounce around ideas about a mountain mining village theme park concept. Those lengthy conversations marked the first appearance of Eoinn in my mind—the visionary founder who was mystical and had lived all the years waiting for someone to find this hidden village. This story would eventually become the heart of Crystal Village.

The story truly found its shape in 2016 during a cross-country road trip with my wife. We spotted a small sign in western Montana that read: "Garnet Ghost Town—>"
and we made an impulsive turn onto a dirt road. After a nerve-wracking drive that had us questioning our judgment and thinking we were heading into an ambush at a meth lab, we discovered Garnet—one of America's best-preserved ghost towns. This former boom town had over 1,000 buildings at its peak, and is now managed by the Bureau of Land Management. It stands frozen in time among the mountains. Walking those quiet streets, the full vision of Crystal Village finally emerged.

My family made regular drives between Seattle and Rhode Island along I-90 for more than twenty years, which deepened my connection to the region. The stretch between Coeur d'Alene and Missoula remains possibly the most beautiful section of highway in America. We've stayed in Kellogg, eaten in Wallace a half dozen times, and explored many corners of this remarkable landscape. Each visit added layers to the story brewing in my mind.

Writing a historical novel presents unique challenges, especially for someone with a History degree who cares perhaps too much about accuracy in the timeline. I've worked diligently to align the real-world timeline with the story's events, drawing from first-person accounts, contemporary newspaper articles, and historical documents. The historical figures appearing in these pages were genuinely present in these locations during these times.

Wyatt Earp, his brother **Jim**, and his wife **Josie**, did in fact found the White Elephant Saloon in Eagle City. **Calamity Jane** also passed through Eagle City during that period, staging her one-woman show and her dancing girls in the White Elephant. **Frank and Lu Worden** truly established the Worden Mercantile before Missoula even carried that name, becoming pillars of the community. **Danny Ferguson**, **Jack Enright**, **Billy Buzzard**, **Sam Black**, **W.F. Hunt**, **Thomas Steele,** and **Sheriff Dunwell** emerged from actual newspaper accounts and historical records.

The Eagle City gunfight described here closely follows contemporary reports. Danny Ferguson's shootout with Thomas Steele is almost exactly extracted from the reporting, as is the aftermath - at least until he heads up to Crystal Village. The real Danny Ferguson did assume the name Danny Miller, but what happened to him is lost to posterity. He did reach out to the authorities years later from an undisclosed location, trying to clear his name. I like to think he was with Eva.

The good ship "Emma Pearl", which carried Mrs. O'Hara across the Atlantic, was a real ship, which transported real passengers from Belfast, Ireland. I pulled the names from the ship's manifest, but invented the back stories. The details of shipboard life come from multiple first-person narratives of similar journeys during that period. I must admit that the ship's name caught my attention because of my daughter Emma, who provided valuable feedback on this book. The seaman, Jed, was named for my old friend and colleague, Jed Nahum, who also was a huge help in reviewing this book.

Historical research yielded remarkable connections. I had envisioned Eoinn as fanatical about intentional communities. The adherents to this movement in the 1800s were sort of the equivalent of todays "crypto bros". They were passionate about their beliefs, thought everyone would agree if they only were educated enough about why it was important, and almost religious about their philosophical stance, even if they were not religiously founded. They wanted to upend society and remake it according to their philosophy. Anyone who's been buttonholed by a crypto bro (Web3 bro) knows of what I speak. The movements regarding intentional communities remade swaths of the country, many of them were religious in origin, but not all.

I was already planning to have **John Roebling** in the book, as I felt like the bridge was an important symbolic element, and he was a celebrity in his day, perhaps the best-known bridge engineer of all time, even today. Then when I was researching him I discovered that he had a similar fanaticism about intentional communities to what I envisioned within Eoinn. His own experiments had failed. The history behind his move from Cincinnati (where I attended graduate school) and New York is accurate, as is the story of his death from tetanus. His son **Washington Roebling** did take over the project when his father died, and his wife **Emily Warren Roebling** did save the project and quietly take it over when Washington was bedridden with Caisson's Disease (decompression sickness). I was tickled when this storyline appeared in the HBO series "The Guilded Age." I'm glad it's been validated by other storytellers.

Andrew Prichard really did stake all those claims, he really did game the system to capture way more claims than legally was allowed, and he really did send that letter (nearly verbatim) to the National Liberal League soliciting a gold rush in order to create an intentional community. I had none of his history when I set Crystal Village there, so it was fortuitous that he was an intentional community fanatic. And it is completely true that Kellogg and its vicinity became the biggest silver mines in history, all because Andrew Prichard was a fanatic about starting an intentional community.

Jonas Brown was a real person, and really was the president of the Idaho County Bank, and by all accounts was a good man and lawyer.

H.C. Davis really was in charge of marketing for the railroad, and did write a memo (almost exactly the one published in this book) that caused the Gold Rush described here, he also is in fact the person who hammered the golden spike that connected the East and West via rail.

More fun coincidences came together around Eoinn's military background and his need for plausible government backing in getting Crystal Village protected for generations to come. The Irish Brigade's presence at the battle of Bull Run, where Idaho's future territorial governor was wounded, provided natural political connections for Eoinn's machinations. Territorial Governor **Gilman Marston** was only appointed for several months before ultimately declining his appointment, and just by chance that timeframe overlapped exactly to the period that Eoinn needed intervention from the territorial government. Even **Ulysses S. Grant**'s ancestral ties to Northern Ireland—in the same county I'd already chosen for Eoinn's crew—felt like historical serendipity.

I encourage readers to explore the fascinating history of this region and period. Visit Wallace, Kellogg, and the surrounding areas. If you go during the winter, ski at Silver Mountain and take the kids to the very cool indoor water park there. The real stories of these places rival any fiction, and their beauty continues to inspire.

To see links to a lot of the background research I've done, although not all of it, feel free to visit:

https://ericpicard.com/crystal-village-tales/
You might also find a few easter eggs.

Acknowledgments

This book owes its existence to many dedicated readers. Dave Smith, Stefan Tornquist, Dane Madsen and Jed Nahum each read multiple drafts, offering invaluable feedback and encouragement. These intrepid readers tackled many complete readings and numerous bits of back and forth, helping shape both story and characters. Stefan provided detailed editorial feedback on the first and second iterations of the book. Their commitment to this project has been extraordinary. Deepest thanks!

Rita DeWitt, Tom Szigethy, Emma Picard, Amelia Picard, and Sullivan Jordan provided crucial early feedback. Dr. Sherri Kurz Descalzo, Scott Tomlin, Terri Giardini and Andrew Sinclair all gave late-stage feedback that offered fresh perspectives that enhanced the final version.

Special thanks to Andrea Lorenzo Molinari, my editor. Andy and I met in college, and our friendship has been one of those lasting ones where any break in conversation picks right back up where it left off. He's a hell of a writer, and among other things he's the creator of The Shepherd series of graphic novels, as well as several literary novels of his own. If anyone needs a freelance editor with great chops, I can't recommend him highly enough.

Hugh Howey deserves special mention. During a chance meeting in Seattle, our shared background as boat captains back in the same periods of our lives led to a conversation about writing. His encouragement to pursue this story, which had been simmering for years, finally prompted me to begin writing during the Covid pandemic. His Silo series was in many ways inspirational to the style of the book, where the environment itself is almost a main character, and large parts of the story unfold as vignettes through the lives of the characters within that environment.

My deepest gratitude goes to my wife, Erynn, fellow historian and perpetual road trip companion. Her willingness to explore ghost towns, mining communities, and historical sites has enriched this story, and my life, immeasurably.

Acknowledgment of Native Stories

When I was in college, I took a course called Native American Anthropology where I read first-person narratives such as Son of Old Man Hat and novels like Ceremony by Leslie Marmon Silko. Reading Ceremony was transformative—not only as a reader but as a person struggling through depression and uncertainty. Through Silko's work and my professor's teachings, I learned that for the Laguna Pueblo people, stories themselves are medicine, that storytelling can be a healing ceremony. In a very real way, reading that book was a healing act for me, and it left me with lasting respect for the living power of stories in Indigenous cultures.

This experience taught me how important it is to honor these traditions and to be sensitive in how they are represented in literature. In writing *Legacy of the Bitterroots*, which includes reimaginings of Coyote and Raven stories, I have approached these figures and themes with respect, humility, and care. I have tried to foreground the living, contemporary realities of Native people and be respectful of Indigenous perspectives both in my research and within the story itself.

That said, I am not Indigenous. I am a settler-descended writer working within a tradition that has too often appropriated, misrepresented, or commodified Native stories. The risks of appropriation and commercialization are real, and I want to acknowledge them directly.

Legacy of the Bitterroots explicitly foregrounds the importance of consultation, permission, and cultural protocol in retelling Indigenous stories. I have been careful to use stories that have already been published rather than attempting to break new ground with sacred or restricted narratives. Within the novel, Coeur d'Alene and Nez Perce elders are depicted as active collaborators in shaping the stories told within the fictional Crystal Village.

The book is also self-aware about the limits of appropriation and the need to honor boundaries around sacred stories.

I have done my best to treat this process respectfully and have reached out to various tribal resources for consultation, unfortunately without much luck. I recognize that consultation is an ongoing process, not a box to be checked. If you are a Native reader and see places where I have erred, I welcome your feedback and hope to continue learning.

This novel is about the power of stories to heal, to change, and to connect cultures across generations. It blends Native and European storytelling traditions while maintaining that Indigenous stories are not interchangeable with European fantasy—I have tried to honor the specificity, agency, and sovereignty of Native cultures and cosmologies. The story acknowledges the ongoing effects of colonization and the need for Indigenous agency and leadership in any project that draws on Native traditions. It is my hope that this book can be a small part of the ongoing conversation about how we tell stories—and who gets to tell them

Stories are medicine, and I hope *Legacy of the Bitterroots* honors that truth. If you are an Indigenous reader, especially from the Coeur d'Alene, Nez Perce, or related nations, and wish to share your thoughts, please reach out at EricPicard.com. Your voice and guidance are valued and important.

About the Author

Eric Picard lives in Newport, RI with his wife Erynn. In a former life, Eric was a commercial boat captain, SCUBA diver, and Lighthouse Keeper. For the last twenty five years he has been a serial entrepreneur and product leader at various tech companies ranging from those he's started and grown, to large companies like Microsoft, Barkbox, and Pandora Music. He has degrees in History and Art from the University of Rhode Island, and an MFA from the University of Cincinnati. He describes himself as a husband, a father, a technology catalyst, an artist and a writer. He loves spending time on, in and under the water, and he walks for exercise every day.

You can connect with me on:

- https://ericpicard.com
- https://x.com/ericpicard
- https://facebook.com/ericpicard
- https://bsky.app/profile/ericpicard.com
- https://ericpicard.medium.com

Subscribe to my newsletter:

- https://newsletter.ericpicard.com

Also by Eric Picard

Frost

In the fog-laden streets of Newport, Jack Frost, an artist with untapped potential, finds his world unraveling as nightmares begin to invade his reality. When his beloved cat is mysteriously killed, he discovers an ancient world of fae and magic hidden within the shadows of his city. Guided by a mysterious woman named Summer, Jack is drawn into a conflict that threatens to shatter the delicate balance between the human realm and the world of the Sidhe.

As Jack navigates this new reality, he encounters allies among the fae, including the enigmatic Dobbs and the wise Duncan Thrift. Alongside his friends Ryan and Chris, Jack must harness his newfound powers to stand against the treacherous Bander of the Host.

Join Jack and his companions in a world where art and magic collide and where the fate of two worlds hangs in the balance. Frost is a captivating urban fantasy that will transport readers to a realm where the extraordinary becomes reality.

Perfect for fans of Neil Gaiman, Seanan McGuire, Charles de Lint, and Emma Bull, Frost is a spellbinding journey that explores the magic hidden in the everyday and the power of hope in the face of darkness.

Sally Braid

Tess embarks on a transformative journey aboard her beloved yacht, *Sally Braid*, as she seeks solace after retiring from a demanding career and mourning the loss of her husband, Robert. The open sea offers her a chance for reflection and renewal, but a brewing storm soon tests her resolve.

As Tess navigates the shifting winds and turbulent waters off the coast of New England, she encounters unexpected challenges that push her sailing skills and courage to the limit. In the heart of the storm, Tess's path crosses with a father and daughter on a fishing trip, leading to an unforeseen adventure that will change their lives forever.

Sally Braid is a gripping maritime tale that delves into themes of resilience, love, and the power of the human spirit. With the stormy sea as both a physical and metaphorical obstacle, Tess's journey becomes one of self-discovery and bravery, as she learns to let go of the past and embrace the unknown.

Perfect for fans of nautical fiction and stories of personal triumph, *Sally Braid* delivers a compelling narrative of courage and the enduring strength found within.